LEARNING TO BEND

BY MICHELLE DAVIS

Learning to Bend by Michelle Davis

First Edition

© 2020 Michelle M. Davis

Cover Design by Melanie Brill

Edited by Kerstin March

Printed in the United States

ISBN: 978-1-7344619-0-9

For more writings by Michelle Davis, please visit:

www.michellemdavis.net

And the day came when the risk to remain tight in a bud

was more painful than the risk it took to blossom.

— Anais Nin

This is your game.

These are the rules.

You get to decide.

– Mike Dooley's word presented by Cynthia LaRoche

Mar De Jade – November 2018

ACKNOWLEDGMENTS

I am extremely grateful to Amy Impellizzeri, Kerstin March, Melanie Brill, and Andrew Cooper for their advice and guidance. And a heartfelt thank you to my beta readers, proofers, and book launch team – I could not have done this without you. Grant and Jack – your support, encouragement, and love throughout this entire process have kept your mom believing that she *could* write a novel. Finally – to my husband, Scott – your unconditional love helps me to grow and discover who I truly am. I am blessed to travel by your side on this beautiful life journey!

CHAPTER 1

Jenna

Sometimes I wonder why he chose me.

Daylight streams in through the lower three inches of the window not covered by the woven blind. Outside, a chickadee sings, announcing spring's eminent arrival while a train sounds its horn as it departs from the station at the end of our block. Hesitant to leave the warmth of our cozy bed, I snuggle closer to Ben, wrapping my leg over his. For a moment I contemplate returning to sleep, but then I remember today's "to do" list. The wedding is less than two months away.

Before I get out of bed, I prop myself upon my elbow and gaze at Ben sleeping next to me. Clearly, he is the picture of perfection. Ben possesses that chiseled, all-American look, like he belongs on the cover of a preppy clothing catalog where everyone and everything seems too good to be true. My fingers graze his lips and then gently brush across the soft skin

1

of his cheek. I watch as his chest rises and falls to the predictable beat of his heart, the heart that belongs to me, just as mine does to him. Ben is my world. Who would I be without him?

But in the midst of studying my fiancé's face, a wave of nausea overcomes me. I involuntarily flinch as that same "pit in the stomach feeling" I experienced last night returns. *Stop it!* It was nothing. I stare deeply at Ben, intently focusing on him as he sleeps, searching for reassurance that I'm being ridiculous. But none comes.

He begins to awaken, murmuring, "Good morning, gorgeous." But then Ben's calm look quickly vanishes.

"What's wrong?" he asks, shifting to his side to face me.

Unsure of what to say because I don't quite understand myself, I force a smile and mumble, "Nothing," as I get out of bed and head toward the bathroom.

I pull back my hair into a ponytail then brush my teeth and scrub my face, hoping to wash away the confusion inside of my head. As I replay last night's conversation, I cannot help but notice the silence that now surrounds me. Even the bird has stopped singing. This dense hush only serves to heighten the impact of what Ben said last night, his words echo in my head. My throat tightens. Was he serious? Is that really how Ben feels?

When I return to our bedroom, all I can see is Ben's dark brown hair – the rest of his head is buried in his pillow. He snores softly, almost in a melodic rhythm. Sam, my golden retriever, snuggles at the foot of the bed, showing no sign of movement. Quietly I put on my bathrobe and head downstairs to the kitchen. I turn on the coffee maker then grab the paper from the front step.

After diligently cutting melon and strawberries, I sprinkle my morning fruit with chia and flaxseed. Slowly and deliberately, I sip a glass of lemon water before rewarding myself with a cup of richly roasted coffee. The heat emanating from the mug warms my cold fingers. This is what I do. Each morning. I like routine. It comforts me.

Settling in at the kitchen table, I open the paper, immersing myself into the headlines. But no matter how hard I try to focus on the article describing the accusations against a local congressman or the one applauding Boston's reduced crime rate, I'm unable to concentrate. I switch sections, hoping that I'll have better luck reading about the Celtics game. But it's futile. I can't shake how I felt last night at The Beehive in South End when Ben uttered those words to Jeff, his boss, and his wife Melissa. *"Jenna's a schoolteacher. But as soon as we have our first child, she's going to stop working and stay home with the baby."*

We never decided this. Sure, we discussed options for when we have kids, but I didn't agree to quit my job. And what is with this schoolteacher bullshit? I have my Masters in Gifted Education from Columbia. How dare he degrade me in front of John and Melissa?

I flip to another page in the paper and try concentrating on today's

3

Sudoku puzzle, but for some reason I'm unable to determine the correct missing numbers. I notice how the pencil shakes in my hand. I'm on my third cup of coffee already, so I make a piece of peanut butter toast hoping that some carbs will help calm my jitters. I assume caffeine's the culprit, but then again, maybe not.

Food doesn't help. Nothing does. Instead, I become more and more agitated. School teacher... stop working and stay home with the baby. Why would Ben say that? And to his boss? Twenty more minutes pass. I'm still as wired as ever.

I just need to sweat, get some miles in. Then I'll feel better. Not wanting to return to the bedroom and wake Ben, I go to the laundry room and change directly out of my robe and pajamas and into the freshly washed running clothes from yesterday, which lay neatly folded atop of the dryer. I shiver as the cool air hits my naked skin, but the cozy turtleneck and fleece-lined tights give me instant comfort. I retrieve my sneakers from the shoe rack in the garage then find a set of headphones in the kitchen junk drawer. Sam, who recently emerged from the bedroom, appears with his bright orange leash in his mouth, nudging me to ensure that I won't leave without him. A good run will clear my mind. It always does. I'm probably stressed from all of the wedding plans, making me second-guess things, or – more specifically – second-guess Ben. But doesn't every bride begin to question her relationship right before the wedding?

Sam and I leave the townhome on Webster Street, the one that I, Jenna Moore, now share with my fiancé, Ben Kelly. Located on a perfectly quiet street in a perfectly quaint neighborhood, we both have perfectly manageable commutes from this perfectly decorated home located in Waban, a small town that sits on the outskirts of Boston.

I start out with a slow jog. Luckily, running comes naturally to me. I've inherited my dad's build. Some people describe me as *willowy* – I'm five nine and weigh just under one hundred and thirty pounds. Still that adjective reminds me of a fragile tree that blooms early each spring. I notice my stiff hamstrings and calves – probably sore from all of the miles I've been putting in. Running helps me manage stress.

Within no time, I hasten my pace to keep up with the music streaming through the headphones. Stevie Wonder's "Living for the City" plays loudly, and I adjust my gait to stay with the music's beat. I must remember to let the wedding band know how much I love this song. Ben always teases me, wanting to know why I gravitate toward these old songs from the seventies. I don't know why, it's just that this music makes me feel safe, protected.

Left. Right. Left. Right. My legs turn over with increasing speed, and I vigorously pump my arms. The morning's cool air circulates through my lungs, quickly exiting in tiny puffs. But then my mind flashes once more to last night at The Beehive and the look on Ben's face when he openly announced my future without even considering what I might want. Left. Right. Left. Right. Focus on the road. Stop thinking about last night. It was nothing.

Sam loves running, especially in this brisk air. My feet gracefully graze the wet pavement. Remnants of an early-March snow linger on the street corners, causing last night's rain to form cinder-laced pools. As my feet navigate around the puddles and ice, my thoughts continue to wander back to the restaurant in South End and the tone of my fiancé's voice as he so matter-of-factly stated that my career, which he showed little respect for, was over once we had a baby. He didn't even glance my way or do anything to suggest that this was a joint decision. No, this was all him pronouncing my future. But Ben was a bit buzzed. Maybe it was just the alcohol.

Splash!

My foot lands directly into a huge puddle. Damn, now my sneakers are soaked! Slow down and think about something else. But I can neither break my stride nor cease focusing on what occurred. What if he continued to act this way after we're married? Have I lost my voice in this relationship? Is Ben trying to control...

Before I can finish this sentence, the screech of tires overrides the music streaming from my phone. I freeze, my feet seemingly cemented into the pavement. The sound of the car's horn reverberates in my ears as it skids closer and closer. Sam veers to the left, pulling me with him. In the process my foot catches the uneven curb, and I stumble onto the sidewalk. Luckily, I avoid hitting my head on the cold pavement as I go down on all fours, bracing my fall. The leash rips out of my hand.

I fail to notice my torn tights and the blood that's now trickling down my legs. All I can grasp is the intense pounding in my chest, knowing that I was almost hit. I stare at the black sedan that is stopped barely a foot away. Literally, it is inches from the sidewalk. The driver, a man who looks to be about seventy, glares at me, shaking his head furiously.

He rolls down the window, staring straight at me as I remain motionless on the sidewalk. "What the hell are you doing? You idiot! You could have been killed! Take out those damn earphones and pay attention to where you're going! Jesus! I could have hit you!" His face reddens as he yells these words.

"I'm so sorry." My body shakes uncontrollably as I get up from the ground. "I don't know what happened. You're right. I need to be aware."

"You're damn right, young lady. You kids today are lost in your own world. Clueless."

I stare blankly ahead as the driver rolls up his window then pulls away, continuing to shake his head, no doubt still cursing me under his breath. That's when I look up and see the stoplight that I'd ignored. How could I have missed that? My body shudders. I could have been seriously injured, or even worse, I might have died. Then the real panic sets in.

Where's Sam? My eyes dart left and right. Please, God, let Sam be OK.

I leave out a huge sigh when I see Sam's sitting obediently on the sidewalk, five feet to my left, staring at me with those big brown eyes. I go to Sam and wrap my arms around my him, bury my face in his neck and cry into his wet fur. What about Sam? He could have been hit. How could I ever have forgiven myself?

I remain on the corner clinging to my dog. This isn't who I am. I need to forget about last night and get my shit together. I'm just overreacting to a stupid comment Ben made. Preferring to err on the side of caution, I tightly loop Sam's leash around my scraped hands, put the earphones into my pocket, and start running again – this time at a much slower, controlled pace. There's nothing wrong with Ben. We're fine. Ben most likely felt the need to assure his boss that his career was our priority, that I supported him one hundred percent. I focus on the road and carefully watch my footing as I make my way home.

Before long I'm back at our townhome, but now Ben's gone. He must have left for his Saturday tennis match, and then he'll probably go to his office to catch up on work. Actually, I'm relieved that he's not here. Usually it makes me sad when I come home from a run and the townhouse is empty. But not today.

* * *

Craving the warmth of a hot shower, I go upstairs and crank the faucet to the highest setting. As the water runs down my legs, the dried blood washes away and the cuts on my knees become visible. Carefully, I pull the skin back so I can clean out the embedded dirt. Yet despite my best efforts at tending to my injury, Ben's words keep replaying in my mind, haunting me. *Stop!* I grab a towel, dry off, bandage my cuts, and dress into a pair of jeans and a long sleeve white tee.

Why, after six years, am I questioning my fiancé? If Ben were a control freak, wouldn't I have seen signs before now? I rub my temples, hoping to massage the confusion away. But instead, my mind rewinds to the early years with Ben, searching for clues. I was only twenty-one, a senior at Boston College, when we first met in Cancun over spring break. My best friend, Liv, was also in Mexico with friends from Colgate, one being Ben. She introduced us at a bar called Señor Frog. Ben and I connected immediately, and we've been together ever since. I can't remember anything to suggest that he's the controlling type. Plus, wouldn't Liv know if this were an issue? Ben's like a brother to her. If Liv had *any* reservations she'd certainly speak up – she always does.

I grab my dirty clothes from the bathroom hamper and go downstairs to throw a load of laundry into the washer before starting my lesson plans for the upcoming week. While passing our living room, I become aware that everything I see is *Ben's*, not *ours*. I moved in almost a year ago, but very little has changed since then. Ben had lived here for three years and already had everything, so I didn't bring much of my stuff – only clothing and personal items. Then I remember my disappointment when Ben suggested that I store my framed photographs, claiming that there really wasn't space for my pictures – we'd create new memories together. I agreed, never thinking twice. Yet, as I glance around, it's clearly evident that nothing resembling *us* was ever added.

I stop and plop down on the sofa, Ben's sofa, and survey the room. Each item is perfectly positioned – the furniture, the rugs, the lamps – even the candles are properly grouped on tables. Nothing is out of place. At first, I thought it kind of endearing that he was so neat. None of the guys I ever dated even made their bed let alone kept their kitchen and bathroom in pristine condition. Then, when I moved into his townhome, I noticed that even his closets were immaculate. In fact, for a moment I wondered if I could meet his standards. Sometimes I still wonder. And that's when memories from when I first moved in surface.

"Jenna, would you mind putting your running shoes on the third shelf of the shoe rack in the garage?" Ben had asked ever so sweetly one day.

On another day, he said matter-of-factly one morning over coffee, "Actually the milk goes in the door of the refrigerator, not on the shelf. And also, please put the sponge in the sponge holder instead of leaving it in the sink."

I just accepted comments like that all of the time. I stand up and begin pacing around the living room. Another memory comes flashing into my head. "Please make sure that you rinse out the sink after you brush your teeth." Ben never said these words in a negative tone. I just thought that he was particular, and since it was his place, I did as he asked. But looking back at these everyday comments and knowing that this isn't his place anymore – it's *ours* – I suddenly feel as if I cannot breathe enough air into my lungs.

I need to move, do something. Remembering that going to the store is on today's list, I grab my purse from the counter and head out the door, hoping that food shopping will help calm my nerves and dispel these looming doubts.

Yet, even when I'm at the store standing in line at the seafood counter, I can't escape wondering whether Ben's been controlling me through this entire relationship. But Ben and I are in love. Sure, he wants to protect me, but control me, why that's ridiculous. Ben just likes things a certain way. I bet most accountants act similarly. They need precision, order.

I tell the man behind the counter that I'd like a half-pound of Norwegian salmon.

After the gray-haired gentleman hands me the fish wrapped in brown paper, I proceed to push the cart through the produce aisle, aimlessly choosing fruits and vegetables. Seriously, we have a wonderful relationship. Ben respects me and what I do. In fact, he loves that I'm in charge of the Gifted and Talented math program at Laurelwood Day School. Then I remember it was his Aunt Catherine, a school trustee, who secured the interview for me. Oh my God, did Ben think I couldn't get the job on my own? Did he ask Catherine to use her influence so that I would be chosen for the position? I keep pushing the shopping cart though it now feels overwhelmingly heavy despite the few items it contains.

Ben knows I want kids, two maybe three. And we discussed moving to a suburb with good schools when we can afford to do so. This has always been our dream. It's not just what Ben wants, it's what I want, too. But as I tell myself this, my throat tightens, constricting my thoughts as well as the muscles around my neck.

I pause at the dairy section, pondering *our* big "game plan" the one *we've* been rehearsing since forever. I open the glass door, and as I reach for a carton of low-fat milk, the container slips from my fingers and hits the ground, splattering milk everywhere. Shit! I am such a mess. An employee eyes the wet floor, shakes his head, and then announces over the loudspeaker, "Clean up needed in the dairy aisle." I quickly grab another carton then slither away, hoping to escape unnoticed. As I continue to unconsciously gather items off of the grocery shelves, oblivious to the other shoppers around me, visions of our perfectly orchestrated future churn in my head. Is this what I want, or has Ben single handedly decided our path? Once we're married will he be calling all of the shots, deciding our future? This question, something I've never asked before now, creates the unsettling sensation that I felt last night at the Beehive and this morning in bed. Once again, I force my brain back to earlier years, before we became engaged.

But then I recall an incident when I was still living at home. Ben came to our house to pick me up for some event honoring his Aunt Catherine. When I opened the door, he sighed and softly said, "Jenna, I love how you look in this dress, but it is a bit tight. Maybe something a bit more conservative would be appropriate." It's the way he said "appropriate" that jarred me. I am so not the type to wear anything revealing or suggestive. But at the time I just shook off the feeling, went upstairs to my bedroom, and chose a simple black dress that was neither too short nor too low cut. Instantly the nausea intensifies, and I notice that I'm starting to perspire under my armpits. And then I remember what occurred later that evening when I asked Ben to get me another glass of wine. He actually looked at me like I was a child wanting candy prior to dinner before saying, "Honey, don't you think you've had enough? Aunt Catherine is being recognized tonight for her work with the Boys and Girls Club, so we have to be on our best behavior."

Ben has been showing signs of trying to control me this entire time – but I've been oblivious. I feel as if I might vomit. After searching the perimeter of the store for a restroom, I abandon my cart and dash into the women's room. Pushing open the first stall I fall to my knees and, as horrible as it is to get sick in your own toilet, vomiting in a public restroom sets a new low. Afterward, I head to the sink and rinse my mouth out with the disgusting tepid tap water. The sight in the dingy mirror causes me to recoil. Who is this unrecognizable stranger staring back at me?

After attempting to get myself together, I return to my cart and sheepishly proceed to the checkout aisle, keeping my head down, praying that no one's witnessed the last twenty minutes of my life. As I make it through the checkout aisle without losing my shit again, I start to question why I just accepted these comments from Ben. Where was my voice?

"Focus" I tell myself as I put the groceries into the back of my Jetta. Just ten minutes till I'll be back home on Webster Street. I'm able to keep my attention on the road, not wanting another accident like I almost had this morning. When I round the corner by the train station, I notice the spot in front of our townhome where Ben parks remains unoccupied. Ben usually doesn't return until one o'clock on Saturdays and now it's almost two. Maybe he's late because he's running errands. Actually, to be perfectly honest, I'm not sure that I'm ready to see him right now.

While carrying the groceries inside, a sharp pain in my right jaw stops me in my tracks, and I immediately raise my hand to my face to help soothe the ache. No doubt I've been clenching. Despite faithfully using a mouth guard, I'll occasionally experience jaw pain. It's been an internal barometer to indicate my unacknowledged stress. I reach into the kitchen cupboard near the fridge, grab the Advil, and pop two – actually, make it three – pills into my mouth and wash them down with a large swallow of water, hoping the pain will subside. My body is definitely acting up.

I put the groceries away, conscious of "where everything belongs."

In an act of spite, I deliberately place the milk on the lower shelf, wondering if Ben will notice. Then I move to "my desk area," a small carved out section in the kitchen that houses my laptop, binders, and school supplies. I grab my teacher's manuals as I begin to tackle my lesson plans for the upcoming week. For the first time today, I forget about what happened last night and am able to immerse myself in my work. I love everything about teaching. It's my life – except of course for Ben.

Finally, I finish and hit "print," sending this week's lesson plans to the printer. I walk to Ben's office and retrieve the stack of papers sitting on top of the printer. Unable to find a paperclip from the top drawer of Ben's desk, I open the side desk drawer searching for an extra box of clips. That's when I see the manila folder carefully placed on top of the supplies in his bottom left drawer. How odd, Ben's so particular with storing his files. Why is this folder not in the filing cabinet with all of his other records? I look at the tab of the folder – neatly printed in Ben's handwriting – *2711 Citrine Court*. There's something familiar about this address, but I can't place it. My intuition tells me that it's important. As I pull the folder from the drawer and place it on the desk, I notice how thick it is, containing multiple papers, some stapled. Slowly I open it. The front page is a real estate flier with a picture of a stately home with off-white siding and dark gray shutters. Five bedrooms and four and a half bathrooms? A three-car garage? Wellesley? Immediately panic and dread envelope me. Why does Ben have this real estate flier?

Needing to know more, I'm compelled to read the description:

Stunning Colonial on an idyllic tree-lined street in a desired neighborhood. A fabulous chef's kitchen flows to an expansive family room with
beautiful vaulted ceilings and a two-sided gas fireplace. An elegant living
room hosts an additional fireplace and connects to a spacious home office.
The second floor offers a spectacular master suite with two large walk-in
closets and spa bath warmed by floor radiant heat. There are four additional
bedrooms and two full baths. The lower level includes a recreation room and
significant climate-controlled storage. The generous mudroom includes
built-ins, a pantry, washer/dryer, and has direct access to the three-car
garage. Private backyard with mature plantings and patio is perfect for en-
tertaining.

Frenzied, I start pulling the sheets of paper out of the file. Behind the
real estate flier is a packet titled "Agreement of Sale" followed by information from a title company. Does Ben own another home? Incredibly
confused I keep flipping through the papers. Then I see a deed – with
Ben's name on it – dated March 2 of this year. That's three weeks ago.
My jaw drops as I realize that Ben has purchased a home for $1,926,000
without telling me.

What the hell is going on? We don't have that kind money. Sure,
Ben has a great job at a large accounting firm, but a house like this in
Wellesley? Sweat begins to drip from my forehead. We did not discuss
this. Ben bought this – on his own – without me. My queasy stomach

16

transitions to an internal fire as I begin to feel pure rage. How could he? And where did he get the money?

And then the dots connect. I know why the address sounded familiar. I've seen that street sign before – on the way to his Aunt Catherine and Uncle Henry's house.

A knife wedges in my heart then twists and turns, almost as if its mission is to sever every artery connecting this organ to my body before ripping it out in its entirety.

This house is in his aunt and uncle's neighborhood. Quickly I take out my phone and google the address. This property backs up to Catherine and Henry's home. It actually seems like the yards are connected.

The nausea returns, stronger than ever. It's one thing realizing that your fiancé has a controlling streak, but it's another to discover that he bought a home, with money you never knew he had, right next to his relatives who you do not particularly like – without discussing it first. Why would he do this?

Devastated, I squeeze my eyes shut, unsure what to do next. If it were a nightmare, I could just wake up. But it's not a bad dream, this is my reality. I collapse onto the office floor, my back against the cool wall as I pull my legs into my chest. In less than twenty-four hours my world's shattered into a million jagged pieces lying at my feet. And if I attempt to put them back together, will I cut myself and be scarred forever? The man who I trusted with my life now seems like a total stranger. What else is he hiding? How can I marry someone who would do this? My jaw's throbbing despite the three Advil.

I hear Ben's car pull up in front of the townhouse and instantly my stomach clenches, forming tight knots expanding from my pelvis to my chest, making it almost impossible to breathe. Ben opens the door. Sam greets him. I remain frozen on the floor.

"Hey, Jenna. How was your day?" Ben says light heartedly as he walks into the living room. I can see him through the open office door. He appears normal. Like Ben. Could I have imagined everything? Was it all in my head? But it's not. That manila file folder still open on the desk holds all of the proof. I stare. It's the only thing I can do.

Ben's startled when he sees me sitting on the floor of his office, huddled against the wall. "What's wrong? Did something happen?"

I try to speak but no words form.

"Honey..." He quickly moves toward me, but as he bends down and attempts to hold me in his arms, I flinch, recoiling away from his touch. I see the obvious hurt in his eyes. He has no clue what's wrong.

"Jenna, talk to me. Tell me what's going on?" Ben's visibly freaked out by my behavior.

I take the deepest breath I can muster, allow the air to dissipate into my lungs, and slowly exhale. "I know about the house you bought... next to Catherine and Henry's." Feeling the heat rise in my chest, I tell myself to remain calm and listen. Ben must have a reasonable explanation.

"That was supposed to be a surprise," Ben says, looking disappointed as if I ruined some grand plan of his. "How did you find out?" His eyes then move to the open file on his desk.

"You never asked me," I say, my voice cracks, sounding wounded and deflated.

He doesn't respond. In fact, Ben seems confused by my reaction.

"How could you buy that house? Where did you get the money? And why would you ever do this without me?" With each question my voice gains momentum.

Ben calmly looks me in the eyes. "Jenna, this is my wedding present to you," he sighs. "I guess it's no longer a surprise."

"A wedding present... Ben, this is a major deal. Where we live is something that we *both* need to decide. You should have asked me. You understand that, don't you?" I stand up to better make my point.

Ben takes a deep breath then loudly exhales. "I thought it would make you happy."

"Make me happy? This house sits next to Catherine and Henry's estate. Why would I want to live there? And it has five bedrooms... *five*... and a *three-car garage*. We only have two cars!" I practically yell even though he's now standing less than a foot away from me. Both my tone and bold statement seem to upset Ben. But I don't care. My cheeks flush with rage.

And then I see it in his eyes. Those blue eyes I so love. I've really hurt Ben. That wasn't my intention. But he needs to know that we can't function this way. Married couples tackle life situations together. They talk about things. So, I sit down on the office love seat, cross my arms across my chest, and tuck my legs underneath me. Limbs close to my body, I feel safer, more protected, ready to spring, perhaps even better prepared for whatever my fiancé is going to say.

Then I remember the price tag. "Where did you get the money? How much of a loan did you need to take? This not only impacts you, but me, too. Remember, we're getting married in two months," I say from my perched position in a rapid-fire manner.

"I didn't take a loan." Ben casts his eyes downward toward the Oriental rug.

"If you didn't take a loan, then how did you buy this house?" I know Ben has family money. After his parents died unexpectedly in a car crash, he inherited a large sum, though I've never asked him how much, that would have been inappropriate to do so. I squirm on the love seat as I wait for his response.

"There is no loan," Ben softly says as he begins fidgeting, his fingers tap nervously on his thigh.

"You spent part of your inheritance?" I ask knowing that it's Ben's money and he can spend it any way he wants.

Ben bites his lower lip and shifts his weight from one leg to the other.

It's as if he's trying to decide what to say. "Actually, the money was a wedding present from Aunt Catherine and Uncle Henry. They knew the house on Citrine Court was coming for sale, and they thought it would be the perfect spot for our first home." He exhales sharply as he makes this pronouncement.

Engulfed with anger, my eyes could not be wider as the shock of Ben's words settles into my brain. "Why would you let them decide what is the perfect home for us? I mean, this is seriously fucked up, Ben. Are they also going to tell us what to name our kids, where to go on vacations, and who are friends should be?" My pulse races out of control and then a clammy, almost claustrophobic sensation shrouds me. I get up and walk out of the office. I need fresh air.

Ben rushes after me. "Wait, you have it all wrong. This was supposed to be a happy surprise. If you hadn't been searching through my drawer and would just have let everything go as I planned, you would have loved it. I was going to take you there next weekend... after the family moved out and everything was cleaned up. I planned to bring champagne... to celebrate. Jenna, the backyard's amazing, and there's plenty of room for a pool. This is a house we could live in forever! There's enough room for a big family. Instead of having a starter home and then moving later, I thought it would be easier to get the perfect home now."

"Big family? Seriously? When did two or three children turn into a *big family*? You just don't get it," I scream as I turn back towards Ben, who now appears more confused than hurt. "I don't care how you were going to tell me or that there's room for a pool. In fact, it doesn't matter if it's the most perfect fucking house in the universe. I wasn't part of the decision! You should never have done this without me!" My left hand instinctively goes to my hip while my right pointer finger jerks back in forth in the air as I make my point, a stance I've picked up from disciplining students. Still, I'd never speak to a misbehaving child in this tone.

I pause and attempt to regain my composure, hoping that a light bulb will go off in Ben's head.

"You're really overreacting," Ben says, looking at me as if I'm a spoiled five-year-old throwing a tantrum. But I'm not – at all. This is big, huge actually. Not only is Ben overstepping his authority in our relationship, but he's also allowing his aunt and uncle to call the shots and choose for both of us.

"I need some time to process this, Ben," I say as I grab my coat and head toward the front door. Maybe a walk outside will help me find an ounce of clarity about what just happened. I open the door and head down the porch steps, never turning back.

I walk slowly, eyes focused on the sidewalk, replaying the entire conversation that just occurred. What if I hadn't found that folder? How would I have reacted if Ben took me to that house and then told me it was ours?

When I finally look up, I'm already four blocks away. Cape Cod homes painted in various shades of gray flank both sides of the street. My mind shifts to Ben's aunt and uncle, who took Ben after his parents' car crash. That was ten years ago when he was just seventeen. It seemed logical. Ben had been close to his mother's sister and her husband. In fact, as a child, he spent summers with them in Nantucket. But he didn't live with them for long. That fall he went to Colgate, returning only during college breaks. Still, there's always been something strange about his relationship with Catherine.

Claiming she's a perfect size eight, Catherine's a tall woman, trim but not too thin. Her sandy blonde bob never has a hair out of place, and her hands are always perfectly manicured. She knows all the "right people," but I've never heard her refer to close friends.

Yet what resonates with me most is that Catherine loves to be in charge. She carefully orchestrates her days, months, and probably years, meticulously planning her life as well as Henry's. And apparently, Ben's and mine as well. Yet no one ever stands up to Catherine, not even her husband. And while there's something absolutely adorable about Henry, who is steadily becoming bald and stands clearly four inches below Catherine in heels, he's not his own man. But in some strange way, I do love Ben's uncle, right down to the way his mustache curls around the pipe that he only smokes when his wife is out of the house. That's his one transgression. Otherwise he always succumbs to Catherine's every wish, or at least that's how it appears.

A young man holding leashes attached to four dogs of varying sizes passes by, catching my attention and pulling me back to the present. I smile at what I presume is a dog walker. But my mind quickly returns to Ben's aunt.

When I first met Catherine, she was cordial but set definite boundaries. She made it clear that she and Ben were quite tight. In fact, I remember teasing Ben that Catherine seemed a bit jealous that I was becoming the other woman in his life.

I think back to when I had just finished grad school and was searching for a job. Catherine actually set up the interview with the director of Laurelwood Day School. Was this because she wanted to help me out, or was she using her power as a trustee to make sure that I had a job close by, ensuring that Ben wouldn't leave Boston to follow me elsewhere, away from her?

Northwestern! I'd forgotten about that. Ben had wanted to go to business school in Chicago after working for a year at Ernst & Young. But once he had been accepted at Northwestern University, Catherine insisted that he defer, telling him he wasn't yet ready for his MBA. Then somehow Ben met Rich Ryder, a partner at his current firm. I think it was at a cocktail party at Catherine and Henry's house. Ben and Rich immediately connected, and Ben's been working there ever since. My foot catches on the unleveled sidewalk, but I catch myself.

As I connect the dots, it's apparent that Catherine's been controlling the show all along. I think of a marionette operating a wooded doll dangling helplessly from the strings anchored in his palms. I feel a shiver go up and down my spine. Are Ben and I puppets that Catherine's manipulating? Unexpectedly everything around me becomes still. Noticing the normally busy block is eerily quiet, I quicken my pace. Goose bumps form on my arms.

No, this is not *my* Ben. Something must have happened that caused him to do this. The Ben I know would never fail to include me in such an important decision. There has to be more to the story. I make a right onto Webster Street. Our townhome is less than fifty yards away.

I walk up the wooden steps to our front porch, resolved to try another approach to help Ben understand why we cannot move into this house. The door is still unlocked. When I enter the townhome, I can see Ben in the kitchen, sitting at the table, his head in his hands.

My heart begins to melt. Yes, I do love Ben. This must all be a misunderstanding. "Honey, I know you meant well, but consider it from my perspective. How would you feel if I had done something like that?" I gently lay my coat on the living room sofa and walk into the kitchen.

Ben just stares at me, appearing incredibly wounded.

So, I continue. "The house is beautiful. But is it right for us? I mean, I'm only twenty-six. We're young. Isn't it a bit too much?" Still no response.

I move toward Ben and pull out a chair, positioning myself so that

I'm sitting directly across from him. "We've got to talk about this. The wedding is only two months away. If we want to have a healthy relationship, we both need to feel free to express ourselves." Nothing. Absolutely nothing. He has retreated.

"Ben, I love that you wanted to surprise me with a house as a wedding present, but you need to understand that I have to be a part of the big decisions. You cannot choose for me." I place my hand on top of his while attempting a small smile.

Ben pulls back as soon as my fingers graze his hand. It's then that his look changes from hurt to disdain as he shifts his glance from his coffee cup to me. It's an expression that I've never seen on Ben before, and it frightens me.

"You always wanted a home in a beautiful neighborhood outside of Boston, and that's exactly what I did – found that place for you." Ben sounds different. There's almost a superiority tone to his voice. "Jenna, for me to be successful at my firm and for us to meet the right people, we need to position ourselves to make these things happen. I don't understand why you're resisting. Aunt Catherine and Uncle Henry were generous to give us this opportunity. Plus, I'm sure it provides them with reassurance that we will be close to them, just in case anything happens."

Oh my God. Ben's brainwashed. He's totally succumbed to his aunt's wishes.

"This is not about the money. Of course, I appreciate their generosity, but if they truly wanted to help us with our first home, they wouldn't dictate where it is located. Don't you see, Ben? This gift comes with many strings attached. And I'm not willing to play that game." I'm talking in circles, getting nowhere, I think while rubbing my forehead.

Confusion seems to settle over Ben. "What are you telling me?" he asks.

"I'm just saying that where we live is *our* decision – not Catherine's, not yours, but *ours*. If we're going to be husband and wife, we have to do things as a team. I can't sit idly by and allow you to decide for both of us." There – I've said it. I can't be more black and white than that. I sit back and wait for his response.

He pulls away emotionally and physically as he rotates his kitchen chair in the opposite direction. Then, with his back toward me, he picks up his coffee mug and takes a long, slow sip. He directs his attention to the newspaper, ignoring both me and what I've said. He's never done this before.

"You're not serious, are you?" I ask with a drawn-out sigh. He still refuses to acknowledge me, which only pisses me off. "Ben, we have to talk about this. You can't shut me out." My voice gets louder as I stand up from the chair.

Then Ben abruptly gets up from the kitchen table and pushes his chair in ever so precisely before retreating into his office. He shuts the door behind him.

What is happening? We've never fought about anything. I sit back down into the kitchen chair in disbelief. It's as if six years of bliss has unraveled right before my eyes. Racking my brain, I cannot recall the last time he asked what I wanted, what I thought, what I wished. He would always take charge, and I allowed it. He picked where we were going on our honeymoon, our china pattern, even the font on the wedding invitations.

But have I ever questioned Ben or his actions? This entire time I've gone along with what he decided, putting my wants on the back burner in order to please him. When did I give up my voice? My hands go to my jaw, rubbing the tense muscles. The Advil has definitely worn off.

Staring up at the ceiling, I wonder how I got myself into this predicament. I've always idolized Ben. In fact, I often wondered what he saw in me. I believed that he had all the answers, especially when I had none. After all, he's gorgeous, smart, successful, and seems to have the perfect response in any situation, aside from this afternoon. But that was the first time I really questioned him or disagreed with what he wanted. My chest constricts with that thought. An asphyxiating feeling begins at the nape of my neck and wraps around to the front of my throat. I massage my upper spine, pressing firmly on my vertebrae to loosen the overwhelming tightness.

We must deal with this now. Standing with purpose, I push my shoulders back and walk toward the office, opening the shut door that is shielding Ben from continuing our conversation. While I know "conversation" is not the appropriate word, I hesitate to call it what it truly is.

"We need to talk," I say with the strongest, authoritative voice that I can muster.

"OK," Ben says in a tone of indifference as he looks up. He leans into his chair, cupping the back of his head with his hands.

"I mean it. I can't live in that house, Ben. Not with the way this happened. Plus, it's *too much*. That house isn't who *we are*." My voice becomes shaky and my fingers dig into my palms as I declare my truth.

The last part of the sentence seems to irritate Ben. I see him flinch as these words exit my mouth.

"I thought you knew what you were getting into. My family is very important to me." Ben exhibits no emotion, just delivers a matter of fact statement.

"I know they are, and I love your family. But this is about us, our life together. We can spend time with your aunt and uncle, but we are separate. You and I – *we* – are a team."

"You're making way too much of this." Ben sits up and pauses, his face seemingly softens as he continues, "How about we drive there now, and you can see the house? I know you're going to love it." He smiles, almost in a pleading way.

Oh my God. He doesn't get it, not in the least. Amazed by his obtuse behavior, my body stiffens as my jaw continues to violently throb.

"No. I don't want to see the house, Ben. I *do not* want to live next to Catherine and Henry. It's nothing against them, but I think we should have our own life, not one where everything we do can be seen by them."

"You're being ridiculous." Once again, the pitch of his voice reverts to disapproving, almost as if he's scolding me. Heat flushes through my torso then travels into my limbs. He's not listening! *He* knows what *he* wants and doesn't seem to give a damn about *me* or *my* feelings. I turn around, stomp out of the office, and head to the kitchen where my purse and car keys are neatly tucked in my designated nook. After flinging my purse over my shoulder, I pick up my keys and Sam's leash and call for my dog to follow me as I grab my coat from the living room sofa. Storming out the front door, I purposely refuse to stop and shut it behind us.

CHAPTER 2

Jenna

I cannot recall how I arrived, as I have absolutely no memory of driving to my parents' house. But just as a lost dog instinctively knows its way home, so do I. Somehow, I manage to park my Jetta in the driveway adjacent to the yellow Victorian on Maxwell Street in Newton. This is the house I grew up in, and it's more of a *home* to me than the townhome I share with Ben.

My legs feel heavy with fatigue as I slowly ascend the newly painted stairs. When I arrive at the doorstep, I realize that my head's pounding. I'm incapable of a single logical thought.

Opening the front door with my key, I slowly enter the familiar foyer while Sam charges ahead. Mac, my parents' Black Lab, runs to greet us. Just before Mac reaches me, he skids on my mother's beautiful Oriental rug, sliding across the worn hardwood floors until he collides into my feet. Seeing him, smelling the special scent of home, this is just what I need. He and Sam immediately take off, running laps around the first floor.

"Jenna! What a nice surprise! I didn't know you were stopping by, Honey." I watch as my mom comes down the stairs. Dressed in sweats and slippers, her shoulder-length blonde hair is pulled up with a clip and she's wearing her glasses instead of contacts. It seems like she's not planning on going anywhere soon.

"I hope I didn't interrupt anything, Mom," I say, suddenly aware that I didn't call before coming over.

"I've just been catching up on house stuff," Mom says. "How are you?"

Margaret Moore, Maggie to her friends and Mom to me, approaches and gives me a sweet embrace. That's what she always does when I stop by, which I do frequently. But as soon as I feel the warmth of her body, I begin to sob and dissolve into her arms.

"What's wrong? What happened? Are you alright?" My mother's face shifts from that of a serene maternal figure to one of a mamma bear displaying great alarm.

"I can't do this. I won't let Ben control me," I spit it out in phrases, my voice cracking as I utter these words.

Instead of immediately probing, digging deeper, Mom just lets me cry. It's who she is, who she's always been. Maybe this behavior can be attributed to working in the Human Resource department of Bain Consulting. She's trained in how to deal with people. Still, this is not an employee breaking down in her arms. It's her daughter. Mom clears her throat as she gently ushers me from the entryway into the living room. We both sit down on the floral living room sofa. "Tell me what happened," she says, her hands resting on my shoulders while her eyes peer into mine, giving me the encouragement to continue.

I take a deep breath then attempt to tell my story. "It all started last night… at The Beehive… we were with Ben's boss and his wife," I sputter. My stomach clenches, and I feel small droplets of sweat forming on my brow. "He just told them I'd leave my job when we had kids… we never talked about it. He just assumed that I'd do what he wants."

"Slow down, Jenna. What exactly did Ben say?" Mom asks now holding me tightly, no doubt in an attempt to diffuse my panic. This is what she'd always do when I was little and became upset. Mom could always calm me down, but not today. Squinting hard as if trying hard to understand what's happened, it's clear to me that she has no idea what I'm trying to say. So, I just blurt it out.

"Ben is trying to control our entire life. He bought a house that cost almost two million dollars, without me knowing it. The money came from his aunt and uncle… and the house is right next to theirs!"

Mom's hand instinctively covers her mouth. "Are you sure? How do you know?" She looks as if someone has punched her in the stomach, a feeling I understand all too well.

Uncertain of how to begin this long and complicated story, I do my best to share the exact sequence of what happened in the past eighteen hours, beginning with Ben's statement about me staying home after we had our first child.

I continue to explain how this got me to thinking about whether or not Ben was controlling me and that when I thought about it, there were little things here and there, but that I'd ignored them, probably because I subconsciously didn't want to make waves. I fill her in on everything that led up to my confrontation with Ben, before slumping back into the soft tasseled throw pillows, tears pouring uncontrollably from my eyes.

Mom leans over and wipes the tears from my cheeks before sitting up straight and saying, "Yes, your dad and I did notice that from time to time Ben would, um, let's say, *influence* you, but always in positive ways. We believed that he was the one for you and that you were perfect for each other." She sighs, brushing her fingers through my hair and looking at me with tenderness. "Ben's felt like a part of our family since you two first started dating. Still, I can't recall him ever saying or doing anything that would make me wonder about a serious control issue." Her eyes, framed in black rectangular glasses, exude a mix of confusion and disappointment.

Somehow this makes me feel better. I wasn't the only one who missed or even ignored any subtle cues.

"As shocked as I am that Ben bought that house, I honestly believe that he'd never intentionally hurt you. He always seemed to want to take care of you. Actually, it was kind of charming, but I obviously had no idea that it went this far." Mom's voice rises and she shakes her head. "And that aunt of his, I never liked her. Always putting on airs around me, as if we weren't good enough and you were lucky to be engaged to Ben."

I had no idea my mom felt that way about Catherine.

"But why didn't he tell me about the house? I mean, it's ridiculously expensive, and if Catherine and Henry wanted to help us with our first home, then he should have shared that, and we could have searched for it together." I clench my fists, the knuckles of my fingers turning white. All day long my emotions have been swaying back and forth, from sad to indignant. Right now, anger's ruling and I want Mom to call Ben some horrible name, to take my side and declare that I've been wronged. "He thinks what I want doesn't matter. How can I fix this, Mom? Our wedding is in less than two months!" Verbalizing my truth causes my heart to pound even faster.

Mom allows me to vent, giving me that "Oh, Honey" glance. She seems to bite her lip, as if she's holding back from saying more.

"Mom, I cannot exist in this charade and allow Ben and Catherine to call the shots." But, if I can't do this and Ben is unwilling to disobey his aunt's wishes, where does that leave us? "Ben's been my life since

35

our senior year in college." I dissolve once again while Mom just holds me, rocks me, loves me.

After I finally calm down, Mom offers to make us some tea. Once again, she's employing another trick she would use to help settle me when I was younger.

Seeing my nod, she slowly rises from the couch and walks toward the kitchen. I remain seated, lost in my thoughts.

When Mom returns, she hands me peppermint tea in the flower-patterned bone china teacup that she reserved just for me when I was a child.

"Where's Dad?" I ask, suddenly cognizant that my father is nowhere to be found.

"He'll be home later tonight. He had a conference in New York that lasted 'til this afternoon. He texted me right before you arrived to let me know that he'd be back around nine."

As I sip the soothing strong brew, I realize that it's probably best that it's just the two of us for now. Mom's the one I have always gone to with my problems. I think that my father would feel useless, unsure of what to say or how to act. That, or he'd become furious with Ben and Catherine, neither of which would help the situation.

"Mom, I'm not sure that I can go through with this wedding. How can I marry a man who doesn't respect who I am or what I want?" I ask, admitting an idea that has been haunting me all day. I feel the air leaving my body at the thought of ending my life with Ben.

"I totally understand how unnerving this is. But before you even consider calling off the wedding, don't you think that you and Ben need to talk about this further?" Mom cautions as she takes a sip of her tea.

"I know. I just can't face him now. I'm still too mad. What if this is who he really is?"

After pausing for a moment, she says, "Then you have to carefully evaluate if Ben's the right man for you." I see tears forming in the corner of my mother's eyes as she continues. "I know how angry you are, and you have every reason to be. Yet, perhaps there is something else going on that he didn't share. You two have a lot of history together. Despite what's happened, you owe it to Ben and to your relationship to try to work this out."

"You're right. But that still doesn't explain why he'd buy the house next to Catherine and Henry," I say, agitation reappearing.

"True, but don't six years together count for something? Running away from conflict isn't the answer. Are you really ready to throw it all away? Aren't you willing to fight for him?" That last comment catches me off guard. Am I?

Mom and I and continue to talk, and finally the scared little girl that fled to her childhood home slowly transforms into a somewhat composed young woman, who, for the first time in her entire life, is questioning her true self and what *she* wants. We talk about what makes a good marriage, compromise, and forgiveness.

"You know, no matter how much you love someone, there may be times when they do things that devastate you. That's when you must search deep within and decide if you're willing to forgive, not forget, and try to make it work despite what happened." I could swear that Mom wants to say more yet instead she purses her lips and waits for me to respond.

After several moments, I stand up, kiss her cheek, and say, "You're the best, Mom. Thank you. I think I know what I need to do now."

I call for Sam, determined to return to Ben and make this work. There must be a solution. These are not the actions of the man who I've loved for the past six years of my life. No, there must be a reason for Ben's behavior.

* * *

I slowly turn the key in the lock of the front door to our townhome, unsure of what I'm going to find when I walk inside. By now the sun is starting to set, and I detect a dim light coming from Ben's office. The door is partially closed, but I can see him sitting at his desk, his head in his hands.

"Hey," I say softly as I cautiously walk into the room.

Ben glances my way, barely acknowledging my presence.

"We need to talk," I say with an optimistic tone in my voice. I go to him and ever so quietly take a seat on the small sofa across from his mahogany desk.

"I knew you'd come to your senses," Ben whispers as a faint smile appears on his face.

I freeze. It takes me a moment to compose myself before saying, "You think I came back to apologize?"

"Not apologize but realize that I'm doing what's best for us."

"Oh my God. You just don't get it. If we are going to be married, then what I want matters, too." How can I be any clearer? But I'm obviously not, as Ben still seems to see nothing wrong in what he's done. My suspicion that something else is going on with Ben instantly vanishes. No. I'm seeing the real him – for the first time – in six years!

"Of course, what you want matters. You can decorate the house however you like. You're very good at that. And you can choose the landscaper." I cannot believe what I'm hearing as he continues, as if this is the most natural conversation in the world. "You've always known that I'm a traditionalist. There are just some things that fall into my category and others into yours."

I'm blown away by his logic. It's no surprise that Ben is conservative in nature, but this philosophy that's he's now expounding dates back to the 1950's.

"I don't give a shit about decorating a house or landscaping a yard that I had no part in purchasing. Ben, this is more than a house – this is our life together that I'm talking about. You just can't make major decisions that impact me without considering my input. *Do you under-*

stand that?" My entire body shakes as I repeatedly ask these questions.

"You're really making this something that it's not. I only wanted to surprise you, give you the wedding present that you deserve." Ben's expression makes it clear that he truly believes his own bullshit. "You've always liked it when I took care of things. I don't understand why this is so different. I mean, you were happy that I handled the honeymoon plans, and you always ask me to make dinner reservations. Why all of the sudden do you feel the need to change things?"

I'm astounded. How can he equate calling Strega's for a dinner reservation to purchasing a two-million-dollar house? "Ben, you're totally missing the point. Those are the little things, easy aspects of our life to delegate. But when you said last night that I was going to quit my job when we had kids, and then I found out that you bought a house, well that's big stuff. I must be a part of those decisions. You don't get to choose these things on your own." I stand up, incapable of remaining still.

"You mean, you wouldn't quit your job when we have kids?" A puzzled expression comes over his face.

"I have no idea what *I'll decide* when or if the time comes. But I'll be damned if you're going to tell me what to do." There – I said it – loud and clear. I'm out of breath, feeling like I just ran a half marathon.

He stares at me, as if he's never seen me before. Maybe he hasn't witnessed this side of me. Have I? Well, it's about time that we both do.

"I thought you were happy with everything, with me."

"I was, I mean, I am... but when did you start thinking this way? Acting like this?"

Again nothing. Ben remains seated, unfazed, appearing incapable of understanding the message I'm so desperately trying to convey. And so, I make it as direct as I possibly can.

"Ben, I cannot marry you if you are going to make life decisions for me. And we have to sell that house. I cannot move in next to Catherine and Henry." I stare deeply into his eyes for any hint that we're on the same page. But I can't find any. No, his mind is made up.

"I really think it's best that we just leave things as they are and that we move into this house. I know you're going to love it. Why won't you just try to see things from my perspective?" Ben asks in a pleading voice.

This is utterly unbelievable. What else can I say? There's only one thing, and so I reply, "No. I can't do that, Ben. I cannot live in that house, and if you insist that we do, then I cannot marry you. It's come down to whether you choose Catherine or me." I wait for a moment to see if he recants and apologizes, assures me that what I want matters, but it doesn't take long to know that none of that is going to happen. Ben won't budge.

So, I do what I must. Without another word, I turn around and go upstairs. I understand what's next. I must pack my belongings, my memories, the life that we've shared together, and leave. I retrieve my suitcases and totes from the top shelf of our closet and begin to place my clothing inside. This luggage is not enough for all of my clothes, so I run downstairs to the kitchen to grab some trash bags and then return to our bedroom, furiously stuffing sweatshirts, jeans, belts, and sweaters into the black bags until they bulge. The sooner I leave, the easier it will be, for both of us. I bring the assortment of bags downstairs and place them by the front door before I pack up my teaching supplies and laptop.

After four trips back and forth to my car, everything that I own is now inside the Jetta. Before leaving, I take one final glimpse at Ben, hoping that he'll tell me he changed his mind, that he's thought things through and reconsidered everything. But instead he says nothing, remaining at his desk. He doesn't try to stop me, but I do see him wiping tears from his eyes.

"Do you really want me to leave?" I ask from the doorway of his office, hoping that this unusual display of emotions is a signal that he's coming around, realizing what has happened.

"No, I don't want you to leave. I love you. But I am who I am. My aunt and uncle expect certain things from me, and I can't disappoint them. They've always been there for me, supported me after my parents died. If it weren't for them..." Ben pauses, staring out the window at the early dusk that has just settled in.

"Ben, I know that Catherine and Henry treat you like their own child. And as good as they've been to you, you've been equally wonderful to them. But you don't have to live your life to please them. This is about *us* and what *we* want, not what they want from us. If you can't see that, well, then I can't be with you." It kills me to say this, but I must be honest with Ben and with myself. Just as he cannot disappoint Catherine, I cannot relinquish my willpower to any man, no matter how much I love him.

Ben's no longer able to hold back the tears, causing me to cry again. I walk toward him and he stands to reach out and embrace me.

"I just don't understand," I whisper, looking deep into his eyes to see if I can figure out the answer even if he is incapable of saying the words. But I can't see it, no matter how hard I search inside of those beautiful blue eyes. Either Ben doesn't want me to know his reason or he has no idea himself – the second possibility even more baffling.

Yet, at that moment, there is a subtle shift in my being. As devastated and lost as I feel, a small part of me unfolds, almost releases. I can't describe the feeling as it's something I've never before experienced. I breathe, inhaling Ben's scent, knowing it's most likely the last time I am going to be this close to him. Then Ben moves his hand to the back of my head, pulling me towards him, passionately kissing me as we momentarily return to who we were. My body instinctively takes over as I languish in his taste, surrendering to him, if only for a few seconds. But I come to my senses and pull away. We are no longer the Jenna and Ben who are about to be married in two months. No, that couple is gone.

It's then that I do the unavoidable – I slowly remove the ring from my left finger and press it into Ben's hand. After all, this is a family antique. It no longer belongs to me. I call for Sam, give Ben a final goodbye kiss on the cheek, and leave.

CHAPTER 3

Jenna

Two hours after leaving the comfort and security of my childhood home, fortified with encouragement from my mother to save my relationship, I return feeling devastated. What I thought I could salvage I now realize has no possibilities. The wedding is off.

When I arrive, she's in the kitchen baking my favorite Toll House chocolate chip cookies, as if she knew how Ben would react and that I'd be back. One look from my mother and it's evident that words are unnecessary. I rush to her, bury my head into her soft shoulder, and melt into her arms.

In moments like these you have no concept of the passage of time. All I know is that the flood of emotions released from my body is nothing like I'd ever experienced before. Finally, fully spent, the tears subside. I gaze up at my mother and see in her eyes that she has experienced similar pain. Of course, she has. She's faced worse. When we lost Annie. How could I forget?

"Don't worry about canceling the wedding," she says. "I'll take care of everything. Your only job is to focus on you, OK?"

I nod without speaking, almost like a young child. Mom will come to the rescue and handle things, save me from the embarrassment and pain of calling the church, the hotel, the florist. She'll let them know that I am no longer going to be Mrs. Ben Kelly. "Discovering this side of Ben right before the wedding, well, it must seem like a terrible nightmare," she says, and once again, I nod in agreement. "But the good news is now you know. Imagine how you would feel if you realized this after you were married?" She's absolutely right.

"Honey, there are two ways to approach this. The first is that you can be miserable, claim yourself the victim, and wallow in your sadness."

"And the second?" I ask, not liking the first option.

A warm smile comes across Mom's face. "The second choice is to accept what is, be thankful that you're aware of it, and then move forward and live your life."

It doesn't take me long to make my decision. "I guess number two," I say as I take a seat at the kitchen counter. Still, being a victim and feeling sorry for myself would be a lot easier. "But how do I do it?" I ask, quite unsure of the answer. After all, I've never truly been on my own. I went from living with my parents to sharing an apartment with a girl from work, and then moving in with Ben.

"Have you thought about what *you* want?" My mother asks as she gives me an encouraging look. No doubt she understands my predicament. The timer goes off. She grabs a hot pad then takes a tray out of the oven, transitioning the hot cookies onto a cooling rack. While I'm contemplating my answer, I reach over the counter and take one of the cooled ones from the rack.

"I have no idea," I admit as I bite into the cookie. "I still have my job, which I love, so that part of my life is intact. And I've kept in touch with some of my friends who aren't *our* friends, so there are still people I can hang out with." I take another bite, savoring the sweetness of my favorite treat, allowing the small chocolate morsels to melt in my mouth. I never understood how something as simple as a Toll House cookie could make me feel better. Then I remember the multiple suitcases, totes, and plastic garbage bags filled with remnants of my life that are jammed into the back of my car. "Mom, can Sam and I move back here until I find a place of my own?" I fidget a bit, hoping my request won't be a burden.

Mom leans over the counter then gently places her hand on my arm. "Of course. We'd love to have you both. Stay as long as you want. And Mac adores Sam. They'll have fun together."

"Thank you," I say, smiling appreciatively. I finish the cookie and then reach for another. After a moment, my mood shifts once again. "Mom, why didn't I see this? If I had spoken up earlier, could I have saved my relationship?" Doubt and shame begin to surface.

"Oh, Jenna, this is not about anything that you did or did not do. You can't change people," Mom says as she places a spoonful of cookie dough on the empty baking sheet. "If Ben needs to control things in his life, you'd eventually come to a crossroad where you'd be in the same predicament."

"But if I couldn't really see who my fiancé is, how can I trust myself to make decisions in *my life*? What else am I misreading? Right now, I don't even know who I am or what I want. I'm so confused!" I spurt out, setting my half-eaten cooking on a napkin so I can rub the sides of my head.

"Jenna, don't over-think things. You've always been able to read people and perceive the good in them," she says before placing the baking sheet in the oven. "You saw the best in Ben, and that's who you fell in love with. Don't beat yourself up and question so much. Try taking it one day at a time." Mom wipes her hand on a tea towel then sits on the stool beside me.

"But where do I begin? I just lost my everything." I look pleadingly at her, hoping that she'll be able to provide me with some direction.

"I can only imagine how devastating this is. But, whenever something horrible happens, I find it helps to reframe things, to search for signs of anything positive that can be gained from the situation."

Mom goes on to explain silver linings, those unexpected benefits to

48

shattering experiences, like losing a job and then discovering your true passion in a totally different field. Slowly, I allow myself to consider this silver lining concept. Could I find *anything* good from this situation?

"What you're saying is that instead of obsessing about breaking up with Ben, I should instead focus on the positives now that our wedding is off?"

"Exactly. I know it sounds kind of crazy, but what other options do you really have?" Mom so bluntly says. Yet, she manages a slight grin, almost challenging me to accept this task. Then she raises a cookie as if to toast a new beginning. *Why not?* I pick up my half-eaten cookie from the napkin and gingerly "clink" it with hers.

After another twenty minutes of delving further into this silver lining concept, Mom glances at her watch. "It's nine o'clock. Let's unload your car, and then I'll make us a proper dinner. You need something more than just cookies. Plus, your father should be back soon."

We put on our coats and head outside to the driveway to begin unloading my things from the Jetta. It's then that the black Ford Expedition pulls behind me into the driveway. Dad's home.

"Jenna, this is a pleasant surprise," he says with a curious expression as to why Mom and I are unloading my car this Saturday night. "What's going on?"

Mom glances in his direction, gently saying "Geoff" as if to clue him in to the severity of the situation. But he should know, so I bring him up to speed as to why we are unpacking my car filled with everything that I own. He says nothing, just stares at me with the saddest eyes I've ever seen him wear. Then Dad embraces me, his tall lean frame holds me tightly before saying, "You two go inside. I'll finish up here."

Twenty-five minutes later, after all of my belongings are safely deposited into my childhood bedroom, the three of us settle around the kitchen table over a bottle of very nice red wine, one that I'm guessing that they reserved for a special occasion but decided that now it might be welcomed. Mom then goes to the fridge, pulls out several Pyrex dishes, and turns on the oven. Suddenly I'm famished.

"Thank you for letting me move back home. I don't know what I would have done without both of you." Attempting a smile, I refill the glass of wine that I had so quickly drained.

Mom puts a casserole of chicken tetrazzini into the oven. The least I can do is make a salad, so I begin to pull lettuce and raw vegetables from the refrigerator then retrieve a knife and cutting board.

Dad remains silent. In a strange way he seems to have the hardest time grasping what's going on. He appears lost, almost in a daze. I guess he's in shock. But aren't we all?

* * *

After consuming a double helping of chicken tetrazzini and another glass of wine, I realize how exhausted I am. I kiss my parents on their cheeks before retreating to the childhood sanctuary of my protective and secure bedroom. No doubt I will find answers here, somewhere within the confines of these pink walls and flowered Lily Pulitzer drapes. Throughout my childhood and teenage years this room provided a safe haven of sorts, a space of solace. It's where I locked myself after being grounded for breaking curfew, it's where I lay crying after my first boyfriend broke up with me, and it's where I buried my sorrow after my grandfather died.

I carefully survey my old room. The bureau shelves still house my track trophies and academic awards, and the drawers remain filled with clothes I could never bear to part with, as well as piles of letters and various trinkets from younger days. My mother hasn't touched a thing since I left for college. Perhaps a part of her wants to keep a piece me in the house. It took Mom ten years to convert Annie's room to our second guest room.

Sam jumps on my queen bed, nestling at the bottom as I search through my suitcase for a pair of pajamas and slippers. Too exhausted to wash my face or brush my teeth, I crawl under the thick down comforter and reach over to turn off the light on my nightstand. Enveloped in darkness, I pull the covers tightly around me and begin to assess the collateral damage from today. Ending this relationship with Ben involves more than just calling off a wedding. Life as I know it is no longer. Aside from my work, nearly everything else will change. Should I get an apartment in the city, or stay in the suburbs? What about dating? I can't even begin to go there, but how long will I be alone? I haven't been by myself for six years. I yank the pillow from under my head, smash it into a ball, and slump my body around it.

Unsure of the next steps, I understand that there's no turning back. I can't rewind the events of today nor can I force Ben to be someone he's not. I know too much to revert to my former naïve self in my "perfectly planned" life. No. I must figure out what's next – where I'm going, who I am, and what *I want*. The path ahead of me is long, but I can't think about all of that now. I need to sleep.

It's then that my phone buzzes. It's a text – from Ben.

Ben: *Please give me another chance. I love you.*

CHAPTER 4

Jackson

Twenty-two, twenty-three, twenty-four... one more, I think to myself, straining to finish the final pull-up. Twenty-five. Done. I then grab a thirty-five-pound kettlebell and begin the first of three sets of twenty swings. The clock on my nightstand says 4:41. I spend the next half-hour hammering my muscles with weights, knowing that is not the end of my morning workout – I still have a run. Welcome to my world. This is my daily practice, my religion. It's the only stable aspect of my life. But I need it, crave it actually. It's what helps me counter the nightmares and the pain.

It's been over a year now. My thirty-four-year old body hasn't *physically* changed since I left the SEALS. At six feet two, discipline and hard work have kept me at a steady weight of 197 pounds. In fact, my only variance from years of following the SEAL's strict codes is that I grew out my hair. Now, it's almost at my shoulders. I think letting it grow was symbolic at first, representing a departure from my former life as a Navy Commander. Yeah, those were the best years of my life. I loved what I did, and my guys were freakin' awesome, totally dependable and loyal as dogs. But afterward, it was impossible to stay. I couldn't trust myself.

Looking around as I lift, it hits me again how small my apartment is. Actually, it's more of a loft, spartan at best. But there's a separate bedroom, a bathroom with a shower, a decent kitchen area, and enough space for my morning workouts. The blinds are ripped, the walls need to be painted, and the furniture's a bit ragged. Regardless, it works. Plus, it's right above my bike shop, so life's simple. All I need to do is go down the back stairs and I'm at work.

I sell bikes. Let me clarify that, I sell mountain bikes. No road bikes here. I hate it when people mix up the two. Technically, I own the shop, but the bank still holds the deed to the building. But that won't be forever. I'm slowly buying both the store and the apartment above it. If my calculations are correct, I'll make the final payment in five years, that is, as long as I can make enough cash. As soon as I bought the bike shop, I christened it "OutRider," the term for a person who is an escort of sorts. One who ensures the safety of others. I guess that's who I am, or at least who I was. But if had I been in the front instead of the back that night, maybe things would have been different.

Running shoes, sweats, and head lamp. That's all I need. I leave the warmth of my apartment and embrace the frigid mountain air. I take in the scent of the pines as I start my run. Bend, Oregon – never thought I'd end up here, but it's home, at least for now.

After starting at a moderate pace, I quicken my stride as I head to the Deschutes River. Morning runs clear my head. It's dark now but soon enough the sun will rise. I don't need the sunlight, however, because I know this route. It's where I run every day.

As I reach the river path, I allow my mind to release, let go, do what it needs to do so that I can be sane for the rest of the day. Yet this escape is only momentary. The clock ticks on, signaling that this diversion cannot last forever. Eventually, I must go to work, where no matter how hard I try, I can't hide from that goddamn memory.

Back at the apartment, I turn on the coffee maker then take a quick shower before downing my daily protein shake mixed with two raw eggs. After grabbing my phone and a travel mug filled with black coffee, I descend the creaky back stairs to OutRider to begin another day of fixing bikes, ordering parts, previewing new equipment, and making sales. I hate selling 'cause I suck at it. It's working on bikes that makes me happy. Each machine has a special language, and it's my job to understand the various dialects. People, on the other hand, well, they require a distinct type of handholding, an ability I no longer possess. I can't be bothered to put on a fucking smile and say positive shit just to sell some product. When people come into my shop knowing what they want, that's fine. I can easily handle them. But when customers have multiple questions or are unsure of what they want, I'm out. I just can't tolerate indecisiveness. To me it's a huge weakness. As a SEAL I was taught to confidently make the best decision in a moment's notice. *But had I done that?*

At the end of the day I survey the showroom. Everything's in place, where it belongs. I stock what sells, not the frivolous gear. I care about the serious riders, not those whose only concern is how they look on the trails. After bringing the outside display inside, I put the "Closed" sign in the window. The day is finally over, and now it's *my time*. This is when I do the only thing left that I love – ride. Even though the shop sponsors group rides each week, I never join them. I only go alone. As I change into my gear in the storage room, I can't hide from what reflects in the cracked mirror hanging on the back of the door. The scar on my cheek continues to haunt me. Although it's beginning to fade, the jagged mark constantly reminds me of Patrick. A part of me wants to forget, yet that would be wrong, weak. I don't shirk my responsibilities. I own them, 'til the end.

I grab my bike, lock the door, and then head toward Phil's Trailhead, the entrance to the Deschutes River State Park. I won't return until after nine tonight, so I'll need my headlamp to navigate the last hour or so. Still, nothing beats gliding through the trails, being alone with nature. It's my solace, my only chance to heal.

CHAPTER 5

Jenna

"Ladies and gentlemen, as we begin our descent, please make sure your seat backs and tray tables are in their full upright position," comes the excessively rehearsed, mechanical voice through the overhead airplane speakers that wakes me with the announcement of our on-time arrival.

As the plane begins to descend, I wonder again what Oregon will be like. I try to envision this Pacific Northwestern state, but my mind draws a blank. Embarrassed by how little I actually know about Oregon, let alone Bend, I search for its location on the map inside the airline magazine that's tucked in the seat pocket in front of me. Bend's literally in the middle of the state. Not much nearby, but who knows, maybe this is just what I need, to get away from Boston, away from Ben, and to see Liv. It's been ages since we've been together. Plus, it will be fun to ski.

Anyway, I can't be home, alone, during break. Not now.

Living this past month at my parents' home had been a godsend, but it's time to move on. I need to find my own place, look for another job, and determine my next steps. The thought of leaving Laurelwood Day School, actually being forced out, kills me. I will never forgive Catherine for what she did. Breathe. Don't think about it. Right now, all I want to do is escape, from my screwed-up life, from the sadness of losing what I thought I had, and from all of the looming decisions I must make when I return home.

The jolting noise of the wheels locking into place startles me. But then I catch a glimpse of the view. The crystal-clear sky – the color of a robin's egg – frames several magnificent snowcapped mountains. Then, in the distance at the foot of the mountain range, I see intermittent houses and farms. Clumps of coniferous trees grace the terrain. But what's most impressive is the wide-open acreage. It goes on forever. I realize it's the exact opposite of Boston where buildings occupy the majority of the land, allowing only pockets of nature here and there. This place is beautiful. Everything appears so natural, untouched.

While descending the jetway, I'm greeted by the scent of pine trees. The Redmond Municipal Airport is nothing like I had expected. It reminds me of the small airports that my family flew into during our Colorado ski trips when I was growing up, but without rows of private planes and women wearing expensive jewelry and fur coats. No, this place doesn't seem to attract the jet set crowd that flocks to other ski towns. Immediately, I sense a totally different vibe. Passing through the revolving doors and into the baggage claim area, I see Liv, wearing leggings, a wool cap, and a black puffy coat. Joy rises within me as I wave.

Olivia Parker, better known as Liv in my family, has been my free-spirited best friend for as long as I can remember. We first met in Kindergarten and have remained the closest of confidents throughout the years, despite our numerous differences. Besides being physical opposites, Liv stands five-feet-two, wears her bleach blonde hair in a short, cropped cut, hosts a nose piercing as well as a lotus tattoo on her left shoulder, we're dissimilar in many other ways. I was the serious student who participated in individual activities such as cross-country, track, piano, and dance. And growing up I had a lot of freedom, so I almost always followed my parents' rules. Not Liv. In spite of being gifted, she did the minimum in school, just enough to squeak by. Liv also had a passion for playing contact team sports such as field hockey, basketball, and lacrosse. In fact, she could get a bit rough during games, always committed to the win. Liv is also the youngest of five in a strict Catholic family and prided herself on *not* listening to authority. If there were a rule, she would figure out a way to break it. No doubt she definitely has an edge to her. But this is one of the things I love most about my friend. She is willing to do what I wish I could. I guess that sometimes I live vicariously through Liv.

Seeing Liv reminds me of the phone conversation we had the day after I broke up with Ben. She listened as I cried, retelling my discovery of the wedding present house as well as the realization that I'd never had a voice in my relationship with Ben.

"Ben texted me late last night and then showed up early this morning at my parents' home with the biggest bouquet of pink peonies," I said after I filled her in on what had transpired the previous day.

"Oh boy, peonies are your favorite." Liv always remembers the smallest details about me.

"It almost killed me, Liv. Yet, I promised myself that I'd stay strong and not give in because I was afraid of being alone. Still, Ben sounded so sad... and sorry. But he wouldn't change his mind about moving into that damn house. He promised that if I'd just accept the house as a wedding present, he'd never make another big decision like that without me. While a part of me wanted to believe him, I couldn't. I made it clear that if he really wanted to marry me, then he would have to tell Catherine that we couldn't live there."

"He wouldn't do that, would he?" Liv asked, already knowing the answer.

Then instead of consoling me, like I had hoped, Liv took a different approach – my best friend gave me five minutes to bitch and moan before telling me to "stop it." Liv emphatically declared that what happened was for the best and that I should consider myself lucky that I found out.

"So, now what?" Liv boldly challenged me on the phone that March

evening, showing little sympathy for my predicament. "Canceling the church, the ballroom at the Four Seasons, and all of the flowers is a pain in the ass and will cost you some money, but that's the easy stuff. What about you? Have you begun to think about your next step?" How typical of Liv to dive right in, wasting no time with small talk or encouraging words. Mom basically did the same thing, but in a more tactful manner. What are the two most important women in my life trying to tell me?

"Laurelwood's closed the week before Easter, right, just like Summit High School?" Liv asked.

"Yes," I sheepishly replied, unsure of where she was going.

"Then come to Bend. We're both off from work so we can ski, spend time downtown, do whatever you want. Plus, I haven't seen you in almost a year." Her voice suggested that this was more of a demand than a request.

Knowing there really wasn't any good reason why I shouldn't accept her invitation, I agreed to visit during the school's spring break. And now, on a Saturday afternoon in April, I rush to Liv and hug her tightly.

The warmth of her embrace provides me with some reassurance that this trip just might be what I need – the perfect tonic for my broken spirit.

"Oh Liv, I've missed you so much," I say as I feel the energy and enthusiasm transfer from her body to mine.

Like me, Liv's a teacher but at a public high school rather than a private academy. She prefers the older kids, however, which is totally different than my classroom experience working with younger students. Teaching at the high school also allows Liv to coach field hockey in the fall and lacrosse in the spring. She reserves winters, however, for the slopes. Skiing is in her blood.

"I've got so much planned for this week. The forecast is crazy amazing – high thirties in the mountains and low fifties in town. I am so excited that you are finally here! Are you ready to have some fun? Tonight, I have reservations for dinner, and then afterwards, if you're not too jet lagged, we can check out some of the bars. You'll probably wake up early tomorrow because of the time change, so I thought we could stop at Sparrow Bakery. They have delicious coffee and these yummy sweet croissants called Ocean Rolls. There's a yoga class I want you to try. Then we can hit the slopes and… " Liv's mouth is moving a hundred miles an hour.

"Whoa! How much coffee have you had today?" I need some time to adjust to Liv's high energy level. "Yes, it all sounds great, but we have an entire week. I came here to be with you, to hang out, and to relax. I'm up for everything, but there's no rush to get it all done in the first three days." I see my suitcase and grab it from the moving carousel. Liv takes my backpack as we walk out of the small terminal toward the parking lot.

"I know, it's just that I'm so excited that you're here. I don't get many visitors. Plus, you're my girl, and I miss you," she says, putting her arm around me as we head toward her burnt orange Jeep Wrangler.

It's a short drive to Liv's home, which is located just on the fringe of the downtown area. God, I've missed being with Liv. She gets me. I can relax, be who I am. I observe the new scenery, surveying the view from the passenger's seat. Everywhere people – young, old, and some with strollers – are walking, biking, smiling, and making eye contact with one another. This casual interaction seems surprisingly different from the suburban Boston town that I know so well.

"I love your home," I say as we pull up next to a small, craftsman style bungalow.

"Thanks. It's my happy space," she replies as she jumps out of the Jeep. "The Deschutes River is just two blocks that way. You should check out the running trails bordering the river." Liv points to her left while I grab my bags from the back.

"It's kind of crazy how the entire town is growing. People keep moving here. There's a ton of construction going on, and real estate is pretty out of control," she continues as we approach the house and she unlocks the front door. "It's hard to find a good rental in Bend. I was incredibly lucky to get this place." She opens the door and I sense a bit of pride on her face as we go inside.

Of course, Liv *was lucky* to find this amazing house. She seems to know how to make things happen. She always has. "But Bend's still cheaper than Boston, right?" I ask as I carry my bags into her small yet impeccably appointed house.

"Almost every place is cheaper than Boston," she responds as she switches on the lights and turns on the gas fireplace.

Decorated in neutral colors, Liv's home is cozy yet has a distinctive flair to it, kind of like Liv. The first floor is open, complete with a modern kitchen, an informal dining area that looks onto a small, fenced in back yard, and a simple, but inviting sitting area. Liv has her desk in a corner next to the bay window. Gazing around the space, I see the perfection in Liv's home.

"Your room is upstairs next to mine. We have to share a bathroom, but I think that you'll be comfortable." Liv winks then grabs my hand, pulling me up the stairs.

After showing me the guestroom, which is decorated with several enlarged pictures of Liv and others from where I assume is Mt. Bachelor, we go downstairs and Olivia hands me a glass of white wine, offers me a seat on her gray couch, and looks at me square in the eyes before asking, "So, how are you *really* doing? You're thin. Are you eating?"

"Yes, I'm eating. I just don't have much of an appetite." I settle into the sofa. "Liv, how could I not have seen this side of Ben?"

"You didn't see it because you were in love with him. And I know you – you tend to only acknowledge what you want to. You've always dismissed the messy parts of life, the things that are unpleasant or un-comfortable," Liv says while standing across from me. "Remember,

Ben's been trying to be who his aunt wants him to be – controlling himself to meet her expectations. Extending this control to you was probably just a natural way of wanting Catherine to accept you as well." She puts her hands on her hips, raises her eyebrows, and projects a "what did you expect" expression.

My best friend's bluntness leaves me a bit speechless, as I'm unsure how to respond.

"So, how did you and Ben leave it? You guys still talk, right?" Liv asks, shifting gears as she pulls down a blind to keep the setting sun from going into our eyes.

"Yes, we still stay in contact. I mean, how can I not? He was my life for six years. And as angry as I was – as I still am – I know that he wasn't intentionally trying to control me. It's just who he is." I pause before adding, "I think I still love him." My voice quivers a bit as I admit this aloud.

Liv plops down on the sofa next to me. "Of course, you do. Ben's easy to love. My God, you two were inseparable for years." She leans over and tucks some stray hair behind my left ear, then looks directly into my eyes and says, "I'm sure Ben still loves you, too, but I guess that he has some weird thing with his aunt. Who knows, it could have something to do with his parents' accident."

"He would never talk about the car crash. When I'd ask him, he'd kind of shrug his shoulders and then change the subject." I say, now wishing that I'd have tried harder.

"I remember one night at Colgate, it was really late – we were all hanging out, smoking – I think it was the first time Ben tried pot. Anyway, he kind of opened up. Really surprised me." Did I hear Liv correctly? Ben smoked weed? He's always denied ever having tried pot.

"What I recall most is that he kind of hinted that the accident had been his dad's fault. Something about the toxicology report showing that he had some heavy anti-depressants or something like that in his system. This didn't make sense to Ben. He said his father never took any pills," Liv sighs. "Who knows, there could be more to the story."

"I never knew. Maybe that explains why Ben's reluctant to take something as benign as an aspirin. But still… why did he choose Catherine over me? That's what I don't understand." I pour myself more wine from the bottle sitting on the coffee table.

"I don't know what else to say. Maybe Ben owes Catherine for some reason."

"What could he owe her? Ben's always been wonderful to her, done whatever she asked. Sure, he moved in with Henry and her after his parents died, but several months later he began college with money his parents had left him. So, he never relied on his aunt and uncle financially. It makes no sense," I sigh, perhaps as a surrender. "And he never called you – to ask you to talk to me or to tell you why living in that house was so important?" I ask, lifting the glass of chardonnay to my lips.

"No. I thought about texting him after you told me you'd broken off the engagement, but my instinct told me that if Ben wanted to talk, he'd reach out to me."

I guess Liv was wise to avoid getting in the middle of things.

"I still remember how Catherine would manipulate Ben. During winter break of our junior year at Colgate, a bunch of us were going on a service trip in Guatemala. But Catherine wanted Ben home. She was throwing a dinner for some candidate she and Henry were endorsing for mayor, and she insisted that Ben attend. Seriously? Who demands that kind of stuff?" Liv can't sit still. She stands up and moves to the wall to adjust a picture frame that's slightly tilting left before returning to the sofa.

"I never knew that," I say, suddenly aware of how clueless I was. "Why didn't Ben share this with me?" I ask staring into my wine glass.

"I'm guessing that the older Ben got, the more he kept hidden. Maybe he was afraid that if you saw who Catherine really was and how she controlled and fucked him up, that you'd have left him, scared about any future you two could have together," Liv says with a shrug of her shoulders.

"Well, that's kind of what happened," I admit. "Sure, I knew that Catherine tried to manipulate Ben from time to time, but I hadn't noticed much more than that. He rarely complained about her. But then when I experienced her malice first hand, well, Catherine's an evil bitch." As I say this, the back of my neck contracts with the memory of meeting with Colleen, Laurelwood's headmaster, only two weeks earlier.

The e-mail only said to stop by Colleen's office after the kids left that afternoon. I didn't think twice about it, but when she invited me to take a seat in the straight back chair across from her, I knew something was wrong.

"Jenna, I'm not sure how to tell you this, but the school's Board of Trustees has decided to make a change in our curriculum." Colleen then gazed down at the floor, as if she didn't want to tell me more.

I remember sitting there totally confused. Why would that affect me?

Colleen sighed then shifted her glance to her desk blotter on top of her antique wooden desk, still not looking at me. "They're canceling the gifted math program." That's all she said. No further explanation. Nothing.

"What?" My heart plunged into my stomach as I tried to comprehend what she just said.

"I argued against this decision, Jenna. Truly I did," Colleen said. When she finally looked at me, her face exuded sympathy. "But apparently one particular trustee initiated this move." Colleen seemed to shrink behind her desk as if avoiding my inevitable question.

"It was Catherine Lewis, wasn't it?" I asked as flames ignited inside my entire body. God damn her! How could she? Ben's aunt was taking

away my job because I called off the wedding. I clenched my jaw, trying to keep the anger inside.

Colleen's silence confirmed my suspicion.

"I can't give you any details. Sharing more information would put my job in jeopardy," she said, deflated. Colleen and I have always had an excellent professional and personal relationship. I believed she whole-heartedly opposed this directive. My eyes moved to the wall directly behind her. There hung a picture, exquisitely framed, of the Board of Trustees with Catherine front and center. It's as if she "chaired" this meeting between Colleen and me and called the shots from the photograph above.

"But what about the kids?" I pleaded, anger shifting to desperation as tears began to stream down my face. "I mean, they are thriving in this program. Just check the test scores! They've soared these past few years. But that's not all," I continued to argue, my voice becoming louder and my gestures more animated, "They love math! None of these kids ever complain. They're always smiling and inquisitive. The parent letters I get at the end of the year say how this is their children's favorite class!" I was definitely losing my shit knowing that the decision was final and that I would not be returning to Laurelwood next fall.

"Why would Ben ever suck up to that horrible woman? I don't get it," I ask Liv, my blood boiling.

She just rolls her eyes and says, "Ben's a people pleaser. And, he not only tries to placate his aunt, but he always tried to satisfy you, too. You know, make you happy and provide you with the perfect world that he thought you wanted. This might explain the house. Maybe he was trying to satisfy his aunt *and* give you a home that would make you feel comfortable and safe." Liv readjusts herself on the sofa before continuing, "Who knows, maybe you felt secure when you were with Ben because there were few risks involved? I'll bet you guys planned your future so far ahead that you already came up with names for your kids."

I gulp. "Marlee and Michael," I respond awkwardly. Liv knows me too well.

"That's all great, but I don't ever recall you talking about fireworks, you know, those sparks. Did you ever wonder about that?" Liv's eyes widen as she leans in closer to me.

I continue listening to my best friend's analysis of my messed-up romance.

"I'm serious. How was the sex?" Liv boldly asks as she raises her wineglass to her lips.

"Good, I guess. Comfortable, predictable." I don't like talking about this, even with Liv.

Liv practically slams her fist on the coffee table. "That's it? *Good. Comfortable. Predictable*? Didn't you wonder if there was more? Where was the passion? The intense orgasms? You know, that feeling where you just can't wait for him to be inside you? Did Ben ever have trouble, you know, getting it up?"

As if to recoil from her direct hit I sit up straighter, breathe in, and clench my jaw.

"Sorry. Too much." Liv backs down. "What I want to know is did you ever ask yourself if Ben was *really* the one for you? You and I have been best friends forever, and as much as you said you loved Ben, I never really saw it." With this challenging statement Liv cups her chin in her right hand, appearing to wait for my response.

I can't believe what just came out of her mouth. "Of course, I loved Ben." I take a big swig of chardonnay. Liv refills my glass then tops off her own as she empties the bottle. It's obvious she picks up on my defensive reaction. There's no hiding anything from her.

"What I mean is that you loved Ben, but did you really *love* him? Did you feel different when he was in the room? Could his touch make you tingle? Was sex with him fucking amazing?"

I just stare out her front window, avoiding eye contact with the woman across from me, the one who always tells me like it is, not the version I want to hear.

Liv continues as she stands up and heads toward the kitchen, putting the empty bottle on the counter. She then grabs a bowl from the cabinet and fills it with a bag of popcorn. When she returns, she places the bowl on the table between us. I can't decide if I want to eat the kernels or throw them at her.

Then she says, "You know, there can be more. You don't need to settle. To me, you've always gone for the safe guy, the one who will take care of you, give you that perfect life you always wanted. But what if that wasn't what you *needed*? I mean, the guy you thought was so perfect, well, now you know he's not." She tosses several kernels into her mouth then offers me the bowl.

Ouch. Maybe she's right. "But will I ever find someone who will love me for who I am?" Now I'm reaching into the popcorn as if the answer lies somewhere at the bottom of the bowl.

"Of course, you will. Jenna, you're beautiful, sweet, and smart. Guys have always liked you. But you need to be with someone who challenges you. Ben could never do that," Liv sits back, tucking her legs underneath her. "So, ask yourself this… did you adore him, or was he just kind, comfortable, and safe, the perfect puzzle piece to complete your perfectly crafted life?"

Liv's question about "adoring Ben" causes waves of guilt to resonate throughout my body. After a few moments contemplating this question, I realize that I never considered it from this perspective. I loved him dearly, and in some ways, I still do. But did I adore him? And, he really could be a bit boring at times, concerned about things I cared little about. Maybe she isn't that far off base.

"Ok, let's say that you're right, then who, or what do I need?" I drain my glass of wine as I play this game with Liv.

"Well, if it were up to me, you would be with someone who has at least two tattoos and maybe even a piercing. He would be a bad ass, and he wouldn't come from a pedigree Irish family like the Kelly's. Also, this guy wouldn't be an accountant like Ben. Are you starting to get the picture?"

"So, you're asking me to go totally outside of my box, to date guys who my dad would slam the door on?"

"Yep, try it. You've got nothing to lose. You might even like it!" Liv winks.

Knowing this is as likely as me marring my own body with permanent ink, I laugh, but deep down inside I begin to wonder what being with this type of man would be like. Would he do things to me that I've only dreamed of? Could I let myself go, trust him? But would someone like this want *me*? Would I be good enough to please him? Resurfacing to the present, I decide it's time to switch the subject. After all, we've pretty much covered every angle of my broken engagement.

"So, what about you and Michael? Are you still seeing him?" I've yet to meet Michael Edison. He and Olivia started dating eight months ago. I only know what she's shared with me – he's recently divorced, has a daughter, and lives outside of Chicago. From her description, he sounds like a traditionalist. But I guess that complements her.

"Yes I am. Things are good." That's all Liv says as she quickly gets up and puts the empty popcorn bowl in the dishwasher. She just cannot sit still and relax.

It's funny how Liv never seems to want to discuss *her* relationships, although she's more than happy to delve deep into mine. But, then again, Liv's never really been that serious with anyone. I wait to see if she's offering more about Michael. After several moments of dead silence, I figure that's all I'll get right now so I ask, "What's it like living in Bend? Are you happy that you moved here?" I go to the kitchen, pour myself a glass of water, and then lean back against the counter.

"When I first came to Bend, I thought it would be a temporary stop, just a change of pace. You know how I talked about moving to Portland or Seattle after a while? But, now that I'm here and settled, I don't want to leave. This town has everything I love – skiing, mountain biking, hiking, plus great food and awesome breweries. I just figured, why not stay for a while?" Liv says as she begins to prepare coffee for tomorrow morning. Now I'm the one cupping my chin in my hand, listening closely.

"Plus, there's a shit load of stuff to do. Everyone here basically lives outdoors. You can paddle or kayak on the river," she continues while pouring water in the back of the coffee maker. "Or, if you don't mind a short drive, you could put in at one of the nearby lakes. Mount Bachelor has the best skiing and is usually open November through May. Plus, there are endless trails in the parks. You'll see. No matter where you are, you're surrounded by nature. Last week alone I saw eight rainbows, and two of them were *doubles*." Liv reaches for coffee grinder then pours fresh beans from a bin on the counter into the grinder and hits the "on" button. "But, my all-time favorite thing about Bend are the sunrises and sunsets. They're out of this freakin' world," she shouts above the harsh shrill of the coffee grinder. Then a serene smile comes across her face as she dumps the pulverized beans into the back of the coffee maker.

I just take it all in while sipping my water.

"Oh my God, it's already eight o'clock. You must be starved," Liv says after looking at her watch. "I forgot that you're still on East Coast time. Let's walk to Zydeco and grab a bite. It's one of my favorite restaurants in town."

"Sounds perfect to me. I could use some real food after drinking half a bottle of wine." Already I feel a bit tipsy. After placing my empty glass in the sink, I head to the bathroom, splash cold water on my face, and quickly apply some mascara and blush. I scrutinize my somewhat crooked nose and thin lips in the mirror, acknowledging that I'll never be as beautiful as the type of women I always envisioned Ben would choose over me. I then go to my bedroom, pull on black tights and a long purple cable knit sweater from my bag, and sweep my hair back into a ponytail.

Resigned to try out my new single self in a new place – perhaps my real self, one that I rarely allow to appear – I put on a smile and grab my purse. Tonight, for the first time in what seems like forever, I'm unafraid, not worried about others' expectations. Being here, on my own, without

Ben by my side, surprisingly it's OK.

* * *

Zydeco is in full swing when we arrive. Waitresses dressed in black jeans and fitted white shirts busily move from table to table. The bar's packed three people deep while the bartender pours various liquors into a shaker then strains the amber liquid into chilled glasses. As the hostess leads us to our seats, I notice the people. Young, old, hippie, chic, Zydeco has it all. There's no typical patron here. Instead, each table has a unique blend of diners. Yet everyone here seems happy, content, relaxed. No one appears to be tense or agitated in the least. The difference becomes apparently clear. This laid-back, friendly environment does not resemble the atmosphere I've grown accustomed to on the East Coast.

It's not long before Liv and I are seated at a corner table and I'm diving into a plate of corn fritters and sipping a "Cardamom New Fashioned," Zydeco's featured bourbon drink.

"What gets me is that despite everything, I still miss Ben," I admit, not wanting to sound like a downer. Most likely the alcohol is stirring up these emotions.

"That won't disappear overnight. You know, the best remedy to get over a guy is to find a new one." Liv tilts her head toward a table of extremely attractive men, all who appear to be in their late twenties. One of the guys catches me staring in his direction and locks his eyes onto mine. Quickly I snap out of it, averting my attention back to Liv.

"I just don't know," I sigh. "After being with Ben for so long, I can't imagine sex with anyone else. It would just be so *uncomfortable*."

"Jenna, it's not supposed to be comfortable." Liv raises her cocktail to tap my glass.

I giggle at the idea – yes – I am feeling the cocktails. Slowly thoughts of Ben dissipate as I become more and more relaxed. Drinking bourbon with my best friend in a hipster restaurant in Bend, Oregon... perhaps, with time, I *could* embrace my new single self.

Eventually, one "New Fashioned" turns into three before we decide to call it a night. Walking back to Liv's house I feel a bit fuzzy. I'm sensing something different about myself. Not quite sure how to label this feeling, knowing that there is a chance it is just the bourbon, I watch as my exhales turn into cloudy white spirals in the cool evening air. With each step, I notice a distinct lightness in my body. Breathing seems easier, more natural. At a loss to identify what's happening, I decide to stop resisting and relinquish control. In this moment, I no longer feel like my life is in shambles. Instead, the enormous weight on my shoulder that's been plaguing me dissipates.

As I marvel at the splendid nocturnal view of the full moon silhouetting the outline of Mt. Bachelor, I begin to wonder if Bend is where I'm meant to be. Could this breathtaking town on the Deschutes River help me forget the life I had and show me the answers I so desperately need?

CHAPTER 6

Jenna

Five hours in snug ski boots cause my arches to cramp. It's been too long since I've skied. My feet and legs are killing me. Time to call it quits. Where is Liv? I scan the slope for my friend as I make my way down Tippy Toe, a black diamond that leads to the main lodge.

After spotting Liv entering the lodge, I continue to the bottom of the slope then stop by the ski racks, happy to take off my skis and lean them against the metal frame. Stomping my sore feet on the metal stairs to dislodge the wet snow from my boots, I remove my helmet as I enter the West Village lodge, still searching for Liv. But instead of finding my best friend, I'm drawn to a solitary man with shoulder length thick brown hair sitting alone at a café table. I try not to stare, but I can't help myself. When I get closer, I see a faint scar on his cheek. It intrigues me. He intrigues me. Yet it's his captivating green eyes that truly catch my attention.

I look in the opposite direction and make it appear as if I'm about to walk away. But I can't, he pulls me toward him. I pause, actually freeze in my tracks before I find my body shifting in his direction. He's drinking coffee and gazing at me. Who is he and why am I feeling this way? Doing my best to regain some composure, I try to avert my eyes, but they won't stop staring at him. What is it? He's not traditionally handsome – he's more of a sensual "bad boy" type – nothing like Ben. Suddenly, I feel my throat tighten and butterflies appear inside my stomach. I become conscious about my hair. I've had a helmet on all day. It must look awful.

Stop it. He's just some stranger.

Although he's sitting, I quickly assess his height and notice his chiseled muscular build. I'm guessing that he's older than me, by at least five or more years. Something deep inside of me begins to stir as I pass by his table. That's when I hear, "Place the weight on your inside toe when you turn. You're using your knees too much."

Startled by his directness, I freeze. Then I realize from the location of his chair that he had watched me ski down the slope. And now he's staring directly at me. The sea green intensity of his eyes mesmerizes me. As much as I try, I cannot look away.

"Umm, thanks for the tip," I say as I tell my feet to start moving and my eyes to stop staring. But my body pulls me to him, captivated, incapable of turning in the opposite direction. It's as though my "True

North" is magnetized to this stranger.

"Jackson," he says in a deep voice as he extends his hand. I notice that we hold on a bit too long for an introductory handshake. As I touch his skin, my fingers, still cold from the slopes despite the hand warmers in my gloves, tingle as if they're cursing with electricity.

"Jenna," I say, my eyes glued to his.

"Jenna, over here!" I glance over my shoulder toward the sound of Liv's voice.

"That's my friend, Liv," I say, turning my focus back to him. "I should leave. Oh, and no more using my knees to turn, I promise." I flash a warm smile, wanting to say more, but forcing myself to turn and leave.

As I walk away, I sense his eyes penetrating my ski jacket, deep into the core of my being. Shake it off. It means nothing. I chastise myself for reading more into this brief encounter and for trying to make it into something it's not.

As I begin to tell Liv about what just happened, a group of people approach us. They're obviously friends of hers. Liv introduces me to everyone, and I quickly learn that this crew of teachers frequently ski together on the weekends. It doesn't take long before the conversation turns to where to meet for après ski. After sufficient debate, Ten Barrel Brewery is the winner. Before leaving, I decide to stop in the ladies' room. I casually pass the table where Jackson had been sitting and observe his chair is now empty. An unexpected disappointment settles over me, but

I quickly dismiss it, reminding myself that those green eyes belonged to just another stranger at Mt. Bachelor. And that stranger was just being nice. No doubt bored while sitting in the ski lodge all by himself, he was probably just passing time watching all of the skiers coming in, analyzing everyone's style. I just happened to walk by him, so he felt compelled to give me some advice. Nothing more. I try to convince myself of this as I continue toward the ladies' room.

"Jenna, hurry up! We're ready to leave." She is always pushing me to speed it up. I prefer moving slowly, deliberately throughout my day while Liv ping-pongs from one activity to another. It's how we've always been, and I hope it will never change.

* * *

Snow flurries fall gracefully, the delicate flakes accumulating on the frozen ground. I can't help but notice the picturesque surroundings as we enter Ten Barrel Brewery, particularly when I eye two guitarists playing bluegrass music under twinkling lights that are strung in the tree branches that surround the outdoor patio. We spot Liv's friends sitting together by the fire pit, so we order two beers at the bar and then join the group. Mark, a tall lean blonde who's wearing a black fleece jacket, smiles in my direction. As I approach Liv's friends, I make a point to stand near Mark.

"Olivia tells us you're visiting from Boston," Mark says as his lips curve suggestively. "What do you think of Bend so far?"

"It's indescribable," I answer honestly. "I loved skiing at Bachelor today. The conditions were perfect. But the people actually intrigue me the most. They seem to be genuinely interested in your story, you know. Where you're from, why you're here. It's so different from home." I start to blush. Am I actually flirting with a man? This seems so strange, but yet there's something kind of fun about it. Freeing. And anyway, it's only flirting. It's not like anything is going to happen.

Liv nudges me and whispers, "Look at you, you're bubbly. Where did that come from?"

I ask myself the same question as I notice that I'm actually sharing what's on my mind instead of mentally rehearsing my words in advance, fearful of doing or saying the wrong thing. Conversation flows freely, and I don't need to force a smile, the norm for the past weeks. Instead it appears naturally.

Mark grins and moves a bit closer.

"Watch out for this one," Liv warns.

"Don't worry, I think I can take care of myself," I say with a mixture of confidence and curiosity. Bottles *clink*. Uninhibited flirtations commence. The rebound begins. It's been so long since I've even kissed a man other than Ben. Am I ready? Could I have a meaningless hook-up with this gorgeous high school English teacher? Why aren't I feeling guilty?

"Bend is just what I needed," I mouth the words to Liv as Mark and I leave Ten Barrel, unsure of what this will lead to.

I forget about my encounter with Jackson. Tonight's about renewal, fresh beginnings, leaving the past behind. It is time to take a risk and see what I've been missing being "perfect, in control Jenna."

* * *

The sidewalks are somewhat slick from the evening's snowfall. Mark places his arm around my waist, ensuring that I don't slip. His hand, resting naturally just below my ribs, feels foreign, yet warm and alluring at the same time. What am I doing? I feel the fall of cold snowflakes on my face. Mark stops, takes off one of his gloves, and wipes away the melting drops from my cheeks before he leans forward and gently kisses me. I almost recoil as his lips graze mine but I catch myself. This is part of letting go, right? I'm no longer Ben's fiancé, so I'm not doing anything wrong. I feel myself relax, moving closer to him, and returning the kiss. Deep inside, something faintly flickers then grows stronger into want, then need. My body presses into his.

"You're absolutely beautiful," he whispers.

I stare into his sensual eyes as his fingertips casually play with a strand of my snow-covered hair. Suddenly I begin to feel a bit surer of what may happen.

We pull apart slowly and continue on our walk, quickening our pace, perhaps with purpose and promise. Could it be that I'm finally awakening from the intense sorrow and pain? Am I ready to be with someone new?

In no time we're inside Mark's apartment. Following his lead, I remove my wet boots and place them next to his on the doormat. He then takes my ski jacket, hanging it on the coat rack to dry.

Mark's place appears to be exactly as I imagine a high school English teacher's home would look. There are books everywhere – on shelves, stacked on tables, and in neat piles on the floor. Fascinating pen and ink sketches hang on the walls. I look closely and see "Mark Rawlins" scribbled in the bottom right corner of one framed piece.

"I like to read and draw," he says with a sense of hesitation and humility in his voice as he bites his lower lip in the most adorable way. This makes him even more intriguing. Ben never did anything artistic, nor did he read, except for *The Wall Street Journal*.

"Your creative side," I say, becoming a bit nervous now that I have an idea as to where this will lead. I seemed so sure of myself ten minutes ago, ready to take the next step, but now that I'm actually in Mark's place and it's just the two of us, alone, I'm starting to second-guess everything. My fingers run through my hair, removing the small clumps of snow that are beginning to melt, as I wonder if I'm going to have sex with Mark. I've never had a random hook-up, ever. Oh God, I haven't even waxed once since Ben and I broke up.

Mark goes to the small kitchenette and returns with two cold IPAs. We sip our beer in silence on his leather sofa while Bill Withers plays soulful music in the background. Then, ever so gently, he wraps his arms around me, drawing me closer. I feel the intense heat of his body next to mine. That's when the stirring sensation I experienced during our walk returns. This feels so different, but so right. My hesitations begin to subside. My body takes over, telling my mind to stop worrying, that I'm not doing anything wrong, that I deserve to feel pleasure.

We sit on his couch and kiss, deeply kiss. It's been forever since I've done this. Mark gently moves his hand from my back to my breasts. Then slowly, he pushes up my shirt. Instead of resisting, I lean back into the leather cushion, close my eyes, and allow myself to enjoy this *new man,* who is doing things so differently than what I am used to. But it feels incredible, so I submit, relax, and completely surrender. Unsure of where this is going, I decide to take the risk and simply let go.

Garlands of white peonies grace the pews, as the flowers' clean scent gently permeates the air. Candle sconces flicker, causing a halo effect in the dimly lit chapel. I step to the rhythm of the pianist playing Pachelbel's Canon in D Major, my father's strong arm guiding me forward, moving me down the ivory runner. We proceed slowly. People turn, smile, and gaze at me with love. I see him ahead of us, standing by the altar's bottom step, between the minister and his best man. He waits, locking his eyes on me. I am almost there... only ten more steps until I become Mrs. Benjamin Kelly.

But midway down the aisle I stop. My feet won't move. I'm frozen in the moment. My father looks at me, quietly asking if I'm all right. The guests nod their heads toward the altar, gesturing for me to continue. The minister beckons with his hands, urging me to proceed to the front of the church, to Ben. But I can't. All I can envision is me – living in that house – with five children running around a newly built pool – Catherine casually walking into our fenced yard, approaching Ben with a list of demands – for him – for me – for us. I attempt to use my voice to say "no" to her, but no words come from my mouth. I look around – I'm still in the church – I see Ben, ahead, but no matter how much I want to, I cannot move forward. My body resists and remains motionless, slowly turning into a stone statue rooted on the ivory runner.

I wake up in a cold sweat from the all-too-familiar nightmare that continues to torment me. Slowly, I lift my head off of the pillow and gaze at my surroundings. *Shit!* This is not Olivia's spare bedroom. No, I'm in a strange bed, partially naked, next to a sleeping man, one who I met just yesterday. I can't believe I went home with him… and stayed the night. At least I stopped things before they went too far. Although I try to tell myself otherwise, my mind and body scream that I've cheated on Ben. As much fun as I had with Mark, everything felt strange, different. I thought I was ready to move on, but maybe not. Ben wouldn't do this. He would never hook up with a random stranger. At least not this soon… would he? Wiping that thought from my mind, I carefully ease out from under the covers, put on the rest of my clothes and then search for pen and paper so I can write Mark a quick note before he awakens. I slink out of his house, pull out my phone, and search for Liv's address, utilizing my nav to find my way back to her house.

Footprints in the snow document my fifteen-minute walk from Mark's place to Liv's bungalow. Her house appears dark. Maybe she's asleep and I can slip in unnoticed. Quietly, I tiptoe up the front stairs, remembering that Liv keeps a spare key under the door mat.

"Have fun?" Liv's voice sounds from the kitchen table as I open the door. Casually seated in front of an open newspaper and a mug of coffee, she gives me a teasing smirk. This reminds me of the time I broke curfew and thought I'd gotten away with it, only to find my mother sitting in the living room, waiting for me to come home.

"Just so you know, I didn't have sex with him." I figure it's best to get that out of the way and avoid an interrogation. "I'm just not ready. It's hard for me to switch gears and sleep with someone else."

"Then that's good." Liv understands me like a sister would. "You don't need to have sex. Just have fun. And, after six years with Ben, you probably should take some time off and just date, keep it casual. Get to know a bunch of guys. Then you'll have a better idea of who's right for you."

"I've just always liked being serious with one person. It takes a lot of question marks out of the equation." I pause to pour myself a cup

87

of coffee. I think I've just identified a characteristic of my old self, the one I so desperately want to break away from. Have Ben and other past boyfriends been my safety nets? I picture the flexible mesh fabric positioned below circus tightrope walkers to protect them should they fall. Have the men in my life functioned in the same capacity? I've always had someone there, by my side, to comfort and encourage me. I was rarely alone. "Wow, that's part of my comfort zone. Being in a committed relationship makes me feel safe, secure. It's when I'm on my own that I am unsure of what to do."

"So you learn to fly solo. The worst thing would be to immediately jump in and get serious with someone else. If you do that, you'll never have time to discover who you are and what you want."

"You're right," I admit. "I need to take a break from men and be by myself." Still, I'm vacillating between grinning about last night with Mark and feeling crappy about it. "This morning when I woke up in his bed I felt as though I was irresponsible, that I had done something wrong."

"Will you stop it?" Liv scolds me as she starts to cut up a large honeydew. "You did nothing wrong. Stop analyzing every aspect of your life, labeling it good or bad. There's a Helluva lot of gray in this world." She throws the rind into the trashcan. "Jenna, you're human. That means that not everything you do will be perfect. Let go and have some fun."

"I'll try, but this will require some serious rewiring," I laugh at the thought of me no longer scrutinizing every little thing that I do. Life would be so much simpler if I could approach things like Liv does. She never obsesses. Instead, she works hard, has a plan, and functions from a "half glass full" perspective.

"So, what will you do with your life? Are you really staying in Boston?" she asks as she offers me a bowl of cut up melon.

My God, she's relentless. I wish she would accept where I'm at and move on.

"I thought I would find a place of my own, but not until I figure out the job situation. I hate Catherine for what she did." My fair skin reddens and my nostrils flare as I reflect on her vengeful behavior.

"I know you're pissed about having to leave Laurelwood," Liv says shaking her head in disbelief. "Does Ben even know what she's done?" she asks as she pours herself a fresh cup of coffee.

"I never told him. I'm not sure I can because I don't want to get Colleen in trouble," I say as I stare at my bare left hand where I used to wear a stunning diamond ring. I'm still not used to it being gone.

Liv nods in agreement and then says, "Look at the bright side. Now that you won't be returning to Laurelwood, your options are endless. It just depends on what *you want* and how *you choose* to look at things."

I stare quizzically at Liv.

"Jenna, you've got so much going for you. I bet there are a trillion schools that would hire you in a minute. But why stay in Boston? You've basically lived there your entire life. Don't you want to try some place new?" Liv asks as she removes eggs from the fridge, cracks four into a bowl, and sets a pan on the stove.

I've often wondered what it would be like to live somewhere else, but Newton's my home, and I never seriously imagined straying too far from it. "Where would I go? My family's in Boston, and so are all of my friends."

"All of your friends but me. Why not move here? I can introduce you to so many people in Bend. And with young families coming to town, there have to be openings for elementary teachers. Plus, you could live with me, like we've always dreamed," Liv encourages as she enthusiastically whisks the eggs and then adds butter to the pan.

"But what about Michael? Doesn't he come here to visit? I'd be in the way."

"As much as I wish he could, it's hard for him to come to Oregon because he has his daughter, Katy, every other weekend. So, mostly I go to Chicago," Liv says. There's a tinge of sadness in her voice.

We've talked about Michael briefly this past week, but Liv's pretty much downplayed the relationship. "Is this becoming serious?" I asked, disappointed in myself that most of our conversations have centered on me.

"He just might be the yin to my yang," Olivia finally admits in a sing-song voice, adding eggs to the pan with a loud sizzle.

"Is he still with the same consulting firm?" I ask. It hits me how little I know about Liv's boyfriend and his eight-year-old daughter. Have I been so caught up in planning my wedding and then the drama of canceling it that I failed to be there for my best friend? Or is she avoiding this topic for a reason? I put two pieces of whole wheat bread into the toaster while I wait for her answer.

"Yes, still with the same job, still votes a straight Republican ticket, and still prefers meat and potatoes. You know, some people consider us kind of an odd couple, but it works. No, it more than works." Liv sweetly smiles. I'm kind of shocked with what Liv's offering up. Then she becomes quiet, almost reflective, and for the first time in forever, I sense an innocence about her. "I think I love him," she says, her eyes drifting out the window.

It's then that the toast pops, but neither Liv nor I are focused on breakfast.

"You love him?" I ask, overwhelmed with the concept of Liv in love. Sure, she's had boyfriends, but never anyone serious. My chest swells with happiness for Liv. "How do you and Katy get along?"

"She's adorable, but I haven't spent much time with her. That's one of the reasons he's bringing Katy to Bend this summer, so I can get to know her better." Liv removes the pan from the stove and dishes eggs onto two plates.

"Then I would definitely need to find my own space. This house isn't big enough to accommodate four people," I laugh, knowing that moving to Bend is as likely for me as packing up to live in Los Angeles, or anywhere else for that matter. I generously spread butter over each piece of toast.

But Liv won't stand down. "They're not coming here until July. That's plenty of time for you to find a place on your own. Or, you could be here while they're visiting. I'm fine with either." Liv hands me a plate and a fork.

For a split second, I allow myself to imagine moving to Bend, starting over, having my own apartment, with no one knowing me, my past, or my relationship with Ben.

"Liv, this would be a really big step for me. I mean *huge*! What would I tell everyone in Boston?" I become giddy thinking of the possibilities, the freedom, and the opportunities.

"People move all the time. It really isn't that big of a deal."

"Well, it is for me," I say, taking a bite of the toast. God, last night made me famished. But is that what's really causing my hunger, or could I be starving for something new?

I pause and consider how dramatically my life has changed in the past six weeks. Looking back, it's evident that most of my decisions were made in fear, meant to keep me safe in my comfort zone. Whether a blessing or a curse, I'm no longer the same person I was a short time ago, even though I'm still not exactly sure who I really am. But can I do this? Am I capable of actually pulling the trigger, uprooting from Boston to move to Oregon?

"Let me think about it. This is happening too fast. And, I don't want to be running away from anything, or anyone," I say as I rub my temples.

"You wouldn't be running away. If anything, you'd be running *toward*. How else can you discover what's out there if you never leave your safe haven? Think all you want, but if you're ever going to change anything in your life, you have to be willing to take a chance and move forward. Staying in Boston and finding another teaching job is fine *if* you want to continue on the same path. But I sense that you want something bigger," Liv challenges me, forcing my hand.

My eyes cast down toward my feet in order to avoid Liv's intense "what will it be?" expression. Truly confused, I want to commit but fear making the wrong choice. I bite my lower lip. What if it's a mistake moving here? It's been so long since I've made a major decision on my own. And if I leave, then everything with Ben is definitely over. Has a part of me secretly hoped to reconcile and return to him?

Liv patiently waits, closely watching me internally debate a life-altering decision. After what seems like an eternity, I finally say, "OK. I'll try it for a year. That's my best offer." I take a big swig of coffee as if to solidify my decision.

"I'll take what I can get," Liv says triumphantly. "As soon as school is over, you'll come to Bend. Sam will love it here! This is the biggest dog town I've ever seen. And, to make things easier, I'll fly to Boston, see my parents for a few days, and then drive west with you. Trust me, OK?" Liv's eyes widen and she speaks even faster than normal. "The two of us can easily make the trip in three or four days, depending how much you're willing to drive each day." She shovels a huge forkful of eggs into her mouth, grinning widely.

"Do you really think this is a good idea?" My old self reappears.

"Absa-fuckin-lutely!" Liv says, a Cheshire cat smirk appears on her face.

I leap from my chair to hug my best friend, hanging on much longer than necessary. The reality is that I'm clinging to her for life. I've just committed to leaving Boston, walking away from my roots and any remaining security – to move to Bend – a small town in Oregon – one that I knew virtually nothing about six short days ago. Am I crazy? Do they even need teachers here? And what about friends? Will I fit in? But then the real question surfaces. Will I discover who I am and what I want out of life if I move here?

CHAPTER 7

Jenna

Three days later I'm back at Logan Airport, waiting for my luggage at the baggage claim. Now it's time for me to "walk the walk." Saying I want to do something is easy, but actually following through and taking action, well that's where the work begins. Although I'm a bit apprehensive about sharing this news with my parents, I have no second thoughts about my decision. In fact, for the first time in what seems like *forever* I feel liberated and hopeful.

I'm pretty sure that my mom will understand, but I'm a bit concerned about how my dad will take it. After contemplating the best way to break the news to them, I decide to speak with them individually. Mom's picking me up at the airport. That should be the perfect time to talk with her.

Rain drizzles down the windshield as I jump into the passenger seat of Mom's silver Audi wagon. Right away I begin to tell her about the amazing skiing, fabulous town, and friendly people in Bend. Of course, I skip certain parts of the trip. Thinking of that night with Mark still causes parts of me to tingle. I secretly wonder if I'll reconnect with Mark when I return in June. We have been texting back and forth. But as much as I'd like to see where things with him could go, deep down I know that jumping into another relationship isn't the answer.

"Liv's so happy. She loves living in Bend. At first, she thought it was just a stop before moving to Portland or Seattle. But, now that she's gotten to know the town, she doesn't want to leave. And, Liv's in love! With Michael, who has an eight-year-old daughter," I ramble on, knowing Mom would want to know how Liv is doing. Liv's always been like a second daughter to her. Third, actually, I don't want to discount Annie.

"You're radiant, which is quite a feat after taking a red-eye home. Honey, it really seems like this trip was just what you needed."

I remember saying those exact words when I left the bar with Mark.

"Yes, it was awesome being with Liv. Her house is adorable. It's a bungalow that's only a few blocks from town. Plus, she has an extra bedroom, and," I pause, looking out the window at the Boston landscape as I search for the courage to say what needs to be said.

"And she suggested you move in with her?" Mom asks in an upbeat fashion as she momentarily turns toward me, with arched eyebrows.

"How did you know I was going to say that?" I'm amazed that my mother saw this coming.

Mom sighs and says, "Honey, I'm not surprised in the least. You're at a crossroad in life. If you've ever thought of living elsewhere, now is the perfect time. Nothing's holding you back. Plus, you have Liv there."

Damn, she's making this so easy.

"I think…," I begin, staring straight ahead into the sea of traffic on the Mass Turnpike. "No, it's more than think, I *want* to do this, Mom. I *am* doing it. I promised Liv and myself that I would try it for a year."

"As much as I will hate you living across the country, I think this will be fabulous for you. A fresh start, a new job, no one knowing about you and Ben. I hadn't heard of Bend before you mentioned it, but if it's half as lovely as you make it sound, it could be an incredible opportunity. And, remember, nothing is cast in bronze, so if you don't like it, you can leave." My mother squeezes my hand, and I continue to tell her about the town that will soon be my new home.

That went much better than I could have imagined. I hope that my dad's reaction is half as good. But I know my dad's inability to express his emotions, and I predict that he will have some trouble accepting the news.

Dad is returning from what I'm guessing is a final training run with Mac and Sam as we pull up in front of my family home. When the Boston Marathon is held next week, it will be Dad's sixth time running the race. Two years ago, we ran it together. But my dad has quickened his pace since then, and I doubt that I could now keep up with him. After greeting me with a big sweaty hug, my father stands back and takes a long look at me.

"You seem relaxed. Guess this trip was good for you," he says, eyeing me somewhat suspiciously.

"I am! Honestly, Dad, Bend is the best. Liv and I had a blast skiing. I have so many pictures to share with you guys! You'll see how beautiful the views are, and the snow at Mt. Bachelor, it's just perfect for April skiing!" I'm speaking so quickly that I sound like Liv.

Figuring I was on a roll, I decide to just go for it and tell him straight out. "Actually, Liv has a spare room, and she asked if I would like to move in with her, you know, until I find my own place. I'd live there just for a year, to see if I like it." I rapidly spit out these words, not taking a breath in between phrases for fear of what my father might say if I were to pause.

Dad's face shows the pain of a father who's learning that his little girl is leaving. He's already lost one for good, but we don't like to talk about that.

"Dad, come on, it won't be forever. I need to do this, for me. Newton is awesome, and it's good to be near you and Mom. But, if I'm trying to figure out who I am and what I want, I need to leave. Can you understand?"

Visibly fighting-back the tears, he nods, saying, "Of course. It just won't be the same here without you." He attempts a half-hearted smile.

I embrace him again, not minding his perspiration-soaked running clothes, and realize how much I'll miss him and how difficult my leaving will be for him. Almost as if on cue, Mac and Sam nuzzle my legs. I'm feeling the love.

While it hurts to see Dad's reaction, telling my parents was much easier than I expected. I go inside, unpack, and throw my clothes into the bathroom hamper. After taking a red-eye and then breaking the news to Mom and Dad, the thought of a shower sounds soothing. I turn on the faucet to the hottest setting and stand there, letting the pulsating shower of water run down my back.

But as I'm drying off, I know that I can't delay the most important conversation any longer, so I reach for my phone to call Ben. He answers immediately.

"Hey, it's me. Are you home?" I ask, nervously fidgeting with a comb lying on the counter as I speak to my ex-fiancé. "Yeah. I just woke up," Ben says sounding groggy. "How was Bend?"

"It was great. Liv's loving life, and she says 'hi.' Ben, will you be home today?" I ask tentatively.

"Yeah. I'll be here for a while. Did you want to come over?" Ben asks, sounding almost excited at the prospect of seeing me.

"Yes, if you're alright with that. Would noon work?" I hold my breath for a moment, unsure of how he will react when I share my news.

Moving away will make everything final between us.

"Sure. See you then. And, Jenna, I've missed you," he says in the sweetest voice before the phone goes dead. I'm not changing my mind. It's over, and I'm moving to Bend. With a new sense of determination, I go downstairs and rummage through the fridge. My appetite has returned, and unlike when we first broke up, I can't seem to feed my soul enough.

* * *

I haven't been in the Waban townhouse since *that day*. It seems so strange now, knocking on the door instead of using my key. When Ben answers, I'm taken aback once more by how handsome he is – that may never change. The conversation is a bit awkward at first, but after a few moments, we settle in.

"It's good to see you," I say truthfully. Being with Ben always comforts me. But I'm cautious about not giving him the wrong idea. He motions for me to come in and offers a cup of coffee. I accept, but as I take my first sip, it hits me how strange it is to be drinking from these mugs, the ones we bought while on a ski trip to Vermont, the ones I used every morning for the past year.

"You said Olivia's happy? What's Bend like?" he asks in an upbeat tone.
"Liv is great, and she loves Bend. The town is pretty awesome." I place the mug on the table and look into his eyes. "Ben, this is actually why I wanted to talk with you. I've decided to move to Oregon – for a year,

maybe longer."

"Wow. I really don't know how to respond," Ben says, staring down at his clasped hands. After a silent moment he straightens up, looks at me again and asks, "You're leaving Laurelwood? That really surprises me. I thought you loved working there."

He doesn't know what Catherine did. For a moment I hesitate telling Ben the truth, as I don't want to jeopardize Colleen's position. But something deep inside tells me that Ben needs to know. I can share this without implicating Colleen.

So, I begin, attempting to leave out my emotions and portray what happened in a clear and factual manner. "Actually, Ben, I'm not leaving Laurelwood. My position was terminated – by the Board members – when they eliminated the Gifted and Talented Math Program."

"What? Why would they do that? You're one of the best teachers there! And the kids love you. I've seen the looks on their faces when I've visited you at the school. Why would the Board ever..." Ben stops mid-sentence as he begins to shake his head and then, with a quiet voice, he says, "Catherine did this." He's put two and two together. Obviously, Ben's more aware of her *influence* than I thought.

"That's what I think. Nothing else makes sense." I tilt my head to the side as I confirm his suspicion without involving Colleen.

"Jenna, this is *so* wrong. Let me talk with my aunt. I can fix it. I can get your job back," Ben says in an almost pleading voice. "Then will you stay in Boston?"

"You can't get my job back, not if Catherine wants to punish me for breaking off our engagement. And anyway, I've promised Liv that I'd give Bend a try." But that's only half the truth. "Actually, I'm doing this for me. I need to leave. The safety, the comfort, the familiarity – that's all I've ever known here. Can you understand?" I look at him, hoping that he'll be able to respect my decision.

Ben nods, though I'm not sure he truly comprehends my reasoning. "I'll miss you, you know that, don't you?" he asks softly, taking my hand.

"I'll miss you, too." And I mean it. This is something I couldn't have admitted a month ago. But time and distance have shown me that while I still love Ben, I am not *in love* with him. I need something else, even though I'm not sure what that is. "Moving to Oregon, to a small town where I have no idea what's ahead, well, that may be my best chance to discover what I'm hoping to find."

Ben remains silent, motionless. So, I continue, hoping he'll understand.

"Liv will help me adjust," I say with optimism. "The town is growing, so they're bound to need teachers. And, if it doesn't work out, I can always move back. You've lived in Pennsylvania, New Jersey, and Massachusetts. Aside from going to grad school in New York, I've never lived anywhere but here. I practically went to college in my backyard.

Boston College is only ten minutes from my house." It seems strange being able to talk so openly to Ben after how things ended.

Then, unexpectedly, he nods, squeezes my hand and says, "I will miss you. You know that. But I think I understand. You need to do this." That's when he swallows hard as if attempting to keep his emotions in check. "And maybe there's a chance that you'll discover what you've always wanted is right here, with me." Hearing him say this and seeing his pleading eyes makes me tear up – not because I don't want it to happen, but because a part of me still does. But it can't. I can't.

"Have you thought about what you're going to do now?" I ask, turning my attention to Ben's future. Maybe I'm referring to the house, but I don't want to directly bring up that topic.

"I'm working on that. I guess I've been hoping you'd come home, back to me." Ben sighs, now taking both of my hands in his. "But that doesn't seem like it's going to happen, so I need to figure out if I'm going to stay here or move into the house." Ben clears his throat.

"You'd live there alone?" No doubt I sound shocked. Why would he move into that huge house all by himself?

"Catherine suggested it. Thought it would be a good idea. She said it would be easier to sell this place than relist the house. Plus, living here, well, it reminds me of you. Of us." This statement somewhat shocks me as the townhome appears exactly the same as it did on the day I first moved in. This space was always Ben's, never *ours*.

The conversation Liv and I had about Ben's relationship with Catherine rings inside my head. At first, I hesitate to share my thoughts, but then my true self stands up and says what's in my heart. "Aside from what Catherine says, what do *you* want to do, Ben?"

He drops my hands and looks at me in a confused child-like manner.

So, I continue, "Seriously, what's best for you, not what's best for Catherine?"

"You just don't understand. Aunt Catherine, well she's..." but he cannot complete the sentence. He leaves me hanging, wondering what it is that she has over him.

"What is it? Why do always do what she wants?" My voice grows as frustration begins to take over. I don't want to pick a fight, but now seems like the opportune moment for me to help him see how his aunt is running his life. "We would still be together if you hadn't chosen Catherine over me!" While I can overlook Ben's controlling tendencies, I cannot and will not ignore this.

"I'm sorry, I can't go there." That's all Ben says as he hangs his head. He refuses to shed any light as to why Catherine will always trump me. I may never know the true reason behind Ben's actions.

After the awkwardness dissipates, we return to small talk and catch up on mutual friends before saying goodbye. As I leave Ben and the home we once shared, my tears start to flow. The first major step of my transformation is complete. Of course, I have to deal with checklist items such as changing banks, forwarding mail, and packing. But, in no way do these undertakings compare to the emotionality of sharing my news with those I love. Everything's moving forward. There's no turning back. I am actually doing this. Please, God, don't let this be a mistake.

CHAPTER 8

Jackson

The weather is finally turning after a crazy winter. Sure, it's normal to have tons of snow in the mountains, but any snowfall in town usually melts right away. Not this year. Schools closed, roofs collapsed, and many streets remained unplowed, causing chaos, especially at the roundabouts. Tomorrow's June first, and the ski company announced that Bachelor will be open for skiing over the 4th of July weekend. As shitty of a winter that it was, the skiing has been pretty epic.

I descend the steps from my apartment into the back of the bike shop, committed but not excited to begin another day. I've owned Out-Rider for just over a year – bought it from a guy who wanted to move East to be with his family. Looking back, it was a bold move. Sure, I love mountain biking, but I knew nothing about running a business. When I saw the "For Sale" sign, something inside just told me to do it. And I've never once regretted the decision.

I used some of my inheritance money as a down payment and applied for a mortgage to cover the rest. Never thought I'd own a bike shop, but then again, I didn't exactly expect to live in Bend either.

After settling everything with the bank, the first "real thing" I did was rename the place to OutRider, a memorial of sorts to my former life – when I was the guard, the one on patrol, the person who watched out for my men. I needed this space to be mine and the original name, Bend Bike Shop, just didn't cut it. I then started to make other changes, gradually transforming the general bike shop into a specialized mountain biking destination. I expanded the merchandise, added new suppliers, and painted the walls to alter the overall vibe of the place. But that was just the beginning. Within a few months, I incorporated a new accounting software system, built a website, and organized sponsored group rides every Tuesday night. And because I lived in the small apartment above the shop, I rarely left the building, except, of course, to ride.

Although OutRider doesn't open to customers until 9:30, I begin my workday much earlier, using the early morning hours in the back office to handle the financial aspects of the business, speak with suppliers, and organize inventory.

With the radio playing "70's Rock" in the background, I find my groove, opening the accounts receivable Excel spreadsheet on my laptop. I work at a steady pace, paying special attention to anyone in arrears of their payment. I'm in no position to be soft with overdue accounts. Then with a click, I generate invoices and send them to print. In less than an hour, I have a stack of envelopes ready to be mailed. It's kinda cool how quickly I figured out what's needed to run this business. Sure, the former owner taught me a few things before he left, but it's crazy how much shit you can learn online. Anyway, it's not like I have a ton of other things to do with my time, except for working out and riding. After checking my watch, I sigh as I unlock the front door to set up the outdoor display.

While the morning's been peaceful, there's no way to predict how the day will unfold or how much time I'll have to deal with customers, something I dread. I just don't have any tolerance for people who are indecisive or aren't serious about biking. And it's more than frustration or impatience. Their half-assed attitudes about the sport really piss me off.

Returning to my desk, I begin processing a pile of invoices before someone walks through the door and needs my attention. It's then that I become aware of the song that starts playing on the radio – "*Loving Cup*" – a Stones classic. Hearing this song takes me half-way across the globe. Before the first verse transitions to the chorus, I'm in the dark Afghanistan desert, leaving the compound with the night's mission perfectly etched in my brain.

The helicopter's humming, ready to transport my team to the remote location where insurgent targets are in hiding. This is the mission we've been waiting for. I'm aware that as much as we rehearsed the details of tonight's operation, things most likely will not run like clockwork. They rarely do. Too many unknowns exist.

We should reach our destination by 2:00 a.m. I expect the entire compound to be in lock down mode, the majority of its residents asleep. As the bird drops my platoon approximately a mile and a half away from the complex, eleven camouflaged men and I slowly make our way on foot heading north. I'm in command of this operation, and platoon leaders are always the outriders, the last men in and out. As much as I hate not being first, it gives me some comfort knowing that I won't leave anyone behind. Still, my men are young, and although they're crazy brave and willing to give their lives for our country, they still lack experience. No amount of tactical training can prepare a soldier for real combat.

Having hiked from the drop-off point, we're less than fifty yards from the compound's outer fence when I first sense something's wrong. No one appears to be guarding this location. If there aren't any snipers, then where are the cameras? With night vision goggles, we can see a great deal. Still, this hellish terrain easily hides surveillance equipment. I continuously scan the surroundings, hoping for a clue that the area is manned or watched. But I can't see a goddamn thing.

Unexpectedly, there's a loud blast. Intense golden flames of fire flash fifteen yards directly ahead of me. Someone's been hit! A lone cry penetrates the silence of the desert while the vivid smell of burning flesh smacks me in the face. A stream of intensely hot air suddenly knocks me on my ass, throwing me onto the jagged terrain. I hear a crack followed by the sensation of a knife being thrust into my shoulder. Recoiling, I rise and lunge forward, running toward the flames. The order of entry is etched in my mind. I know who's been hit. It's Patrick, my first gunner and best friend.

I reach Patrick, or what remains of him, and quickly access the damage. It was a fucking landmine. He's hurt bad… his legs… there's nothing below his knees…blood is everywhere… I have to stop the bleeding.

"Hang in there, Buddy. You've got this, Patrick. You're gonna be OK. You hear me? God damn it, don't you close your eyes! Stay with me."

I radio the pilot as two of my men and I attempt to stop the hemorrhaging. I send the rest of my platoon back, ordering them to make sure that our pilot knows what's happened and is ready for us when we arrive. Then, carrying Patrick, we retreat back to the copter, trying to avoid any more hidden landmines. I pray that the medic on board will able to help him. That is, if Patrick makes it back.

Five weeks later, after submitting my resignation to my commander, I return to the States. He had tried to talk me out of leaving my position,

110

but there was no way I could stay. Not after what happened to Patrick. I no longer had faith in my abilities to lead.

Bethesda, Maryland – actually Walter Reed Medical Center – was my first stop on my way back from Afghanistan, not my hometown of Ross, located just outside of San Francisco. After the cab dropped me off at the hospital, I navigated my way to Patrick's room. But when I saw him – the three quarters of Patrick that remained lying on a hospital bed – I lost my shit, unable to deal with my best friend's reality. Both of his legs had shattered during the blast. The landmine sent bone fragments into his upper torso, and Patrick also lost significant hearing in his left ear and suffered burns on various parts of his body.

As painful as it was being there that night when he was hit, it was worse to see Patrick in that damn hospital bed with sample prosthetics on the counter by the window sill, a bedpan by the sink, and vases of various phases of dying flowers on the tray beside of his bed. I couldn't accept the harsh truths of Patrick's new world. My hands shook uncontrollably. I tried to speak to him, but nothing came out of my mouth. That's when I began to shut down. Although there was so much I wanted to say to Patrick – how sorry I was, that it was my fault, and that I should have been first in – I couldn't form the words. Instead, I refused to allow my pain to surface, and so the remorse tunneled deep down into the dark recesses of my soul. I needed this shame. It was all I had left.

At first Patrick appeared confused by my reaction, but then he *calmly explained all that had happened since he arrived at Walter Reed, the past and upcoming surgeries, and how the doctors were fitting him for prosthetics. Despite Patrick's unwavering determination to return to "normal," I knew that his surviving wasn't enough. Patrick was my responsibility. One of my men came home without his legs, and this is something I owned.*

I never returned to visit Patrick in that sterile hospital room, or anywhere else for that fact. Instead, well, I keep to myself, desperately seeking solace in places where no graces flow.

The song ends, jolting me back to the invoices at my desk. I brush my hand across the scar on my cheek, knowing that even as it fades, it will forever mark my disastrous last mission. But it's my broken soul that constantly haunts me, something I know will never heal. It will always remind me of how I failed Patrick that night in Afghanistan.

Concentrate. Stay busy. Stop obsessing about Patrick.

I try to distance myself from the memories by returning to my bills. Twenty minutes later the door chimes. It's the blonde from the Northwest who keeps dropping by. Yes, her legs are non-stop, and she is definitely attractive in a natural, wholesome way, something I actually prefer. Plus, I've heard she shreds the trails. Still, I'm not interested. I've spent enough time trying to find comfort from women, all beautiful and all very eager to develop a relationship, but I'm incapable of being with someone. Dating requires honesty about the past, and there's no way in hell I'm doing that. My brother, Matt, suggested I try counseling or join a veterans' support group, but I have no interest in talking to a shrink or sharing my story with other soldiers. Before I left the SEALs, I had enough debriefings with psychologists to last me a lifetime. Maybe one day I'll be able to fully open up to Matt. But not yet.

I watch the blonde while seated at my desk in the back of the shop. She struts around, casually pausing at the helmet display then suggestively glancing in my direction. This is not the first time she's acted this way.

"Can I help you with anything?" I ask in a disinterested voice without getting up from my chair.

"Do you think this top will fit me?" she asks, holding up an extra small Cannondale bike shirt. This woman is relentless. Her not-so-subtle gestures are actually a turn off.

In a monotone voice I say, "You're welcome to try it on. Fitting room is on the left." Finally, she gets the hint and leaves the shop. What's wrong with me? Seriously, this is f'ed up. Jackson, get your shit together. You can't hide forever.

CHAPTER 9

Jenna

Liv, Sam, and I pile into my new – actually, gently used – Subaru wagon. Dad had insisted on buying me a car for our roughly 3,000-mile trip west. While great around Boston, my Jetta had over 95,000 miles on it. For weeks he repeatedly expressed his concern that the Jetta was not a safe vehicle for two women to take across the country. I normally don't want my parents helping me out this way, but I gladly accepted Dad's generous gift, thanking him profusely and promising that we would stop whenever we became tired.

The car is packed to the brim, allowing just enough space for Sam's dog bed on the back seat. What doesn't fit inside is stuffed into the roof box above. As I pull away from my parents' house, I suddenly stop the car in the middle of the road. Staring straight ahead, I clutch the steering wheel in a death grip. My hands are shaking. Am I making a mistake?

Should I really be leaving Boston – everything I know – to go live in Bend? Where I know only one person?

"You OK?" Liv asks as she touches my shoulder.

Her voice snaps me back to reality. I breathe deeply. My fingers start to relax a bit. "I'll be fine. I just need a moment." I glance in the rearview mirror at the home where I grew up, where I celebrated Thanksgiving dinners and had sleepover parties on my birthdays, where I first made out with my ninth-grade boyfriend, and where I retreated after ending it with Ben. The bittersweet emotion of leaving the safety and security of my parents and this house resonates strongly. But I need to do this, try something new, something that's for me. Leaving the past behind me, I look ahead, check the side mirrors then confidently press down on the pedal and drive away.

* * *

Two and a half days later, Liv directs me to make the final turn off of Newport Avenue. I drive down the block until we reach Liv's home. Strangely, the house is illuminated.

"Shit. I thought I turned off those lights. I don't want to see my electric bill after being away for eight days with the house totally lit up."

As we park in front of Liv's home, I can tell that not only are all of the lights on, but also there are people moving about inside. In fact, it seems like there is a party in the living room. Liv grins.

"You don't think I'd just let you arrive here, what, and quietly crash after the drive? Are you kidding? It's time to have fun!" Liv's already taken off her seatbelt and is half-way out of the car.

"You're crazy. How did you manage to organize this?" I ask as I tentatively open my car door.

"Before I left for Boston, I asked a couple of people to put something together. Figured that after days of driving, it might be kinda nice to be greeted by a houseful of new friends and neighbors." Liv smiles as she grabs my arm, pulling me out of the car. She leads me up her front stairs as Sam comes running behind us.

Just before she opens the door, Liv stops and says, "I wanted everything to be perfect for you, Jenna. You're going to love living here. We always wanted to be roommates. Now it's actually happening!"

* * *

My first days in Bend with Liv feel more like a vacation than a relocation. Sam and I explore different running paths each morning and then Liv and I tube on the Deschutes River, hike the trails, or kayak at one of the nearby lakes. At night, we check out the different breweries and restaurants in town. I ran into Mark once. As nice as it was to see him, I resisted the urge to do a repeat "date." After all, that is not why I'm here.

While I've had a carefree week playing in Bend with Liv, I remind myself that I have to get serious and stop playing tourist. Michael and Katy arrive on July 2, and four people in Liv's bungalow is two too many.

After grabbing a bag of red licorice – my favorite treat – my laptop and a notepad and pen, I become comfortably situated on the couch in Liv's living space. Using her coffee table as my makeshift desk, I begin my online search for open teaching positions. Bend has several public schools as well as a few private elementary academies. I canvass the various websites, searching for availabilities in my area.

Before I left Boston, I made sure that all of my teaching credentials were in order. Luckily, my Massachusetts teaching certification transferred to Oregon. Colleen wrote a glowing letter of recommendation and attached four strong reference letters from parents of former students. Hopefully, I'll be able to find something close to a Laurelwood in Bend.

Just as that thought crosses my mind, I notice an opening for a math coach at the Northwest Crossing Elementary School. It could be perfect. After all, I've spent the last several years coordinating a gifted math program. How different could this position be? And, tomorrow's the last day to apply. I click the link to learn more details about this job. After reading the fine print, I can't suppress the grin that appears on my face. This job sounds ideal. Suddenly, I feel a surge of energy pulsate throughout my body.

It takes an hour to upload the necessary information onto the school's portal. I hit "submit." Now the waiting game begins. Will I be called for an interview? Not wanting to focus entirely on one opening, I find several other available positions online and provide the necessary documentation. Still, I want the math position at Northwest Crossing.

As I open the bag of licorice and pull out a piece, "Old Jenna" starts worrying about a callback for the math coach position. *Stop it!* That's not who I am anymore. I take a deep breath and envision myself working with struggling math students. Suddenly, I feel a new sense of confidence and trust that it will work out. I take a bite of licorice. Now, a place to live.

I wish that searching for an apartment was as easy as applying for teaching positions. Let's just say that by the end of the afternoon, the half-pound bag of licorice is empty, but I had yet to find a place to live. What I like is too expensive, and what I can afford, well I wouldn't want to live there. Frustrated, I lie down on the couch, grab the remote, and turn on *The Office.*

Just as I'm about to watch a fourth episode of this show, Liv comes in the front door and stares at me before saying, "Come on, change out of your pajamas. Why haven't you gotten dressed yet? It's four o'clock in the afternoon. We have a yoga class in thirty minutes. The first class is free. Then, if you like it, we can both get a monthly membership."

"What? You know I'm so inflexible. My hamstrings are super tight from running. I can't even touch the floor. How can I do yoga?"

But Liv's look makes it clear that I'm going to yoga, so grudgingly, I change into gray leggings and a light pink tank top. My belly's swollen from that half pound of licorice I ate earlier today. I'll be the worst person there. Yet I pull back my hair, put on a light jacket, and follow Liv out the front door. As we walk toward the yoga studio, I wonder if my inflexible body could ever transform, could ever submit, could ever relax.

* * *

A beautiful, lithe woman in her mid-forties stands gracefully behind the desk, warmly greeting clients as they arrive. Her welcoming smile and soothing voice immediately calm my nerves. Olivia and I find spots for our mats near the back of the room. Instantly, I notice the balmy heat coming from the humidifier, which gives a somewhat peaceful effect on this space. Peering around the studio, it's obvious that the men and women here could model for lululemon. Their clothes, their bodies, even their hair reflect a perfect, "Om." My eyes dart to the mirrored wall in front of me. Examining my outfit, my body, and my ponytail, I shrink. My shoulders grow closer to my ears, and I feel less than everyone else, in every way.

"Jenna, these people have been practicing yoga for years. Just have fun. Yoga isn't a contest. Just be you on your mat and see what happens. No judgment, no expectations. Try to stay present and focus on yourself," Liv says as she warms up, twisting her body in ways that I know mine will never go. Still, no matter how hard I try, I feel defeated before I even begin.

When class begins, the instructor's voice flows effortlessly. Everyone seems to easily follow her directives. Everyone, that is, except me. I'm in awe with the height that these women and men can kick their legs, the manner in which they can bend their backs, and how they can balance effortlessly with their legs perched on their triceps. I can't even touch the floor without bending my knees. No one else has that issue. How long is this class? I can't believe Liv wants to sign up for a month. Shit! She'll never let me live it down if I quit. Whatever... But I don't quit. Instead, I take a deep breath, try to follow the instructor, and hope that no one notices how bad I am.

Yet, I'm busted. As I attempt a lunge twist, I lose my balance and fall right onto the mat of some gorgeous man directly to my right. He's not amused, not in the least. No one else seems to be, except Liv, who has the nerve to laugh out loud. I'm mortified.

After what feels like an eternity, we finally put away our props, roll up our mats, and exit the studio.

"You know, I'm kinda proud of you," Liv says as we walk back to her house.

"Are you serious? I was a disaster in there. I can't believe that you told the instructor we'd sign up for the monthly membership, especially after I lost my balance and landed on that guy's mat." Just the thought of my sweaty, rigid body so clumsily falling onto his clean pristine mat makes me never want to walk into that yoga studio again. I had absolutely no business being in that class. What was I thinking?

"You're missing the point. What's important is that you *tried*. You

120

did something that was really hard for you, and you stuck with it, gave it your best shot, even if you really do kind of suck at yoga." The quirky look on Liv's face causes me to laugh.

"But what if I never get better, if I continue to be the worst person in the class? Will I ever be able to touch the floor?"

"Yoga isn't about flexibility or the physical poses, the good stuff is what happens inside, what the poses teach you about yourself. The challenges you face on your mat prepare you for what happens in life. It's all connected," she says. "Ultimately, it's about surrendering, trying not to control every aspect of your body, your pose, or your life." Could I learn about life from attending yoga classes? Is it possible that my in-flexible body is connected to my perfectionistic personality? If I could learn to surrender on the mat, let go, could I begin to find the answers I'm searching for?

CHAPTER 10

Jackson

"*Come on, Mattie, it's gonna be OK. We can do this.*"

We're visiting our dad this weekend, for the first time. My mom, Rachel Tait, enters our playroom, tells me it's time to leave, and then picks up Mattie – my almost three-year-old brother who is busy playing with Lincoln Logs – and carries him into the garage, plopping him into the car seat in the back of her Volvo. She lets me buckle my own seatbelt, almost as if she forgot that I'm there. Looking at my brother as we pull out of our driveway, I see streams of tears slowly falling from Mattie's sad blue eyes. He sniffles, wiping the snot from his nose onto his shirtsleeve.

Within moments, Mattie starts to yell, "No go to Daddy's, stay with Mommy!" as he struggles to get out of his car seat.

Watching my Mom's reflection in the rearview mirror, I see the im-

pact this outburst has on her as she drives away from our house. Unsure if it makes her more angry or sad, all I know that she hasn't been herself. I sort of remember her before Dad left. She used to laugh and smile a lot. She didn't have those lines between her eyes, and she didn't cry and yell, like she does now. But everything changed.

The ride seems to last forever, even though Mom said it would be about thirty minutes. Finally, the car stops. I look out the window and see that we've pulled up in front of a large stone house, one that's even bigger than ours in Ross. Is this where Dad and Bridgette live? My eyes open wide as I hear the engine turn off.

Mom quickly opens the car door behind her, unstrapping Mattie then whisking him out onto the curb. I guess I'm old enough to get myself out of the car. Hesitantly, I grasp the door handle and slowly pull on it, unsure of what will be inside the big home where I'll be spending the next two days. I take Mattie's hand. Mom's already depositing the small bag that contains our toothbrushes, two changes of clothes, pajamas, and Mattie's Teddy bear by the front door. She rings the doorbell, and within seconds, it opens. Dad's standing there, happy to see us. I look at the Mickey Mouse watch on my right wrist. Mickey says it's three o'clock. Dad must have come home early from work.

I hear words exchanged between my parents, but knowing that they aren't nice words, I tune them out and stare down at the brick walkway. Mom pulls Mattie and me close to her to give us one last embrace *before she leaves. Mattie dissolves into sobs, desperately clinging on to her leg. Dad reaches down, gently prying Mattie away from Mom, and envelopes him into a bear hug, telling him about all the fun we are going to have together this weekend. Dad then brushes his hand through my hair and pulls me into the group hug. We all watch Mom drive away, but she never looks back at us.*

I wake up suddenly, sweat beading on my chest. That goddamn dream! Looking back now as an adult, I better understand the intense emotions that my mother felt during that time period. Not only did her husband betray her, but he also had a child with another woman, his secretary. And all of this started when she was pregnant with Matt – the little boy who grew out of his nickname, Mattie, by the age of six. But it took several years for Dad to finally leave home. And when he did, well that's when everything changed.

Of course, my dad and his new family were Mom's perceived enemies. I get that now. But we had no clue when we were kids. My parents were so involved in their own shit that they never thought about how it would impact us. The truth is, I had fun staying at my dad's. Bridgette didn't scream all the time, and Mollie always giggled at me when I made faces.

While this dream is an instant reminder of how messed up my parents' relationship was, I will gladly take this memory over the others that continuously haunt me at night. Even though it's been seventeen months, the Afghanistan nightmares and vivid memories of Patrick's accident, the one I should have prevented, still jolt me awake, propelling me off my mattress, drenched in my own sweat.

It's only 3:30 in the morning, a bit too early for even me to get up. The stars shine brightly through my bedroom window. The Oregon light shows never fail to impress me. I think the constellations actually help ground me, show me how small I am in comparison to what's out there.

Yet, this dream makes my mind drift to my mother. Still resentful of her deceased ex-husband and his widow, Mom now lives alone, in the same house where we grew up. She spends the majority of her days playing tennis and golf, hanging with her middle-aged divorced friends, gossiping and drinking chardonnay, too much chardonnay. I shake my head. How could she allow her life to become so pathetic?

It's been over a year since I've seen her. When I left the Navy last February, I flew to San Francisco right after visiting Patrick at Walter Reed. My plan was to go home and get my shit together. But being around my mother and her dysfunction was unbearable. She never tried to understand what I was going through. She actually suggested that I forget about what happened – it wasn't my fault so I should just *let it go*. All she seemed to care about was me going back to college and finishing my degree. Mom could never stomach the fact that I'd left the University of Washington with just one semester to go. It's as if she couldn't release *her* dream of me becoming that civil engineer, the one she wanted me to be.

Finally, I couldn't take being around her any longer. I bought a used pickup truck with money from my savings account and drove north, working odd jobs along the way. Eventually I landed in Bend.

I look at the clock. It's now 4:00 a.m. Knowing that my alarm will sound in ten minutes, I kick off the covers and stretch my legs, resigned to commence the morning's grueling workout. As if on autopilot, I gladly relinquish my free will. Choice requires thought, and thought leads to emotion, something I avoid at all cost. Sticking to my routine is safe. It protects me.

CHAPTER 11

Jenna

The email's subject line states "Math Coordinator." I hold my breath as I point the cursor onto this email from Northwest Crossing Elementary School and click it open. I am one of three contestants for the math position! This makes my day. All week long I've been glued to my inbox, waiting for responses from schools while scanning real estate websites for apartments. I decide to text my mom, happy to share some promising news.

As soon as I hit "send" on my phone, I grab my running shoes while calling for Sam. "Time to celebrate, Sam. How about a long run? Afterward, we can try those tacos from the food truck lot."

He wags his tail excitedly and, while he may not know the words "tacos" or "truck," Sam definitely understands the meaning of "food" and "run."

While running toward the Old Mill District, Sam and I merge onto the river trail. After completing most of the loop, I feel particularly strong, so I decide to exit near the shops and head toward Pilot Butte. Everyone talks about this place and what a great workout it is to run up to the top. I remember asking Liv what a butte was. She said that it's an inverted cinder cone, caused from volcanic eruptions years ago. Apparently, there are tons around here.

When we arrive at the base of Pilot Butte, I feel a burst of energy and decide to go for it, taking the mile-long incline at full force. As I near the top, my right IT band twinges. It's nothing, just an old injury. Assuring myself that I'm fine, I continue to push forward, even though Sam seems to be slowing down. Finally, the pain subsides as we reach the summit. But thirty-some minutes later, when we're back on the river trail, the outside of my right leg begins to pulsate. Still, I ignore this warning sign. It's when we're three blocks from Liv's that I feel a slight snap, immediately reminding me of an injury that occurred during grad school, on that training run for the New York Marathon.

"Crap!" We will not be eating tacos at the truck lot.

Sam looks relieved that I'm finally stopping, even if that means no food. Hurting just to walk, I slowly hobble home, cursing myself for being so foolish.

"Ice, Advil, and get off your feet!" Liv, who witnessed me limping into the house, chides me for pushing it too hard. "You should know better. What exactly were you thinking?" she asks as she hands me a glass of water and two pills.

"I don't know. I was in a groove, and I wanted to keep running, to prove to myself that I could. I ran all the way to the top of Pilot Butte and back," I announce, my voice tinged with pride for this accomplishment. "Anyway, you're the one who's always telling me to take risks." I declare as I swallow the Advil then make my way to the floor. I'm too sweaty to lie on the couch.

"Well, yeah, but not to the point where you're injuring yourself. I bet you just ran close to twelve miles." Liv says as she offers Sam a bowl of cold water. "Don't worry, you'll be fine, just lay low for a while. Think of the bright side, now you'll have time to prep for your interview and maybe find an apartment." Liv walks over to the kitchen counter, grabs the latest edition of the *Bend Bulletin*, and tosses it to me.

As I open the paper to the real estate section I say, "I wanted to talk to you about that. Michael and Katy are coming next week…"

"Don't worry. If you still can't find something, you and Katy can share the guest room." Liv says seemingly unconcerned as she begins to empty the dishwasher.

"Seriously, I've been at it non-stop for three weeks. I haven't come across any leads to follow up on. Absolutely nothing!" I rub my temples with my fingers. "Why is everything so difficult? Less than four months ago, my life seemed to be perfect, and now, I'm a mess. I don't have a job, I don't have a place to live, and I certainly no longer have a fiancé!" I look to Liv, hoping for some sign of encouragement.

"Really, your life was perfect?" Liv responds in a sarcastic manner as she walks back into the living room, puts her hands on her hips and looms directly over me. "Let me remind you of some things. Your fiancé, who we both still agree is a great guy, had just bought a two-million-dollar home – adjacent to Catherine's house – without you knowing about it. Does that sound perfect to you?" Somehow all five-feet-two-inches of her seems to have grown to seven feet tall. Then she continues, "And that perfect job of yours was always contingent on Catherine. She called the shots at that school. In a way, I guess you could say that you actually worked for her." *Zing!*

The thought of Catherine as my boss makes me shudder. I prop myself up on my elbows in an attempt to shorten the distance between Liv and me.

But Liv's not done. "And you lived at home – with your parents! Jenna, you're twenty-six years old. You are perfectly capable of living your life without Ben, your parents, or anyone else taking care of you. When are you going to believe in yourself?" Liv turns around sharply and returns to emptying the dishwasher. Except for the clatter of silverware being placed into a drawer, silence fills the room.

Five minutes later, Liv plops down next to me on the floor. "You know," she begins, her tone much lighter, "I can't believe I didn't think of it sooner. Elizabeth, one of the Spanish teachers at my school, is leaving to move back to Seattle. She has a really nice two-bedroom apartment that's about ten blocks from here. I wonder if it's rented yet. Do you want me to call her and see if it's still available?"

I sit up, my eyes widening. Liv's helping me again. Aren't I supposed to be doing this on my own? But I need a place to stay. "I don't want to depend on you to find a place to live, but if you think it's a possibility..."

Next thing I know Liv jumps up, grabs her phone, and calls Elizabeth. In less than two minutes, she's giving me the thumbs up sign. After hanging up she says, "Apparently, Elizabeth's landlord still hasn't found someone to take the rental. Since she's breaking her lease, you're actually helping her. She's leaving in five days, plenty of time for you to move in before Michael and Katy come. But there is one thing, rent's $1,700 a month."

"I think I can make that work," I say, knowing I can dig into my savings if necessary. I stand up, hesitant to put too much weight onto my leg, and hobble over to Liv, wrapping my sweaty, smelly self around her. "Thank you. Not just for making the phone call, but for reminding me that my 'perfect life' was anything but."

In a rare moment, Liv gives me a quick kiss on my cheek. "You've got this, Jenna. You don't always have to do it all alone, but it's important to know that you *can* if you need to. Everything you need is right here." She pokes her finger into my stomach causing me to laugh. It's moments like these that cement friendships.

* * *

Later that evening, as the ice and Advil start to do their trick, I contemplate the extent of my injury. When I can't run, I get cranky. Like Sam, I need exercise or I'm a pain in the ass to be around. I hobble to the kitchen, where Liv's started to make dinner, and sit on a stool by the counter.

"You know, if you feel OK in a few days, it's probably safe to do things like restorative yoga. Actually, that class might help with your recovery," she says while reaching into the refrigerator for a head of lettuce. "There're a ton of things to do besides running that won't bother your IT band. Like kayaking. And soon it might be OK to get on mountain bike." Liv rinses the lettuce and throws the wet leaves into a salad spinner.

Grinning, I say, "Remember when we were kids, I was absolutely pathetic on a bike. I would always fall and scrape my knees and elbows. One time you laughed so hard you wet your pants."

"Yeah, I remember that," Liv then begins to rip the dried lettuce into bite-sized pieces. "But that was years ago. You're an athlete now. Why not give it a try? OutRider, one of the local bike shops, sponsors rides on Tuesday nights. Sometimes, I lead the intermediate group. Let me see who's scheduled to guide the beginners next week."

"That is, if my IT band is feeling better. And don't you think I should try it first, beforehand? Plus, I don't have a bike." I'm coming up with every excuse I can think of.

"Good point, but there are free demos Tuesday nights. So, *if* you're better, you could rent a bike next weekend, and I'll take you on some easy trails. That will give your leg a good week and a half to rest." She opens the cabinet and reaches for the olive oil and vinegar.

Liv's not one to take "no" for an answer, so I resolve that I'll be leaving my comfort zone once again and most likely embarrassing myself on a bike, albeit this time on a mountain bike, not the hot pink Schwinn from my childhood, the one with sparkles and a matching helmet. Anyway, isn't this why I'm here? To try new things. Guess it's time to "walk the walk."

* * *

I lay low for the next week, elevating and icing my IT band and religiously taking Advil three times a day. Liv's recovery plan seems to have worked. While not yet ready to tackle running, I feel capable of giving biking a try.

During a shopping trip downtown yesterday, I came across a journal with a picture of a beautiful lotus flower on the cover. It reminded me of the tattoo Liv has on her shoulder. I used to journal when I was younger, but that was long ago. Yet, I remember liking it, found it soothing. Something compelled me to buy the lotus journal. Maybe writing will lead me to the answers I'm searching for. And now, as I sit quietly on my bed before going to sleep, I open to the first page of my new journal and begin.

I've been in Bend for two and a half weeks, and I rarely think of Ben. He texts me occasionally, but it's about the small stuff — a new restaurant, a mutual friend, or his latest tennis match. I've reached out a few times, but I don't want him to get the wrong idea. How can feelings change so quickly? This is the man I was going to marry. Now we're down to talking about places to eat, acquaintances, and tennis scores. It's sad, but I guess that's what happens when people break up.

Tomorrow Liv's taking me mountain biking. Since my leg's better I promised her that I'd give it a try. Still, I'm nervous. Last night Liv said that facing your fears is necessary to figure out who you are and what you want in life, so I guess I'm on the right on track because the thought of mountain biking scares the pants off of me!

On Tuesday morning I have an 8:00 a.m. interview at Northwest Crossing Elementary School for a math coach position. I spent a lot of time prepping for this interview. But there could be a ton of qualified candidates, so maybe I won't get the job. I'm not used to all of these uncertainties in my life. Boston was so much easier, more predictable, safer — but look where that got me.

CHAPTER 12

Jackson

The front door chimes as two women enter OutRider. I recognize the short blonde. She's been in the shop before. Parker… think that's her last name. Yeah, she leads some of those Tuesday night rides. But, the other one, although vaguely familiar, escapes me. I'm positive that she's never been here before. Yet, there's something about her. Damn, I've met her, but where? I remember that chestnut hair, and that smile. I probe my memory, searching for a time and place that connects me to this woman.

"Hey there, we're here to rent a bike for my friend. She just moved to Bend, and she's never been mountain biking. Actually, she doesn't really bike much at all. I thought she should check out the Tuesday night beginner rides, but beforehand, she wanted to rent a bike and try it out. You know, to get the hang of things," the short blonde says in rapid sentences without pausing, speaking for her friend, who is standing right next to her in silence.

Then I realize that she's another beginner, the type of customer I dread. This woman will need to have everything explained to her, be fitted for a bike and helmet, and be coached about the rules on the trails. But for some strange reason, I'm not feeling it. No, today my body's telling something else. I eye "the friend," conspicuously checking her out from head to toe. Who is she? I know that we've met. I get up from my desk and approach the two women, without realizing it a slight smile forms on my face.

"Olivia's right. I'm not a biker, I'm a runner," the woman finally speaks for herself. "Actually, an injured runner." She bites her lip, kind of cute and sexy at the same time. "I thought, I mean Olivia thought, that maybe I should try mountain biking." She looks at me as if she's trying to figure something out.

"By the way, I'm Jenna," she says, flashing a beautiful smile.

The ski lodge, that's it. I watched her ski down to the slopes. That was in April, when my hair was much longer. But it's shorter now, back to a more military high and tight style, better for riding in the warmer weather.

"Jackson," I say as I focus my full attention on her. This woman, who stands about five foot nine, looks stunning, radiant actually. I notice how her dark hair shines from the sunlight coming in through the front window. That's when I sense something that I haven't felt for quite some time. Curiosity. Who is she? And, how come I keep meeting her?

"I think I can help you," I say, moving closer toward her. "So, you've never been on a mountain bike before?" I grab a pen and rental form attached to a clipboard from behind the counter.

"No," Jenna says, fidgeting from one foot to the other.

"And not too much time on a road bike either?" I ask, as I check off the appropriate boxes on the form. However, I really want to know her answers, I'm not just reciting the typical pre-rental questions.

"Not really. I'm kind of challenged in this area," Jenna admits.

"No worries. Think I have something that will be just right for you," I say, giving her the best reassuring grin I can offer.

I guide Jenna to the back of the shop where I keep the rentals. Fitting her ever so carefully, I explain the mechanics and elements behind mountain biking. I help her find a helmet and adjust it so that it fits just right. When my hand casually brushes her chin as I tighten the strap, I notice that she blushes. I find myself using encouraging words and phrases – not something I'm accustomed to doing – whenever Jenna shows apprehension or hesitancy about biking on the trails. Although I can't pinpoint the reason, something inside me desperately wants to protect her.

Twenty-five minutes later, Jenna's outfitted with all of the necessary equipment. She's ready to ride. Or, at least she's as prepared as she can be. "Thank you, I really appreciate your help with all of this," she says as she hands me her credit card.

"No problem. I'm here if you need anything." I look deeply into her brown eyes as I hand her my business card, the first time I've ever shared one of the newly embossed cards that sit, unused, on the counter by the register. "I remember you from the ski lodge," I say, wondering if she recognizes me as well. "You need to use your toe to turn, not your knee." Then I give her my best wink before I begin to process her credit card. Did I actually just do that? Jesus!

"Yes, I thought that was you, but your hair, it was longer, right?" Jenna's voice becomes animated and her eyes sparkle as she seemingly puts two and two together.

"It was longer, but..." I consider saying more but decide to change the subject. "Anyway, you know, since you're new to Bend and you're just getting started biking, maybe we could go on a hike sometime. I could show you the trails on foot, until you become more comfortable on a bike" Shit! Did I really say that? What am I doing asking a girl I don't know to go hiking? I never hike – I ride.

"That would be awesome." Jenna doesn't waver. In fact, she quickly adds, "What about tomorrow? Are you working then?" Her friend snorts in the background, apparently amused at our conversation.

Monday *would* work. In fact, it's the only day that OutRider is closed.

"How about I pick you up at nine? Then we can head out to Benham

Falls." I hand Jenna her card, the receipt, and a pen. I then look at the address on her rental form. I know exactly where she lives.

"That's perfect," Jenna replies as she signs the receipt.

"You're only a few blocks from the shop, on Indiana Street?" I ask envisioning the location of her house.

"For now. I've been staying with my friend," Jenna says, nodding toward the blonde who is going through the rack of women's biking shorts. "But next week I'm moving into my own place."

I smile wondering why she moved here and what her story is. But I figure that I'll learn more tomorrow, so I say, "See you at nine sharp. Remember to bring water and use a lot of sunscreen. You can easily become dehydrated or burn at these high altitudes." I sound authoritative in my directive, a habit from my former life.

"OK, see you Monday at nine!" Jenna says, flashing that smile, the one I remember so clearly from that afternoon on the mountain.

After the women exit the shop with the rental bike and helmet, I return to my desk. I just asked someone out, for the first time in over a year. There was absolutely no hesitation. It was almost as if I were on autopilot, sensed that she was safe, believed that she wouldn't try to "fix" me. Maybe she'll be like the rest and want a serious relationship, becoming clingy, a trait I despise. Regardless, I have a date, if hiking with someone qualifies as a date. Maybe it does. Either way, I guess I could use a hike, be in nature while not on my bike, hang with someone who knows nothing about me, my past, or my demons. I just hope I'm ready. I rub my forehead. I still can't believe I just asked her out. Fuck. Now I have to actually go through with it. Clearly ironic, a decorated SEAL who led countless missions in the Middle East, expressing anxiety over being alone on the trails with a woman. If only my men could hear this. They would burst out laughing, totally give me shit and call me names. But maybe hiking with Jenna is a test, a kind of measure to see how ready I actually am to fully assimilate back into civilian life. It's been close to a year and a half. I'll never forget Afghanistan, but am I capable of feeling normal again? Could I actually have a relationship with someone? Am I ready?

CHAPTER 13

Jenna

The alarm sounds. As I yawn and stretch, I notice a slight sting on my right shin, so I pull my leg out from under the covers to inspect it. Oh yeah, that's from yesterday's "easy bike ride" with Liv. Can't believe I fell into the bushes. Think I took off five inches of the skin on my shin from that spiky pedal. *Ugh*. At least my IT band is feeling almost back to normal.

My next thought is today's Monday, the day I'm scheduled to hike with Jackson, who I just met yesterday at the bike shop. Actually, that's not true, I'd also met him at the ski lodge in April.

Liv's already up. But before she can even say "good morning," I begin to deluge her with questions as I walk into the kitchen.

"What kind of hike will this be? I mean, it won't be crazy hard, will it? What should I wear? How hot will it get?" Without even tasting my first cup of coffee I'm already wired.

"Seriously, you've never been hiking?" Liv asks as she looks up from the morning paper.

"Well, no," I admit, reaching into the back of the cabinet for a coffee mug. "Not unless you count that overnight field trip to New Hampshire in ninth grade."

"Ha!" Liv laughs aloud. "That wasn't real hiking. The trails were asphalt."

"Oh," I say as I begin to realize how little I know about the outdoors. "But it's not my fault. I never went to camp as a kid, and my family went to the beach, not the mountains. To be honest, the wilderness makes me a bit uneasy." I pour the dark steamy liquid into my cup, savoring the aroma.

"You're impossible," Liv says while shaking her head. "The most important thing is what's on your feet. What shoes were you planning to wear?"

"My running shoes." Oblivious as to where she's going, I check the fridge to see if there are any berries left from our trip to the Northwest Crossing Market.

"Yeah, running shoes are fine if you want to fall on your ass. Jenna, you need thick socks and hiking boots, or trail shoes at the least. Are you still a size eight and a half?" Liv asks as she gets up and goes upstairs toward her bedroom.

"Yes!" I shout back as I put berries into a bowl and rinse them under the faucet. Despite Olivia's small frame, she has big feet. "Do you have something I can borrow?" I ask, hoping that she does. This would not be the first time Liv has exactly what I don't.

"Try these on." Liv returns to the kitchen, handing me a pair of hiking shoes along with a thick pair of gray wool sock. "I bought these boots at a clearance sale last fall, but I haven't worn them yet, so they might be a bit stiff. And wear these socks. They should help prevent blisters."

"Thanks, this is huge, Liv," I say as I inspect the heavy treaded, unattractive dark suede boots.

"Listen, I don't know Jackson at all. My only contact with him has been when I've been at OutRider before group rides. The thing is, I never see him out. Not at bars, restaurants, never anywhere but at his shop or on the trails. And then, he's always riding by himself. I think he's totally safe, but I don't know his story. Somehow, he seems a bit, well, complicated. He might be pretty different from the guys you've dated." Liv normally doesn't warn me like this.

"I know. There's definitely something unusual about him. I can't explain it, but for some reason, I want to know more," I say, pouring cereal into the bowl and topping it off with a generous helping of milk. Silently, I sit down at the kitchen table and slowly eat my breakfast, my mind envisioning possible scenarios that I might encounter during this "hike" in the wilderness with a man I just met.

* * *

Forty minutes later, I change out of my pajamas and into shorts, a tank top, and a sweatshirt. I put on the wool socks before pulling on the hiking shoes, carefully double knotting the laces. Luckily, they fit perfectly. Next, I go into the bathroom, apply generous amounts of sunscreen, put my hair into a ponytail and add just a hint of make-up. I spot my Red Sox cap and decide to bring it along, just in case there are ticks. I have no idea what I'll encounter. Are there bears in Bend? I'm terrified of them. However, a part of me senses that it won't matter – I'll be safe with Jackson.

"I think he's here," Liv yells to me. I glance at my watch – it's 8:59. Wow, he's punctual.

Hurrying into the living room, I look out the front window as Jackson emerges from the driver's side of a black pick-up truck. I quickly grab my sunglasses from the counter and a bottle of water from the fridge before heading outside. As I open the front door, Jackson, dressed in gray gear pants and a navy t-shirt, is walking toward the house. I can't help but notice how his lean, muscular body flexes with each movement. He greets me warmly, casually touching my arm as he holds my gaze a bit longer than expected. Sam begins barking, conveying that "don't leave me" sound.

"Do you want to bring him?" Jackson asks as I begin to head out

144

the door.

Instantly comforted at the thought of having Sam by my side – it's always good to have a wingman or a wing dog in this case – I call for him to come. But before I can say his name, Sam bounds out of the house holding his leash in his mouth.

"So that's a yes," Jackson laughs as we head down the porch steps. I climb, as gracefully as possible, into the passenger side of the truck after Sam jumps into the back. Jackson closes my door, never once taking his eyes off of me.

We're off, Jackson, Sam, and I on a date – or perhaps it's only a hike. I can't tell which. Either way, something inside whispers that this is just the beginning. Unsure of what exactly this is the beginning to, I have a sense that it will certainly not be what I expect. No, Jackson is not Ben, not in the least. And Bend is most definitely not Boston.

"So, where are you from?" I ask Jackson, attempting the awkward first conversation that accompanies being alone with someone you don't know.

"Ross, California," he responds in a pleasant tone, but that's all the information he gives.

I look back at Sam. His head rests on the rolled down window and his mouth has the biggest dog smile possible as the wind blows into his face. I continue to try to engage Jackson, "Do you have any siblings?"

"One, a brother, Matt. He lives nearby, in Northwest Crossing, with his girlfriend." Jackpot. He's given me something. I continue to ask away, yet Jackson carefully weighs his responses, offering just the minimum to answer my questions. Is he not interested in me, or is he just private? Ben was always so open, but with Jackson I feel like I'm pulling teeth to get more than a basic response.

When we arrive at the trailhead, Sam bolts from the truck and heads toward the path beautifully nestled between high wild grasses. The Deschutes River flows majestically on the left while a variety of wildflowers inhabit the vast meadow on the right. Jackson and I walk on the dirt path while Sam darts ahead, behind, sideways, and between us. There is so much for this dog to explore.

"Sometimes, early in the morning, you can see elk at the other end by those pine trees," Jackson says, pointing toward the meadow laced with evergreens to our west. I envision how amazing it would be to spot such majestic creatures, but then I nervously wonder where they are right now and if we'll encounter them or some other kind of big animal on our hike.

High reeds line the riverbanks, but Sam easily maneuvers through the thick growth. He makes a loud splash. Goldens love the water, making this the perfect playground for him. Paddle boarders glide upstream, utilizing their muscles to battle the strong current. The trail is not crowded, but we see other hikers and several runners.

The beauty of the flowing water is a calming background, which helps me relax. I'm nervous, not only about my lack of hiking experience, but also about being alone with Jackson. Yes, there was Mark, but alcohol infused that situation, and there wasn't exactly a lot of real conversation happening that night. Before Ben, I dated some guys, but that was so long ago. I always preferred relationships, shying away from casual dates and the unease that accompanies them as well as the unpredictability of what might or might not happen.

Yet, something about today suggests otherwise. I watch as his powerful, sinewy body navigates the trail with ease, pausing from time to time, allowing me to catch up. Only twice do I trip on rocks. Each time I catch myself, avoiding a tumble. I remind myself to be careful, I can't afford to reinjure my leg. Still, my mind's focused on Jackson. Hugely curious, I crave to know more about this man and discover what makes him tick. Yet, he keeps giving me mixed signals, almost appearing standoffish at times. Perhaps that makes him even more intriguing.

Eventually, we arrive at the falls.

"It's gorgeous," I say as we climb the final steps to the lookout in front of the cascading waterfalls and sit down on a large boulder.

"I know, it's beautiful. Benham is one of my favorite spots in Bend. Sometimes I come here just to think." Jackson offers me a glimpse inside of him, but only for a moment.

Sam sits by my side, recuperating from the hike. I hold onto him tightly just in case he gets some crazy idea about going into the water by the waterfall. "The sound of the rushing water is incredibly soothing. If any place could provide a sanctuary, this might be it," I say as I pour water from my bottle into my cupped hand for Sam to drink. "That's why I run... it's where I solve all of my problems, or at least try to. And if I can't figure them out, then it's therapy just pounding the pavement. I miss it."

"Is that how you hurt yourself? Running? Were you trying to figure something out?" Jackson must have remembered me talking about my injury yesterday.

"I'm trying to figure out a lot right now," I admit, staring straight ahead while stroking Sam's head. "Three weeks ago, I left Boston, where I grew up, and moved here. When you first saw me at Mount Bachelor, I was just visiting Olivia, kind of a last-minute trip." I turn toward Jackson.

He remains silent, looking intently at me, allowing me to continue.

"You see, I was with someone... for six years." Stop. Pause. Don't continue. Then, for some unknown reason, I do.

"I was engaged." All of a sudden, my throat tightens. Yesterday would have been our wedding. After forcing myself to swallow, I admit this to Jackson, "Actually, we were supposed to be married yesterday." I look down, fixating on the gravel below. How could I not remember my wedding day?

"What happened?" Jackson asks, placing his hand on my shoulder.

The tenderness of his unexpected touch brings me back to the present. I glance up at him, noticing that his face has turned serious. He probably thinks I'm crazy to be here – with him – the day after I was supposed to be married – to someone else. If I could take the words back, I would. But I can't.

I hesitate, unsure that I can share my story with someone I barely know. Staring at the water that's cascading off of the falls, I momentarily become lost in its melodic rhythm. Churning water crashes over the boulders at the fall's base before joining the flow for the long trek downstream. I gaze up and see Jackson looking at me in a knowing way. Without using words, those sea green eyes focus solely on me, giving me strength. So, I share my story, telling Jackson about Ben, his controlling behaviors, Aunt Catherine, the house he bought, and the ultimatum I gave.

"He wouldn't change his mind, even after you left?" Jackson questions as he leans in a bit closer. Damn, this man is gorgeous.

"No, it came down to his aunt or me… and he chose his aunt." There, I've said it. But somehow, I feel OK, like a heavy weight had been lifted from my shoulder. Being honest with Jackson seems so natural.

"Better to find out now, right?" Jackson states in a tender but somewhat provocative voice, pulling me deeper into his eyes as he tilts his head slightly and bites his lower lip. This distracts me, and my thoughts leave my failed engagement and center only on Jackson. Just hearing his deep voice stirs something inside.

"That's what Olivia and my mom said." I allow myself to laugh.

"He sounds like a good guy, but it seems that he's got some stuff to work out," Jackson says without criticizing Ben. He picks up a pebble and starts rubbing it between his fingers. Watching him makes me wonder what it feels like to be that pebble. Then Jackson tosses the stone into the water below.

"Yeah, well, I still feel pretty shitty about the whole thing." I stop myself from saying more, having already revealed enough. I cannot believe I just bared my soul to Jackson about another man – the one I was going to marry yesterday.

"Things have a way of working out." Jackson places his hand on top of mine, causing my heartbeat to quicken.

Is this a sympathy move, or could it be something else? I'm not sure how to read Jackson. But he doesn't pull away, instead his fingers carefully weave into mine, and I realize he's now holding my hand. Suddenly Ben, who despite being more than three thousand miles away, has completely vanished from my thoughts. It's Jackson who is captivating me. Moved by just his touch, I sense that this man is different. With Jackson, I know I would have a voice.

"So, what do you think about when you come here?" I lean toward Jackson.

"There's some shit I've been dealing with." He unlaces his fingers from mine.

Noting the hesitancy in his voice, I don't want to push him, so I remain silent and wait patiently. It's now *me* who is looking intensely into *his* eyes. I feel as though I am intimately connected to Jackson, almost as if known him for most of my life.

"I usually don't discuss it," he says as he jaw seems to tighten.

I refrain from saying something as trite as "no worries" or a phrase equally as unoriginal. Instead I give him time.

Jackson pulls a few blades of grass from the ground and then, without looking up, he begins to tell me about a fateful mission in Afghanistan. I'm in awe, totally amazed that he was once a SEAL. When he relays the blast, my heart breaks for Patrick, but my body yearns to embrace Jackson and to tell him that it wasn't his fault.

Finally, he concludes his story by saying, "Patrick was in my platoon, under my command. It was my job to make sure that all of my men returned home safely. He didn't, and I'm responsible for that." Now it's Jackson who stares into the foam at the bottom of the waterfall.

Searching for a way to offer comfort, I reach for his hand. His warmth penetrates deeply into my fingertips. "I know nothing about being a SEAL, but I would guess that Patrick knew the risks involved. This was not your fault." I emphasize the last three words.

"Yeah," Jackson smiles briefly, then pulls his hand away. "Let's head back."

Damn it. I said the wrong thing. I should have kept my mouth shut. Sam and I follow Jackson – in silence – as we wind our way back along the path high above the river's bank. Trying to be light and engaging, I ask Jackson about mountain biking, reminding him that I have the group ride tomorrow and ask if I can return the bike afterward. I ramble on awkwardly, recounting yesterday's trail ride with Olivia and sharing how nervous I am about tomorrow's interview for a math coach position. Although I notice that he's become mentally absent, I continue this one-way dialogue in hopes of filling the void that now exists between us.

Jackson remains quiet, nodding every once in a while, but not saying a word. I've lost him. I had a glimpse, but then he disappeared.

CHAPTER 14

Jackson

"You took a girl on a date today? Really? Who was she? Tell me about it." Relentless, my brother, Matt, who stands six foot two and prides himself on his Cross Fit body, drills me during our weekly Monday night dinner at the home in Northwest Crossing that he shares with his girlfriend, Simone. Matt and I debate the proper name for today's excursion while Simone busily chops zucchini on a thick wooden cutting board.

"Matt, I took her to Benham Falls, it wasn't a date. She's new to Bend. Thought I would show her around." I sound too defensive.

"First of all, *you* never *show people around*. Since you've moved here, when have you ever done that? And, secondly, it was a date," Matt argues, pushing his blonde hair across his forehead.

"What's she like?" Simone, a fiery red head who always seems to have the last word, asks as she puts down the knife and joins us at the table. I'm usually cautious about what I say around Simone. She has her doctorate in Psychology, and I don't want her psychoanalyzing me.

"Her name is Jenna, and I met her at the shop. Actually, I first met her in April at Bachelor, but just for a moment. We remembered each other, so I kind of felt like I should reach out. She just left Boston, broke up with some guy she was with for six years. They were supposed to get married yesterday," I say then casually sip my beer as if this always happens to me.

"Wow, this is so, um, so unexpected." Simone sits up tall and give me her full attention. "She was supposed to get married yesterday but she was on a hike with you today? Way to go, Jackson. Didn't know you were such a stud," Simone says in a teasing tone. I hate being teased. "So, when do you plan on seeing her again?" Damn Simone's direct. Her green eyes seem to grow bigger as if to make a point.

"I don't know. We didn't go there. The day started out really well. When we reached the falls, we started talking, you know about stuff. That's when she told me why she left Boston. And, then, somehow, I'm not sure why it happened, I...um...well, I told her... about Patrick." I shift uneasily in my chair.

Both Matt and Simone freeze.

"Wow, I mean, you never talk about this with anyone. We hardly discuss it. It's just kind of surprising that you opened up to someone you just met," Matt says, eyes wide with disbelief.

I clam up. I've said enough already.

After an awkward pause, Simone leaves us briefly to put together a plate of chips and salsa, which she then places between Matt and me. "You know, this Jenna seems kind of special. Maybe you should get to know her better. It's hard to find someone who you can be honest with. Why don't you call her?" Simone isn't suggesting this. From the tone of her voice it's more of a command.

"Easier said than done. The day sort of ended uncomfortably," I confess as my shoulders hunch closer to my ears. "I kind of freaked out that I told her about Patrick, so I was quiet the entire way back to the truck, maybe even bordering on being an ass. I think I blew it." As I admit to fucking up the day, I can't help but remember how good it was to be around Jenna. Just touching her skin and inhaling her perfume – being with Jenna felt easy and natural.

"You didn't blow it. Maybe you just confused her a bit. More of a reason to contact her," Matt says before taking a swig of his beer.

Then it hits me. "Shit, she's coming to OutRider tomorrow night for the beginners' group ride." How could I have forgotten? Plus, she'll need to return the rental. I can't avoid seeing her again.

"Why don't you go with her, Jackson? Or you could offer to lead the beginners' group," Simone encourages as she returns to preparing dinner. Simone just can't sit still.

"Well if you do that, you should really call her first," Matt says. "Otherwise, it might be weird." He scoops the salsa with a big tortilla chip.

Feeling the pressure of them ganging up on me, I reluctantly give in.

"OK, OK. I'll text her, but I'm definitely not leading a beginner's group."

Simone gives me that look. Damn it!

"Fine. I'll offer to take her out on the trails, but just the two of us. You good with that?" I finish my beer then go to the fridge to reload.

Smiling in response to my compromise, Simone says, "It's settled then, so ask her. Now!"

Simone can be such a demanding woman. How does Matt deal with her? But then I look at my brother and see how happy he's been since they met. After all, Simone's intelligent, motivated, and athletic. She teaches Psychology at Oregon State University's Cascades campus, here in Bend. But my favorite thing about Simone is that she's an amazing cook, one of the reasons I never refuse their Monday night dinner invitations. I grab my phone and text Jenna.

Me: *Hey, how about I take you biking tomorrow night instead of you going on the group ride? And if you're up for it, we could grab dinner afterward.*

"Done. Let's see if she responds." I put my phone onto the table face up.

For the remainder of the dinner, I can't stop watching my phone, waiting to see if Jenna texts me.

Matt and I do the dishes while Simone places slices of freshly baked warm cherry pie on the table. From across the room I hear my phone sound. I toss the dishtowel on the counter then quickly grab my cell from the table. It's her.

Jenna: *Are you sure? I'm kind of a mess on a bike. But, if you're up for it, then yes. Same time as the group ride?*

I answer immediately.

Me: *How about 5:15 at the shop? We can leave before the groups take off. I'm totally up for it.*

Proud of myself for the somewhat suggestive comment, I can now focus on Matt and Simone. I complement my brother's girlfriend on her baking skills and ask Matt about work before sharing how things are going at OutRider.

Matt and Simone catch each other's eye, perhaps in validation that they are witnessing a different version of me, one Simone's probably never seen before. In fact, I can't remember the last time I had so much fun during one of our Monday night dinners. Instead of leaving by nine o'clock, as has been my norm, I stay to watch the Giants play the Dodgers. Matt and I cheer for our team while trash talking the Giants players. Instinctively, Simone knows that this is relished "bro time" and claims the need to grade papers for her class. But the look on her face gives her away.

"I'm not sure who this Jenna is, but if she makes you this happy, don't let her slip away. Good to have you back, Jackson," my brother says, slapping my back as we watch outfielder Steven Duggar slam a homerun.

* * *

For the first time in over two years, I sleep through the alarm. It's 6:15 when I finally wake up. Jesus, what was in that cherry pie? I haven't racked so many hours since – I can't even remember. Crap, I don't want to miss my workout. I bolt out of bed, grabbing some sweats and sneakers.

Somehow this morning's routine flows flawlessly. I even had the urge to turn on music, something I stopped doing during workouts. The kettle bell floats through the air, pull-ups seem effortless, and I set a personal record for sit-ups. No, she has nothing to do with that. Wipe that thought from your brain. It has to be the warmer weather or the carbs from the pie.

Despite my attempts to rationalize this ramped up performance, I can't help but wonder if Jenna is the source of my renewed spirit. Could a woman, one who I just met, really have this effect on me? Unable to put it into words, all I know is that I somehow feel better prepared to move throughout my day. I'm not dreading the thought of dealing with new riders who come into the shop. In fact, knowing that I'll see Jenna tonight energizes me for whatever might happen today. I turn off the lights in my apartment and head downstairs.

CHAPTER 15

Jenna

Leaving Northwest Crossing Elementary School, I'm pretty confident that I nailed the interview. However, three hours later my winning streak comes to an abrupt end when Marjorie Rider, the school's principal, calls to tell me that I am not the chosen candidate. My heart drops to the bottom of my stomach.

"I understand, Mrs. Rider, truly, I do." But I don't. I could do the job, probably better than the chosen candidate. "Do you know of any other positions open at Northwest?" I want to work there. The school seems pretty spectacular.

"Unfortunately, no, and please call me Marjorie. Jenna, I can tell that you are an excellent teacher, and if we were hiring for other positions, I would seriously consider you. But, there's nothing available."

We say our goodbyes and I hang up the phone. I look at Sam and sigh, "This is going to be harder than I thought." Perhaps on instinct, he gives me a big lick on my cheek then nudges me to pet him. It's pretty incredible how intuitive animals can be.

Five minutes later the front door opens. Olivia juggles several grocery bags as she attempts to pull her keys from the lock. I jump up to help.

"You look like you lost your best friend, but that can't be because I'm right here." Liv's always one to instill humor into any situation.

I place the heavy bag on the kitchen counter. "The principal from Northwest Crossing just called. I didn't get the job." I pause, still trying to connect the dots as to why I wasn't chosen. I fill Liv in on the conversation as we unpack the groceries.

"Did you ever think about doing something besides teaching?" Liv asks as she puts the last item, a carton of eggs, inside the refrigerator.

"What do you mean?" I say taking a seat on the sofa.

"What I mean is if there aren't teaching jobs available, then what else can you do?" She asks as she closes the refrigerator door. "Maybe something *will* open up and *then* you can add your name to the hat. But in the meantime, why not try another avenue? What about a job like bartending? I've always wanted to be a bartender." Liv says as she unpeels a banana and takes a big bite.

"I'm a teacher, Liv. That's what I do, what I've always done. I can't even imagine starting over." I bury my head into the sofa pillow in an act of frustration.

"And, if I may remind you, you also always lived in the Boston area, and you always had a boyfriend, and you always tried to please everyone, and you always tried to be perfect, and you always..." She takes another bite before tossing the peel into the trash can.

I throw the pillow at Olivia, a reluctant smile forming on my face. "Stop it! I get where you're going. I'm not here to do what I've always done. But a career change? That's huge. What could I do?"

"That's what's so fucking awesome. You get to play, have fun, apply for jobs that you would never have considered because they didn't fit into what you thought you were supposed to do. Seriously, let's look online and see what's out there." Liv goes into her bedroom.

While Olivia retrieves her laptop, I decide to make some tea. Something tells me a stronger beverage might be more in order, but it's only noon and we've got a lot of work ahead of us.

An hour later, we've identified five possible leads – a hostess at Drake, a barista at Spoken Motto, a salesclerk at Patagonia, a program director for a summer camp, and a manager at Tanager, a downtown art gallery.

"God, what a random group of jobs. What do you think? Could I do any of these?" I ask, still not convinced that I should venture outside of the classroom. I find a pad of paper and a pencil and settle in on the couch.

"You'd be great at all of them. Think about each one and consider how you would be spending your day, the hours that you'd be working, and how much you'd make," Liv suggests.

I take a few moments and write down some pros and cons for each position. "I don't like the thought of working at night, so forget the hostess and barista-bartender jobs. That leaves Patagonia, the summer camp, and Tanager. Any thoughts?"

"Well, the camp director seems like a solid match because you're awesome with kids. But, I'm not sure about the pay. Plus, what happens in the fall when the kids return to school? Have you ever worked in retail?" Liv asks as she sits down in the navy armchair across from me and pulls up Patagonia's website.

"No, I haven't. I sometimes find salesclerks to be annoying, almost like they're watching everything I do, checking to see if I've shoved a piece of merchandise into my purse. Either that, or they try to pressure me into buying something I don't want, claiming it will look *fabulous* when I try it on." I roll my eyes.

Laughing, Liv says, "Well then, that pretty much narrows it down to the position at the gallery. Do you know anything about art?"

I pause before responding. "I know I like it. But, no, I only took one art class in college." Renaissance to Modern Times – with Professor Braden – that was the course.

"Remember, it's all how you sell yourself. Consider what a director of a gallery does." Liv encourages me to think outside the box.

"Well, I guess you'd need to be organized, set up showings, ensure that items are properly categorized and displayed." I reposition myself on the sofa, shoving a pillow behind my back.

Liv moves her hands in a circular motion, encouraging me to continue.

"Plus, you'd need strong interpersonal abilities to deal with clients and artists," I sit up straighter.

"Yep. Keep going," Liv nods her head as I speak.

"It would be important to have efficient computer skills, as I doubt that there is a staff or an assistant. Plus, you should know a bit about marketing and advertising events, kind of like an event planner." As I speak, I detect confidence slowly rising inside.

"Exactly! Maybe you don't know a Cezanne from a Picasso, but you can figure that stuff out." Liv jumps out of the chair. "This job encompasses organization, planning, and people skills. You are gifted in all of those areas. I am sure that you will be able to compensate for what you lack in background knowledge about art. Here's the number for the gallery. Call them now." From her behavior you'd think Liv had been a cheerleader in high school, not a star on both the basketball court and the lacrosse field.

Once again, Liv does what Liv always does to propel me into forward motion. Resigning to the fact that this moment is as good of time as any, I dial the number.

The owner answers after the second ring. Within two minutes I learn from her that the current manager just had a baby and requested to take up to a year off. Presently, they're looking for someone to run the gallery while she's at home with her newborn.

"Have you ever worked at a gallery or a museum?" she asks in a precise manner.

I admit that I haven't, but energetically begin my sales pitch as to why I believe I would be a qualified manager for Tanager.

The woman, who then introduces herself as Claire Reese, shares that she and her husband, Don, opened Tanager five years ago.

"We showcase local artists each first Friday during the Art Walks downtown. Tanager also hosts monthly exhibits, featuring a variety of genres. Instead of focusing on a particular style, we prefer to offer our clientele a diverse display of artwork."

This job sounds so interesting. Maybe I *could* do this. Losing out on the math job made me question my professional abilities. But for some reason, maybe it was Liv's coaching, I'm beginning to feel capable, ready to put myself out there and try something new.

I must have made a positive impression because Claire suggests that we meet the next morning to discuss the position.

"What did I tell you? Believe. Your thoughts become your realities," she says in an "I told you so" fashion.

And so, I begin to prepare for tomorrow, taking copious notes as I research gallery operations and brush up on the Bend art scene. After reading multiple articles, I wonder why I didn't take more art courses in college.

But then my mind wanders to later this afternoon and my ride with Jackson. As much as I want to see him, yesterday didn't exactly end well. Plus, I'm kind of nervous about getting on a bike again. I glance down at my leg, hoping I don't fall and embarrass myself.

Knowing what I need to do, I shut my laptop and change into a t-shirt and a pair of bike shorts that Liv lent to me. After remembering to put on my helmet, I carefully climb on the rental bike and slowly start peddling. A bit wobbly at first, I begin to feel more at ease as I practice laps around Liv's neighborhood. Please let today's ride with Jackson be easier than Sunday's fiasco. But as I glance down at my newly formed scab, I feel anything but encouragement. The smooth pavement that's beneath my tires is a totally different feeling than the rocky terrain of the trails that I'll encounter tonight. Still, I try.

CHAPTER 16

Jackson

Figuring it's easier to start from Phil's Trailhead, I put our bikes into the back of my truck. Jenna's fairly quiet. I'm not sure if she's acting this way because of how yesterday's hike ended or if she's nervous about riding.

Fifteen minutes later we pull into the Phil's parking lot. I brought my fat bike, figured the wide wheelbase would be fine on the easy trails that I have planned for today. I hand Jenna the purple Santa Cruz Juliana bike that I fitted her with on Sunday. I normally wouldn't rent a Santa Cruz to a beginner, but I wanted to make sure that Jenna had a solid bike.

"Follow me," I say in a relaxed manner as I lead the way down to "Kent's," one of the easiest trails. When I look over my shoulder several minutes later, I don't see Jenna. Where is she? But then I spot her, cautiously rounding the corner. She stops, putting both feet on the ground, then struggles to start up again.

She wasn't kidding when she said that she's challenged on a bike. Keeping this thought to myself, I patiently wait as Jenna furiously tries to catch up. Seeing the look of determination on her face, I grin, amazed that despite how difficult this appears to be for her, she keeps pedaling, slow and steady. Dressed in black bike shorts, which look incredibly short – or maybe it's just because her legs are so long – and a loose-fitting Patriot's t-shirt with Tom Brady's number on the back, Jenna doesn't come close to resembling a mountain biker.

Already she'd taken a few tumbles on the down hills. The trail must seem pretty narrow to Jenna because she freezes whenever she rides close to tree trunks. There are just too many things wrong with how she is approaching this. Jenna takes her feet off the pedals to steady herself, even when the bike is moving. She starts by sitting on her seat then tries to peddle like crazy. She brakes constantly while navigating the down hills. Still, Jenna looks adorable.

I don't correct her. Instead, I only encourage Jenna, offering bits of advice, hoping that eventually she'll catch on. I wait patiently when she gets off her bike to walk around protruding rocks, and I pretend not to notice when she falls into the low brush.

But after about an hour, I decide that she's had enough. "How about we ride back to the parking lot and then drop off our bikes at OutRider? We can change there before heading to dinner."

Relief sweeps across her face.

Forty minutes later, after storing our bikes and changing clothes, we arrive at Parilla Grill, a Mexican restaurant several blocks from Outrider. We go to the counter. Jenna orders a margarita and a fish burrito while I decide on a Modelo Especial with a Jambalaya Wrap. While I pay, Jenna takes her food and drink with her and goes outside to check for an empty table.

When I walk out onto the deck, I see Jenna at a corner table. As I sit down next to her, she asks, "How come people in Bend are so relaxed? Is it because they're always outdoors doing things that they love?"

A night breeze passes by and I catch her scent, the one I remembered from yesterday. Momentarily distracted, I force myself to refocus and then answer her question. "I think people here seem to accept themselves and others for who they are. There's not a lot of judgment or comparison." I think back to growing up outside of San Francisco. That vibe was definitely different than it is here in Bend.

"Also, what's with all of the dogs in Bend? Look, there are two dogs over there at that table." Jenna's eyes grow wide as she tilts her head in the direction of the two enormous yellow labs. "People seem to bring their dogs everywhere. Do you have a dog?" Jenna asks as the tip of her tongue suddenly grazes her lips. Damn, that does something to me.

"No. I've thought about it, but I wanted to wait until I could properly care for a dog." Not a false statement. But the truth is I cannot imagine having anything depend on me right now.

"Maybe you should, especially since your business is right below where you live. If you like, we could stop at the local shelter and see if there are any dogs that you connect to. I would love to help you find one," Jenna says with excitement. Too much excitement, if you ask me.

Not one who likes to be pushed, my immediate reaction is to tell her "no," but something prevents me from doing that. Instead, I lean back in my chair and enjoy my view of her.

"Well, it's something to think about," I say, resisting the instinct to ask her to back off.

She gives me that smile, and I think that I'd take an entire litter of dogs if she would look at me that way every day.

"So, have you heard anything about your interview from this morning?" I ask, feeling confident that she will be chosen for the job.

"Well," Jenna starts, "apparently I didn't do as well as I thought. They hired someone else." Her eyes momentarily shift to the plank flooring of the deck below before turning up toward me.

"I'm sorry." I see the hurt in her eyes and sense that she would be great with kids.

"Olivia's trying to convince me to try something different, something besides teaching, until there's an opening at one of the schools. This afternoon we looked at job posting online, you know, non-teaching positions," she says as she takes a sip of her salt-rimmed margarita.

"Really?" I ask, genuinely interested.

"I ended up calling the owner of an art gallery about a position." Jenna laughs under her breath. "Apparently the manager just had a baby, so they need someone to fill in until she returns."

"Do you like art?" I ask, fixated on Jenna's lips, still moist from the margarita.

"My art skills are pretty much limited to painting the walls of my former living spaces." Jenna grins as she says this. "Truthfully, I know nothing about it, but Olivia's convinced that I have the necessary skills. So, I figured I'd try. I'm meeting with the owner tomorrow morning." I detect a hint of adventure in Jenna's voice. She takes another sip of her drink. Once again, my eyes are drawn to her lips.

I shift in my seat, positioning myself closer to Jenna before saying, "Is this something that you would have 'tried' when you lived in Boston? Or, is this part of the new Jenna?" I tease as I casually brush a bit of salt from the corner of her mouth.

A faint blush appears on her face, but she doesn't miss a beat. "To be honest, I'm not very comfortable trying anything new. I could really screw up, disappoint someone, or maybe myself. And I don't like doing that." I'm amazed with the casualness that Jenna admits her shortcomings. That sure as hell isn't something I'd do.

"But, for some reason, here, well, it's different. I'm not sure why, but I seem to be taking more risks – like mountain biking." Jenna points to her leg as she makes her point. Her right shin has two fresh cuts from tonight's ride. But it's her thighs, gently exposed from the bottom of her sundress that catches my attention.

My eyes meet hers. "Yes, you are, and I have to say that it intrigues me. Why now? Is it Olivia's influence, or is there something else behind the *new Jenna*?" I act like I'm kidding, but I really want to know.

"I have no idea." Jenna looks away. "I think it's all part of the aftermath of ending things with Ben. It made me question everything – who I was, what I wanted to do, who I wanted to be. I realized that I loved teaching, but I wasn't really that passionate about the other parts of my life." She takes a bite of her burrito.

"Like your fiancé?" I put it out there, plain and simple, before digging into my dinner, instantly remembering why I always order the same thing at Parilla.

"Ouch." She laughs as she finishes her bite. "Maybe, yes...Ben's great, but he's not what I need." Jenna quickly says as she takes a sip of the margarita and returns her gaze in my direction.

"What do you need?" I regret the words as they come out of my mouth. What the fuck was I thinking?

Jenna pauses before answering. "I'm hoping to find that out," she says ever so softly, leaning her body closer all while staring straight into my eyes.

Almost on cue, I shift my chair closer to Jenna then place my hand on her back, pulling her into me as I gently kiss her, tasting the tequila that lingers on her lips. I pause for a moment, but then it is Jenna who kisses me.

CHAPTER 17

Jenna

I'm scheduled to meet Claire Reese at eleven this morning. Normally I'd wake up early, eager to prepare for a meeting like this. But not today. I slept through my alarm, and now I'm walking aimlessly around the house. I leave some half-eaten toast on the kitchen table and then go upstairs to my bedroom, put on one earring then return to the kitchen before I remember about the other. I can't stop thinking about Jackson, about last night. The memory of how he felt, his taste, it still lingers.

I leave breakfast behind and take Sam for a walk along the river path, hoping that fresh air and sunshine will help me refocus. Already, the trail's packed with runners. Normally this would depress me, as I hate seeing others doing what I cannot. But I feel none of those emotions today. Instead, still high from last night, I soak in this magical setting and inhale the faint scent of the surrounding juniper trees.

Gazing into the water, my mind shifts to last night with Jackson. I close my eyes and try to return to that moment, when for several minutes everything felt intoxicating, nothing like I ever experienced with Ben.

Becoming impatient, Sam starts pulling against his leash, prompting me to continue down the trail. For the remainder of our walk, my brain vacillates between being totally absorbed with blissful memories of last night and becoming anxious about today's interview at Tanager. I prefer to think about Jackson, yet I know that I need to be on my game when I meet with Claire.

As we finish the loop and head back to the house, it hits me that in two days Sam and I will have a new route to the river. I move on Friday. Between meeting Jackson and looking for a job, I've barely thought about my next home. But for some reason, I'm not worried about having things perfect when I move in. Instead, I know that everything will be fine.

* * *

Large stained-glass windows framed in weathered metal border the gallery's front door. I feel a twinge in my belly as I enter Tanager. But then a soothing chime sounds, announcing my arrival. The space is larger than I expected, and the décor is a mix of modern and mountain.

A small woman with short dark hair, wispy around her face, greets me. "You must be Jenna. I'm Claire."

Spoken in an almost mystic tone, her voice captivates me. This petite woman, who looks to be in her late fifties, is elegantly stunning. I can't help but notice Claire's gorgeous jewelry – an exquisite silver and turquoise necklace complements her black tunic.

"It's a pleasure to meet you." Immediately my breathing calms, and I feel my pulse slow down.

"Please, come in. Let me show you around, and then we can sit and chat."

I'm captivated by the stunning paintings perfectly hung on the rustic plank walls. It's almost as if the pictures are positioned to tell a story. I then take note of the gallery's flooring. It's a unique mixture of forged metal and aged hardwood.

Claire motions to a seating area in the center of the gallery. As we sit down on matching Mid-century wooden upholstered chairs, Clair asks, "So Jenna, why do you want to manage Tanager?" No small talk. Claire's direct and to the point. She picks up a leather-bound notebook and opens it. Pen in hand, she's poised to begin the interview.

And so, for the next hour we discuss the position, my qualifications, and the vision she and her husband have for the gallery.

Finally, she closes her notebook and says, "You shared that your first love is teaching, but I believe that you have an inherent talent to do this job. I normally wouldn't hire someone with no experience, but I'm going to go on instinct. It's served me very well in the past. Jenna, I'm offering you the position."

Upon hearing her words, energy pulsates through my entire body, boosting my confidence. After finalizing the terms of my employment, Claire and I agree on my start date – this upcoming Monday – only five days from today. She must trust me... maybe I can do this.

Walking out of the gallery, having just been hired as the interim manager of Tanager, I'm beaming, incredibly proud of myself for taking this risk and trying something new. Never in a million years would I believe that I'd be a director of an art gallery. But, did I ever expect to leave Boston or Ben?

Continuing down the main street, I begin to check out the storefront displays. Knowing that there's a ton to do before I move – and begin working at Tanager – I spend the remainder of the day shopping for my new apartment. Things are changing, quickly. I've found an apartment... and a job. Plus, there's definitely something happening between Jackson and me. I'm not sure what it is or if it will last, but he's unlike anyone else I've ever met. Slowly, the pieces of my life are starting to fall into place.

Hours later, I return to Olivia's bungalow.

"You look exhausted," Olivia says, taking a break from her laptop and a pile of bills.

"I am, mentally, physically, and financially," I say as I crumble onto the couch. But, in a strange way, this past week's been like a fresh start – almost a life makeover – one I've desperately needed for quite some time.

"What did I tell ya?" Liv proclaims as she begins to clean up her workspace. "You have to learn to trust, Jenna. You know, believe it's all going to work out."

* * *

The next morning, as soon as the alarm sounds, I grab my journal and favorite felt tip pen from the bedside table.

I never thought I'd be qualified to work in an art gallery. But maybe I am. A side of me is scared, yet there's another part that's energized. In a few days I'll be starting at Tanager and living in my new space... MY place. And, then there's Jackson... it feels so right being with him. It's not just physical. I sense that he's different in other ways - that I can trust him. Sometimes I feel like I am on the top of the ceiling looking down at this new version of me who is living an entirely different life. But somehow, I'm ok with it... I think I'll just see what happens.

Although first hesitant to bare my soul through writing, this practice forces me to remain focused on my goals and helps me from falling into comfortable, old patterns. Somehow, putting my thoughts on paper make them more real, more tangible, more possible.

My phone rings. As I pick it up, I see that familiar number – calling me – here in Bend. Do I let it go to voice mail or should I answer?

"Hello," I say tentatively.

"Hey, Jenna, it's me, Ben."

CHAPTER 18

Jackson

It's early Thursday morning, just two days since being with Jenna. My life is ordered, disciplined, but not this week. It's as if my game is off. Since Tuesday night it's been a struggle for me to focus. I constantly have to push thoughts of her aside and get back to work.

Radiohead plays in the background as I review my monthly financial statements. Damn, why isn't the balance higher? Sales have been strong. This makes no sense. I begin searching for a pattern, something to explain why my monthly residual is not larger. The only red flag is the check I write each month to my sister, Mollie.

Unable to hold a steady job, Mollie rarely asks for help, but she needs it in more ways than one. Paying rent in San Francisco poses a big problem for her. And since her, rather *our* dad died when she was still young, she's never had a backup for when things become tight. Still, if

Mollie had any idea that my monthly "gifts" negatively impacted me, she would never have agreed to utilize the funds from the account that I set up for her. That's why I make it appear as if its extra cash from the shop, that I can barely keep inventory in stock. Yet, the truth is that while OutRider does well, I'm not killing it, at least not yet. And the $1,000 that goes into Mollie's account each month could definitely help me with my mortgage.

But Mollie has no one else, just Matt and me, and even Matt's not totally aware of the situation. When she had her first breakdown, it was me who she called, and me who held her and nursed her back to health. It was our secret. She didn't want to burden her mom, Bridgette, who deals with her own emotional issues. Mollie is my duty, my responsibility. I'm the oldest, and she's the baby of the family.

My next mortgage payment is due in five days, but I've barely got enough cash to cover it. There's got to be a better way. I consider my expenses. There's no rent because my apartment is part of this building. I own my truck, and my bike keeps me busy during any free time. But then I pause, considering Jenna. Dating costs money, money that I don't have. I start to question if it makes sense to begin a relationship. But then her image floods my brain, and I know that I'd regret walking away. The bottom line is that I need to figure out a way to make more money.

Already it's nine-thirty. Time to unlock the front door. Within fifteen minutes, a group of men enter OutRider, eight Texans who appear to be on a guys' bike trip. The biggest in the crew, a forty-something guy wearing a bright yellow XXL bike shirt and shorts that are a bit too tight, shares that he crashed yesterday and needs to buy a new bike. From the bling he's wearing and the comments he makes within earshot of me, it is clear that he's loaded.

Hmmm, this is exactly what I need. I force a smile and approach the customer in an outgoing, friendly manner, something foreign and uncomfortable for me.

It isn't long before I'm accepting an $8,949 credit card payment for an all carbon bike from Specialized, a new helmet, gloves, and a muted gray short-sleeve top with matching shorts – one size larger than what he's currently wearing. I throw in a water bottle, one bearing OutRider's logo, just because. Two other men in the group purchase new shoes, and four ask about dropping off their bikes at the end of the day for full tune-ups. All in all, this morning's sale is almost $10,000. Could my luck be changing?

Exuding confidence, I pick up my phone and text Jenna.

Me: *Are you free for dinner tonight?*

Maybe we'll try that new Italian restaurant. But then I remember, I should be saving, not spending. This morning was just lucky. So I pick a different spot, one that has great food but is more within my budget.

My phone sounds.

Jenna: *Yes! Just have some final packing to do before tomor-*
row's move. Can't wait to tell you about my meeting at the
gallery.

That settles it. For the first time in a while, it appears that there is
a lot to celebrate.

* * *

I have no regrets giving up my evening ride to be with Jenna. After
work I run upstairs and change out of my Cannondale t-shirt and REI
shorts into a striped button down and a pair of well-worn jeans. Fifteen
minutes later I pull up outside of Olivia's place. I'm feeling good as I hop
out of the truck. As much as I hate to admit it, Jenna's pretty much all
I've been thinking about. But when I ring the doorbell, instantly I sense
that something's off.

Why is it so quiet? I know Olivia left for Chicago to see her boyfriend. Even though it's been a year and a half since I've been on active
duty, I'm still wired to notice subtle changes in an environment. Why
isn't Sam barking?

Jenna answers, dressed in a short white dress, her long legs instantly
catch my attention. I kiss her hello then ask, "Where's Sam?"

"He's in the living room on his dog bed," Jenna says, looking somewhat confused.

"I thought you said he barked when people came to the front door." I sense that something is wrong. Listening to my intuition has always saved my ass, as well as some of my buddies' in high school and college – but more importantly in Afghanistan. I never doubt this feeling.

"Sam," Jenna calls, walking around and searching the hidden spaces and corners of the main level that I presume are his favorite spots. "Oh my God, you're right. He's not here."

Together we do a more thorough search of Olivia's home and yard, combing through every nook and cranny for the eighty-five-pound golden retriever. He's nowhere to be found. It isn't until we go back inside that I hear the faintest whimper. Following the noise, we find Sam upstairs. He's tucked into the back of Jenna's closet, hidden behind her suitcases, curled up in a ball.

Unable to coax him out, Jenna and I do our best to gently pull Sam out from his hiding place. Immediately I notice that his coat is matted from sweat and he's drooling uncontrollably.

"What's wrong with him? I've never seen Sam like this before?" Tears stream down Jenna's face.

"I don't know, but we need to get him to a vet. Do you have a blanket?" Jenna brings me a comforter from the hallway closet, and I wrap Sam in it before carrying him to the back seat of my truck. Jenna sits next to him, holding his head on her lap.

Instead of a romantic dinner, Jenna and I spend the night at Pine Mountain Veterinary Clinic. Jenna paces back and forth, clenching her jaw. After I convince her to sit down, I hold her hand as we wait while Sam is treated in the clinic's emergency facilities. Several hours later we learn that Sam had eaten grapes, seven of them to be exact. He'll be fine, but the doctor wants to keep the golden overnight for observations.

"I threw some old grapes into the trashcan this morning. I never thought Sam would find them. I know dogs can't have grapes." Jenna's eyes begin to fill with tears.

Recognizing that Jenna's on the way to beating herself up for Sam becoming sick, I quickly intervene, stopping her before she goes down that rabbit hole.

"I saw that trashcan in the kitchen when we were looking for Sam. It has a lid. He must have figured out how to open it," I tell her while rubbing her back, hoping to calm her down. "This is not your fault."

"I don't know what I would have done if he…" she turns around then cries into my chest.

"Come on, let me take you home. The doctor sedated Sam so he can rest. We'll come back in the morning to get him," I say as I wipe the tears spilling down her face.

I place my arm around Jenna as we leave Sam under the care of the vets at Pine Mountain. Being that it is now close to eleven and no restaurants are open, we decide to order a take-out pizza before returning to

Olivia's place.

Once we're back at the house, Jenna claims she's not hungry, but I know she needs something to eat. I grab a bottle of red wine that is on the counter, find two glasses and plates in the kitchen cupboards, and bring everything to where Jenna's sitting in the living area.

"Sam just has to be OK... he is all I have... I can't let him get sick... he's my responsibility... he can't... " she rubs her forehead then pauses, appearing unable to say what would naturally come next.

"Sam will be fine. He's a big dog. Yeah, he ate some grapes, but from the X-ray, the vet said it was enough to make him sick, but not enough to harm him," I reassure Jenna while pouring her a glass of wine. "They'll take good care of him. Try not to worry." I sit next to her on the sofa and pull her close to me, cradling her in my arms, hoping to help her relax.

But she doesn't. I feel her body stiffen even more as she asks, "Do you *really* think he'll be OK?"

"He's gonna be fine, better than ever. Here, eat something." I offer her a slice of the white pizza. "By tomorrow afternoon, Sam will seem like his old self. Trust me." I wink and kiss the tip of her nose.

"I believe you... it's just that I can't lose him... " she says as the scared look on her face intensifies and her body begins to shake. "I can't let him die... I can't deal with that... having it be my fault... again... " Trembling, Jenna sinks back into the sofa, pulling her knees into her chest.

"What do you mean again?" I sit up straight, concerned about the word "again."

Jenna shuts her eyes, squeezing them tightly. "I can't be responsible for someone else dying."

Caught off guard, I'm not sure how to react. I definitely don't want to push her, she's incredibly fragile right now. "Jenna, who died?" I ask as I softly brush the hair from her face.

After a long pause, Jenna opens her eyes, looks at me, and then utters, "Annie..."

"Annie?" Jenna's never mentioned anyone by that name before.

"My little sister... she died when she was two years old." Jenna buries her head in her hands. I pull her toward me then begin to rock her back and forth as she quietly sobs.

"Jesus, Jenna – I can't even imagine." I wish I had the right words, but I've been around death too many times to know that there's nothing I can say to make this memory any easier for Jenna. So, I just hold her.

After several minutes Jenna sits up, takes a sip of wine – as if wine could provide the courage she needs – and begins to tell her story. "I was five. It was summertime. We were at the playground with our nanny, Jane," she begins as her tears slowly subside. "I had scraped my knee after tripping over a curb, so I ran to Jane, crying." Jenna pauses then shakes her head. "Jane was paying attention to me, not to Annie... that's when... " Jenna abruptly stops.

I kiss the top of her head and wait to see if she will say more.

Jenna takes a big breath, sighs it out and then says, "Annie walked in front of the swing set. One of the bigger boys who was on a swing didn't see her..." She stops, swallows, then continues in a hushed monotone. "His feet struck Annie... sending her tumbling backwards... into the metal bar of the jungle gym. We ran to her right away, but we couldn't revive her. She just lay there... limp... lifeless. The emergency room doctor told us that either the initial hit or the fall into the pole caused an instant brain hemorrhage, causing Traumatic Brain Injury." Jenna gazes into space, and without looking at me she continues, "Sometimes I have nightmares about this. I'm at that playground... watching her fall backwards... hitting her head. In one instant she went from being this vibrant toddler to..." but Jenna stops. Once again, she swallows hard.

"And you were only five, way too young to see something like that." I momentarily recall some of the gut-wrenching deaths I've witnessed during my years in the SEALs. But I was an adult, one who signed up for the entire package.

"This wouldn't have happened if I hadn't gone to Jane," Jenna insists speaking rapidly, her hand now clutching my leg as if she's trying to convince me. "Jane always watched us... she was a wonderful nanny... she just missed seeing Annie walk in front of the swings because she was focused on me. It was my fault! I shouldn't have distracted Jane!" Jenna's practically shouting.

I take Jenna's hands and look directly into her eyes. "You were only five, and you were hurt. You did exactly what you were supposed to do. What happened to Annie wasn't your fault. Annie was in the wrong place at the wrong time. It was a freak accident." I know that she hears me, but I doubt that my words are making an impact.

"Yeah, that's what everyone told me. But, if I had been more careful, then the accident never would have happened." Jenna pulls away from me, sits back into the sofa then crosses her long legs beneath her. She then reaches for her glass of wine, slowly sipping it, as if to give me time to digest her point.

Knowing that I cannot convince her that this accident had nothing to do with her, I say, "Some things in life make no sense. But that doesn't mean it's your fault. You gotta let go of the guilt." As the words leave my lips, it hits me that she feels responsible for Annie's death the same way I do for Patrick's injury.

Jenna takes another sip of wine and then says, "It's why I hate making mistakes. Olivia says I have a 'disease to please.' But, if I do the right thing, then maybe bad things won't happen again. I can't imagine what my parents went through, losing a child. I never want them to experience that pain again. That's why I have this thing with being perfect. I think that if I never screw up, then, well maybe, everything will be alright."

"Oh, Jenna," I reach over and pull her onto my lap, her back melting into my chest as I wrap my arms around her waist. "You can't prevent bad things from happening by being perfect. Life's full of dark and light, and sometimes shit just happens."

Jenna lifts her chin, turns, and looks toward me. "I *know* you're right, but sometimes it's hard to *believe* it."

Interlacing my fingers with hers I say, "Part of living is accepting what comes your way. It's hard for me, too. You know how much I beat myself up about Patrick. Intellectually, I know it wasn't my fault, but I still *believe* that it was."

Jenna nods. Maybe I'm helping her understand the parallels between our situations. "After it happened, I couldn't be a platoon leader anymore. I'd lost all faith in my ability to lead. I guess I was afraid that I'd let one of my men down… again… not be there when one of them needed me. I didn't want to resign. Being a SEAL was my life. But I knew that I couldn't stay. Not after what happened."

Jenna just stares at our clasped hands.

"Maybe we could help each other work through our guilt." I kiss the back of her head waiting for her response.

Finally, she utters, "OK…"

Although she agrees, I sense that she still has more to reconcile about her little sister's death, just like I do with Patrick's accident.

"Pizza's getting cold. Want me to heat it up?" I shift gears.

"No thanks." Jenna picks up the slice from her plate and nibbles on it. When she's finished eating, she repositions herself on my lap, tucking

189

her head beneath my chin. Slowly, the rhythm of her breath stabilizes and before long, she falls asleep. So, this is how it's supposed to be. I want Jenna to feel safe. Can I do it? Can I take care of her?

I spend the night on Olivia's sofa, sleeping intermittently while Jenna snuggles next to me. As much as a part of me wishes that last night had been different, her sharing Annie's sudden death seems to have brought us closer. I can't remember the last time I've felt so much compassion for another – except for Patrick.

CHAPTER 19

Jenna

It's been almost three weeks since I've opened my journal. Everything's been so crazy - but good crazy. I haven't had time to collect my thoughts on paper, something I had promised myself I'd do. Well, here goes... my last three weeks...

Ben called me, and by the sound of his voice, I think he had a few drinks. He told me that he'd been doing a lot of thinking, trying to understand why I did what I did. That's when he surprised me and actually apologized for not taking my side — for doing what his aunt wanted. He went off on her taking my job away from me. Then Ben asked if I was happy, but I think he wanted to know if I missed him. I have, but not in the way he'd like me to.

The night I told Jackson about Annie shifted our relationship to a higher level. Jackson took the following morning off from work to go with me to get Sam. He then helped me move into my new place. This apartment is awesome, in fact it's perfect... so is Jackson. Even though I've only known Jackson for a month, I'm amazed with the way he lives his life — so assured and in charge. Ben didn't do this. I think the difference is that Ben did what he thought he should do, and

Jackson does what he feels is right. A part of me will always love Ben, but I now realize that he never was "the one."

Jackson and I spend most evenings together. Still he hasn't spent the night — except that one time when Sam was at the vets. We've definitely tried to take things slowly, at least physically. But it's hard, the more I'm with him, the more I want him. I can tell he feels the same.

And I never thought that I'd be managing a gallery. Sure, there's a lot to learn, but even though I've only been there less than three weeks, I feel like I'm actually helping Claire and Don — that I'm making a difference.

A part of me misses living with Liv, but she's so busy since Michael and Katy have been in town. Still, we make sure that we meet for lunch and go to an occasional yoga class.

Everything's changing since I moved to Bend. But I'm not afraid because it feels so right.

Sipping my coffee that I purchased on the way to work, I lean toward my laptop, carefully contemplating everything left to do before my first showing that's in two weeks. Already I'm nervous about the event even though I meticulously planned each minute of Trinity Love's debut. This new artist resides in Sisters, a small town located between Bend and Redmond. Trinity specializes in intaglio, another word for printmaking. The majority of the pieces that she'll be showing depict the trees of Oregon, her trademark.

While reviewing the set of prints from the e-mail that Trinity sent, I hear the UPS truck idling outside. Maybe the invitations have arrived. I leave my desk to meet the deliveryman at the front door. Observing the box he hands to me, I can tell from the return address that this is what I've been waiting for. After unwrapping the package, I carefully proof the forest green print on ecru card stock, checking once again for typos. Everything seems perfect. I have to send these invites today, so I begin stuffing the envelopes while printing the invite list. Choosing to add a personal touch, I hand write the addresses, hoping this will entice recipients to open the envelopes. The last thing I want is for my invitations to be tossed, unopened, into the trash.

I look at the clock. Where did the morning go? Famished, I retrieve my lunch from the refrigerator located in the storage room and then return to my desk. As I'm about to bite into my sandwich, I hear the front door chime. Covering the BLT with my napkin, I leave my desk and greet the three women who've just walked into the gallery.

"Good afternoon. I'm Jenna. Please let me know if I can help you with anything."

"Thanks," the tall brunette responds off handedly, avoiding eye contact, "but we're just browsing."

"Take your time. I'm here if you have any questions," I say, trying my best to exude confidence and warmth. Customer service is an entirely new world for me. Or is it? Hadn't I learned some tough lessons as a teacher? Actually, this job might be much easier, especially considering some of the demanding parents I've encountered.

As I begin adjusting paintings, keeping myself available should the women have any inquiries, I can't help but overhear their conversation.

"This is an interesting picture, the one of the bike," the redhead says as she approaches an oil painting of a classic Schwinn propped up against a split rail fence. "That reminds me, I wanted to share what my husband told me last night. You know, the yummy guy in that bike shop that you're always drooling over," she says to the long-legged blonde who's wearing somewhat revealing yoga clothes. "Well, apparently, there's a chance that the bank might begin to pressure him." Then she whispers, "You know, *foreclosure*." She returns to her normal voice. "His mortgage payments are always late. As his personal banker, my husband *tries* to advise him, but apparently he doesn't exactly have a head for numbers."

Shit, they're talking about Jackson. But he told me that he owned the shop. If he's in financial trouble, then the last thing he should be doing is spend money on me. Why wouldn't he just tell me if things were tight? And what the hell was that comment, "Who you're always drooling over"? It takes every ounce of self-control not to move closer to these women. Although I'm dying to learn more, I'm conscious not to appear to be eavesdropping. I attempt to compose myself while still listening from the far end of the gallery.

The blonde shows no compassion for the news her friend just revealed about her apparent crush. Instead she only rolls her eyes, casually stating, "Who cares if he's broke? I don't have to marry him; I just want to fuck him."

Instantly, I transition into an internal rage, incensed by what I just heard. My gut instinct is to leave Tanager and run to Jackson, but that's impossible. I can't take off with these three in the gallery. After several minutes, they depart without acknowledging me or offering even a small pleasantry before going. Too upset to finish lunch, I decide to call Jackson. Learning about his financial issues and hearing that this stranger wants to have sex with my boyfriend have rocked my world. Can I even call him my boyfriend after a month? As soon as the door shuts, I reach for my phone and dial his number. I notice my trembling fingers and racing heartbeat.

"Hey," Jackson says as he picks up. "Love this surprise. You never call during the day."

"Just wanted to hear your voice." I try to sound upbeat, but right now it's hard to breathe.

"Are you OK?" he asks.

"I just miss you," I say as I bite my lower lip. Do I tell him what I've heard?

"One awesome surprise after another. Must be my lucky day. What time can you leave the gallery today?" Jackson sounds like he really wants to see me. I sigh, realizing that I've worked myself up unnecessarily.

"We close at five, so I could probably cut out by five-fifteen," I say. Already I can feel my pulse return to its normal pace.

"Great. I'll swing by your place around five-thirty. Would you be up for trying paddle boarding? It should be light till about nine or so. That will give us plenty of time on the river."

"That sounds awesome." Knowing that we'll be together in a few hours is just what I needed to calm down.

"And why don't you pack a bag, you know, don't you think it's time you spent the night?" There is almost a pleading in his voice.

Considering this tempting offer, I remember Sam. Knowing I can't leave him alone overnight, I ask in my best suggestive voice, "How about you pack *your* bag... because of Sam."

"Yes, ma'am. I've been waiting for you to ask me that." The energy in his tone picks up decisively.

Now I'm feeling better. Maybe it is time to take it to the next level with Jackson. We've waited long enough, haven't we? Even though it's only been a few weeks I'm falling for him hard. It's strange how I rarely think about Ben.

My mind then wanders to this afternoon's double discovery, and I question if I should broach either topic with Jackson. But it really isn't my business if he's having trouble paying his mortgage. And, he's never shown any signs of a wandering eye. Plus, that woman didn't seem like his type. I decide to let things go.

Almost back to my new normal, a much calmer version of the "Boston Jenna," I decide to finish my sandwich before any other customers come into the gallery. As I eat, I carefully review what needs to happen prior to Trinity's opening. Everything seems to be under control. I've arranged for a bartender, a caterer, and flowers. And I'll send the invitations later this afternoon. All that's left is to hope people show up. I'm used to handling a classroom of little kids, all with different personalities and needs. So, compared to that, how tough could this opening really be?

CHAPTER 20

Jackson

Jenna's careful maneuvering of her stand up paddleboard makes me grin. Tall and lean, she looks adorable in that flowered bikini. I watch as her long arms work furiously to advance the board against the river's strong current. These past weeks have been unbelievable. My life is changing... quickly. I've kept up with my morning workouts, but I can't remember the last time I rode after work.

Taking her on the river was a last-minute idea. But this won't be a typical paddle. Actually, I'm pretty proud of myself. I packed a bottle of wine, two plastic glasses, and some cheese and crackers in my dry bag. The plan is to paddle upriver, then chill as the Deschutes carries us downstream. If my timing's right, we'll arrive at the riverbanks by the Les Schwabb Amphitheatre just as Jack Johnson begins to play. Then we can anchor ourselves and our boards by the shoreline and listen to the concert from the river. I think Jenna will love it. She's mentioned that he's one of her favorite artists. While it's great to be at the actual concert, nothing beats experiencing it from the river. Not a bad date.

* * *

Not only does Jack Johnson kill it, but this entire evening – complete with a classic Bend sunset – could not get any better.

"This is so cool," Jenna says, reclining on her paddleboard.

"I'm glad you like it," I say, intently staring at Jenna. The setting sun's reflection off of the water's surface illuminates her in light.

"How can anything be this beautiful? I mean, you can see the outline of the mountains against that watercolor sky, all while hanging on the river and listening to 'Better Together.'" Jenna then carefully sits on her heels, balancing the board as she glances up at the sky.

"We are better together," I say, but my look turning serious. "You know that, don't you? Before we met, failing Patrick was all I thought about. Now, that's changed. I've changed. *You've* changed me."

After this deluge of more words than I ever say, Jenna adeptly paddles her board closer to mine, wedging us tight against the riverbank. Carefully shifting her position, she reaches for my hand, pulling me closer. "You know, you're making me fall in love with you," Jenna says as she leans toward me, pressing her lips into mine.

"And it keeps getting better," I whisper, lost in Jenna's kiss.

* * *

After the concert and our riverside picnic comes to an end, we put on headlamps and paddle upstream to where we parked. I grab both boards and we make the short trek to my truck. Heading to Jenna's apartment for the night feels so damn natural. In fact, it makes me realize how sad, almost pathetic, my life actually was before Jenna came along. I wasn't living – I was merely existing, going through the motions. But not anymore.

"Sam!" Jenna laughs as the dog bounds toward us, barking like a watchdog when she opens the door. After we take him for a quick walk around the block, Jenna locks up the apartment and then lights some candles in the living room while I uncork a bottle of red that I'd brought along for the occasion. Settling onto the sofa, we sip wine and share more stories from our pasts, comparing tales of previous relationships.

"Every woman I met wanted something from me that I couldn't, or wouldn't, give. I don't know what it was, but they pushed me until I'd shut down and end it," I admit as several particular women come to mind.

"And I don't do that to you?" Jenna asks as she tucks a strand of hair behind her right ear.

Slowly shaking my head, I say, "No you don't. I want to open up with you. You just have to be patient with me." I sit back and take a sip of the Shiraz.

Her eyes lift as she quietly says, "You know I will be."

And that's when Jenna begins to offer more insight about breaking off her engagement. "Leaving Ben was the hardest thing I ever did." Jenna's eyes narrow as if remembering a former lifetime. "He's a super nice guy, handsome, successful – one of those people who has it all. We moved in together last September. Figured we'd save some money before the wedding. As a couple we were fine. But that's all it was. Just *fine*. It was comfortable, and I felt safe and secure." Jenna pauses for a moment.

I hold her gaze, allowing her to continue.

"Then, when it was over, I became afraid... of who I was without him. I felt lost... so alone. I began questioning everything in my life, not just my choice in men." Jenna rolls her eyes. "I started doubting myself, and I had trouble making decisions. When I lost my job, well, that almost put me over the edge. But then Liv convinced me to move to Bend." Jenna sighs before taking a sip of wine. "And, well, you pretty much know the rest." Jenna grins at me as she leans back into the sofa, her eyes glistening. The woman in front of me is not the person she described, the one engaged to Ben.

"Do you still doubt yourself?" I ask as I move closer to her. I assume I already know the answer.

"Not so much," Jenna smiles as she shakes her head. "Maybe it's being with you. You constantly encourage me to try new things."

"Like biking, for example?" I tease, leaning in to kiss her forehead.

"Among other things," she laughs as she playfully pushes me away. "When we're together, everything's right. I don't know how to describe it, but I don't have the urge to be 'perfect' like I did in the past."

"Well, you're definitely perfect for me." I take her wine glass, set it on the table, and pull her into my arms. My hands move from her shoulders, to her spine, then down to the small of her back. The softness of her skin, the electricity of her touch, and the sweet scent at the nape of her neck drive me crazy. I cannot get enough of Jenna. I kiss her fully on her mouth while my hand travels beneath her t-shirt to her bikini top underneath. Her hands caress my back, instinctively moving downward till her fingertips linger at the top of my board shorts. Intertwined, I cannot tell where her body ends and mine begins. Every inch of me craves her. I now know she's what I need, what I've waited so long to find. When I can't stand it any longer, I carefully shift her body from me to the sofa and kiss her fingertips before blowing out the candles. Then I take her hands and lead Jenna to her bedroom.

* * *

The next morning, I look over at the beautiful woman sleeping next to me. As I brush the hair from her eyes, she stirs from my touch, blinking several times as she awakens. A warm smile lights up her face, and her eyes begin to sparkle as she gives me a sweet, long good morning kiss. The aroma of strong coffee begins to permeate the apartment. "Want some coffee? I set it up so it would brew at 6:00 this morning,"

Jenna says as she lazily exits the bed, throwing on a t-shirt that doesn't quite reach the top of her thighs. She heads toward the kitchen. Stretching my body then folding my hands behind my head, I feel complete. It's a totally new sensation. I actually slept through the night without nightmares. Wondering how it could get any better, Jenna reappears with two mugs of coffee. She places the mugs on the bedside table, but something tells me that our coffee will be cold by the time that we get to it.

CHAPTER 21

Jenna

Tonight's Trinity's opening. I leave my home – with Jackson in my bed – before eight that morning, armed with a huge cup of coffee and the best attitude I can muster. Slightly nervous, I review my checklist – four times – just to make sure that I haven't forgotten anything. Relax, it will be fine.

When Trinity arrives at the gallery, I'm immediately struck by her dramatic make-up and the abundance of grey that's sprinkled throughout her enviable thick, black hair. From her online bio I know that she's in her late sixties. Trinity possesses an ethereal element to her, gliding about the gallery with her silky Oriental wrap flowing gracefully behind her. I watch as she and Clair switch several framed prints around, adjusting their location in order to take better advantage of the lighting. Claire suggests I put on some mood music, so I choose an acoustical jazz station – not too vibrant, but energetic enough to match Trinity's artistic style.

As the chill music plays softly in the background, I sense my shoulder blades beginning to slide down my back and my jaw softening. I had no idea how tense I was in anticipation of tonight. Looking around, I sigh. Everything's exactly as I imagined, even better. According to the schedule, the caterer and bartender should be here at 4:45, allowing ample time for the final set-up before the guests arrive at six. The turn-out appears to be higher than Claire and I expected. Fifty-seven people responded that they would be attending, but I've told the caterer and bartender to plan for seventy, just to be safe.

Checking my watch, I see that it is 3:30, time to go home and change into that new black dress that I bought for tonight. Everything that can be done has been. Trinity and Claire went to the cafe next door for a cup of tea. I know that Claire was hoping to discuss future collaborations. I smile as I head out the door. Tonight's going to be perfect! Jackson's coming and so are Liv, Michael, and Katy. Otherwise, I doubt that I'll know many people, except for several of those frequent gallery browsers.

As I'm taking my new dress off of the hanger, I hear my phone. It's a text from Liv, but it makes no sense.

Liv: *Will be running late tonight. Katy and Michael went to Elk Lake and won't be back until 4:30. Don't think that we can get there till close to 5:30.*

Me: *But it doesn't start till 6.*

After several minutes, my phone pings again.

Liv: *Invitation says 5.*

Oh my God! I put the wrong time on the invitation. I need to call the caterer and bartender... and Claire! My heart races as I reach for my phone, desperately searching for the bartender's number. Sam wakes up, comes over, and gives me a lick on the leg.

Unable to reach Joe, the bartender, I leave a message for him to call me back immediately. Luckily, I connect with the caterer. Although a stretch, she will do her best to show up by four. While on the phone, I quickly apply make-up and get dressed. Now the tough call, the one to Claire.

"I am so sorry. I don't know what happened. I proofed it so many times, but I guess that I was checking for spelling and grammar. I didn't think that the time would be wrong." My voice cracks as I hesitantly add, "I totally understand if you no longer want me at the gallery." I take a deep breath as I wait to hear her response.

"Jenna, don't be ridiculous. Of course, I want you at the gallery.

We'll just need a Plan B. Thankfully, the caterer can be there earlier. Since you haven't heard from Joe, I'll grab some plastic wine glasses and then head straight to the gallery. Don can stop at the liquor store in case Joe can't arrive till later. Try to relax." Despite Claire's reassurance, I cannot calm down. I rummage through my closet for the shoes that I bought to go with the dress.

After throwing my wallet, lipstick, and phone into the small purse that matches my new shoes, I run out the front door, mentally rehearsing possible scenarios of a ruined evening. Then, in an instant, my heel catches on a slight crack in the stairs, and I tumble to the sidewalk. Blood oozes down my right calf, paralleling the still visible scar from my biking debut, and I see that the heel of one of my new, expensive shoes has snapped in half. *Great, just great.* But when I stand up, I cannot put any weight onto my right leg – it's my IT band. *Damn it!* On top of everything else, this fall just added more time to my rehab, further delaying my return to running. Hobbling back inside, I clean the cut and then quickly bandage it and switch into lower heeled shoes.

By the time I arrive at the gallery, Jill, the caterer, is pulling up, ready to unload trays of appetizers. While thanking her for her flexibility, I see Claire walking toward us.

"What happened to you?" Claire inquires after seeing my bandaged leg.

"Well, in my rush to get here, I fell down my front steps. And, I think I may have reinjured my IT band," I say, trying to hold in my anger and pain.

"Jenna, slow down. Take some deep breaths," Claire says as she puts her arm around my shoulder.

"Thank you for being so understanding and for giving me a second chance." My voice begins to quiver, and I hang my head in defeat. "I really screwed up."

"No, you made a simple mistake. Believe it or not, you aren't perfect." Claire speaks in an authoritative tone as she opens the stained-glass door and walks into the gallery.

"But not tonight, it's supposed to be flawless, for you and Trinity," I say as I follow her into Tanager.

Claire stops then turns to face me. "We could have the most beautiful, elegant opening, but if none of Trinity's pieces sell, then what is it worth? Let's just wait and see how the night goes. Stop beating yourself up."

As I consider my boss's words, it becomes evident that under stress I revert to the "Old Jenna" who thrives on perfection. I'm slipping back into those bad patterns, the ones that I want to get rid of. Maybe I can't change what's on the invitation, but I can do my best to make this night a success.

The first guests arrive a few minutes past five. Nothing suggests that the start time was otherwise. The realization that all is fine allows me to breathe and take in the moment. Observing the interaction within the gallery, I sense electricity in the air. People genuinely seem to be enjoying themselves. Jill passes trays of lobster salad on endive while Joe generously pours glasses of chardonnay and cabernet. Thievery Corporation Radio plays in the background, adding a nice touch to the evening. Trinity's glowing, engaging with the guests as she answers their questions about her various pieces.

While speaking with a prospective client, I notice that Jackson's arrived wearing his best pair of jeans, a crisp white shirt, and a dark gray jacket. His mere presence causes me to stop and stare. Despite being in this crowded gallery, the sight of him electrifies me, and I suddenly long for his touch. As he makes his way toward me, I notice several heads turn and gaze at Jackson, only to show visible disappointment when he places his hand on *my* back and kisses *my* cheek. Inhaling his scent, I relax even more as I introduce him to the gentleman next to me. Immediately, he and Jackson connect, discovering that they are both from the Bay area.

Claire approaches with another woman and says, "Jenna, this is my *older* sister, Marjorie. Marjorie is the principal at Northwest Crossing." She emphasized the word "older" with a hint of mischief in her voice. I recognize the petite dark-haired woman as the one who interviewed me for the math coach position.

I'm shocked. I had no idea that the woman who I so desperately wanted to work for is my boss's sister.

"Actually, I already know Jenna," Marjorie says grinning, yet not sharing with Claire how we're acquainted.

"Marjorie, it's good to see you again. As you can tell, I'm trying something besides teaching," I say as Claire scatters off to speak with an elegant looking couple standing in front of one of Trinity's prints.

"I can't believe that this is your sister and brother-in-law's gallery." The family resemblance is so strong, I wonder why I didn't notice it before.

Marjorie nods, saying, "I've been meaning to stop by Tanager, but work's been so busy. When Claire told me that she found a replacement for Paige, it never occurred to me that it was you. Still, promise me you won't stop looking for teaching openings at Northwest."

Happy that I connected with Marjorie, I continue to move through the crowded room, doing my best to do whatever gallery managers do.

* * *

Several hours later, after the last guest leaves, I survey the gallery as Jill clears empty plates and glasses. Where are all of Trinity's pieces?

"Did Trinity load the remaining paintings into her van?" I ask Claire, unsure how I could have missed her departure.

Humored by my question, Claire glances at Don and then responds, "No, almost every piece sold. The buyers took the prints with them."

The expression on my face makes Don chuckle. I watch as this stocky man in his early sixties shakes his bald head. But then his pale blue eyes glisten as he says, "Tonight's sales totaled just over forty-eight thousand dollars. After Trinity receives her cut, that leaves us with a profit of nearly twenty-five thousand! I'd venture to say that tonight was a success." Don takes his wine glass and toasts it into the air.

While I was responsible for planning the event and intermingling with clients, Don's role for the evening, besides making an unexpected stop at the liquor store, was to process the sales. Being incredibly focused on interacting with our guests, I totally missed how many people were purchasing Trinity's prints.

After hearing Don's report on sales, Jackson, who's been waiting in the background, steps closer to give me a congratulatory kiss.

"But as profitable as tonight was, I believe that there is a bigger take away for you," Claire says. "Five hours ago, you were ready to quit because you made one small error. The reality is that this mistake had very little impact on tonight's event. As soon as you became aware of the typo on the invitation, you acted appropriately. Things don't need to be perfect all of the time. In fact, if they are, you probably aren't pushing yourself enough." Claire tilts her head as she makes her point.

* * *

As I drive home, I can't help but reflect on Claire's comments, conceding that she may be right.

Jackson arrives at my place just after I do.

"It always seems to come back to the same theme," I say to Jackson, as we walk up the front stairs. "Part of me keeps focusing on *every* small detail, hoping to make *everything* just right. But the thing is, I really can't control much. And if I want to grow, then I've got to start taking more risks. Things might not turn out like I want. But, maybe that's the point." I unlock the front door, then we take Sam for a quick walk around the block.

Jackson interlaces his fingers with mine as we stroll down street. "Have you ever considered that maybe if you relinquish some control, things could turn out even better than you ever imagined?"

Jackson pulls me into his warm chest, and we stay that way for several moments, Sam patiently sitting on the sidewalk. And then I have an "aha" moment – everything *is* turning out much better than I ever could have hoped when I left Boston. I lift my chin, locking my eyes on Jackson as I run my fingers through his thick gorgeous hair. "Things are better than I ever imagined. You, Jackson Tait, are beyond my wildest dreams."

CHAPTER 22

Jackson

My phone rings, something that rarely happens. Almost everyone I know texts. It must be Jenna. Wonder what's up? But when I see the number I quickly answer. "Hey, are you OK?" I ask before even saying hello.

I only hear sobbing. "Mollie, what's going on?"

A meek voice comes across the phone.

"Jackson… I'm really scared."

"Where are you?"

"Home," but after that, she doesn't say another word.

Mollie's cries fluctuate from soft weeping to full out sobbing. Although it's only one in the afternoon, I'm already shutting down OutRider, phone in hand, trying to get her to talk to me as I hang the "CLOSED" sign on the door, lock up the shop, and head to my truck. I know what

I must do, and I'm the only one who can do it. She sounds bad, even worse than before. "Hold on, Mollie. I'm coming. I'll be there as soon as I can," I assure her as I climb into the truck and turn the ignition. "Just stay put." My foot hits the accelerator.

"Thank you," she mutters between snivels. Then the phone goes dead.

It's an eight-hour drive to San Francisco, but it could take even longer to find a flight. Mollie needs me now.

Ten months ago, Mollie called sounding terrified and totally out of it. And now it's like déjà vu – once again I'm driving to San Francisco hoping to prevent my sister from losing her shit. Yeah, I suspected Mollie was getting dark again, but I had no idea had bad it had gotten. Damn it, why didn't I pay more attention? I know she's fragile. I should have checked in to make sure she was OK.

After what seems like an eternity, I finally cross the Golden Gate Bridge. Glancing at my watch, I see it's almost nine-thirty. The elevator's not working at her apartment building, so I climb the stairs and let myself into her fourth floor one-bedroom apartment with the spare key I keep on my key ring.

The scene is worse than I had imagined. The apartment is sparsely lit with blinds drawn, and the only light comes from a lone lamp on a side table. Dishes crowd the kitchenette; the smell of old food permeates the air. The television is on with some sort of reality show playing in the background. Otherwise it's silent. Panicked, my mind jumps to the worst possible scenario. But, when I enter her bedroom, I see Mollie lying on her bed in a fetal position, just rocking, her long blonde unbrushed hair draping over her shoulders. Her jaw quivers, but no noise comes from her mouth. Rushing over, I sweep her into my arms and hug her tightly. I can't believe how boney she feels.

"Mollie. It's OK. I'm here now." Despite my attempt to reassure her, my little sister continues to shake.

Memory reminds me that doctors and hospitals are *not* an option right now. When I tried that last time, she became totally hysterical – begged that I check her out of the hospital immediately and made me promise I'd never take her there again. Where are her pills? I know she's supposed to be taking them daily.

Searching her apartment for the medicine, I finally find the bottle in the bathroom cabinet. It's unopened. The fill date was four months ago. She hasn't been taking her medication. That was the one thing she promised to do. But she hated the side effects. Mollie probably thought she didn't need it, that she'd be fine on her own. But her psychiatrist specifically stated that she had to take these pills, possibly for the rest of her life.

I know what I must do. I need to bring Mollie to Bend, help her get healthy again. Searching her closet, I find a small duffle and grab some clothes and personal items, adding the bottle of antidepressants. I put the duffle over my shoulder and then carefully pick up Mollie and carry her down the four flights of stairs. I'm surprised by how light she is.

After gently placing Mollie onto the back seat of the truck, I jump in, start it up, and begin the trek back to Bend. If I drive it straight, I should get there by six in the morning. I've pulled all-nighters before – it's nothing I can't handle.

Mollie falls asleep as soon as we leave the city. Even though she's twenty-eight years old, her face still looks the same when she sleeps as it did when she was a little girl. Her lips purse and her eyes flutter behind her eyelids, something Matt and I used to kid her about when we were younger. But now I wonder where she goes when she sleeps. Maybe these dreams feed her fears.

Shit. I never told Jenna. As soon as Mollie called, all of my thoughts centered on her and the urgency of driving to San Francisco. I reach for my phone to call Jenna, but the battery is dead. Damn it, I forgot to bring the charger. It's late. Jenna's probably asleep anyway. I can call her as soon as I get back. Right now, my focus is Mollie and getting us safely back to Bend.

I put country music on the radio, keeping the volume low, hoping not to wake my sister, and drive.

The sun is rising as I pull up outside of OutRider. Mollie's still completely out, so I carry her up the back stairway to my apartment then carefully tuck her into my bed, hoping she can sleep for a few more hours.

I'm starved. Haven't eaten since lunch yesterday. I look but there's nothing in the fridge. The coffee shop down the street should be open. They have some decent food there. So, I plug in my cell phone and lock the door behind me, leaving Mollie to sleep as I go down the block to grab breakfast.

While walking the three blocks to the breakfast café, I soak in the early morning sun. Still, I'm preoccupied by the past sixteen hours. Should I have taken Mollie to the hospital? The doctors there would have known how to treat her, given her the right meds. But I promised her I wouldn't. No, she wants to be here, with me, in Bend. That's what she said. Accepting that I did what was best for Mollie, I inhale the familiar mountain air. Unsure of what lay ahead, the challenges my sister will face, I'm committed to be there for her. That's what big brothers do.

CHAPTER 23

Jenna

Obsessed with worry, I pace my apartment most of the night. Part of me wants to drive over to Jackson's, but I keep waiting, hoping that he'll call and let me know that he fell asleep and didn't hear his phone. Even though we spend most nights together, occasionally we'll stay at our own places, so I don't want to overreact. I try sleeping, but it's futile because I'm constantly checking my phone, hoping for a response.

By 5:50 I can't wait any longer. Maybe he's sick or had some kind of accident. Although unlikely, it is still a possibility. Regardless, I'm heading over. Two weeks ago, we exchanged keys. It just made things easier. I stare at his key on my keychain.

When I get there, Jackson's truck is parked directly in front of his shop. Why didn't he answer my calls? I run up the backstairs and unlock his door. Everything's quiet when I enter. His car keys lay on the kitchen table, alongside of a strange bag. It's odd that Jackson's bedroom door is shut. I decide to check if he's sleeping. But as I enter the darkened room and turn on the light switch, my heartbeat explodes as soon as the cold fluorescent light reveals a beautiful woman wrapped in *his* sheet, her long blonde hair flowing across *his* pillow. How could he? Who is she? How long has this been going on? Has he been screwing her the entire time we've been together?

Yet, at that exact moment my mind detours to, a distant memory, no doubt triggered by the sight of this woman. Another image appears, crystal clear, like a silent movie streaming in my head.

But in this scene, there's a different bed and an unknown woman's lying on that bed. It's not Jackson's room that I recall, or even Ben's. It's my parents'. In a flash, everything comes back, each disturbing detail meticulously magnified, invading my mind, projecting images no five-year-old daughter should see.

My dad. No. How could he have done that to my mom? I feel nauseous. I want to vomit. My entire body shakes. I've got to get out of here! I turn and sprint toward the door, almost colliding into Jackson as he returns holding two paper cups and a pastry bag from the local café. Oh my God! That is the same place he bought breakfast after he and I first spent our first night together at his apartment.

"Jenna, my phone died, I tried to call," Jackson begins, only I'll hear none of his bullshit.

Hitting him in the chest with tightly clenched fists, I yell, "How could you? How long have you been fucking her? Since I knew you or before?"

I can't bear to hear his lies. So, I run. Away. From him and that woman in his bed.

Jackson chases after me.

"If that is what you want, then fine, but I'm certainly not putting up with that crap!" I sprint as fast as I can and climb into my car. Jackson yells for me to stop, he wants to explain things. But I can't – I won't listen. So, I slam the car door in his face and pull out onto the street, never looking back. First my dad, and now Jackson. Why did I ever trust him?

CHAPTER 24

Jackson

When I return upstairs Mollie's awake, peering from the bedroom door and looking scared. "Jackson, what's going on?" she asks with a shiver in her voice. "How did I get here? Who was that yelling?" Slowly, Mollie emerges from my bedroom.

"Don't you remember? You called me yesterday, really upset. I drove to San Francisco and found you curled up in your bed. I brought you here, to Bend," I explain as point to her duffle bag. "You were still asleep when we arrived early this morning, so I put you in my bed. I just left for a few moments to get us something for breakfast."

"But who was that woman?" She asks, her eyes somewhat squinting in confusion.

"That was Jenna, my girlfriend. She's super pissed at me because she saw you and thought I had cheated on her. I guess I can understand her

221

reaction. I never told her that I was going to San Francisco. Then, once I remembered, my phone was dead. She probably came over to check that everything was all right – and then she saw you." I run my fingers through my uncombed hair.

"This is all my fault." Mollie's voice sounds faint. She doesn't make eye contact, only looks down at the floor.

"It's not your fault." I walk toward her and gently put my arms across her thin shoulders. "It's just a misunderstanding. Actually, it's on me. I should have called Jenna. Here, I got you some muffins and tea." I hand her the bag and the take-out cup of tea. "You need to eat. I'm going to Jenna's apartment to try to explain. Call me if you need anything, promise?" She nods as I kiss the top of her head then turn toward the door.

My heart races as I drive to Jenna's apartment. She needs to understand what really happened. I try calling, but she won't pick up her phone. Four minutes later, I'm knocking at her door, and Sam's barking on the other side. Jenna doesn't answer, but I know she's there because her car is parked outside. I stay, but after fifteen minutes and no response, I begin to walk around and look into the windows, hoping to find some evidence of whether or not Jenna is inside. Finally, I decide to leave. If she won't hear me out, maybe she'll at least read what I have to say. After finding a pen and post-it-note in my truck, I carefully write a note and then place it through the mail slot of her front door.

JENNA, IT'S NOT WHAT YOU THINK. THE GIRL YOU SAW
IS MY SISTER, MOLLIE. I'M SORRY I NEVER TOLD YOU ABOUT
HER. IT'S A LONG STORY, AND I WANT TO SHARE ALL OF IT
WITH YOU, IF YOU'LL LET ME. PLEASE BELIEVE ME. I LOVE YOU.

– JACKSON

When I get back to my apartment, I feel some relief when I see that the muffin's gone and Mollie's back asleep. Still, I'm glued to my cell, constantly checking for any sign that Jenna read my note. Sure, it seemed suspect, but if she'd let me explain, it would all make sense. Exhaustion hits, the trip back and forth to Mollie's apartment begins to take its toll. I need sleep. But my analytical mind won't permit my body to rest. The scene replays vividly in my head. I know it looked bad, but why wouldn't she listen to me? But, can I blame her? How would I feel if he walked into her apartment and saw some guy sleeping in her bed? *Shit.* I should have called her yesterday on my way there. I'm such an idiot.

There must be a way to talk to Jenna. *Olivia.* Maybe she can get through to Jenna. I dial her number.

"Olivia, it's me, Jackson. Have you heard from Jenna?" I ask while pacing around my kitchen.

"Actually, she's here right now," Olivia pauses, her voice sharp and distant. Maybe Jenna never saw the note.

223

"I need you to listen to me. I didn't cheat on Jenna. The girl she saw, well, she's Mollie, my sister – actually, my half-sister. Olivia, please. Hear me out." My voice grows louder.

"Go on." Olivia's curt, but maybe she'll give me a chance to explain.

"Yesterday, sometime after lunch, Mollie called me, freaking out. She has some, um, issues, and I'm the only one she'll reach out to when she needs help. I immediately shut down the shop and drove straight to San Francisco to see what was going on." I know I'm speaking fast, but I need to make my point.

Then I share the rest of the story until reaching this morning's incident. "That's when Jenna walked in and saw Mollie. I'm guessing you know what happened after that," I say, hoping that Olivia can see my side. "The timing couldn't have been worse. If I had been there, I could have explained everything before she went into the bedroom. But I wasn't. I tried to tell Jenna, but she wouldn't listen. She stormed out, refusing to speak to me." After a moment I add, "Guess I would have done the same." My head hangs as I make this statement.

"Jackson, you know I like you. I want to believe what you're telling me," Olivia says.

I quickly respond, hoping she will. "You can ask Matt about Mollie. I know I was wrong not telling Jenna about her. I just never discuss Mollie, with anyone. I guess it's my way of protecting her."

"Keep talking," Olivia says, her voice softening.

"Can you pass the phone to Jenna? She has to hear it from me. Plus, now Mollie's blaming herself for what happened, which is only making things worse. She doesn't even remember the drive to Bend, so when she woke up to Jenna screaming, Mollie was totally freaked out. She just knows that my girlfriend may no longer be my girlfriend because of her." I sit down on the kitchen chair and lean my head into my hand.

"Jackson, here's what I'll do. I'll tell Jenna that you shared your side of the story and that it all makes sense. However, she must hear it from you," Olivia says. There's something about her delivery that makes me think that she's leaning toward believing me.

"And, I want her to. But, when I went to her apartment, she wouldn't answer. Was she here with you that entire time?" I rub my eyes, mentally and physically exhausted.

"She was home. It wasn't until after you left that she came here," Olivia admits.

"I left a note in the mail slot." Why Jenna didn't see it?

"Jackson, I've never witnessed Jenna react like this. I doubt that she even saw the note." After a moment, I hear Olivia sigh before saying, "You must be wiped out. Back and forth to San Francisco in less than a day, dealing with a messed-up sister, and walking into a total shit show at your apartment." Olivia almost sounds sympathetic at this point.

"Will you talk to her? Now?" I ask in a pleading tone.

"Yes, I promise. Hopefully, she'll come around." Olivia sounds optimistic, but I'm not so sure.

Jenna has to listen to Olivia. I lean back in the chair and close my eyes, trying to ignore my throbbing head. Every inch of my body craves sleep, but I can't risk it. What if Jenna tries to contact me? No, I must stay awake, regardless of how difficult it is. Years of sleepless missions kick in, enabling me to remain focused, present.

Twenty-five minutes later, I receive a text. It's from Jenna.

Jenna: *Liv said it was a misunderstanding.*

Me: *I would never be with anyone else. I love you.*

I wait, but no response. So, I continue typing.

Me: *I need to see you. Are you home?*

Jenna: *No. I'm at Liv's.*

Me: *I'm heading there now.*

Jenna: *No. Meet me at my place.*

I race to her apartment, knowing I'll get there before Jenna does.

Then I remember Mollie's asleep. Unsure how long I'll be away, I quickly call Matt, bring him up to speed, and then ask that he stop by and take Mollie to lunch, keep her occupied – and safe – while I do whatever I can to fix things with Jenna.

I pull up outside of Jenna's place and stay in the truck, waiting for her Subaru to round the corner. After what feels like an eternity, but is actually less than ten minutes, she finally pulls up. Before Jenna's able to turn off the engine, I'm already out of my truck and approaching her car. As the car door opens, I pull her close to me, look her straight in the eyes, and slowly say, "I would *never* cheat on you. I'm not that guy."

Jenna just clings tightly to me. She's shaking. "I know that now, but when I saw that woman... in your bed, well I lost it."
"I totally understand that it looked really bad. And I take the blame for not calling you about going to San Francisco. But, why wouldn't you listen to me?" I pause, hoping she'll say something, but she doesn't, so I continue. "Didn't part of you believe in me?" I ask as I gently stroke her hair.

"I wanted to. I really did. But I was so angry I couldn't think clearly. And then I thought you were bringing her breakfast, just like you had done for me. I can't explain how much it hurt." Tears start to fall from Jenna's eyes.

I hold her tightly, kissing her wet cheeks. We walk together into her apartment.

"But, there's more." Jenna pauses and looks away as she takes a seat at the kitchen table. "When I saw her wrapped in your sheets, it triggered something, a memory from the past, flooding my mind with horrible images." Jenna's body slumps in the chair then her legs begin to tremble.

"What images?" I do my best to keep my voice calm and steady, sensing a traumatic flashback, almost like a PTSD.

"I must have forgotten about it... until this morning... but this time it was you..." Jenna sputters the words, pausing for a breath between phrases.

Aware of the immense strain on her face, I sit down in a chair next to hers. "What did you remember?"

She starts crying. Her body trembles. "It's so long ago, I never understood the disjointed memories, not until this morning."

"It's OK. It's over. Tell me, what happened?" I place my hand atop of hers.

Slowly, she begins to recount the incident from her childhood. "I was little, five, I think. I didn't understand it, but deep down, I knew it was wrong."

She pauses to wipe her tears, and I patiently wait for her to continue.

"Both my mom and dad were away on business trips, so I was staying with my grandmother. I'm guessing it was in the fall because I remember Halloween decorations in the house," she says as she tightly wraps her arms across her chest.

"It was just you then?" I asked, wondering if Annie was still alive.

"Yes, Annie had died that May." She swallows before continuing. "I was at my grandmother's, in Beacon Hill, and it was time for bed. I realized that no one packed my favorite stuffed animal, my bunny, and I wouldn't sleep without it. That's why my grandmother drove me to our house, instructing me to hurry quickly to my room and retrieve the stuffed animal." Jenna stops and takes a breath before continuing. "There wasn't supposed to be anyone home... he said he'd be away. But when I went upstairs, I heard noises coming from my parents' bedroom. This really confused me. I probably should have gone downstairs and told my grandmother, but I didn't. Instead, I walked to the doorway of their room and saw..." Jenna pauses, shuddering. "They never knew I was there. I quietly backed away, grabbed the bunny from my bed, and ran downstairs. I guess I buried it deep inside my mind. It probably would have stayed there, but then I walked into your bedroom, and, well, it brought everything back." She rubs her forehead as if attempting to erase this disturbing memory.

"Your dad was with another woman? Oh, Jenna." I take hold of her hands. "Now I understand why you became so upset this morning."

"I remember that my parents were really sad for a while. I always attributed it to Annie's death. Why did he do that to my mother? I thought that they were so in love."

I pull her onto my lap, and we stay that way, tightly embraced in each other's arms. After a few moments, I say, "Losing a child is traumatic for everyone in the family. Some marriages never survive it. It looks like your parents experienced some tough times after Annie died, but they made it work. My parents weren't so lucky. Their marriage ended over an affair, after mom my found out about my dad and his secretary... and the daughter they were expecting." It's then that I see the irony of our situations. We both suffered from memories of unfaithful parents.

"What? You mean Mollie was born while your dad was still married to your mom?" she asks, her eyes wide in disbelief. "Did you hate him? And weren't you mad about Mollie?"

I begin to tell her the story of Mollie. "I was young when this happened. I didn't understand the entire situation. Matt and I would stay at our dad's place every other weekend and some holidays. We loved Mollie and her mom, Bridgette. They were our second family," I say as I think back to how much fun we had those weekends – away from my mom.

"But why didn't you tell me about Mollie?" Jenna asks, sounding hurt.

"I'm sorry. It was wrong of me to keep it from you. You have every right to be angry. It's just that Mollie, well, she's been pretty sick lately. She struggles emotionally. I don't like to talk about it." Just thinking about Mollie zaps the energy from my body. I'm never sure what to say or do to help her.

"That's what Olivia said." Jenna abruptly stops. "Sorry. I wasn't supposed to tell you that. But you know Olivia... she is horrible with secrets and keeping her mouth shut."

"Did you tell Olivia about your dad?" I ask, wondering how Olivia would have reacted.

"No, I couldn't talk about it. The flashback was so confusing. I'm still trying to process everything." Jenna stands up, goes to the fridge, and grabs two bottles of water off of the top shelf. She returns to place them on the table in front of us and sits back down. "I'm so sorry that I flipped out. I should have listened to you, but I was so mad about what I saw *and* what I remembered. I can't believe he did that to my mother. Who was that woman? Were there others? I need to know. I'm going to confront him about this. I can't ignore it, pretend it didn't happen." She unscrews the cap of the water bottle and takes a long sip.

"It is probably best to wait, let things settle for a bit. Somehow, you'll figure out what to do," I say, trying to reassure Jenna that calling out her dad now would be a huge mistake. She's way too emotional.

"I always thought that my parents had this perfect marriage. What if my mom doesn't know? What should I do?" Jenna's voice gets louder, and her allegiance to her mother becomes quite obvious.

"Sleep on it," I suggest. "Maybe it's something you want to talk to your dad about. But not now."

"Fine, I'll wait. Besides, I'm too furious to have a rational conversation with him at this moment." She's suppressed this for twenty years, so what's another twenty-four hours? Jenna inhales deeply before switching subjects. "So, tell me about Mollie. What happened to her?"

I lean back into the chair and share the entire story about my sister and my parents' ruined marriage.

"I'm so sorry. I was really a bitch to you and Mollie this morning. Does she hate me?" Jenna asks. Sam puts his head on her leg, and she begins to rub his ears.

"No." I shake my head. "She's beating herself up over this, says it's all her fault. Today was difficult for Mollie, too. When she became old enough to understand why Matt and I didn't live at her house all of the time, she instantly blamed herself for my parents' divorce. I think it could even be the root to her depression. And, after this morning, she's feeling like she ended our relationship. I'm going to text her to let her know we're all right. We are, aren't we?" I gaze at Jenna, eyebrows raised, waiting for her confirmation.

Jenna gives me that look, the one I love.

"Good," I say as I squeeze her thigh then send a reassuring message to my sister.

"Jackson, I need to see Mollie, to tell her I'm sorry about losing it this morning."

"She totally understands why you were upset. Mollie's pretty special. I think you two would get along. Do you want to meet her, I mean officially?"

"Give me a minute to shower first, I'm a mess." Jenna smiles, finally.

"You know, I haven't taken a shower in at least a day. Driving back and forth to San Francisco, and then everything else. I could probably use one, too."

Although physically exhausted, make up sex in a steamy bathroom gives me a surge of energy. Another emotional barrier crossed, our connection becomes even closer. With trust reestablished, desire and thirst return. We both have the need to please and to be pleased. She is freak'n unbelievable. I never thought a woman could mean so much to me. Despite what has happened during the last twenty-four hours, I still feel like the luckiest bastard alive.

CHAPTER 25

Jenna

Wanting to meet his sister, but in no rush to end our make-up session, we eventually head to Jackson's, bringing Sam along for the ride. When we walk into his apartment, I see Matt watching TV on the sofa and the woman I saw in Jackson's bed mulling about the kitchen, sipping from a mug. She looks nervous and on edge.

"Mollie, there's someone I want you to meet," Jackson says to his sister as he puts his arm around me. As beautiful as she is now, no doubt Mollie looks even more stunning under better circumstances.

Approaching her, I do my best to appear welcoming while still trying to overcome my initial jealousy. But Mollie makes it easier, sweetly offering a hug as she starts to apologize for the earlier misunderstanding.

"I am so sorry. I didn't even know where I was when I woke up. It must have looked horrible, Jenna," Mollie's voice radiates regret.

"Yeah, it was pretty bad," I admit as I inhale deeply. "But I overreacted. And, I am sorry about that." I reach out to give her hand a gentle squeeze.

"No, it's not your fault. When we become upset, sometimes we're past the point of reasoning. It just takes time for us to hear, to listen."

Grateful for his sister's reaction, I consider telling her why I overreacted. "When I first saw you this morning, it caused a memory to resurface, a bad one, from my childhood, something that I must have suppressed for years. That's why I ran. I was unable to separate the two realities because they merged into one terrible nightmare." I then look at Jackson, our eyes meet.

"I understand, really I do," Mollie says with a sigh. "I'm not sure what Jackson's told you, but there's stuff from my past that has impacted me, too, pretty badly."

For some unknown reason, Mollie starts to relax. We sit down at the kitchen table while Jackson starts a pot of coffee. Matt turns off the television and joins us. Slowly, their sister begins to share her story. "Growing up, it all seemed great, I mean, I had everything I wanted. And when my two brothers would visit me," she pauses as she looks at Matt and Jackson, "we'd have so much fun. But then I started asking my parents some tough questions. I still remember that rainy November afternoon when they sat me down and told me about their relationship, my being born, and then my dad's divorce from Jackson's mom. I was old enough to put two and two together. I was the cause of Jackson and Matt's back-and-forth between the two households. I took their dad away from them. If I hadn't been born, our dad may have never left Rachel. But I was and he did. Now my dad is dead, my mother's lonely, and I'm a total mess." Mollie buries her head in her hands. Matt instinctively rubs her back, telling her it will be all right.

Jackson shakes his head as he gets up to pour coffee for everyone. "Mollie, how many times do I have to tell you? Matt's and my parents had a horrible marriage. My mom is a very difficult person to live with. You know that." Matt shakes his head in agreement as Jackson hands each us each a mug.

"I was too young to remember them living together, but from the stories I've heard, it was awful," Matt says as he goes to the refrigerator to get milk for his coffee.

Mollie sits up. "Sure, I know that intellectually, but emotionally, I still don't buy it. If it weren't for me, your dad may have still continued his affair with my mom, but I doubt that he'd ever leave you guys. You know, I think his heart attack was caused by the guilt he felt for abandoning you," Mollie contemplatively says as she casts her eyes toward her hands folded neatly on her lap.

"He didn't abandon us," Jackson counters his sister. "He took excellent care of us, *and* of our mom for that matter. We always had everything that we wanted, and then some. Plus, he constantly included us whenever he took you and Bridgette on vacations. He referred to us as his three kids. Never did he utter the word 'half' or 'step,' before saying 'brother' or 'sister,'" Jackson reminds Mollie while Matt nods in agreement.

"Mollie, you were a gift. Maybe your being born is exactly what was needed to give your dad the courage to leave Rachel," I say before lifting the warm mug to my lips. As the hot liquid travels down my throat, I watch Mollie trying to take in what we're all saying. She still seems confused, so I add, "You didn't cause the break-up. Their marriage was already hopeless. Blaming yourself is only hurting you."

"Thank you," Mollie says as she meets my gaze. "Every therapist has told me the same thing, I just never believed them," she admits as she grimaces and shrugs her shoulders.

Jackson looks lovingly at his sister. "We all keep telling you the same thing," he says, "but until you accept it, things won't change, and you won't get better." The conversation then shifts to inconsequential subjects, the small talk that we revert to when we've said enough. That's when I realize how exhausted I am, both mentally and physically.

A half-hour later, Mollie yawns before excusing herself to go to the bedroom and lie down. Matt then says goodbye, sharing that he and Simone are meeting friends downtown at Deschutes Brewery. Once they leave, I take the opportunity to speak privately with Jackson.

"You know, Mollie can't make herself believe this, but maybe, if we could give her some proof, then she might listen." My forehead furrows as I quickly devise a plan. "Let's talk to your mom. Ask her some questions about her marriage to your dad before Bridgette and he became involved. Do you think she would be honest, if not for Mollie, for your sake?" I ask, hoping that this unconventional approach could help Mollie accept the fact that the divorce wasn't her fault.

"You want to meet my mom?" Jackson asks as he laughs aloud. "Seriously, you're prepared to spend a day with Rachel Tait?" Jackson's clearly amused as he puts the four mugs in the dishwasher.

"Yes, I want to meet her. She's your mom after all," I say as I stand up and place my hands on my hips. "And remember the stories I told you about Ben's aunt? I mean, how much worse could your mom be?"

"If what you said about his family is half-way true, then you're right. My mom may be difficult, but she's definitely not bat-shit crazy like you've described Ben's aunt." Jackson walks toward me, and I move into his arms. "Alright. You can meet her. Plus, at some point, Mollie needs to go back to her apartment."

"Do you really think that she'll be ready to return to San Francisco so quickly? She just got here. It will take time until she's capable of being on her own," I offer with concern evident in my voice.

"You're right. In a few weeks we'll drive Mollie back, and then you can meet my mom," Jackson says as he begins to kiss the nape of my neck and run his fingers through my hair.

I pull back from his embrace. "No, this can't wait. I mean it. Your sister's recovery depends on this. It's critical that she understands that she didn't cause your parents' divorce. Otherwise, she'll continually blame herself for all that happened. You said so yourself."

Jackson remains silent, so I continue to state my case.

"Flying gets us back and forth to San Francisco in one day. Plus, you *should* see your mom. I'm sure she misses you." I give him that look, the one I learned so well from my mother, the one she'd use to invoke a bit of guilt when trying to sway my dad.

"You are relentless," Jackson sighs. "I give up. I'll call my mom and see when she's available. You're sure that you're ready to do this? Aren't there already enough parent issues?" he asks in a solemn tone, while sitting down onto the couch and then pulling me onto his lap.

"Of course, I am." A slight grin momentarily comes over my face before letting out a sigh, remembering the situation with my father. "But first, I need to deal with my dad. I can't ignore it any longer. Just thinking about it makes me crazy." I clench my jaw as I contemplate what to do.

Jackson rubs my shoulders. "What are you thinking?"

"I've decided to email him, tell him what I remembered, and then ask him why he did it. This way I can plan what I want to say and how I want to say it. He owes me an explanation." My voice escalates, and I can feel the tension form in my neck muscles. "I trusted my dad. He was my role model in so many ways, and now it's all shattered."

"I know you're upset, but this happened a long time ago," Jackson says as he continues to massage my shoulders. "Yes, your dad made a huge mistake, but give him a chance to explain. Maybe there is more to the story than you know."

"Really? What else could there be? He cheated on my mom. And as soon as I get home, I'm emailing him. I can't wait any longer," I declare as I remove myself from Jackson's lap and sit next to him.

"Wait until tomorrow. It's been an emotional day, and we're all exhausted. You don't want to say anything that you'll regret. In the morning you'll have a clearer head." He pulls me toward him and kisses me lightly on her cheek as I promise that I won't send an email until the next day. But that doesn't mean that I can't start working on the email tonight.

* * *

Two hours later, I'm back at my place sitting in front of my laptop, the blank email screen staring me in the face. How exactly do I tell my father that I had a flashback of him screwing some woman who wasn't my mother? Unsure of how to begin, I just start writing, deleting, rewriting, and revising. Finally, forty-five minutes later, I hit "Save as Draft" as I dig my fingers into the back of my tense neck. Wiped out, I head to bed, Sam at my heels. What a nightmare of a day. Tomorrow has to be better.

Although exhausted, my sleep is restless. The day's events keep invading my mind. By five the next morning, I finally accept that I won't fall back to sleep. Reluctantly, I crawl out of bed, head to the kitchen to turn on the coffee maker, and then return to the saved email.

Dad,

I need you to tell me the truth about something that happened when I was little. Yesterday, a memory resurfaced, one that I've suppressed for years. It happened several months after Annie died. You and mom both had business trips, so I was staying with Gran. But I had to go back to the house that first night because Mom forgot to pack my bunny. When I was headed to my room, I saw you with a woman – in your bed. At the time I didn't understand what was happening, but now I remember every detail. Why did you cheat on Mom? Who was she? How long did this relationship last? Does Mom know? I am so angry with you. Part of me doesn't believe you could do this, but I remember it, and the vision is crystal clear, so I know that it happened. I hate saying all of this in an email, but the truth is that I don't really want to see or speak with you right now.

Jenna

I hit "Send." Done. The ball is in his court.

CHAPTER 26

Jackson

The thought of my mother, Rachel Tait, brings up anything *but* maternal feelings. She isn't a bad person, she just never made her children a priority. Even though I dread talking to my mother, I promised Jenna that I'd make the call. As much as I hate to admit it, Jenna may be right – maybe my mom will tell us something that can help Mollie. Plus, it's been a while, and I probably should reach out to her. I walk outside and sit on my back steps so that Mollie doesn't hear the conversation.

"Mom... hi. It's Jackson." My voice sounds constricted as I hold the phone to my right ear.

"Hello, Jackson, how are you?" my mother politely asks.

"I'm fine, Mom," I say before pausing, taking in the early morning sun, hoping the warm rays will give me the extra energy I need right now. "I'm just calling to see if we – I mean, my girlfriend, Jenna, and I – could visit you sometime this week. Would that work with your schedule?"

"What a nice surprise," she says tentatively, seeming to ignore the girlfriend comment. "Yes, I'm in town all week. What day were you thinking?"

I suggest Wednesday, just four days away. I just want this to be over.

"All right. Is there any particular reason for this trip?" my mother asks. She does not like surprises.

"Actually, Mollie's with us, in Bend. She's having some issues again. I'm hoping you can provide some information that will help her get better," I say while looking down at my left hand and noticing that the calluses are starting to heal, a sign that I haven't been on my mountain bike in a while.

"I'm not sure what I could tell you that would help Mollie, but I'll do my best to answer your questions. I look forward to seeing both of you on Wednesday." The words are kind, but the tone is cold and controlled. Then the phone clicks. I walk back inside.

This will definitely be interesting. As I turn on the stove and grab a carton of eggs from the fridge, I call Jenna to let her know that we're all set. But when she answers, I notice distance in her voice.

"Jenna, are you OK?" I ask but my instincts tell me otherwise.

"I think so… no…. I'm not sure." Jenna pauses for a moment then continues. "I waited until this morning to send the email, like I promised. Forty-five minutes later, my dad responded."

"What did he say?" I turn off the stovetop. She's got my full attention now.

"He said that he was deeply sorry that I witnessed what happened and carried it inside of me for so long. Yes, my mother knows. Oh, and, he's flying to Oregon, *today,* to see me." Jenna becomes silent.

"You've got to be kidding." I run my fingers through my hair, realizing that as bad as yesterday was, today is going to be anything but normal. "Did you expect that kind of response?"

"I had no idea how he would react. But I never thought he'd come here, especially not right away. He said he's leaving on the next available flight, arriving tonight. What should I do?" I can hear the heaviness of her voice.

"You need to hear your dad out," I say while taking the carton of orange juice from the fridge and pouring, myself a glass. "He's owning up to something pretty big. Obviously, it's important for him to see you and explain in person. Are you ready to give him that chance? After all, you're the one who emailed him." I knew that she should have waited longer before contacting him.

"I know I did. But what else could I have done? I couldn't ignore it," she says, yet I sense a tinge of regret in her voice.

"Now everything is out on the table," I say as I return to making breakfast. "You and your dad can have an honest conversation. It doesn't mean that you approve or even forgive him for what he did. Just listen to what he has to say."

"I know," Jenna pauses. "Can you be with me when he arrives? I don't think I can do this alone."

Even though this is the last place I want to be, between a father and his daughter when he explains why he cheated on his wife, it's clear that Jenna's feeling incredibly fragile and needs support. The past two days have been pretty disturbing, for everyone. And, the quicker things are resolved, the better. I guess that means on all ends, including visiting my mom. I crack three eggs into a bowl, turn the burner back on, and add butter to the pan.

"Since there's no sense in just waiting around for your dad's flight to land, why don't I come get you, and we can spend the day hiking at Smith Rock?" I suggest to her. "Afterward we can head to the airport to pick him up. Sound good? I can ask Matt to hang around OutRider and take care of anyone who comes in. And, Simone told Matt she wanted to get to know Mollie, so she and my sister can do something together."

"Are you sure that's not imposing too much on Matt and Simone?" Jenna asks, her voice sounding less heavy. Maybe she's relieved that I'll be with her when she sees her dad.

"Nope, in fact Matt just told me that they have nothing going on this weekend." When my brother and I spoke yesterday, we talked about the five of us having dinner tonight. But now that Jenna's dad is flying to Bend, it will just be Mollie, Matt, and Simone. I toss the eggs into the hot buttered pan. "I'm making breakfast now. How 'bout I pick you up in forty-five?" Eggs sizzle as we say goodbye and I tuck my phone into the back pocket of my jeans.

* * *

Ten hours later, we're waiting inside the Redmond terminal for her dad's Saturday evening flight to arrive. Jenna tightly grips my hand. She had become more and more unraveled as the day progressed. What started out as a fun hike ended up being a tearful walk back to the truck. As fired-up as Jenna was last night about confronting her dad, she's now second-guessing her actions.

"It would have been so much easier if I never remember it. Or, if I just left it alone and didn't email him," she fidgets while we wait in the baggage claim area.

"But the memory still would have been there, deep inside, somehow affecting you. Now you both have a chance to say what needs to be said. This is you taking control of your life. Isn't that what you wanted?" I place my hand on the small of her back, pulling her toward me. "And from what you've told me about your dad, he seems like a great guy. This happened so long ago, right after Annie died. I can't even imagine the pain he and your mom were going through."

"I know, but that doesn't give him permission," she says as she looks directly at me, frowning.

"Of course not. But it does give *you* perspective." I lean down to kiss the tip of her nose.

Fifteen minutes later, a tall, lean man with thick hair that's graying at the temples walks toward us. Unsure as to what's about to unfold, I'm committed to stay by Jenna's side, supporting her however I can.

"Jenna…" Geoff Moore raises his arms and moves to hug his daughter. Jenna flinches, and he respectfully steps back and keeps his distance.

"Mr. Moore, I'm Jackson," I say, offering my hand.

"Please, call me Geoff," Jenna's dad responds as we shake.

I carefully observe Geoff with his red eyes and creased forehead. It took a lot of guts for him to drop everything and fly to Oregon to talk to Jenna in person. Not many fathers would have done that.

The ride back to Jenna's apartment is basically silent. Once inside, Sam jumps up on Geoff, obviously happy to see him. At least someone is.

"Jenna, I am so sorry," Geoff begins before we've even entered the living room. "What I did was wrong. I wish I could tell you why it happened, but I can't. It just did."

"How could you do that to Mom?" Jenna, who stands at least ten feet away from Geoff, finally questions her father. I watch as her jaw clenches and her nostrils flare. Here it comes. This is going to be painful, but it's what Jenna must do to let go of her emotions and release what's been haunting her. I watch as tears stream down her face now that the elephant in the room has been addressed. I move closer, offering an arm around her shoulder, attempting to comfort her.

"That's the thing," Geoff says, his voice slow and steady as he looks at the floor and shakes his head. "There was nothing wrong between your Mom and me. It just happened. I know that's not an excuse, but I wasn't myself. Neither of us was back then. Losing Annie five months earlier, well it basically destroyed your mother and me." He slowly lifts his head, looking toward his daughter. I can see tears forming in his eyes.

"But you were supposed to be away... for work... that's why I was at Gran's." Jenna starts pacing between the edge of the sofa and the front door.

"That's right, but my flight was canceled. Linda, the woman you saw," Geoff swallows, "was my coworker at the time. We were both trying a case and needed to travel to Minneapolis for a few days to finish the proceedings. However, the airlines postponed our flight to Minnesota until the next day, so we decided to have a drink at the bar before going home." Geoff awkwardly shifts his weight back and forth while wringing his hands. "One drink turned into way too many, and it just happened. She was lonely, and I was hurting." His eyes momentarily shut, and he once again shakes his head. "There was no excuse. What I did was wrong. Immediately I told Linda that I had made a huge mistake and that as soon as we finished our business in Minneapolis, I would submit my resignation. And that's exactly what I did. Three weeks later I began working at another firm." He looks up at Jenna.

"When did you tell Mom?" Jenna questions, her tone sharp and direct.

"Right after she returned from her trip. I couldn't stand it, couldn't stand myself." Geoff stops talking for a bit, gazing out the window into darkness. "When I told your mom, she just looked at me then started crying. I'd crushed her. Not only did we lose Annie, but for a while, we had lost each other." Tears slowly fall down his face. His left hand quickly wipes them away as he says, "I've spent every day since telling your mother how much I love her. She knows it's true. She never stopped loving me. It took some time, but she eventually forgave me." Geoff looks from Jenna to me and then back to his daughter, almost as if he's trying to gage whether or not we believe him. "This whole thing has been in our past for quite a while. But then you emailed me, and, well..." Geoff stops talking, struggling to hold himself together.

"Does Mom know that you're here and why?" Jenna's tone sounds a bit softer.

"Yes, she wanted to come, but I told her that this was something I needed to do by myself," Geoff admits, eyes cast downward.

Immediately, I respect him for that comment. Geoff's definitely owning up to his actions. He isn't giving his daughter excuses and isn't asking for her forgiveness either.

"So, now that I know, what happens next?" Jenna faces her dad with hands on her hips.

"That's not something I can answer for you. I know what my hope is, but that is too much to ask. You need to decide. It's up to you," Geoff says, his voice cracking a bit as he speaks.

Suspecting that it's an appropriate time to cut in, I say, "Geoff, it means a lot that you came here to explain what happened. It's just a lot for Jenna to handle. It's been a tough couple of days." Protectively I put my arm around Jenna. Geoff reflectively stiffens as he watches me stake claim to his only daughter. No doubt I've encroached on his territory as his father. But he is not my concern at the moment, Jenna is.

Jenna takes a few steps closer to her dad and says, "I need to process what you've told me, Dad. I can't promise anything right now. But, thank you for coming here, for being honest about what happened."

Without saying another word, Geoff nods and pulls out his phone from his back pocket.

"What are you doing?" Jenna asks.

"I'm getting an Uber back to the airport. I can take a red-eye to Boston if I first catch the 9:45 from Redmond to San Francisco," Geoff answers as he appears to pull up the app.

I look at Jenna and give her the "come on" glance.

She sighs then says, "Stay here. I have an extra room. You can fly back tomorrow. It's been a long day."

"Are you sure?" Relief appears on Geoff's face.

Jenna just nods. "I'm wiped out. I didn't sleep well last night. The guest room bed is all made up, and there are fresh towels in the bathroom. If you need anything, Jackson knows where everything is. I've asked him to stay tonight. Goodnight, Dad." Then, before retreating to her bedroom, she gives me a quick kiss whispering, "Thank you."

"How about a drink? I know I could sure use one," I say to Geoff once Jenna leaves, while entering the kitchen to retrieve two glasses out of the cabinet.

"Please," Geoff sighs as he takes a seat on the sofa.

"She'll come around. Jenna wasn't kidding when she said she's exhausted. She's had a hell of a few days." While I prepare two scotches, I fill Geoff in on what triggered Jenna's memory. Geoff just listens, appearing deep in reflection.

"You know, Maggie and I, well, we dealt with it. Never in a million years did we think that Jenna would find out. There was no point in telling her. What I did had absolutely nothing to do with her." Geoff rubs his graying temples.

"I know that. From what you said, you had just lost your younger daughter and you were distraught." I hand him his drink.

"True, but that's no excuse. I know you haven't known my daughter for very long, but you two seem to have a connection. Do you think she'll forgive me?" Geoff asks while looking me directly in the eyes.

Giving him a brief nod, I say, "I do. She loves you very much. I'm not sure if you know how much she's missed you both since she's been here."

"Well, we've missed her," Geoff says as he takes a deep breath. "I didn't want her to move, but I guess she had to leave Boston. Watching Jenna grow up, her life always flowed. She worked hard, got great grades, always made the right choices – pretty much achieved whatever she set out to do. We thought she was happy. But, when she told us about Ben, that's when we knew that her life wasn't all we thought it was. And then, when she lost her job, well that's when she really started coming apart." He takes a long sip of his scotch.

"Jenna's changed since we first met. She's not as afraid of making mistakes." I pause and smile as I think about how much she's grown. "And, she's beginning to stand up for herself, going out of her comfort zone. Her emailing you is a good example of that. I don't think that she would have taken that risk two months ago. She would have been afraid of ruining your relationship." I sip my scotch, savoring its soothing peaty flavor.

"We always knew she was hard on herself. Jenna constantly strived to be perfect. Maggie and I think it's because she saw how devastated we were after losing Annie. In an instant, Jenna became our only child. It's as if she wanted to be the best she could be, so that she didn't disappoint us." Geoff momentarily appears to be somewhere else, at another juncture of his life.

"Your theory sounds pretty solid." I unexpectedly smile as I consider how Jenna may have acted when she was younger. "Jenna's already admitted to me how much she tries to please others. It's one of the things that she's been working on, you know, doing things because she wants to, not because she thinks she's supposed to."

"Her mom and I didn't impose demands on her…" Geoff declares, a bit defensively.

"She knows that. Jenna's shared that she created a lot of this on her own. It's no one's fault. But, in order for her to figure things out, she needed to leave Boston. I think, at least I hope, she's finding the answers here." I look at Geoff's empty drink and nod toward the bottle of scotch. He shakes his head yes, so I refresh both of our drinks.

While I fill the glasses with ice he says, "I think she might have." Geoff looks at me then smiles.

We stay up for another round, and I fill him in on how I ended up in Bend and how Jenna and I first met. We talk about our mutual love of baseball, and he asks me what life was like as a SEAL. But eventually the wear and tear of the day takes over, so we call it a night.

Jenna's sound asleep when I crawl into her bed. Finally, she looks at peace. Tonight, things happened the way they were supposed to. She received the answers she needed, and her dad had the opportunity to apologize and tell his truth. People can make bad decisions, but they can also correct their actions. I guess there's always hope.

* * *

Sleep does wonders for Jenna. She wakes up early that Sunday morning in a surprisingly good mood. After preparing a large breakfast, she waits for her dad to get up, and then they talk – not about what happened twenty years ago – but about what's occurring now, in both of their lives. I closely watch their interaction. Time, combined with a good night's sleep, can heal. I doubt that she's forgiven him, but maybe the process has begun.

On the drive back to the airport, we give Geoff a quick tour of the town. Jenna makes her dad promise that he and her mom will come to Bend soon, maybe to ski at Mt. Bachelor. Geoff readily agrees. I notice his eyes. They're brighter, and he appears about ten years younger than he did last night. He's a good man. I like Geoff Moore.

This time, Jenna doesn't flinch when her father tries to embrace her before leaving the terminal. She hugs him tightly, even tells him that she loves him.

CHAPTER 27

Jenna

"We are now boarding all zones," the cheery voice comes over the loudspeaker as Jackson and I head toward the counter and the airline attendant scans our tickets. We walk outside onto the tarmac to board the small plane headed to San Francisco.

I feel tingly knowing that today I get to meet Jackson's mother, and yet I sense that he's not feeling the same way. Perhaps visiting his mother will help me understand why their relationship is so estranged. Still, the main purpose of this trip is to find out anything that might help Mollie get better.

Since Mollie's been in town, Jackson's been staying at my apartment – his space is way too small for two people. Mollie usually sleeps late and then spends her afternoons at OutRider, helping Jackson with various projects.

"So, what's on your mind?" I ask as the plane heads down the runway. The look of dread appeared on his face as soon as he awoke this morning, and it's only gotten worse.

At first, he does not respond. Instead, Jackson sits back into the turquoise upholstered airplane seat and closes his eyes before he speaks. "I hate the idea of my mom. It's who she's become. My only happy memories of her were before my dad left. Since then, she's turned mean and bitter." Jackson stares out the plane's window, his eyes narrow, forming creases above his nose. "She blames everyone else for anything that's wrong in her life. When she found out that I wanted to join the Navy, she snapped." Jackson gives out a big sigh. "I don't know why she hated the idea so much. I waited until I had already passed the SEAL Qualification Training before I told her." He rubs his forehead before continuing. "It's always been about her and what she wants. And while that pissed me off growing up, it devastated Matt." The muscles in Jackson's face tense when he speaks of how his mom impacted his younger brother. "Matt was so young and needed her. She wasn't there for him, or for me. It's almost as if my mom vanished when my dad left, replaced by this empty shell of an angry woman who lacked compassion and purpose." He stops and stares into space.

"Wow." I'm speechless. I thought that maybe Jackson would open up a bit, but I never expected him to divulge so much. After a moment of quiet between us I say, "Your mom sounds pretty complicated. I'm sorry." I place my head on his shoulder, cuddling closer as we hear the plane's wheels retract and lock into place. "I mean, that's pretty messed up. But then I just found out that my dad had an affair, so what's worse?" At least now I understand Jackson's hesitation about today's visit.

* * *

It's a quick flight that puts us back on the ground in just over an hour. After exiting the terminal, we grab an Uber to Jackson's childhood home in Ross. Before long, we're standing outside of a red brick Tudor with overgrown shrubbery that's crowding the entrance. Despite this, or perhaps because of it, the house has an air of elegance in a strange, detached way. A lone flowerpot sits on the front porch, the petunias wilting from lack of water.

"My mother was never one for gardening," Jackson comments sarcastically as he walks past the limp flowers and rings the doorbell.

A tall, thin woman answers the door, and the first thing I notice is her light blonde hair, almost gray, that she wears pulled back in a dig- nified manner. She appears quite fit dressed in a white tennis outfit. By the tone of her face, I'm almost certain that she's had some work done. As soon as she sees Jackson, her expression softens. She hugs her son, although somewhat awkwardly, then eyes me as if to determine whether I am friend or foe.

"Hi, Ms. Tate, I'm Jenna," I extend my hand to Jackson's mother.

Her cool thin fingers lightly graze mine as she says, "Hello, please call me Rachel. It's nice to meet you. Come in. I thought we'd sit and chat before we leave to have lunch at the Club. Jackson said that you have a five-thirty flight to catch, and I've scheduled a tennis lesson at around the same time, so our afternoon should work perfectly." Wow. Strong boundaries set right away.

Rachel leads us through a perfectly appointed foyer. I look around as I follow her, noting that unlike the outside, the house's interior is spotless, and everything is in its proper place. But, something's missing. It takes me a while, but then I realize what it is. Where are the photographs? There are no baby pictures, no graduation photos, nothing from vacations or every-day life. It's as if she has no family.

I take a seat on an elegant upholstered floral print sofa while Jackson and his mother sit opposite one another on coordinated stuffed arm-chairs. There's an exquisite Oriental rug beneath the antique mahogany coffee table that separates the three of us creating a natural boundary of sorts. This living room's impeccable – but it's almost like a museum – it certainly doesn't seem like anyone actually sits in here.

"I was so surprised when you called, Jackson. How long has it been?" Rachel asks, looking directly at her son as she sits with perfect posture in her perfect living room.

"February, a year ago? Does that seem right, Mom?" Jackson sounds authoritative, refusing to take her bait. "I think that the last time I was here was right after I returned from Afghanistan, before moving to Bend. I spent less than a week at home, but I seem to recall that you and I were both relieved when I left." He keeps his eyes locked on her, creating a standoff of sorts.

Jackson won't play her game. He's not letting her get away with anything.

"Yes, I think you are correct." Rachel doesn't miss a beat in this back and forth volley. "You were suffering so." All of the sudden, Rachel exudes an expression of panic as she glances in my direction and her hand goes to her throat.

"It's OK, Mom. Jenna knows about Patrick. Things are better now." Jackson leans over and reaches for my hand.

"Good, and Jenna, if you've helped my son, then thank you. I certainly couldn't," she says with regret in her voice.

Unable to get a solid read on this woman, I awkwardly smile, confused as to whether Jackson's tone was too harsh or if Rachel is carefully choosing her words and actions, trying to maintain some control.

Hoping to break the ice, I withdraw my hand from Jackson's, lean toward Rachel, and ask, "What was Jackson like as a child?" After all, there are no baby pictures in sight.

Smiling fondly, Rachel relaxes a bit then says, "Jackson was quiet, perhaps pensive. Everything came easily to him – sports, school, even girls for that matter," she laughs. "But, as talented as he was, he was also reserved, hated to take risks. But that all changed when he joined the

Navy." Once again, her voice turns heavy. This twist in the conversation sheds a light on Rachel's obvious grief and inability to comprehend her son's decision to become a SEAL. I think she may actually miss Jackson.

I can tell that Jackson's not planning to respond to his mother. So, in an attempt to keep the peace, I bring up the reason we made the trip. "Rachel, when Jackson called you, did he tell you about Mollie?" I ask, shifting in the sofa, so I can face both Jackson and Rachel.

"Why, yes, he mentioned that she was having some troubles again and that she's in Oregon with both of you at the moment." To my surprise Rachel's face turns serious, and a hint of empathy appears in her eyes.

"Some troubles are probably an understatement, Mom," Jackson interrupts and sighs heavily. "She's had another breakdown, and I need to keep her with me until she's more stable and can return to San Francisco."

"Oh, I'm sorry." Rachel sits even more erectly. "I had no idea things were that bad. Can her mother do something?" she asks.

"Unfortunately, Bridgette is not in the position to help." Jackson says, biting his lower lip a bit as he glances down toward the floor. I guess he doesn't want Rachel to know about Bridgett's emotional struggles.

"Rachel, Mollie blames herself for your divorce and for Jackson and Matt growing up living between two households. She believes that *she* ruined your marriage," I say rapidly, just putting it out there. Why waste time? After all, Rachel strikes me as a woman who would appreciate directness.

Reflecting for a few moments, Rachel wipes her brow, leans back into the cushioned chair before softly saying, "But it wasn't the child's fault. She had nothing to do with it. It was John… and Bridgette." She pauses. The corners of her lips crease. "He's the one who cheated on me, on *us*." I sense a tone of anger, perhaps even jealousy in Rachel's delivery. "He left before he ever found out that Bridgette was expecting. That was just the icing on the cake." Rachel shakes her head, looking down into her lap. As I hear this, I can't help but be reminded of my own parents' history and how that ended so differently.

"So, the divorce wasn't because of Mollie?" I want to clarify this important detail. After all, this is why we flew to San Francisco – to discover whatever we could to help Mollie get over her guilt.

"No. John learned that Bridgette was pregnant after he filed for divorce." Rachel's voice is clear and crisp as she confirms her prior statement.

Shocked to hear this, Jackson sits forward and asks, "Why didn't you ever tell us this?"

"You've never asked, have you? In fact, there's a lot that you don't know about me." Rachel's eyes narrow as a somewhat devilish grin surfaces. "I understand. I truly do. Our relationship became, shall I say, 'cordial'? We exchange gifts at Christmas and on birthdays, send the obligatory cards, and make the necessary phone calls. But has there been sentiment behind those actions? I doubt that either of us has taken the time to figure out the other. Perhaps you and I aren't that different after all." Rachel purses her lips as she crosses her long, tanned legs.

Jackson becomes silent and the muscles in his face seem to loosen. I watch as he looks at his mother, who's seated across from him, in a new way, almost as if he's seeing her for the first time.

This afternoon – no, this entire week – couldn't get any stranger. I can only imagine what is going through Jackson's mind at this moment. No doubt, the plane ride home will be interesting.

Glancing at her watch, Rachel suggests that we leave to have lunch at the Club. The remainder of the afternoon is smooth, small talk prevails, and no one ventures into the delicate matters discussed earlier. At around three in the afternoon, Jackson and I say goodbye before leaving for the airport. As I thank Rachel for her hospitality, I quietly slip a piece of folded paper into her hand. It's my phone number.

I watch as Jackson awkwardly hugs his mom goodbye. Maybe there's hope for their relationship. Still, he's harboring a lot of anger toward his mother. There's a lot they're not discussing. But today was a start. I wonder if she'll contact me.

* * *

Before I know it, we're back in Bend. As we open the door to Jackson's apartment, we hear the Grateful Dead playing. Mollie's folding laundry, softly singing the lyrics to "Sugar Magnolia."

As soon as she sees us, she abruptly stops asking, "How'd it go?"

We relay today's conversation with Rachel.

"I just don't get it. Why would Dad leave Rachel if he didn't know that my mom was pregnant?" A perplexed look forms on her face as she takes a seat at the kitchen table and puts her feet on the chair next to her, wrapping her arms around both knees.

"None of this was your fault. It never was. John and Rachel's marriage was already over before your mom knew she was expecting," I say before sitting down next to Mollie and placing my hand on her knee, giving it a slight squeeze

It's then that Mollie's expression begins to show a bit of optimism.

"We picked up some Thai on the way home from the airport. Anyone hungry?" Jackson asks as he raises the take-out bag. The smell of Street Noodles permeates the apartment when Jackson opens the lid to the one of large container.

"That sounds awesome. All of the sudden I'm starving," Mollie says is an upbeat tone as she pops up from the table to get three plates out of the cabinet. Thai's Mollie's favorite, which, of course, Jackson knows.

After dinner, I clear the plates while Jackson and his sister continue talking about their childhood. "Jackson, could you help me for a moment?" I ask, interrupting as I put leftovers in Tupperware containers.

"What do you think? Does Mollie believe us?" I whisper as Mollie transitions to the couch and picks up the remote.

"I'm not sure," he says as he looks back at his sister. She's turned on the television, scanning the available Netflix series.

"I can see why you care about her so much," I say while putting the containers into the fridge. I already have a special place in my heart for Mollie.

As I turn away from the refrigerator, Jackson's hands reaches for my hips while he says, "She and Matt, well, they're my family."

I lace my fingers behind his neck. "Don't forget about your mom. You know, the two of you seemed to connect for a bit. I could tell by how she hugged you before we left. You've already lost your dad. Don't lose your mom, too."

Jackson gives a slight nod, as if he acknowledges that I have a point. "I guess I'm still pissed about her not being there when we needed her." I see the pain in his face.

"People change. Don't be so hard on her." I brush my lips against his. "Give her a chance."

"You want me to be nice to her? Give her a second chance?" He says this in a mocking tone as his eyes begin to dance, suggesting something else altogether.

"Yes," I say seriously. "She's your mother. I think it would be good for you." I kiddingly smack his butt to make my point.

"For you, Jenna Moore, I will give her a chance," Jackson teases, happily playing my game. "But there will be a price to pay later tonight when we get back to your place." Jackson grins as he lifts me up and places me on the countertop. The TV plays loudly in the background as we kiss in the kitchen and tease one another for what will come when we're finally alone.

CHAPTER 28

Jackson

Tomorrow's the twentieth of August. I can't believe how quickly this summer has gone. Jenna and I, with Sam in tow, head to my favorite outdoor bar – Crux – which is unusually crowded for a Tuesday evening. Strings of white lights hang between trees, food trucks line the back fence, and little kids and dogs run around while the adults hang out on the lawn. Tonight, a cover band's performing classic Johnny Cash with the lead singer playing a harmonica for extra effect. This is Bend.

After ordering Crux's latest IPA, we look for Olivia and Michael. I spot them at a high-top table near the band. When Katy sees us, she stops playing with her dolls and rushes over to greet Sam. Immediately, she attaches herself to the dog, giving the four of us time to talk.

"So, Jenna, it's been over two months since you've been in Oregon. Are you happy you moved here?" Michael asks as he adjusts his dark-rimmed glasses over his angular nose.

"It sucks!" she jokes, then clamps her hand over her mouth as she glances toward Katy. But Katy's mesmerized with Sam and appears to have no interest in her dad and his friends' conversation.

Jenna leans in closer, then answers Michael's question. "Seriously, I love it here. Bend's got it all – trails, the river, awesome yoga classes, great restaurants…"

"Hey, aren't you missing something?" I say to Jenna as I take a swig of my beer.

Seemingly confused, Jenna starts guessing at where I'm coming from. "Hiking… paddling… breweries? What did I forget?" She wrinkles her forehead, visibly perplexed.

"Me." I sit there smirking.

Olivia and Jenna exchange a quick glance.

"My God, you've changed," Olivia says amused. "What happened to that solitary dude from the bike shop?"

"He's transformed." I'm still smiling as I reach for Jenna's hand and gently kiss her fingers.

"I've been working on his 'dark side.' You know, trying to soften those hard edges." Jenna giggles as she leans back in her high-top chair.

"Well, I believe I like this Jackson even better. Keep doing what you're doing. And, by the way, I think he's been impacting you as well. I hardly see the 'Little Miss Perfect' who I grew up with." Olivia takes a sip from her water glass. Wonder why she's not drinking beer? "I mean it. You actually seem relaxed. It's really awesome how you guys are, well, helping each other grow."

I quickly lose the thought of Olivia not drinking as soon as I look back at Jenna. She's beaming, her eyes sparkling from the reflection of the outdoor lights. Damn, she is beautiful.

"So, the reason we asked you to meet us here is because there's something we want to tell you," Olivia says as she squeezes Michael's thigh.

"I'm listening," Jenna says, sitting up and focusing on Olivia.

"Actually, it's two things, kind of related." Olivia hesitates as she glances over at Michael.

Katy bursts out, "I'm gonna be a big sister!" She doesn't even lift her head from playing with Sam. That kid's been listening to us the entire time.

"Oh my God!" Jenna shouts out, obviously happy about the news. "You're going to be the coolest mom ever!"

"That's only half the news," Michael begins as he takes Olivia's hand from her lap, lifting it for us to see. "The rest is that we're getting married." Olivia flashes a beautiful diamond on her ring finger as she grins uncontrollably.

"And you're my maid of honor!" Olivia announces, skipping "the ask."

Jenna jumps up and hugs her best friend. Then she walks over to

Michael, giving him a warm embrace.

"I'm really happy for both of you," I say, looking at them and then at Katy.

"So, when's the wedding?" Jenna cannot contain herself.

"Since we're kind of on a timeline," Olivia places her hand on her stomach, "we're planning to get married at the end of September."

"September!" Jenna's jaw drops.

"I know," Olivia's eyes widen. "It's only five weeks away. My parents were a bit surprised, but now that the news has settled in, they're excited. Mom booked the club in Brookline and is handling all of the details, with me being here and everything," Olivia exhales a sigh of relief. "My principal is being cool and letting me to take a week off for the wedding. We'll wait till next summer, after the baby is a bit older, to take our honeymoon." Olivia polishes off the remaining water in her glass.

"So, you'll get to see Massachusetts next month." Jenna says to me, her eyes lighting up.

It's time for her to return home, to see her parents. After what happened with her dad, well, they need to reconnect. Plus, I can tell how much she misses her mom. Jenna becomes pretty distant after they talk on the phone. Jenna's come so far, but she needs to be able to be her true self, the one she's still discovering – in Boston, not just in Bend.

While the women talk about wedding plans, Michael and I go to the bar to buy another round, three beers and a seltzer.

"Michael, this is great news, all around," I say while patting my new friend on the back.

"The baby kind of hit us by surprise, but Olivia and I always knew we wanted to be together. This just accelerated our decision. My divorce only became final four months ago." Michael leans toward the bar and gives our order.

"That must have been tough," I say, having watched my parents go through their divorce.

"I guess it went as well as it could, but still, it is a brutal process. Having Katy in the middle of it all, that was pretty shitty. But her mom and I did our best to keep her out of it as much as we could. The challenge now is where to live." Michael takes a big breath then slowly exhales as he looks toward Olivia. "My consulting firm has an office here, so I could easily transfer. But Katy's the issue. I doubt that her mom will let me bring her to Oregon on a permanent basis, and I can't stand to be so far away from her." When Michael speaks about his daughter something shifts in his body. I watch his face relax as he looks at Katy playing with Sam. "Olivia and I had a long conversation about this, and she agreed to move to Chicago. She understands, but she hates leaving Bend, and she especially hates leaving Jenna." Michael says as the bartender hands us our drinks.

"You're making the right choice," I say as we walk toward Jenna and Olivia.

"Yeah. I just hate separating those two. They are both so different, but at the same time, they're like sisters," he says as he watches Olivia and Jenna interact.

"Michael, they've been apart before. It won't mean the end of their friendship. Jenna needed Olivia when she first moved to Bend. But, Jenna's not that same person who arrived in June. Sure, she'll miss Olivia, but she'll be OK. And besides, I've got this now. *I've got Jenna*," I say with the utmost confidence.

Michael smiles then nods his head. He gets it.

We return to the table, and I hand Jenna another IPA while Michael sets a glass of seltzer in front of Olivia. The conversation returns to Boston and wedding plans. Katy curls up next to Sam, her tiny arms wrapped around the golden as she falls asleep on his soft fur. After finishing this round, we say goodnight.

* * *

Jenna's unusually quiet as we walk to the car. I thought she'd be talking nonstop about Olivia and all of the changes she has coming in her life. But instead, she's silent.

"What are you thinking?" I ask as I put the truck in gear and pull out of Crux's parking lot.

"I'll miss her." Jenna solemnly says while searching through the radio channels. She chooses a country station, not her normal choice, and Keith Urban sings, "Blue's Not Your Color."

"I know," I interlace my fingers with hers. "But this is what's right for them, as a family. Michael will be miserable if Katy's not nearby." I pause, remembering my own childhood as I look into the pitch-black sky. "Katy has a tough road ahead of her. This baby will be to Katy what Mollie was to Matt and me. She'll love the baby, but it will change her world in many ways."

"You're absolutely right. It has to be about Katy. That's what's most important." Jenna leans her head on my shoulder then becomes quiet again.

After the song's over, Jenna clears her throat. "There's something that Liv told me that you should probably know." She has my attention. "Liv's inviting Ben to the wedding... cause they were best friends at Colgate, she figures it would be wrong for her to not include him, just because of me and, well, our past."

Hmmm. So, I get to meet the guy Jenna almost married. I can't ignore the competitive sensation that arises. But Ben doesn't threaten me. Actually, I've always wondered what he's like.

"There's one more thing," she says. "Ben most likely won't be coming alone." Jenna lifts her head from my shoulder and looks at me. "Liv heard he's engaged... to someone named Maria." And with that, Jenna stops talking.

Unsure of how to react, I take my time. "How do you feel about that?"

"I don't know. We left on good terms, the best considering the circumstances. But, a fiancé… how did that happen so fast? It's been less than five months since *we* were engaged," Jenna says as she stares down at our interlaced fingers.

"Well, things happen quickly sometimes," I give her hand a squeeze. "Look at us."

"I know," Jenna smiles briefly. "I think it would be fine seeing Ben, if he was alone or even with a date, but meeting the woman he's planning to marry… well, that's pretty huge." I hear a quiver in her voice. Quickly I glance sideways and see that she's pressing her lips tightly together as if she's keeping herself from saying more.

I return my focus to the road as I ask, "How do you think he'll react when he sees me with you?" Curious about her answer, I pause, waiting for her response.

"Probably the same as I will feel about seeing him with someone else." Jenna turns toward the window, leaning her forehead into the glass. "I don't know. The more time that's passed, I kind of realized what a jerk I was. I mean, I broke up with him two months before the wedding, after invitations were sent…."

"You weren't a jerk. You just realized that you shouldn't marry him. And, lucky me for that." I pull the car over into an empty coffee shop parking lot so that I can give Jenna my full attention. "Listen, I don't know the guy, but if he's half as nice as you say he is, then good for him that he's found someone. Haven't you?"

Slowly she sits up and our eyes meet. Her lips begin to curve upward.

"Well then, what exactly is the problem? He's happy, we're happy. Win-win."

"Let's go home," she says before sliding closer and giving me the most delicious kiss. After a few moments, I reluctantly pull away from her and put the car into drive. Although Jenna seems momentarily all right with seeing her ex, something tells me that this is not the end of this conversation.

CHAPTER 29

Jenna

I barely slept last night. Thoughts of Ben marrying another woman kept invading my mind.

Eventually, I get out of bed and call Liv, hoping to learn more. "How can he have proposed already?" I ask, jealousy raging as I begin to hammer Liv for information. "It hasn't been that long… my God, just a month ago, he wanted *me* to reconsider."

"Why does it matter so much to you? I mean, you're with Jackson now," Liv replies with a yawn.

"Were you sleeping?" I ask, hoping I didn't wake her. I look at my watch – it's a quarter past eight.

"No, I'm awake. That's the problem. This baby is keeping me up at night, giving me indigestion. Keep talking."

"Well, sure, I'm with Jackson, but we're not *getting married*. I mean,

Ben and I were together for six years…SIX! We had our lives planned out."

Liv laughs at my outburst. "Jenna, what did you think would happen when you broke off your engagement?"

"I don't know. He'd wait before getting involved again? Tell me that he had become serious with someone else?" I feel a lump form in my throat. After all, I haven't told Ben about Jackson. Yet I'm not caving that easily – *we're not engaged.* "Who is she? What do you know about her?"

"All I heard was that they met at work, and that they connected pretty quickly."

An unexpected snort releases from my mouth. Instinctively my free hand flies to my face, perhaps in an attempt to shove it back down my throat. I hear Liv laughing at my reaction.

"Come on, be happy for Ben. Wouldn't you rather that he's with someone than miserable by himself?" Liv asks. "And, besides, I thought that you and Jackson were getting pretty serious."

"We are, and I *am* glad that Ben's found someone." I guess I am. I take a banana from the fruit bowl and begin to peel it. "He never even hinted that he had met someone. And they work at the same firm? Was he attracted to her while we were together?" I ask, suddenly realizing that this relationship could have been going on for some time. I pause, contemplating that thought as I bite off the top of the banana and swallow it in one gulp. "This hurts. I know it's not supposed to because I'm with Jackson, but it's really hitting me hard. Am I really that replaceable, Liv?" And then it hits me. "Do you think he gave her my ring?" I ask, envisioning this other woman with the three-diamond ring set in platinum – the one that was once mine. I put the rest of the banana on a paper towel and sit down, dejected, at the kitchen table.

"Stop it. Neither the ring nor Ben is yours any longer. You made a choice," Liv says in a trite tone, as if she's tiring of me already.

"I know, and it was the right choice." I stare at my partially eaten banana then say, "I'm so happy that Jackson will be there." For a moment, I envision what it would be like to go to the wedding alone. My jaw clenches involuntarily.

"From what my friend relayed, this woman sounds very sweet," Liv says, which makes me feel even worse. I take another bite of the banana.

"It's just going to be so uncomfortable," I say while chewing. "What will I say to them?" Leaning back into my chair, I can already anticipate the awkwardness.

When Liv and I finally hang up, I am only slightly more relaxed and a tiny bit happy for Ben. After finishing breakfast, I change out of my bathrobe and pull on a pair of running shorts and a tank top before lacing up my sneakers and heading outside.

Finally, I'm back to running. This is only my third time out on the trails. The last two runs felt amazing. My body seemed to move so freely after weeks of not being able to do what I love. Yet, this obsession with Ben and Maria impedes my ability to concentrate on the undulating river path. The idea of seeing them at Liv's wedding freaks me out. I'm also uneasy about staying with my parents. Things with my dad still aren't back to normal. Plus, I'm not sure how my mom will act, now that I know.

I quicken my pace, running with these scattered thoughts as I play out multiple doomsday scenarios in my head. As I take a particularly steep turn, my foot catches a rock on the dirt path, throwing me forward. Immediately, the pain rips through my right ankle. *My Achilles – shit!*

My ankle violently throbs, registering at an entirely different pain level than any previous injury. I wince as soon as I try to put weight on it. There's no way I can make it home. I take my phone from my armband and call Jackson.

"I hate to bother you at work, but I fell running… can you pick me up by Reed Market Bridge?" I whimper, there's no hiding how much this hurts.

"I'll be right there," Jackson says. "Stay put."

Since it's only forty yards to the bridge, I hold onto Sam's leash as my dog gently pulls, helping me navigate the narrow footpath. The warm breeze dries the accumulated sweat on my body, but with each additional step, the pain heightens.

Jackson arrives in only six minutes, but to me, it seems like sixty.

He picks me up and carries me the remaining distance from the top of the footpath to where he's parked. After he gently places me on the back seat of the truck, Sam hops up front onto the passenger seat. Although I resist, Jackson insists on taking me to the Urgent Care, just to be safe.

An hour and a half later, I learn that I have a partially torn Achilles and that I must refrain from strenuous activities for at least two months. The doctor's orders are to rest, elevate my foot, and take two Tylenol twice a day. Then, in two weeks, I can begin stretching and resume light exercise. Returning to running is nowhere in the discussion. I'm tempted to ask, but I don't want to hear the answer.

I kept it together while the doctor delivered the prognosis, but as soon as we get into the truck, I melt down. The past weeks have worn me out, and tearing my Achilles was the final straw. Jackson keeps the truck in park, turns toward the back seat, and allows me to vent.

"First, I saw Mollie in your bed, triggering that memory of my dad cheating on my mom. But I dealt with that," I gasp as tears start to flow. "Then I learned that my best friend is pregnant, getting married, and *leaving me* to move to Chicago!" I utter between sobs. "On top of that... Ben is getting married... *already*. That's an incredible amount of shit for anyone to handle, but I dealt with all of it. But not being able to run... again... after spending weeks rehabbing my IT band..." I stare straight ahead, ignoring the flood of tears streaming down my face.

"Let's take it one day at a time," Jackson says in a soothing tone as he places his right hand on my good leg. "Just because you can't run now doesn't mean that you're done forever. You just need time to recover, to get stronger. It's gonna be alright."

While I appreciate his support, I don't think that he gets it. It's then that I snap. "How would you feel if you couldn't ride? Ask yourself that. Then maybe you'll know what I'm going through." My words come out harshly. I'm unable to take them back – I own them.

Jackson abruptly turns around, shifts the truck into drive and pulls out of the urgent care parking lot, remaining silent the entire way back to my place. Minutes later he shuts off the engine then dutifully helps me out of the truck and up the front stairs, still saying nothing.

At midday the temperature is near ninety, but I'm even hotter than that. My pulse is racing with a mixture of anger and frustration. My sweet golden retriever greets us at the front door, wagging his tail as he licks my ankle, almost as if he's trying to soothe my pain. I hobble to the sofa while Jackson goes to the sink and fills a glass with water. Without looking at me, he places it on the table next to me. It's then that I realize that I've been a bitch to the most amazing guy I know. "I'm sorry," I say as I reach for his hand. "It just sucks not being able to do anything." Jackson lets out a sigh before sitting down on the chair next to the sofa.

"Jenna, try stopping for a moment to ask what the universe is trying to tell you. Have you ever wondered why you keep getting injured from running?" I sense frustration with a tinge of anger in his voice.

"No," I say then quickly add, "but I don't want to give it up." My head drops at just the thought.

"You won't have to." Jackson leans back into the chair still keeping his distance, emotionally and physically. "But you need to take a break and get stronger. Maybe focus on yoga for now."

I think about what he's just said as I reach for the glass of water. I take several gulps, just now realizing how thirsty I am.

Jackson gives me a slight smile then leans over and kisses my forehead. "I have to go back to work for a bit. Are you OK for now?"

I pull him closer, giving him a proper kiss. "I'll be fine. Thank you. I'm really sorry that I acted like a brat."

"Hey, so you're human," he winks, kisses me one more time then grabs his keys and heads out the door.

Jackson leaves me with a lot to consider. Unsure of how to process my thoughts, I hobble into the bedroom, take my journal from my nightstand, return to the sofa, and begin writing.

For as long as I can remember, I've needed to run. It helps me stay in shape, clears my boggled mind, and keeps me strong - both mentally and physically. Running's been my safety net... it's what helps me make sense of life. But could this activity that I love actually be harming me? Am I really weakening my body every time I run?

Is it possible that yoga's more than I first thought? Besides helping me become more flexible and less hyper, could yoga actually have the potential to make me stronger? Maybe I will focus on yoga, start with the restorative classes, and then as I get better, try some of the more advanced flow classes.

In the midst of journaling my phone pings. It's a text from Rachel.

Rachel: *Thank you for visiting. It was good to meet you.*
I appreciate what you're doing for Jackson. He needs you.

I respond without hesitation, somewhat shocked that she reached out to me.

Me: *I enjoyed meeting you, too. Jackson means a lot to me. I know he sometimes struggles to express himself, but I can tell how much he loves you.*

Even though Jackson would be pissed if he saw what I wrote, I believe it's the truth. Both Jackson and his mother share a stubborn streak; perhaps it's a family trait. In order for this relationship to heal, I might have to intervene a bit. Not much, but just enough to set things in motion.

Rachel: *Thank you for sharing that.*

Instantly I *know* that I've done the right thing.

CHAPTER 30

Jackson

With Jenna unable to run, I feel a bit guilty as I head to the trailhead. Yet, I can't limit myself because of her injury, and she wouldn't want me to. I need to get back on my bike and ride, especially if I want to compete in the fifty-miler next month that I signed up for. It's probably the toughest race in Bend. Mileage isn't the issue, it's the course – steep and technical.

My mind returns to Jenna. I hated seeing her so down after her fall last week. But she's turned a corner and is now committed to yoga. Maybe that will help fill the void while she rehabs her Achilles. Still, she places too much emphasis on her need to run. It's not the answer, but she has to figure that out.

As I head toward Phil's Trailhead, I notice how much the grasses and shrubs have grown. The single track's definitely narrower than it was in early July – the last time I rode here. Although it's been a while, it doesn't take me long to find my groove. Effortlessly steering through the tight trees and over large rocks and logs, I easily maneuver the rugged terrain.

My best ideas come when I'm on the bike, and today is no different. My thoughts revolve around Jenna and how I want to spend every possible moment with her. It seems ridiculous for us to both have apartments. With Mollie now at my place, Jenna suggested I sleep at her apartment and give Mollie my bedroom. Plus, if I'm honest, the space above Out-Rider isn't exactly fabulous. It's pretty small, equipped with just the basics. Before Jenna, it felt fine. But now, well, now's another story.

Mollie also occupies my mind. Will she be ready to return to San Francisco? Is that even a good idea? What if she stayed in Bend? Out-Rider's growing – she could help me in the shop. She's already filled in part-time. But would Mollie be open to the idea? I guess I won't know unless I ask.

Two hours later, I'm back at the trailhead, feeling spent after finishing a hard ride. From here it's easy getting home, all downhill. But something tells me that the effortless ride back isn't the real reason I'm feeling so good. No, it's more like I now have a plan. The time on my bike has helped me see what I need to do next.

When I get back to the apartment, Mollie is sitting on the couch watching some home improvement episode on TV.

"Jackson, I'm really starting to get bored. I need to return to San

Francisco and find a job," she says, momentarily looking up from the screen. I can sense her low energy.

Now's the perfect moment to share my idea. "What if you didn't? What if you stayed here, in Bend?" I ask as I sit down on the sturdy wooden coffee table across from the sofa.

"What would I do here?" she asks as she picks up the remote and turns down the volume before turning her full attention on me.

"Actually, I need some more help at the shop. Would you be open to working full-time? And, you can stay here, in my apartment." I watch Mollie's expression shift as my idea begins to sink in.

"Come on, I already feel like I'm a huge imposition to you and Jenna. That won't work."

"No, both of us living here on a permanent basis wouldn't work. But what if I moved in with Jenna? Then you could fix this place up, you know, give it your feminine touch." I try to sound convincing.

"Really?" Mollie's eyes widen. "You'd want me to stay here *and* work for you? What does Jenna think about this?" she asks as she pulls her legs beneath her and sits up straighter.

"I haven't asked her yet. Thought I needed to speak with you first, to find out if you're interested," I say, even though I'm feeling pretty positive about this idea.

"But are *you* ready to move in with a woman? Is this the same brother who wouldn't even date anyone a few months ago?" she teases, her little sister personality emerging.

"Point taken," I say, clearing my throat. Shit – she's totally calling me out. "But Jenna's different. What we have is unique."

"I know," she lets out a slight giggle. "I see it every time I'm around the two of you. Talk to Jenna, see what she thinks about the idea, and then we'll figure out my end." With that, she gives me a big hug.

Happy for Mollie's support, a definite role reversal, I head to Jenna's apartment. I arrive just as she's returning from yoga.

* * *

"How's the Achilles doing?" I ask as I watch her stretch out her legs using the porch railing to assist.

"Tight at first, but then it loosens up," she says in an upbeat fashion as she transitions to the bottom step and begins to massage her injured ankle.

I sit down next to her on the steps. "Hey, there's something I want to talk to you about." I wait for some kind of signal to proceed.

Jenna stops then turns toward me, giving me her sweet smile – that's my sign.

"I've been thinking. Mollie shouldn't return to San Francisco. She's not ready, plus she doesn't have a support system there. But if she lived here and worked in the shop, then Matt and I could keep an eye on her. Plus, I'd have some help at OutRider." I look deeply into Jenna's eyes trying to gauge if she sees where I'm going.

"Makes total sense. Is Mollie on board?" Jenna asks, obviously missing my point.

"Yes, but the issue is where she lives." I intentionally raise my eyebrows, hoping Jenna will connect the dots.

"Do you want her to move in with me?" Jenna offers, seemingly excited about the idea. She's still clueless to what I'm asking. "I'd love that. Remember, I have that extra bedroom."

"No, Jenna, *I* want to live with you, not just spend the nights," I say, as I gently take both of her hands in mine. "Do you think this would work?"

Knowing that Jenna and Ben had lived together, I'm unsure about her response. Yet, in typical Jenna style, she surprises me.

"You do? You want to move in?" she spurts out. "That would be perfect! And your place is ideal for Mollie. Well, maybe, if she paints a wall or two and adds some touches to it."

"Is that a…" Before I can finish my sentence, Jenna crawls on top of me, as I lean back into the porch steps. Jenna's playful at first, kissing me all over. But she then turns serious. Focusing on my neck, her mouth lingers at the top of my shoulder. Her warmth envelopes me, and all thoughts leave my brain. My body's natural urges take over, causing my back to arch, begging for more. I can't help but groan as Jenna's hands graze the top of my thighs. Knowing where this is going to lead and being that we're on the front steps to her house, I take her hand and lead her inside toward her, now our, bedroom. I never did remember what I was going to say. It no longer matters...

* * *

The clock reads 4:30 in the morning. I can't recall the last time I woke up so early. I stopped those intense morning workouts a while ago, and now, with Jenna sleeping next to me, there's a reason to remain in bed. But, not this Saturday – I need to be at the Athletic Club in an hour, for the start of this fifty-mile race.

I've been riding hard these past several weeks, adding more miles while challenging myself with technical down hills. Today will definitely test me. Quietly, I go into the kitchen, turn on the coffee maker, and review the map even though I already have the course memorized. Still, this fifty-mile race boasts a 75 percent completion rate. And it has a high number of accidents, ranking well above the percentages of typical competitions. But, I'm ready.

I hear Jenna rumbling in the next room.

"Hey, you're up already?" she murmurs from our bed.

I go to the bedroom and sit on the edge of the bed, sweeping the hair off of her face. "Why don't you sleep? I'll see you at the finish line."

"No way," she says, sitting up straight and pulling her knees to her chest. She swings her legs out of bed then makes her way into the bathroom. "I told you I'd be at each aid station, and that I'd bring the cooler with those pickle sandwiches, orange slices, and that Tailwind drink that

288

you like." I hear water and the sound of her electric toothbrush.

Shaking my head, I return to the kitchen where I check the contents of my pack, three more times, just to be sure. Knowing I'm properly prepared, I smile and pour myself a cup of coffee.

* * *

Crammed with Sprinter vans, trucks, and cars with bike racks, the parking lot outside of the Athletic Club pulsates. Riders warm up, stretching and conducting last minute rituals prior to start time. When the horn sounds for the participants to line up, Jenna gives me a big kiss and says, "You've got this," before I join the other racers.

The air horn signals the start of the race. It's begun. There must be over three hundred riders. The starts are always crowded as it takes time for the pack to spread out. I feel good out of the gate. My legs seem strong as they effortlessly pedal my black Flagline Transform, one of the newest models in the Flagline series. It's an easy four miles of pavement up Century Drive before I hit the beginning of the trail. I love the dirt. That's when my bike shows what she's got. During the first leg of the race I pass my share of riders, yet there is still a crew ahead.

There are two aid stations on this course, one at the twenty-mile mark and the other at mile thirty-five. Knowing that Jenna can easily access them from Century Drive, I accepted her offer to meet me at each. This way she can hand off items from the cooler that I packed this morning. Sure, the race provides replenishments at each stop, but half of that stuff is crap, not what I want to put into my body.

By the time I arrive at the first aid station, Jenna's there waiting for me. She diligently hands me a sports drink and a sandwich and offers words of encouragement. Focused solely on my ride, I quickly consume the food then shove the bottle into the bike's bottle holder, saying little and making minimum eye contact. I can't afford distractions. In no time, I'm back in the game.

This interchange is the same at mile thirty-five. The only difference is that I'm dirtier, bloodier, and less present than I was at the previous aid station. While I've had no major crashes so far. I did catch a rock with my pedal, causing me to jump off the bike to avoid a fall. So, I have a few scratches and minor bruising. Probably looks worse than it really is.

It's as I approach mile forty that I face my greatest challenge. It's a four-mile trek uphill, and the sandy terrain makes the climb especially tricky. But I dig deep, engaging my quads as I carefully navigate the vertical trail. Once at the top, I know that the next section is all downhill. Speed will be critical, but so will my ability to handle the demanding course. As I grapple with the uncertain terrain, I surprise myself with the ease at which my bike and I move, almost operating as one unit. Six miles left. Keep it at a steady sprint.

When I finally emerge through the trees that frame the entrance to the Athletic Club, I'm part of the lead pack. Directing every ounce of my energy into the finish, I suspect that Jenna, Matt, and Simone will be waiting for me, cheering me on. Mollie stayed behind, offering to man OutRider for the day, but Matt and Simone, who bike a lot themselves, wanted to see the finish. Still, I can't sacrifice losing my concentration by searching the crowd for them, so I steady my mind, eliminate all distractions, and ride.

Four hundred yards later, I cross the finish line. I'll be damned. I never thought I would place in the top three! By the time they reach me, I'm sitting on a fold-out chair with a cold towel over my head. Bruised with dried streaks of blood on my leg and arms, I continue to breathe incredibly hard. Jenna leans down and hugs me, pressing a bit too enthusiastically on a tender part of my right shoulder. Still, I don't care. After she seems confident that I'm OK, she offers to get some food for me at one of the nearby tents. Simone goes with her. Suddenly I'm cold, so I hand Matt my keys and ask that he grab me a sweatshirt from my truck.

As I catch my breath, a tall muscular man with light brown hair wearing khaki hiking shorts and a button-down bike shirt approaches. I don't think that I've ever seen him before. He introduces himself as Chris and shares that he's in town to watch the race.

"Congratulations! Great ride! How do you like your bike?" he asks, pointing to my Flagline Transform that's leaning against a tree, caked with mud.

"It helped me huge today. Honestly, the rocks were a bitch and the corners were tight. For the most part, this bike handled extremely well,"

I say as I take a swig of what's left in my water bottle. "There were just a few things about it that I would change,"

Intrigued, Chris lingers. "Really? Do you know bikes pretty well?"

"I own a bike shop in town, so I see and work on a lot of different models." I wrap the cool towel that they handed me at the finish line around my neck. It slowly lowers my elevated body temperature.

"What would you suggest to improve the Transform's performance?" Chris asks as he moves closer to my bike, examining its carbon frame.

Speaking in engineering terms, I share some ideas about how to increase the bike's ability to climb more efficiently and better handle sharp turns, using angles and ratios to support my recommendations.

"This is really interesting feedback. I'll be in town for a few days. Would you have some time to meet with me, maybe grab coffee and talk?" Chris asks as he hands me his card.

CHRIS O'DONNELL - VP OF DESIGN - FLAGLINE

I stand up, carefully stretching my quads. After reading this card I now understand why he wanted to know about the bike's performance. "How about Monday at nine? Thump Coffee on Minnesota?" I ask, remembering that I kept Monday morning's schedule light as I predicted that I'll still be recovering from today.

"Works for me. See you then. Oh, and again, congratulations! Impressive finish," Chris says as he leaves.

CHAPTER 31

Jenna

I'm not excited to go to work this morning. Something's nagging at me. It's when I see a yellow school bus parked down the block, waiting for students to board, that I realize how much I miss teaching. Sure, I've learned a ton working at the gallery – how to properly display artwork, assist clients in finding appropriate pieces for their space, manage showings from beginning to end, and work with the various artists. But the seasonal visitors have left, and already things are starting to slow down at Tanager.

"What's wrong?" Jackson asks while getting ready to leave for his meeting with Chris O'Donnell.

"I don't know. I think I'm starting to lose interest in the art gallery," I admit. "You know, it's becoming kind of routine. Now that I understand the main aspects of the job, it's kind of boring. And you know how

I hate not being busy. I miss teaching." Just verbalizing these emotions helps me feel better. I finish getting dressed then meet Jackson in the kitchen for a quick breakfast.

"Have there been any openings at the elementary schools?" Jackson asks while chugging a glass of orange juice.

"Nothing. But if there were, I'd be very tempted to apply. I've just been thinking, you know, about other opportunities. Yet, I feel indebted to Claire and Don. They're both wonderful and gave me a chance when I needed a job." I begin to cut into a papaya.

"What other kinds of opportunities?" Jackson asks, pausing while grabbing his biking gear and a change of clothes so he can ride after work. He then reaches for a banana. It's crazy how quickly he rebounded after the race. But, then again, he's a former SEAL, something I'm forgetting more and more.

"What if I could combine both worlds? Before this summer I knew next to nothing about art or running a gallery. Maybe I could help kids better understand the various types of art, expose them to different genres and various local artists?" I sprinkle flax seed and chia on top of the papaya slices.

"I'm listening," he says, pausing before heading out the door.

"I was reading about an organization in Portland that provides meaningful art experiences to students. It's called Art Goes to School or AGS. In fact, similar programs exist in cities throughout the country. Since many school districts struggle to fund arts education, these non-profits finance and run an arts-based curriculum to supplement what schools can offer. The Portland operation focuses on public elementary schools downtown. It sounds pretty fabulous."

"Why don't you drive to Portland and speak with them?" he suggests in an encouraging tone.

"That's what I was thinking... but it would be kind of a long shot to make it happen here, don't you think?"

"Sure, but what if it takes off? How rewarding would that be?" He walks back into the kitchen and kisses me goodbye, leaving me with a lot to contemplate.

It would be exciting to develop a similar program in Bend. But where would I begin? Would there be enough support to make this happen, because this will definitely cost money?

It's a beautiful fall day, so I decide to walk to work. Pausing at a stoplight, I look up at the majestic mountains framed by the clear blue sky. Something inside me shifts, becomes inspired. Why can't I make this happen? After all, isn't this why I moved here, to figure out what I want? Taking a risk and bringing this program to Bend could impact kids' lives, especially the students who have never visited a gallery or art museum.

My inner voice is not just speaking, it's actually shouting at me to do this, take the next step, and see if I can make this idea a reality in Bend. Without second-guessing my intuition, I take out my phone and quickly compose an email to Trisha Frazier, the Executive Director of Portland's AGS program. After checking it twice for typos, I hit "send." A burst of electricity suddenly races through my body. Unsure as to what will happen next, I decide to trust, surrender control, and allow what's meant to be to happen.

Step number one.

* * *

I arrive at the gallery twenty minutes later and waste no time before reviewing the tentative plan for Tanager's next showing. This one will be a bit more complicated than Trinity's. Instead of just one artist, Claire invited three to showcase their artwork, all centered around the theme of Bend's gorgeous sunrises. I work straight through lunch, determined to finalize the layout, ensuring that the combination of acrylic, watercolor, and oil pieces will intermix to create the feeling that Claire and I envisioned. Finally, at around four-thirty that afternoon, I come up for air and give myself some time to carefully scan my phone for messages. It's then that I see the email from Trisha Frazier inviting me to Portland. She wants to meet with me.

As soon as I leave the gallery, I phone, hoping she's available to talk. As luck would have it, we connect.

"Are you free this Saturday?" Trisha asks.

Quickly, I open my phone calendar to ensure that I am. "How's two o'clock?" I ask.

That works for Trisha, so it's settled. I'm going – to Portland – this Saturday. *Step number two.*

In the meantime, I've got some research to do. I can't wait to dive into learning more about the Portland program. But first I'm scheduled to meet Liv at the yoga studio for a restorative class. Just the thought of the warm room, the scented air, and the mesmerizing voice of the instructor helps me relax, take a step back, and appreciate what is.

CHAPTER 32

Jackson

When I arrive at Thump, Chris O'Donnell is sitting at a high top by the front window, drinking coffee, and reading a copy of *The Source*, Bend's local paper. I'm surprised by his physical presence. His sheer mass didn't register when we met briefly at the finish line. But then again, a fifty-mile mountain bike race will do that to you. Creases along his forehead also suggest that he's a bit older than I originally thought. But I bet he can ride. I wave to him before walking to the counter and ordering a medium black coffee.

"How do the legs feel today?" Chris asks as he closes the paper when I join him at his table.

"Surprisingly, not too bad," I say, shaking his hand before I pull out a chair across from him and sit down.

I sense a positive vibe from Chris as we begin to talk, but I'm still

299

unsure as to why I'm here. After several minutes of recapping the race, Chris shifts the conversation. "I bet you're wondering why I wanted to meet with you," he says as he sets down his coffee mug.

"I've been curious about that all morning," I reply with a smile.

Chuckling, Chris says, "It's clear that you understand bikes. As you know, I head up the design team at Flagline. While we have a solid line of products, I admit that there are a few areas where we could improve the Transform."

I nod and take a sip of coffee.

"We found that one of the best ways to gain productive input is through meeting with people who know and use our bikes. That's why I'm here in Bend – to get feedback from racers who rode a Transform in Saturday's race. And knowing that you have a bike shop gives your comments even more weight in my book."

Now things are beginning to make sense.

"So, where did you pick up so much knowledge about bikes? From owning a shop? And how'd you end up in Bend – or are you from here?" Chris asks with interest.

I settle into my hardback chair, shifting several times to prevent the plastic arm from poking into my sore ribs, and carefully tell my story, intentionally omitting certain details about my past. "My path is a bit unusual. The plan was a Civil Engineering degree from the University of Washington, but I left school just a few months before graduation.

My dad passed away suddenly, and I took it hard. After some time off, I enlisted in the Navy and eventually trained to become a SEAL. In a few years, I advanced to Platoon Leader. That experience, well, let's just say it was a game changer. But to answer your question in terms of specific skills, my main technical knowledge is in the construction of bridges and buildings." I pause and wait to see if Chris has any questions.

"You have a Civil Engineering background, but the Navy is where you really learned how to think and understand how things work. Makes total sense. And since you're a skilled rider, you figured out how to transfer that knowledge to the mechanics of the bike. I think you have some untapped talent." Chris leans back and folds his hands on the table.

"Thank you, Chris." Where is he going with this?

"The areas of mechanical improvement you suggested on Saturday targeted some of the problem areas we're experiencing with the Transform. My team has been struggling to devise a viable solution to address those issues. I have to admit that so far, nothing we've implemented has worked. But you clearly identified reasonable suggestions that I'd like to explore further."

I sit up straighter, intrigued that he finds my feedback helpful.

Chris takes a big sip of coffee and then asks, "Have you ever considered working for a bike manufacturer? With your training and hands-on knowledge, you would be a valuable addition to our engineering department. Your ideas for improving the bike, well, that's exactly the type of thinking that we're looking for. I've been planning on adding another person to our team in Santa Rosa, and I think that you'd be a strong fit. Flagline's already approved the position. I just need to find the right person to fill it. And I think I have."

I'm totally caught off guard. This is the last thing I expected to happen. Working at Flagline would be freak'n unbelievable. But they're located in Santa Rosa. I can't move there. Not with Jenna in Bend, especially not now that Olivia's leaving. Plus, I finally have OutRider operating smoothly and generating good income. And what about Mollie? No, it's not the right time. *Damn it!*

For a moment I allow myself to consider what it would be like to work with Chris and his team at Flagline. However, accepting this offer would jeopardize everything that's starting to go right in my life. So, I give him the only possible answer. "Chris, I'm flattered. If we'd met three months ago, it might have worked. But there are too many reasons now for me to stay." I swallow hard thinking of Jenna and Mollie. "Thank you. But I have to say no." Then a big exhale comes, and it's not just air that exits my body, I also let go of the biggest opportunity I've had in some time.

Judging by the look on Chris' face, I don't think that's the answer he expected. He remains silent, as if waiting to see if I offer more.

Finally, he says, "I can see how Bend's an awesome place to live. I mean, who wouldn't love it, especially if you're a rider. But, let's keep this dialogue open. You never know when things may change." Chris gives me a nod. He doesn't give up easily, a trait I admire.

"I will, and thank you. Maybe it might work out at some point," I say still wondering if I could ever make this happen.

"Oh, and if you're ever near Santa Rosa, please let me know. I'd love to show you our facility. I think you'd be impressed."

"I'm sure I would," I say, already feeling regret for refusing his offer.

"My flight leaves in two hours, so I have to head out. But, please give me your contact information. I'd like to stay in touch," Chris says, extending his hand.

I watch as Chris leaves the coffee shop, deciding not to mention this conversation to anyone. Shit, I want this job. But, now's not the right time.

CHAPTER 33

Jenna

I finally admitted to Jackson that I've been in contact with his mother. Initially, he became angry, accusing me of butting in. But after I explained my intention, he calmed down. I know I overstepped my boundary, but I think it was worth it. Since then he's called his mom a few times. Hopefully this is the beginning of a stronger relationship for both of them. It isn't easy for him to reach out to her. Watching the vault to Jackson's heart slowly crack, well, it's pretty incredible.

Yet, his dreams persist. Just last night, I woke up to him shaking and murmuring in his sleep. After a few seconds of thrashing under the covers, his body quieted. What's happening in his dreams? Is he reliving Patrick stepping on an IED? Or is it something else? Does it have to do with his parents' divorce or maybe with his dad's death? As far as Jackson's progressed these past few months, in order to fully heal, he must ultimately face those remaining monsters.

Closing my journal, I take a few moments to refocus. Today I'm driving to Portland to meet with Trisha, and I need to be on my game when I get there.

After the three-hour trip, I arrive at AGS's headquarters located in a renovated brick warehouse in Cedar Mills, a suburb just west of the city. The impressive steel doors open into a foyer displaying several colorful tile mosaics. After ringing the AGS buzzer, Trisha meets me in the lobby, welcoming me to the Portland office.

"I've been at AGS for three years, but two women started this branch after our public school cut arts funding. Single handedly, they raised the necessary dollars to create a local program modeled after the national AGS organization," Trisha shares as we walk down a hallway adorned with student artwork and photographs. "We offer assemblies and workshops at Portland's elementary schools once a month where local artists present their craft." Trisha points to photo showing children working with clay. "It's a win-win. Students gain exposure to the arts at no cost to the district." We come to Trisha's office, and she motions for me to enter.

"Could this work in Bend?" I ask as I take a seat across from her desk.

"Bend has one of the fastest growing populations in the state. If you're willing to coordinate the program, then yes, it can work. The biggest hurdle will be funding," she says as she takes an annual report from the shelf and opens it to the donors page.

"I've never fundraised before," I admit while looking at the pages of contributors.

"You are more than welcome to replicate our solicitation letters and donation packets," Trisha says while searching her filing cabinet. "Your first step is to find a partner school, one that's willing to host the program. Aha – here it is," she says, handing me a packet of information.

"I know the principal at Northwest Crossing. She may be interested," I share, immediately thinking of Marjorie. "Also, I've met local artists and clients through the gallery who might support this project." Now is the time to commit. Am I willing to do this? "If you're serious about establishing a branch in Bend, then I'm all in."

"It's been my dream to expand the program," Trisha says as she leans closer to me. "But I have to be honest," she pauses and gives me a serious look. "This will require a lot of work – meeting with school administrators, fundraising events, grant writing..."

"I've never been afraid of hard work. Combining teaching with the arts, well I believe it's what I'm meant to do." Observing Trisha's face, I can see that this was the perfect response. *Step number three.*

* * *

Early Monday morning on my drive to work I call Marjorie, hoping to gain her support to pilot AGS at Northwest Crossing.

"I love the idea, but first I'll need the superintendent's and School

Board's backing. Unfortunately, there are lots of hoops to jump through before anything moves forward in public education." Although her words are cautionary, her voice exudes promise.

I just remembered one important detail as I unfasten my seatbelt and grab my purse from the passenger seat. "Oh, and I spoke with Claire yesterday. Apparently, Paige approached her, wanting to come back to work next month, part-time to start but then permanently this February. It sounds as if she's going a bit crazy staying at home with the baby." I chuckle at the thought.

"Jenna, with Paige back at Tanager, this could become a full-time endeavor for you."

"I know it sounds strange, but I'm trying not to plan too far into the future. That's how I've always lived my life, and, well, it hasn't necessarily been the best strategy for me." I surprise myself with these words.

"Good for you," Marjorie laughs.

I get out of the car then head down the sidewalk.

"As soon as we hang up, I'll call my superintendent. Then, if he's in favor of this proposal, I'll ask him to bring it to the School Board president. It may take some time, but I will let you know as soon as I hear back from him. Jenna, I always hoped that we would work together one day. Maybe it won't be as principal and teacher, but this could be even better," Marjorie says just as I reach the gallery's front door. My thoughts, exactly.

Later that day, soon after I arrive home from work, I receive a text from Marjorie.

Marjorie: *Great news - Superintendent has School Board president's backing. They'll vote on it during next Monday's meeting. He feels confident that it will pass.*

Step four – check.

Even though we're waiting for the School Board's vote, I see no reason why I shouldn't get started. After developing a list of potential donors, I'll begin to map out possible programs and workshops for the upcoming year. I grab a notepad and immediately jot down some ideas.

When Jackson walks in the front door, I share my news with him.

"Can you believe it?" I ask as I throw my arms around his neck.

"I'm not surprised at all. You just needed to believe in yourself and take a few chances." He gives me that "I told you so" glance before planting an absolutely yummy kiss on my lips.

He's right. Slowly, I'm rebuilding my life. And Jackson's right there beside me, providing support when I need a bit of encouragement. After only four months in Bend, I'm coming closer to discovering what I came here to find.

* * *

Marjorie calls the following week right before Jackson and I are about to take Sam for a walk. "The motion passed, 9-1. It's official." I can hear the joy in her voice.

"This is amazing!" I say to Marjorie as I give Jackson a thumbs up. "Claire's been helping me with a list of potential donors. I'll send the first batch of solicitation letters this week. Marjorie, it's happening!" After hanging up I do a little victory dance in the living room while Jackson just looks at me and laughs.

* * *

Before long, responses start arriving. While most regretfully decline my funding request, slowly but surely, checks begin trickling in from interested community members and businesses. This growing support provides the necessary seed money, enabling me to plan a workshop for the end of October. Trinity's agreed to be our first official artist. The kids will love her.

I am beginning to love my life... the pieces are finally connecting. I no longer focus on what others think about me. Sure, I'm still apprehensive about Liv's wedding... seeing Ben and my dad. So much has changed since I left Boston. I've changed. But can I retain who I am in Bend when I go back East?

CHAPTER 34

Jackson

Olivia and Michael's wedding is this weekend, and we leave for Boston tomorrow. While packing my bag, my mind starts spiraling in all directions. First, I revisit Chris's offer. Was I right to refuse? I regret not involving Jenna in my decision, and now, it feels as if I've lost the chance entirely. This just isn't the right time for a major change. OutRider's revenue increased forty-seven percent this past month. It feels good to watch money accumulate in my bank account.

My thoughts switch to Jenna. She's so happy, going one hundred miles an hour working on AGS. Yesterday, she shared that *The Source* promised to run an article about the first workshop in its Sunday Edition. Plus, her Achilles is becoming stronger, and Jenna's entire outlook regarding her physical self has shifted. I think yoga's impacting her confidence level. She's calmer and not so overwhelmed all of the time.

Mollie's also on my mind. Fully up to speed, she's rocking it at OutRider. Living in Bend seems to be the fresh start that she's needed. Mollie's even tried mountain biking. Before long, I bet she'll be leading a beginners' group. I couldn't be prouder of my little sister. And she and Jenna are getting close. For the first time ever, my life feels on target.

* * *

Jenna and I reach our gate just as the attendant calls for our zone to board. Once we're seated with bags stowed, we finally begin to unwind. The next three days are ours.

We have no trouble sleeping on the red-eye. I awake to the sound of a flight attendant offering paper cups of coffee prior to landing. I take two and gently nudge Jenna. Before long, we're on the ground at Logan Airport.

Geoff said he'd be waiting in the cell lot. Shortly after our bags arrive, he pulls up outside of the terminal, ecstatic to see Jenna. Respectfully, I hold back, allowing this father daughter reunion to occur.

It's a quick ride to Jenna's house. Jenna's mom is waiting at the front door when we arrive. Immediately I notice the resemblance between Jenna and Maggie. While Jenna favors her father's physical build and hair color, she has her mom's eyes and smile.

Maggie's prepared breakfast – bacon, blueberry pancakes, eggs, and endless cups of richly roasted coffee. And I'm starved. We settle around the kitchen table, the conversation flowing naturally. This must be what it's like when you're part of a real family.

An hour later when plates are empty, but coffee mugs are still being refilled, Maggie gingerly asks, "So, what do you guys have planned for this afternoon?"

"I have a bridesmaid's brunch at noon in Brookline," Jenna says as she glances at her watch. "Dad, do you mind showing Jackson around town? Maybe grab lunch somewhere? I'll be back by three, but we have to be at the club for the rehearsal by five."

"I'm sure we can entertain ourselves," Geoff glances at me. Despite the purpose of his spontaneous trip to Bend last month, we seem to have formed a bond. So, this is your family, Jenna Moore. And I feel like I belong. Must be a sign.

CHAPTER 35

Jenna

When I return from the bridesmaids' brunch, my mother's the only one home. "Where are they?" I ask Mom, who's busy marinating a flank steak. Secretly I'm thrilled that my dad and Jackson are still out.

"Your dad mentioned taking Jackson to see Fenway then having lunch at the Union Oyster House. He probably showed him Faneuil Hall. Think he wants to give him the full Boston experience," Mom says as she makes quotation signs with her fingers, accentuating the world "full."

I take a seat at the kitchen counter. "So, Mom, what do *you* think about Jackson?" I've been dying to ask her this since we arrived.

"I like him," Mom pauses. "It's obvious that he's totally in love with you." Then she looks at me in a thoughtful way. "Jackson's different, not in a bad way, just unlike anyone else you've ever dated." She picks up the pepper grinder and begins seasoning the raw meat.

"I know. But, here's the thing. When I'm with him, I'm a better person. Not that I was a bad person when I was with Ben, but Jackson inspires me to try new things and believe in myself. It's almost like he has no expectations of me, so I can be who I really am. Does that make sense?" I ask looking into Mom's eyes.

"He makes you happy?" she asks as she washes her hands before rinsing fresh green beans in a colander.

"I've never been happier. And, the more I know him, the more I love him," I say leaning forward onto the counter. "He's faced some challenges. Jackson's parents divorced when he was young." I pause, wondering how much I should reveal. But I trust my mother. "Then his dad passed away during his senior year of college. So yes, he's dealt with a lot." I then share that Jackson spent time in Afghanistan as a SEAL. Finally, I tell her about Patrick.

"Did this man live?" she asks, eyes wide with alarm.

"Yes, but he lost both of his legs." I frown thinking of how difficult Patrick's life must be. "Jackson blames himself for this. It still affects him, but its impact appears to lessen each day." I wonder if I've said too much.

"Jackson definitely seems special, but has he faced *too* much sorrow? Can *you* deal with that?" My mom turns away from the sink and looks at me. It's then that her eyes reveal a mixture of sympathy for Jackson and concern for me.

"I know where you're coming from, but if you saw what he was like when I first met him compared to where he is now, you'd be pretty amazed." I think about how much Jackson's changed.

"The power of love," my mom says, leaning over the counter and placing her hand on mine. "You're saving him. Just know that it won't always be easy," she warns, but her expression only exudes compassion.

"He's worth it, believe me." My heart flutters as I admit this. Then I shift gears, asking something I've wondered since knowing the truth about my father. "Is that how you felt about Dad, that he was worth forgiving?" I stop, unsure if I've crossed the line.

"I thought you might want to talk about that." My mom sits down on a stool next to me. "After Annie died, it seemed like I was living in a fog. I passed through the days emotionless, barely functioning. Realizing how low I was going, I worried that it might affect you." She leans on the counter. "So, I found a counselor, and slowly he helped me return to life. I tried to convince your father to do the same, but he was so stoic and felt he had to be strong for me. But he was broken, too, maybe more so than I realized. He dealt with it differently." She stops and looks intently at me before continuing.

"As crushed as I was, I was already so numb. I'm not sure that it fully hit me. Your father told me right away and proved to me that it was over. He left his firm and found another position. Your dad took full ownership for his actions, never blaming what he did on anything else. I never doubted his remorse. For a while, I guess that I hated him.

It took me some time, but I eventually forgave your father. I knew it was a mistake, that he always loved me, and that it was his way of escaping his pain. We attended therapy together for quite some time. That was my condition. But I never thought that you would find out about it." Tears begin to stream down her face. After reaching for a tissue, she lightly touches my cheek.

Now I'm crying. "It's just that I thought you and Dad had the perfect marriage. And, now I know it's not."

It's then that Mom's expression brightens. "Jenna, we're incredibly happy now. Yes, we had our problem, a big one. But we worked through it. I learned to trust him again. I don't know of any perfect marriages. There's usually some issue for every couple."

I try to take in what my mom says, but I must admit that it's hard.

"So, here's a question for you," Mom begins, shifting the subject. "Have you thought about what it will be like to see Ben?"

"I know it will be awkward. I mean, how can't it be... and at a wedding, of all places?" I roll my eyes. "Today at the brunch Liv told me Catherine no longer speaks to Ben – because she doesn't approve that Maria is Costa Rican. Also, Ben and Maria are moving to the South End. He actually sold his townhouse *and* that house next to Catherine's... the one he bought for *us*." Just sharing this nearly knocks the wind out of me.

"I know that's tough to handle." Mom tucks a wisp of hair behind my ear.

"I guess I'm happy for him. I mean he found someone and so did I. I just don't get why he sold that house for her and wouldn't for me." I lament as I look at my mother.

"Oh, Honey. Try to remember that things happen for a reason. If he had sold the house, would you have ever moved to Bend or met Jackson? Both you and Ben are special people, and something tells me that you'll have no trouble seeing each other at the wedding. If things become uncomfortable, maybe try some humor to get you through the awkward moments."

Suddenly the front door opens. Geoff and Jackson enter loudly. No doubt their afternoon included a stop or two at one of the local bars. After all, my dad did say that he wanted to provide Jackson with a "true Boston experience."

As we leave for the rehearsal at Brookline Country Club, I look back at my parents standing in the doorway. Both are smiling. They like him. And, they're OK. Their marriage is fine.

* * *

Jackson continues to be a hit, but this time it's at the rehearsal. He comfortably jokes with the other bridesmaids' dates while the wedding party practices for tomorrow's service. It appears that he's honestly having fun.

In less than an hour, the entire wedding party loads onto a chartered bus and heads to Nico's, a small Italian restaurant in the North End that Michael booked for the rehearsal dinner. While dining on Caesar salad, pumpkin ravioli with sage, and chicken saltimbocca, an a cappella quartette serenades our group.

"You know, I love Bend, but Boston's not too bad," Jackson admits before putting a forkful of chicken into his mouth.

"It's pretty fabulous, isn't it? Totally different from Bend, but there's something about this city," I say. "Now that I'm back, I see how special it is. Maybe you need to leave home to truly appreciate what you always had." As I consider that thought, I look over at Liv and see that she's beaming. I'm so happy she's found Michael.

CHAPTER 36

Jackson

Seated next to Jenna's parents on foldout chairs that line the Brookline Country Club's front lawn, we stand when the wedding procession begins. Olivia looks beautiful. Still, it's the maid of honor who I'm staring at. Jenna rarely wears makeup or fusses with her hair. Seeing her in a long sage green dress and carrying a bouquet of tulips takes my breath away.

The ceremony's short. After the exchange of vows, the bridal party goes to the garden for pictures while guests move to the outdoor patio. I head straight to the bar and wait for Jenna to finish her maid of honor duties. Surveying the crowd, I try to identify Ben. Jenna's described his personality but was never that specific about his looks. I pick three possible candidates. As Jenna returns to the tented patio where the rest of the guests are already enjoying cocktails and appetizers, I watch as one of these three men approaches her, introducing Jenna to the attractive woman by his side. He and Jenna embrace warmly. Must be Ben and Maria. Anticipating that perhaps she could use some support, I walk across the patio and approach the trio, wondering what it will be like to meet the man Jenna almost married. As I gently place my hand on Jenna's back, the man extends his hand and says, "Great to meet you, Jackson. I'm Ben, and this is Maria." Damn, he's better looking than I thought he would be.

No doubt, this reunion of sorts attracts attention from those who know Ben and Jenna's history. While our conversation was a bit awkward in the beginning, over the next fifteen minutes or so it becomes natural. Ben and I discover we both love soccer while Jenna and Maria talk about yoga. Then, at an appropriate break, Ben and Maria excuse themselves and head to the bar.

"That wasn't so bad, now, was it?" I ask, giving Jenna's bottom a slight pinch.

She giggles, saying "No, it went well. Actually, I think that they make a lovely couple." I must appear surprised by her response because she immediately follows up by saying, "No, I mean it. It's nice to see him happy."

A bell rings, signaling the guests to move inside toward the ballroom. As we walk into the building, I notice that there are tulips everywhere. Jenna explains that they're Olivia's favorite flower. A four-piece band plays "Isn't She Lovely" as a waitress hands us our name cards with the assigned table number. Our table is up front, reserved for the bridal party and their dates.

When I look over to where Olivia and Michael sit with their parents and Katy, I sense that this all makes sense and is happening just as it's supposed to. These two are headed for a great marriage. And Katy seems so happy when they're all together. Sure, Jenna will miss having them in Bend. But isn't that's what life is all about – new beginnings?

CHAPTER 37

Jenna

Following dinner, the bride and groom begin the customary wedding traditions. Together, they cut the elegant four-tiered dark chocolate and butter cream cake before gently feeding it to one another. Katy stands by their side, sneaking fingers of icing, the evidence remaining on her face. Then, the band signals for Liv to throw her bouquet into a recently assembled crowd of single women. I'm reluctant to venture onto the dance floor for this tradition. It's just not my thing. When Liv notices my absence, she marches over to our table and drags me toward the group of women. Jackson looks extremely amused. I'm not. Of course, she throws the bouquet directly to me. Blushing, not only from the wine but also from embarrassment, I smile awkwardly.

After removing the "borrowed blue" garter from Liv's thigh, Michael tosses it into the sea of single men. For some reason, unknown to me, Ben, not Jackson, stands smack in the middle of the crowd, right where the garter lands. It appears to be somewhat of a magnetic attraction. At least fifteen people in the audience let out a loud gasp, perhaps my dad's being the most noticeable.

"Why was Ben on the dance floor? He's engaged! And where was Jackson?" I ask Liv. But my best friend continues to laugh loudly, almost to the point of convulsing. "Stop it, it's not funny!" I mouth. Yet, Liv ignores me, signaling for Ben to come up front.

Now it's Ben who is bright red. "Jenna, I'm so sorry," he says. "I wasn't paying attention. I didn't see you catch the bouquet. I wasn't going to go out there, but Maria said I had to because we weren't married yet. Something about bad luck..." Ben grimaces with embarrassment as he kneels down in front of the chair that Liv puts me on.

"Well, I hope that Maria has a good sense of humor," I whisper while Ben carefully slides the garter up my leg, stopping just above my knee. I give him a quick hug before hopping out of the chair and rushing back to Jackson, who's clearly as entertained as Liv.

Within a few moments, Maria approaches our table and warmly says, "Jenna, you're a good sport. Not many people could carry that off as gracefully as you just did."

"Oh, Maria, I'm so sorry. How uncomfortable for everyone," I say before taking a long sip of wine.

"Actually, it was funny. In fact, it's encouraging to know that we

323

can all laugh about it. You and Ben have a lot of history. You can't erase those years together." Maria places her hand lightly on top of mine.

"I'm glad you see it that way, Maria. Not everyone would." Instantly I feel myself relax. She's very understanding. Maybe we could be friends, under different circumstances.

It's then that I notice that the band begins playing "You've Made Me So Very Happy." Jackson looks at me and extends his hand. "Shall we?" he asks before leading me to the dance floor. He pulls me close, quietly singing the lyrics in my ear. "*I chose you for the one. Now I'm having so much fun. You treated me so kind. I'm about to lose my mind. You made me so very happy, I'm so glad you came into my life.*"

So true.

CHAPTER 38

Jackson

We return to Bend late Sunday night. Mollie's busy at work when I arrive the next morning. She's organizing a new display of helmets and bike accessories. "Looks great, Mollie. In fact, this whole place seems more put together since you've been here," I say as I hug her hello.

"How was the trip? Tell me about the wedding. How did Olivia's dress look?" She fires questions while she continues to adjust the row of helmets.

I give her a play-by-play description of the weekend, including the garter story.

"No way! I can't believe she had to sit there in front of all of those people while her ex-fiancé slipped a garter up her leg. How mortifying."

"Actually, it was pretty funny," I recall as I move to my desk and turn on my laptop.

"Oh, I forgot," Mollie says, handing me a large envelope, "this arrived on Saturday. Looks kind of important."

Immediately I recognize the return address – Boulder, Colorado. More than curious, I carefully open the manila envelope and remove the contents.

"What is it?" Mollie asks impatiently.

"It's a photograph. This must have been taken about three years ago." The muscles in my face relax, as I momentarily drift into the past.

"Let me see," Mollie says, reverting to her little sister ways as she peers over my shoulders.

The photo shows several men in fatigues playing soccer, but not on a typical soccer field. Instead, the ground is dusty. Objects, not lines, indicate the boundaries of the playing space. Large, barren mountains form the backdrop.

"Was this in Afghanistan?" she asks with wide eyes.

"Yes, those are men from my platoon," I say, suddenly overwhelmed with a sense of pride.

"Who are they? Tell me about them!" Mollie pulls up a chair next to mine.

As I begin my narrative on each man's background, Mollie's captivated, listening intently. I highlight where each man was from and his specialty as a SEAL. Suddenly I pause.

"Jackson, who's that short blonde man?" Mollie asks.

"That's Patrick," I say, my voice solemn.

"I always wondered what he looks like." A smile and a sense of awe warms her face.

I remain silent.

"Well, that's a really special picture. How about I find a frame for it?" She leans down and picks it up from my desk, glancing toward me for approval.

Gently touching my sister's arm, I nod.

As far as I've come, seeing this photo propels me backwards, to another time. Sure, my life's been getting back on track, but what about Patrick? I've never once stopped to ask how he's doing. Instead I've chosen to beat myself up, focusing on how it was my fault. Why haven't I reached out to him? The last time we spoke was in that hospital.

Knowing Patrick, I bet he's moved on. That's the kind of guy he was, is. But not me, I've been stuck in the past, selfish, only focused on how this impacted me. Why didn't I stay by Patrick's side – help him, show how much I cared? But, I ran, turned inward, and shut everyone out. I was a coward.

"Jackson, are you OK?" Mollie asks from the other side of the room.

"Yeah. Hey, there's something I need to do." I look down at my keyboard and begin typing.

* * *

"So, something pretty interesting happened today," I tell Jenna during our dinner together, after taking the last bite of chicken curry. "While we were in Boston, an envelope came in the mail." I get up and dig in my backpack for the photo now preserved in a shiny back frame. I return to the kitchen and carefully place the frame on the table. Jenna lights up, taking in the picture.

"This was when you were a SEAL?" she asks, eyes totally locked on the photo.

"Yes, we were in Afghanistan. See the mountains in the background?" I point to the rugged terrain.

I share stories similar to those I told Mollie earlier in the day. Jenna sits on the edge of her seat, captivated by the picture and my narrative. This is her first glimpse into my life as a SEAL.

"And this is Patrick." My voice cracks a bit when I mention his name.

"Wow! He seems so vibrant, alive. It's hard to think of the struggles he's been enduring." Jenna leans closer to the photo.

"Exactly. That's what I haven't been doing. I've been spending all my time focused on *my* guilt, and in the process, I've ignored Patrick." I exhale loudly. "Guess I thought that punishing myself would eventually absolve me of everything. My shame's kept me away. It wasn't until I saw this picture this morning that I realized what I've been doing."

Jenna lightly places her hand on my arm before picking up the framed photograph. "Jackson, did you see this?"

"See what?" I have no idea what she's referring to.

"What's written at the bottom of the picture. *How about a rematch? P.*" Jenna looks confused as she hands me the framed photo, stands up, and then heads to the sink with our dirty dishes.

"Jesus. I totally missed that. This morning I sent Patrick a long email. I can't believe I didn't see the writing in the bottom corner." I shake my head in frustration.

"What did you say?" she asks as she puts our dishes into the dishwasher.

"Well, pretty much what I told you. That I've been focusing on my guilt and how I'm embarrassed that I haven't reached out and connected with him," I admit.

"Has he responded?" Jenna sits down after placing a plate of peanut butter cookies on the table.

"I haven't checked my phone since I got home." I walk over to grab my cell that's charging on the kitchen counter and begin scrolling the screen for unread messages. I pause when my eyes lock on Patrick's response. I can't believe what I'm reading. "He invited us to visit him in Boulder, for his 35th birthday party in January."

CHAPTER 39

Jenna

The roundabouts glow from the shimmer of Christmas lights draped over the unique metal sculptures that grace these central islands, business is picking up downtown from the influx of skiers who have arrived for the early December snow, and the kids at school are bursting with energy, excited about the approaching holiday. Overall, life couldn't be more beautiful.

But there is one thing weighing me down. "This is the first time ever that I won't be with my parents on Christmas," I mention to Jackson while sorting through the day's mail, pulling out the Christmas cards to open first.

"We could visit them," Jackson proposes, looking up from his biography about Ulysses S. Grant.

"That's sweet of you. But it wouldn't be right to leave Mollie during the holidays. I remember hearing how this time of year can be tough for people dealing with depression," I say, throwing the envelopes into the trash and setting the cards on the counter.

"Then why don't you invite them here?" Jackson suggests as he puts his book down on the table.

I walk over and sit next to him. "Do you think they'll come?"

"You'll never know if you don't ask. Maybe see if they want to ski Bachelor," he says.

We always talked about them visiting, but the logistics seemed tricky. "Our apartment is too small for everyone, and the guest room only has a twin bed. I guess we could check out rentals and see what's available." I get up and walk over to the kitchen counter where my laptop's plugged in.

"What about Olivia's place? I'm sure they could stay there while she's in Chicago with Michael and Katy," Jackson suggests as he stands up to grab a beer from the fridge.

Several phone calls later, everything is settled – Liv's place is available and so are my parents.

"We're in! I'm about to book flights. This will be so much fun. You know, it's been tough thinking of celebrating Christmas without you," Mom says. It's nice to know that she, too, was struggling with the thought of spending Christmas apart.

As soon as we say goodbye, I begin making lists of places to see, activities to do, restaurants to try, and breweries to visit when my parents are in Bend. I even decide to cook my first traditional Christmas dinner, knowing that Mom will be more than happy to jump in and help.

"Relax, Jenna. Remember, it's their vacation, too," Jackson gently reminds me. I now understand how Liv felt when I arrived last April.

"I know, but this means a lot to me. As incredible as these past seven months have been, I've missed my parents. Having them here for Christmas, well, it just makes me happy," I say as I continue scribbling "to dos" on a pad of paper. Grabbing my coat, I yell to Jackson, "Come on, let's get a tree. And lights. And decorations!" Unable to contain my newly found energy, I scurry out the door.

CHAPTER 40

Jackson

Sam's barking prompts me to look out the front window just as Jenna's car pulls up to a stop. I walk outside to greet Geoff and Maggie. I immediately pick up on Jenna's elevated mood. This is the way it's supposed to be, especially during the holidays, and it feels good.

Jenna insists on giving her parents a tour of Bend. She's made reservations at a local pub, knowing her dad's love of craft beer. Watching Jenna around her family fascinates me. As outgoing and bubbly as Jenna can be, she becomes even more animated, especially around her mom. She's really missed them.

That next morning, Christmas Eve day, the four of us take Sam for a long walk along the river path and then head to the Lot for lunch. Afterwards, Jenna and her mom make cookies, which is apparently a tradition, while Geoff and I check out Deschutes Brewery. In the evening, we attend a candlelight service downtown before sitting down for dinner at Joolz.

As nice as this day was, I'm happy when we finally drop off Jenna's parents at Olivia's. This is our first Christmas together, and I want some time alone with Jenna.

"I know tomorrow will be a bit crazy, so I want to give you your present now," I say, taking her hands in mine.

"Really?" Jenna asks with visible surprise. "I thought we were exchanging gifts tomorrow. I can't give you yours until then."

"I can wait. But tonight, I have something, for you." I hesitate. "I hope that you like it. Come with me. It's in here." I guide her into the spare room, leading her toward her present.

Wrapped in a candy cane plastic holiday bag, the shape of the package gives it away.

"You got me a bike?" Jenna asks excitedly as she begins to unwrap her present.

"Yes, but not an ordinary bike. It has a comfortable seat, non-clip-in pedals, and it's designed for roads and minor trails. I altered it just for you. I think you'll be more comfortable riding this and then, maybe someday, you can exchange it for a mountain bike – that is if you want to," I say hopefully, knowing that it's up to Jenna.

Jenna runs her hand over the silver metallic frame.

"I figured that a mountain bike could be a bit, well, too much. I know you prefer running, but this will help make your legs stronger, hopefully preventing any more injuries. Anyway, it's something we could do together," I say while I retrieve a new helmet from the closet and give it to Jenna.

"It's perfect. I love it," she says with a big smile on her face as she tries on the helmet.

"That's not it. There's something more. Look closely at the bike." I nod toward the wheels.

"Where?" she asks, but then she sees it, tucked between the chains. It's a small satin bag. Slowly, she unties the satchel and peeks inside.

I smile as she discovers the drop earrings. Carefully, she examines the intricate metal work and the blue gemstones embedded in the silver earrings.

"They're beautiful! Let me try them on," she moves toward the mirror behind the door, takes off the helmet, and puts on the earrings. "I love them," she says as she admires her gift in the mirror. "What is the stone?"

"The stone's lapis lazuli, the universal symbol for truth and wisdom. I saw it and immediately thought of you." I pause as I look at this beautiful woman standing in front of me. "I've never been this happy before," I say as move behind her and seductively kiss the back of her neck. Slowly, I brush my lips across her skin and linger at the top of her right shoulder.

"Oh, how I adore you, Jackson Tait," Jenna says as she turns around, gently kissing me before demurely removing her dress. Right then, another side of Jenna emerges as she skillfully unbuttons my shirt and slowly continues downward. While she can't give me my Christmas present tonight, there are certainly other gifts that she is more than willing to share with me.

* * *

The following morning, Jenna leaves to pick up her parents while I start making omelets and bacon for the four of us. Twenty minutes later the door opens, and Jenna and Geoff walk inside carrying brightly wrapped packages.

"Merry Christmas," I say to Geoff while helping him with the gifts.

"Where's Maggie?" I ask as I shake Geoff's hand, somewhat confused by her absence.

"Oh, she'll be here in a few minutes. Let's place the packages under the tree," Jenna suggests somewhat coyly. Now I'm curious. Jenna's not exactly gifted at secrets.

Jenna pours her dad a big cup of coffee as she invites him to sit near the warm fire. There's a knock at the door.

"Mom must be here," Jenna says excitedly. "Do you mind getting the door?" she asks me.

I go to the front door expecting Maggie, but instead, a tethered puppy comes bounding in, followed by Jenna's mom who's holding the other end of the red leash in her hand, a mischievous look across her face.

"This is my present to you. I wanted you to have a dog of your own. Of *our* own," Jenna kind of fumbles her words. She seems nervous as she squats down to pet the puppy.

"Jenna Moore... are you nuts?" I scoop up the black lab puppy, appraising the size of his paws. "This is going to be one big boy." The grin on my face grows by the second.

Jenna retrieves the rest of the presents hidden in the guestroom – chew toys, dog bowls, a fleece dog bed, and a medium-sized crate – all perfectly suited for a lab puppy.

"So, what are you going to name this little guy?" Maggie asks as the puppy tugs at his leash.

After the four of us banter over appropriate names, Geoff suggests "Bryce."

"I like it. What do you think?" I ask the wide-eyed puppy. He licks my nose.

Winking at Jenna, I say, "Bryce it is."

"Sam, meet your new buddy," Jenna says as the golden retriever walks hesitantly over to sniff the puppy, a large knotted rope in his mouth.

"That's a bit big for him, Sam. But, before long, he'll be able to play tug with you." Jenna hugs her dog, scratching him behind the ears.

After brunch, Jenna and Maggie get busy chopping, dicing, stuffing, and stirring in preparation for tonight's dinner. Geoff's sprawled on the sofa, watching "It's A Wonderful Life" with Bryce snuggled against his chest. I carefully pick up the puppy and call out to Sam. It's time for Bryce to have his first proper dog walk.

Two hours later, Matt, Simone, and Mollie arrive. Our small home seems about to burst at its seams, filled with positive energy and holiday spirit. The night proceeds better than I could ever have anticipated. Bryce passes out on his new puppy dog bed while Sam cuddles next to him. I look across the room and see everyone in my life that matters – everyone, that is, except for Patrick. Amidst the laughter and wonderful meal, I excuse myself from the table. There's one thing left to do.

Me: *Merry Christmas, Patrick. I miss you, Buddy.*

Since receiving that photograph, I've been reaching out to Patrick regularly. It's almost as if we are rebuilding our friendship, just starting from a different place. But it's then that my mind wanders to another person who I've ignored – my mother. I feel a lump form in my throat as I question why we didn't include her tonight. After all, Matt and Simone are here… and she could have met Jenna's parents… and spent time with Mollie. Knowing what needs to be done, I pick up my phone, walk into the bedroom, and call my mother to wish her a Merry Christmas.

When she answers, I can hear women's voices and Christmas music playing in the background.

"Jackson is that you?" my mother asks.

"Yeah, Mom. I just wanted to call and wish you a merry Christmas. How are you?"

"I'm well, thank you." But then she pauses, and her voice softens. "I have a several of my neighbors over for Christmas dinner tonight. They're also alone, so we thought that we'd celebrate together."

Instantly guilt courses through my veins. "Mom, I'm sorry. I should have invited you to come to Bend." How could I have been so thoughtless?

"It's fine. We've been doing this for years. It's our tradition, Jackson," my mother says without a hint of being hurt.

"Well, what about next year, Mom? Will you promise me that you'll come here then?" As I make this ask, I realize that I *actually want* her to come next year.

"I'd be delighted, Jackson. Truly, I would."

After hanging up, a sense of calm comes over me. Even though I didn't include her this Christmas, she now knows she is missed. And, maybe she will come to Bend next December. Returning to the living room, I rejoin my family around the long wooden table. My family. I like the way that sounds. So, this is how Christmas is supposed to be.

CHAPTER 41

Jenna

It's been the most amazing week ever, but it had to end. During our tearful goodbyes at the airport, I promise to visit my parents in Boston this spring. As sad as I am to see them leave, I realize that I'm building a new life here in Bend. The past is truly in the past, and although I am unsure as to what the future holds, for the first time in my life I'm embracing the uncertainty.

Once I'm back at home, the phone rings and interrupts my thoughts on this Saturday afternoon. It's Liv. After a brief conversation, I plop down next to Jackson, my cheeks damp from crying.

"Hey, what's wrong?" he asks, giving me a sweet hug.

"They found a house. It's exactly what they wanted, near Katy's school, too." I snivel as I bury my head into his chest. "I know I should be happy for her, but selfishly I'm sad for me."

"It's normal to be upset that your best friend is moving. But you can be sad for you *and* happy for Olivia at the same time," Jackson says as he kisses the top of my head.

"I guess you're right, it's just tough," I sniff as I reach for a tissue on the table next to me.

"I'm going to miss them, too. But you'll find a way to see each other. Friendships like yours don't just dissolve." Jackson pulls me closer toward him.

I nod, gulping down tears. But, it's no use. Dissolving into sobs, I curl into fetal position and lean into Jackson's strong body.

This is one of those times when words are useless. I need to cry, to let out my emotions so I can move on without my best friend. Liv was my safety net in Bend, the main the reason I moved here. And, now, less than a year later, she's leaving.

Trying to regain my composure, I straighten up and say, "I know it's for the best, but I didn't expect it to happen so soon. I kind of hoped that they'd have the baby here and then move afterwards." Jackson hands me another tissue.

"It's gotta be difficult enough moving when you're pregnant, but with a newborn? Did she say when they'd be closing on the house?" he asks.

"Next week. Michael is staying to finalize everything, and Liv's flying home on Tuesday to start packing. Then she heads back the next week to stay. Permanently." I shake my head then say, "Soon she won't be able to fly. It will be too close to her delivery date. She officially resigned from school yesterday."

"Why don't you offer to help her move? Can you take a few days off?"

I like this idea. I stand up, grab my phone, and open up the calendar. "We have an artist visiting this week, but then there's a break. Plus, Paige can probably cover Tanager. After all, she'll be back to a full-time schedule next month." I sniff. My tears have stopped.

"Then do it," Jackson says, walking toward the kitchen to feed Sam and Bryce.

"But that weekend is Patrick's birthday party," I say as I point to my phone calendar. "You promised him we'd go to Boulder."

Without seeming phased Jackson says, "You help Olivia in Chicago, and I'll go to Boulder. That way, we can each be where we're needed."

As much as I've looked forward to meeting Patrick, I want to be there for Liv. Plus, Jackson said that this birthday party is more of a reunion for the men in his platoon. So, maybe this is best. Jackson needs that time to reconnect with these guys, not babysit me.

* * *

Today is an unusually warm Sunday in January. The sun's brightly shining, and the view of Bachelor is perfect enough to be a post card. I decide to take advantage of the break in weather and take Sam for a

342

run. I make my way to the river. The path is crowded. Apparently, I'm not the only one with cabin fever.

I keep a steady, cautious pace as my mind turns to the upcoming days. Liv returns on Tuesday, and I'm taking off part of this upcoming week to help her pack. Then we're flying to Chicago to set up their new home. I hate watching my best friend leave.

The river moves swiftly. Ice along the banks reflects the brilliant sunlight as the water flowing by glistens. I focus on the moving ripples. Constant change. Nothing stays the same, in nature, or in life. Liv and I are also no longer the same two people we were last spring. Liv is now a wife and will soon become a mother. And, while I can try to envision what that will entail, I honestly have no idea. Just as a flowing river must divide and choose the best route when it comes to a fork, Liv must also change course and move in another direction. Growing as individuals often requires us to say goodbye to parts of our past. As difficult as this can be, it is what allows space for the new.

Yet, it doesn't have to be heartbreaking. I've made those shifts, too, as I've said farewell to so much and am now living a totally new existence in Bend. Jackson's been pivotal in my transformation. Yet as important as he is to me, I am also fine when I'm alone. I don't *need* Jackson. I *want* him. And there is absolutely no doubt – I know that he's the one.

For the rest of the run I take in my surroundings. Sam greets other dogs while I happily acknowledge oncoming runners. My senses come alive as I notice aspects of my surroundings that I've taken for granted – the pine scented air, the breeze rippling through the branches, the sound of the rushing water. Yes, Liv's on her path, and I've found mine. Right here. In Bend.

CHAPTER 42

Jackson

Jenna's in Chicago helping Olivia unpack. I miss her, but I've been looking forward to this weekend since Patrick invited me last September. The trip to Boulder is uneventful, and I appreciate the solitude. It gives me time to collect my thoughts and think about this reunion with Patrick and my men. It's been two years since I've seen any of them. I wonder how they've changed since they've been back. But my main concern is Patrick. The last time we were together was in the hospital, and I cringe when I think of how I behaved.

The sun's set by the time I arrive at his house. But I can easily see the scene through the front window – men – my men – reuniting. With a renewed sense of confidence, I ring the doorbell. Mary O'Brien answers, appearing even more beautiful than her photos that Patrick showed me when we were in Afghanistan. Their kids, Ryan and Shannon, stand shyly by their mom's side. The little girl's a spitting image of her dad while Ryan resembles his mom. Mary warmly embraces me before leading me into the house and toward the crowded kitchen. There, in his wheelchair, sits Patrick. He looks strong and vibrant. The men surround him, beer bottles clinking in toasts. But then, for a moment, everyone freezes as Patrick's attention turns to me. He starts crying as he yells, "Fuck, I've missed you, Buddy! Get over here!" His arms open widely, waiting to give me a hug.

As the night flows, stories are told and retold, bottles drained. Memories, some embellished, others pared down in respect for Patrick's family, are rehashed. We drink to each other, to our families, and to our country. Slowly, we start to fade, retreating to sofas, blow up mattresses, and empty spaces on the living room floor. Mary's pretty incredible to deal with all of us. Guess it worked out that Jenna didn't come. Those are my last thoughts as my head hits the pillow.

The next morning everyone nurses their hangovers with multiple cups of coffee accompanied by hash browns, fried eggs, and bacon. Mary once again proves herself a saint. It's been great reconnecting with the guys, the ones I trained, depended on and supported. One by one they say goodbye, leaving Patrick and me at the kitchen table. Patrick had asked me stay through Monday so that we'd have some time alone after everyone else left.

"So, tell me about this Jenna. Is this serious?" Patrick asks while he snacks on some of the leftover bacon.

"She may be it for me," I say as I take a seat next to him. "We've only been together since June, but it's like we've known each other forever."

"I feel the same way about Mary. If it wasn't for her, I don't think I could have made it. You better not let this girl go." Patrick slaps me on the back.

"Yeah... and Mary's pretty special. Not many women would deal with all of us, right?" But then things turn serious. "You know, Patrick, I've always felt like I let you down. Maybe if I'd planned the operation differently or changed the timing..." I wait to continue, harnessing more courage to say what's in my heart. "What I mean is that I've spent so many hours trying to figure out what I could have done to prevent the accident, but I can't go back and fix it."

"How many times do I have to tell you? Shit happens. This had absolutely nothing to do with you or your planning," Patrick says as he adjusts his chair to face me head on. Then he pauses and his demeanor shifts. "But I have to ask, why did you disappear? You came to see me once, but I never heard from you again?" I hear the pain in his voice.

Here it is. This is when it gets real. He's hit the nerve, where my guilt lies deepest, what's been eating me alive for the past two years. The rawness of his question constricts my throat. But I owe him an explanation.

"I couldn't. It just killed me seeing you that way." I gather more strength to continue. "I didn't know if you could handle living your life in a wheelchair," I say, swallowing hard. "You were the most physical guy I knew, always on the move, never sitting still. But, when I saw you there in the hospital, I knew that you'd be confined, the thing you hated most. So, I blamed myself." There, I said it. I look at Patrick's face. It shows a mixture of anger and pity – not for his situation in life, but for *me*.

"What you're forgetting is that I wouldn't be here today if it wasn't for you. Your quick reaction saved my life, kept me from bleeding to death." His puts his hand on my leg for emphasis. "Jackson, don't feel sorry for me, be proud of how you performed that night." He removes his hand then takes a deep breath. "Sure, it fucking sucks being stuck in this chair. But I have my life. I get to see my kids grow up. I am able to love my wife," Patrick says with deep conviction.

I can't look at him. My eyes remain glued to the floor.

"That's why you received those medals. *You* were the hero." His voice escalates with the word "you."

Those damn medals. I buried them deep in my closet, wanting them out of sight forever. They served as a reminder of what happened that night to Patrick. But, right now, it's not about the medals' merit. At this moment my friend's absolving me of my guilt and shame. I can either accept what he's saying, or I can spend the rest of my life condemning myself for what happened.

Almost as if Patrick knew where my mind was, he says, "You have

348

two choices. You can leave here, still blaming yourself for me being in a chair, or you can decide right now that you're done shitting on yourself. What's it gonna be, Jackson?" Patrick asks wheeling himself back a few feet, creating a bit of a distance between us, almost as if to dare me to make a step toward him.

He's right. It can't continue like this. "Fine. It's done, finished, time to move on." With that I stand up, cross the divide between us, and give him the biggest bear hug.

"Good decision," is all that Patrick says. But from the corner of my eye, I see him getting choked up.

After a moment I ask, "So, how are you? I mean you look freak'n great, even fitter than before."

"Hey, I just make it my priority to do as much as I can. I need to be strong to remain mobile. Sure, there's still shit that I can't do, but I try not to focus on that. Instead, I keep busy with my job, Mary, the kids, and working out."

"How's the insurance business treating you?" I ask as I grab a piece of the bacon from the plate still sitting on the kitchen table.

"Better. It was tough breaking into it, but once I figured out what I needed to do, it's been pretty manageable. I don't love it, but it's a solid paycheck, if you know what I mean," Patrick says as he pushes his palms into the table's edge, stretching his shoulders.

I nod, empathizing with Patrick's dilemma of remaining in a job for the financial stability it provides. For a moment, I consider sharing the Flagline offer with Patrick but decide against it. I don't want the conversation to focus on me.

The rest of the day continues with thoughtful discussion, evolving into Sunday's typical activities at the O'Brien household. While outside with Shannon and Ryan, Patrick shows me how he maneuvers his chair, holding specially designed paddles to kick the soccer ball. The kids follow suit, and this adapted game becomes totally normal. Mary joins us, taking a break from cleaning up after last night. Her patience, compassion, and love shine through all of her actions and words. Mary's a special lady. I can't even imagine the challenges they've faced.

* * *

The next morning, I head to the airport, but after one more serious conversation with Patrick and Mary. They ask me if I'd be their children's guardian, just in case anything happened to both of them. Without hesitation, I accept this highest honor. After everything, they both trust me with their children. I thought that some part of them blamed me for what happened, but that can't be true. Maybe I really did save Patrick's life. Finally, I grasp what everyone else has known all along.

CHAPTER 43

Jenna

The last of the winter snow has melted, except for what remains on the mountains. Spring slowly arrives in Bend. I read the most recent text from Liv, loving the attached picture of adorable Hannah. When this beautiful baby girl was born on the fourth of March, I immediately booked a flight to Chicago to meet my godchild. Since then, Liv's been keeping me updated with daily photos of Hannah in her latest pink outfit, Katy holding Hannah, or Hannah sleeping blissfully in her bassinette.

Never in a million years did I picture Liv with a daughter or enjoying motherhood. She could handle boys, but a little girl? If Hannah grows into a typical female, she will certainly broaden Liv's world, exposing her to dolls, tea sets, endless baubles, and dress up, only to be followed by short dresses, make up, bras, piercings, and boyfriends. No doubt Katy's been "breaking in" Liv, but this is different from being a stepmom.

I laugh at the thought of Liv and Hannah playing with Barbie dolls or with Liv taking Hannah shopping for a prom dress.

While I'll occasionally help out at Tanager, Paige is now a fulltime employee. I appreciate being able to focus on AGS. Marjorie's given me a small office at the school, allowing me to better immerse myself into the building, getting to know the teachers and the students. I love what I do. Plus, the program is taking off and making a difference. Just last week I received two letters from parents expressing how pleased they were that AGS is exposing their children to local artists.

"Hey, how was your day?" Jackson asks when he returns – covered in mud – from Phil's Trailhead.

"Good," I say, giving him a quick kiss as he heads to the bathroom to shower before dinner.

I stir the homemade chili simmering on the stove, take a small taste from the wooden spoon, then add more garlic and a hint of paprika. Searching inside the cabinet, I find the bottle of cab that's tucked away in the back. Just as I'm pouring two glasses of red wine, Jackson emerges, smelling of coconut and shea soap. I turn the heat down on the stove and put a lid on the chili pot before giving him a warm embrace. "Hey, next Friday we have our final event for the year. I have five local artists coming, one for each grade level. They'll rotate through the various homerooms all day long. I asked a reporter to stop by and bring a photographer so they can capture the kids working with the artists. Why don't you come, too? You still haven't seen any of the workshops."

"I'll be there," he promises as he softly brushes his lips across mine, slowly pulling me closer. I trace my fingers down his back, still slightly wet from the shower. Then I slide my hands beneath his jeans, leisurely running my fingertips across the lower portion of his spine. Jackson's reaction tells me not to stop. I feel myself stir inside. Knowing that the chili needs about forty more minutes until it's ready, I take his hand and lead him toward the bedroom.

* * *

On Friday morning, I arrive at school before seven to prepare for the final workshop. Today could be a bit chaotic, so I want the extra time to ensure that everything flows as smoothly as possible.

Anticipating that one of the artists, Paul Simmons, a potter from Redmond, may be somewhat temperamental around younger students, I've placed him with the fourth graders. Kids this age usually follow directions and listen attentively, somewhat different from the younger children. While I focus on Paul and the fourth grade, Marjorie, Claire, and two all-star parent volunteers cover the remaining artists in the lower grades.

I carefully watch as Paul demonstrates his craft. There's not enough time for the kids to work with the wheel, so he distributes clay and asks the students to create an object, promising to later fire their artwork at his shop. As I rotate among the kids, I eye Jackson in the doorway of this fourth-grade classroom. My tall boyfriend awkwardly towers over these students. But he blends in easily as soon as he begins talking with the kids, asking them what they're making.

I watch him approach Jeffrey, one of my favorites in this class. An extremely smart and talented kid, Jeffrey is confined to a wheelchair, the result of a viral infection from his earlier childhood. Curious, I move closer to Jackson and Jeffrey and silently observe.

"Hey, Buddy, that is an impressive bike you're making," Jackson says as he bends down toward Jeffrey. Jackson seems genuinely impressed with this nine-year-old's ability to mold the clay into a realistic looking mountain bike.

"Thanks. My dad rides, and I think that he'd really like this for Father's Day," Jeffrey spouts out, pride in his voice. "He bought me a trailer that he attaches to his bike, but he thinks some paths are too rocky for me. He's worried that I'd get tossed around too much." Jeffrey makes a silly face showing his amusement with this idea.

"You like riding with your dad?" Jackson probes deeper as he gently places his hand on the back of Jeffrey's chair.

"Yeah, it's so much fun. And, my dad's really awesome. He does downhill races all of the time. Mom and me watch him almost every weekend. Last month he was a top five finisher!" Jeffrey proudly shares, his eyes almost popping out of his head.

"That's so cool," Jackson's mouth opens then closes. It appears as if he wants to say more but doesn't. I'm guessing that this young boy in a wheelchair reminds him of Patrick.

Hours later, after an exhilarating day, I walk in the front door of our apartment, exhausted. There's a note from Jackson on the kitchen table saying that he's at OutRider and will probably be working late. At eight, there's still no Jackson so I text him about dinner.

Me: *How about I grab some food and come to you?*

Jackson: *Sounds good. Thanks.*

I pick up pizza on the way to OutRider. When I arrive, Jackson's in the workspace located in the rear of the shop, totally enthralled in a project. He has welding glasses on, and it seems that he has taken a small bike apart and is reassembling it.

"What are you working on?" I put the box of pizza on the only spot on the counter that's not covered with tools.

"I'm just trying something. You know that little kid at school, the one in the wheelchair?" Jackson asks, momentarily glancing at me. His face is solemn, focused.

"His name is Jeffrey, yes," I pause. "What about him?"

"Well, I saw him sculpting this bike for his dad, and we started talking. Seems that his dad takes him out on the trails, but they have limited access because the trailer his dad hooks onto the back of his bike can't maneuver all of the paths. I started wondering if I could adapt one of my kids' bikes for Jeffrey, you know, make it more of a hand cycle, so that someday he could do the trails on his own with his dad." As Jackson speaks, his eyes never leave his project.

I stare in amazement as my boyfriend diligently welds, measures, and welds again. My love for this man swells to a level higher than I ever thought possible.

Jackson stops momentarily, only to eat a slice of pizza before returning to his venture. Knowing that I'm useless here, I climb the stairs to Mollie's apartment, lie down on the couch, and watch TV with her. Several hours later, I wake up alone. Mollie must have gone to bed. Then I look at the clock. It's one in the morning. Is Jackson still working on this bike?

I walk down the back stairs and open the unlocked door. "How's it going? You must be tired," I call into his shop. "Let's go home. We both have to get up early tomorrow. Besides, Bryce and Sam can't be alone this long." There's no response so I walk to the back.

Jackson's face has a serene expression, and his eyes deeply project a trancelike state as he turns the wheel of his creation, making sure the tire moves with ease.

"Hey, it's late. I think we should go home," I say again, still half asleep.

"OK, but before we leave, come here. I want to show you something," Jackson says while he wipes the frame of the small bike with a clean cloth.

With pride, he demonstrates how the adaptive bike works, how Jeffrey's dad can help him get strapped in, and how the hand crank totally powers the bike.

"You did all of this for Jeffrey?" I examine this handcrafted bike, totally in awe of what he created.

"He should be able to ride with his dad. It's only right. Could you reach out to his father and let him know that I have something for his son to demo?" Jackson asks as he continues to make minor adjustments to the bike.

"Of course. I'll ask Marjorie to contact the parents on Monday." I know that student information is confidential and cannot be given out. "I'd like that," is all Jackson says.

He gently lays the bike on the workbench, grabs his coat, and reaches for my hand. His work is done.

CHAPTER 44

Jackson

After finishing my early morning workout, I throw my sweaty t-shirt by the washer. Jenna's not home yet, she's at yoga – *her* new ritual. Jenna and I have both settled into our own morning routines. Sure, she still runs three or four times a week, but running no longer consumes her. She's committed to these early morning classes, and they seem to be impacting her in more than one way. Not only is her flexibility increasing, but I've also noticed a new calmness about her.

As I pass through the kitchen on my way to shower, I see that I have a text from Chris O'Donnell. He wants me to call him. It's been over a year since we last talked. I wonder what this is about.

I decide to phone him as soon as I get to work. Just as I'm about to leave for OutRider, Sam and Bryce come charging at me. The force of their tag-teaming effort pushes me over. Bryce, who now weighs in at fifty-three pounds, jumps on top of me and relentlessly licks my face.

"I give up. You win!" Grabbing their leashes, we head outside for a walk before I go to work.

An hour later, I'm at my desk when I remember that I need to call Chris. On the third ring, he picks up. "Hey, Jackson, thanks for getting back to me." The conversation starts with small talk and catching up. I patiently wait for Chris to transition into the purpose of his text.

"Listen, I heard about what you did for that little boy, how you redesigned a bike to make it adaptive for him, allowing him to ride with his dad. Where did you learn to do that?" he asks.

"Whoa. Back-up. First, how did you hear about it?" I sit up straight, totally confused.

"Well, the boy's father was in the same fraternity at Stanford as my chief engineer, Jeff Mills. They just had their twentieth reunion, and the guy shared what you did. It impressed the hell out of everyone, especially Jeff. He told me about this yesterday, and when he said that the guy who designed and built this adaptive bike was from Bend and owned a bike shop, well I connected the dots," Chris explains.

"Seven degrees of separation, right?" I laugh aloud, amazed that this story reached Chris. "I gave it to him about six weeks ago, but we agreed not to make a big deal about it. I didn't want any props, just wanted the kid to be able to get out on the trails with his dad," I say as that feeling of satisfaction resurfaces, the one I felt when I gave Jeffrey the bike.

"That's a huge thing that you did for that little boy. How exactly did you know what adaptations to make?" Chris asks with a tone of sincerity.

Thinking back to the night when I built the bike, I can't specifically recall how the ideas came to me. They just did. "I'm not sure. Everything kind of made sense to me as I altered the original bike. I guess that my intuition guided me," I admit as my fingers scratch the side of my head.

"Listen, the real reason I'm calling is to revisit my offer, but with a somewhat different emphasize. What would you say to designing adaptive bikes? For adults and kids?" I swallow hard when I hear Chris's proposal.

But, before Chris can continue, I say, "As much as this interests me, I can't leave Bend."

"You wouldn't have to. With our technological capabilities, you can design from Bend, and then we can build in Santa Rosa. You'll need to join us for meetings at our headquarters from time to time, but the majority of your work week would be spent right where you are."

Intrigued with this new twist, I ask numerous questions. Each of his answers only deepens my interest. Chris promises to send me a specific job description in addition to a detailed salary and benefits package for this newly created position.

"Think it over," Chris says in an upbeat voice. "I believe that we can make this work."

"I will," I say with conviction as I stand up and begin to pace back and forth. "Being able to operate from here, well, that's a game changer." I need to talk to Jenna about this, as well as my sister, because for this to work, Mollie would need to take on more responsibilities at OutRider.

"I understand. It's a big decision. Let me know when you have an answer. We could do some very special things together. Flagline needs someone with your abilities and talents."

As I hang up, my mind's spinning with possibilities. Unable to wait until tonight, I ask Jenna to meet me for lunch.

Less than an hour later, Jenna's sitting at an outdoor table when I arrive at Chow restaurant. Looking radiant, she's dressed in jeans and a white t-shirt, my favorite.

"So, tell me what's so important that prompted you to ask me to lunch?" she teases. Lunch dates are not part of our normal routine.

"Do you remember last summer when I did that bike race?" I ask as the waitress brings us mason jars of water with lemon.

"Of course," Jenna says as she takes a sip of water.

"Well, there was that guy, Chris O'Donnell, who I met for coffee at Thump." I pause to see if this registers with Jenna.

"Oh yeah, but you never really told me what he wanted." She squints her eyes, either from the bright sunlight or confusion of where I'm going.

"I know. He actually offered me a job that morning, with Flagline,"

I say before taking a sip of water.

"Why didn't you mention that?" Jenna seems hurt.

"Because the job was in California, and I didn't want to leave Bend, *or you*." I look her directly in the eyes to emphasize my reason.

"So, why are you telling me now?" Jenna asks, her forehead furrows and she appears totally puzzled.

"Because Chris reached out to me again this morning. He wanted to know if I would work for his design team, but this time he said I could work remotely from Bend."

"What?" Jenna asks, her jaw drops.

"I know. It blew me away, too. He heard about the bike I designed for Jeffrey. And, I guess that piqued his interest in me again." I tell her the details of the offer and the connection with Jeffrey's father. "Specifically, he wants me to design a line of adaptive bikes for kids and adults. It's a new area for Flagline, something that they've considered venturing into for a while. And, when he learned that I built that bike, well, it set things in motion, and that's when he reached out to me."

"This could be the perfect job for you," Jenna says as she reaches for my hand that's resting on the table.

"I want to hear your thoughts about it, Jenna." And I do.

After reflecting for a few moments, she says, "You have my total support if this is what you want to do. But can you still run OutRider? Or will you have to sell it?" Clearly, she's looking at this from a practical perspective.

"I'd still oversee the shop, but I need to ask Mollie if she's open to taking on more responsibilities. I can design for Flagline while still keeping an eye on OutRider. I just can't be in charge of the day to day operations," I admit right before the waitress stops by to share the daily specials.

"From what Mollie's said to me, she loves working at the shop. I bet she'd be willing to do more. She's certainly capable. Have you thought about the downside to saying 'yes'?" Jenna asks as soon as the waitress leaves our table.

"Basically, I'd be reporting to someone else, and I'd have to travel to Santa Rosa every few weeks. Also, my workload would increase dramatically."

Jenna's eyes narrow. "Would this job make you happy?"

I sit back in the chair and consider her question. "Yes, I think that it would. Working for Flagline would definitely challenge me. Plus, financially, it would open up an entirely different world, give me – *give us* – new opportunities. But what attracts me the most is that I'd be creating something to help people." Instinctively I know that this job would give me what I'm missing.

"So, what will you tell him?" Jenna asks as she closes her menu and interlaces her fingers in mine.

Kissing her hand, I say, "That I'll do it."

* * *

I make the call first thing the following morning, and this time Chris is pleased with my response. Sharing the tight schedule between design and production, he'll need my blueprints by September 15 so production can create prototypes for the October 14 board meeting.

"Have any plans for the next few weeks?" Chris asks.

"Not anymore." I say, committed to making this happen.

After a few more formalities about onboarding with the organization, the conversation ends. I stare at the wall in front of me. Instead of seeing the calendar, the memos, or the various posters of the newest mountain bikes or apparel lines, my thoughts are elsewhere – already calculating what needs to happen next. Invigorated, I begin sketching. While I crumple some of these thoughts, others, I pin on the bulletin board, the critical space which houses those important items that previously organized my business. However, at this moment, they've lost their significance. It's the designs that matter now.

Mollie walks in. "Hey, what are you doing?" she asks as she leans against the back counter.

"Do you have a minute?" I ask, putting my pencil down.

"Sure, is everything OK?"

"Better than OK," I say as I feel another surge of energy… here goes… "But I'm going to need more help at OutRider. Be honest. Are you interested in taking on more responsibility at the shop?"

364

"Sure, if you need me to," Mollie says a bit hesitantly.

I relay the details of my conversation with Chris. "I'd maintain responsibility for anything financial, but most of the day-to-day operational items would be yours – the ordering, advertising, sales. Do you think you'd like that?" I lean forward and place my hands on my knees, waiting for Mollie's response.

"Wow, Jackson. You'd trust me to do all of that. Do you think I'm ready?" She asks as her fingers start playing with her long blonde hair, a nervous habit from her childhood.

I stand up, walk over to her, and place my arm around my little sister. "You're more than ready. Mollie, you're smart, talented, and skilled with the customers. And, I'll be right here if you need anything."

Mollie beams. "If you need me to do this, then I'm in."

Maybe that's been part of Mollie's struggle. She wants to belong.

Then Mollie gives me the tightest of hugs before saying, "Thank you for believing in me."

A short while later, as Mollie's begins reviewing past months' orders at a makeshift desk area that I set up for her in the front of the store, I decide to call Jenna.

"Mollie's on board," I quietly say, knowing that Mollie's out of earshot. "This may be exactly what's missing in her life – responsibility and the sense that she's needed. I think that she always considered herself a burden. Managing OutRider will give her purpose."

"Mollie will do an outstanding job. She has a lot of talent, but she's the one who must realize that." Jenna's response reinforces my thoughts.

"And, I spoke with Chris this morning. He shared the department's internal timeline. It's pretty tight. I'll have to make Flagline my focus for the next month and a half, which means really long days. Are you sure about this?" I ask, already knowing her answer.

"Of course." Jenna understands the demands of starting something new. After all, she's been in the same position with AGS. There have been numerous nights when she's on her laptop till early in the morning.

"But, tonight, no work, just us. I made a reservation at Ariana's. I'll be home before seven-thirty to pick you up."

"Can't wait," Jenna says.

Later that evening, tucked in a quiet corner of Ariana, we talk about my new job, Jenna's upcoming plans for the second year of AGS, and possible trips we might take next spring. We have become a true couple, committed to one another while continuing to challenge ourselves individually.

CHAPTER 45

Jenna

The guest room looks cozy and inviting. I've put fresh daisies on the bureau and assembled a small basket of toiletries for Liv's use. Despite her resistance, saying that the Pack n' Play would be fine for Hannah, I insisted on renting a crib for this upcoming week. I also went to Home Depot to buy a thicker shade to help keep the room dark for naptime. I want my godchild to feel safe while visiting.

Jackson's been so busy finishing the final designs that I barely see him. In fact, he leaves in six days for California to share his progress with Chris and the team. Last night he told me that he reached out to his mother and asked if he could stay at her house in Ross, as it's less than an hour from the company's headquarters. He claimed it would prevent him from dealing with a hotel, but I know that's not the real reason. The last time he stayed with Rachel was after he returned from

Afghanistan, right before moving to Bend. That visit certainly didn't go well. But my intuition tells me that this time will be different. It's almost like they're getting a do-over.

* * *

This was Hannah's first plane ride, and Liv looks wiped out when they arrive. The stress and strain of motherhood appears to be taking its toll. My best friend crashes for a quick nap while Hanna and I curl up on the sofa.

Unsure of what to do, I prop the baby against my knees, looking straight into Hannah's pale blue eyes. "You are such a combination of your mommy and your daddy." She seems to have Michael's length, but her hair's thick and light colored, just like Liv's. I gently cradle the six-month-old, carefully ensuring to support her neck. Hannah makes bubbles with her tiny pink lips as she smiles. God, she's beautiful. What would it be like to have a tiny being dependent on you for everything? That thought sounds terrifying.

But the more time that I spend with this baby, the more my shoulders relax. Could I do this? Would I be a good mother? Jackson and I have never talked about children. We haven't even discussed marriage. I wonder what Jackson will think when he sees Hannah. How will *he* be with a baby?

Lost deep in my head, I'm jolted when Liv, looking somewhat refreshed, walks into the living room. Hannah eyes her mom, but she doesn't appear to want to leave my lap. In fact, she stares back and forth between the two of us before a big grin appears on her face.

"It's almost as if she knows how close we are," I say while gently stroking Hannah's back.

"This one may be an old soul. Sometimes her reactions overwhelm me. It seems impossible for a little baby to seemingly understand all that she does. Michael and I talk about it frequently. I'm glad that you noticed it, too," Liv says as she looks adoringly at her baby girl.

"You could be right. I've read that babies are closely connected to the universe and are more aware of their gifts," I say staring straight into Hannah's endearing little face.

"When did you start reading about that stuff?" Liv asks while she takes a seat on the chair across from us.

"The more yoga and meditation I've done, the more questions I've been asking myself. It seemed natural to search for information in articles and books, even podcasts. There's so much I want to know. I'm not sure that I believe everything, but I'm definitely thinking differently and considering new possibilities," I say as I shift Hannah to face her mom.

"No doubt part of *you* finding *you*?"

"You know, I don't talk with many people about this, except for Jackson, of course, but I can't begin to tell you how at peace I am. Sure, I love Jackson, but it's more than that. Me being happy doesn't center around him. It's much more." I pause to make a face at Hannah before continuing. "I know I'm not doing a very good job explaining myself, but lately, I've felt *grounded*. And, I'm more content with where things are going. Instead of constantly striving to do or be the best, I'm starting to become comfortable in my own skin, accepting the good and the bad. Sure, I like to do well, but I'm not as afraid of making mistakes. Do you know what I mean?" My nose scrunches, as I'm unsure whether or not Liv understands.

"That is fucking awesome," Liv says. "I could see the small changes before I left for Chicago. But to be honest, I was so consumed with being newly married and pregnant that I probably didn't notice much."

Liv gets up and goes into the kitchen, takes a bottle of formula from the fridge, and then places it into the bottle warmer that's plugged into an outlet by the kitchen counter. "You realize how much of a mess you were after breaking up with Ben, don't you?" She waits till the bottle warmer beeps. "But something told me that you needed this, you know, a change of scenery, a new place, to sort things out. That's why I pushed you so hard to move here," she says while shaking the bottle. Droplets of milk form on her wrist as she checks to ensure it's not too hot.

"Really? I was that bad?" I ask. But then I remember the episode in the grocery store, sitting huddled in Ben's office, and crying on my mother's shoulder.

"Let's just say you're in a much better place now," Liv comes over and takes Hannah from my arms and begins to feed her child.

"Please don't think that I have it all figured out. There's so much more to learn," I say while shifting into a crossed-legged position on the couch.

"Do we ever have all of the answers? If we did, then what's the point? Where's the adventure?" Liv lifts her head and gives me one of her looks while Hannah sucks away at her bottle.

* * *

Liv, Hannah, and I are inseparable over the next six days. We take the baby everywhere in Bend, alternating who carries Hannah in the front pack. Sam and Bryce dutifully guard anyone from getting too close to their baby. In fact, Hannah became instantly attached to these two dogs, and they to her. At first, I worried that they could hurt Hannah, so I kept them in my bedroom. But, after they whimpered for two hours, I introduced them to the baby. Instinctively, both dogs sensed how delicate this child is and have dutifully glued themselves to Hannah, lying right next to her crib or aside of her Pack n' Play, attentively watching her every move.

After a week of endless hours refining his designs, Jackson joins us for our final dinner at Zydeco, Liv's favorite restaurant, the one she took me to when I first visited. We order a round of the "Cardamom New Fashioneds," just because it reminds us of that first night in Bend.

Sitting across from Hannah, Jackson appears captivated by this tiny being. Without the distraction of work, he's able to give this baby his full attention. He entertains Hannah, entirely memorized, while Liv and I chat over our cocktails, happy to have a break from the responsibilities of watching the baby.

"I had no idea what I've been missing, holed up in my office all week," he says as he makes faces at Hannah, causing her to smile her toothless grin.

"She gets under your skin, doesn't she?" Liv says, full of motherly pride.

For a moment, I permit myself to wonder. What if? Could he possibly want a baby?

As expected, Hannah behaves perfectly throughout the entire dinner, attracting unending attention from the other patrons and the wait staff. While Liv and I giggle over past antics and joke about former boyfriends, Jackson remains quiet, appearing lost in his thoughts. This does not surprise me because he leaves early tomorrow for California – to meet with the team at Flagline, but first to spend the night at his mother's. I understand his uneasiness. After all, it's been quite a while since he's been part of a group or seen his mom. But, I'm not worried. His designs seem flawless. And Rachel's told me she's looking forward to having him visit. I sense that some of the missing pieces to his puzzle are finally coming together.

CHAPTER 46

Jackson

The bunk beds, trophies, and posters from my childhood are long gone. Instead, I'm lying in a barely used queen bed that's equipped with a linen upholstered headboard set against gray walls. The expensive white cotton bedding and thick down comforter have replaced my Spiderman sheets and navy bedspread. When I first walked into my former bedroom, I laughed at the number of throw pillows carefully arranged on the bed. Mom's put a lot of effort into transforming my childhood bedroom into a proper guestroom, a space that most likely hosts few visitors. Still, I have to give it to her. She definitely has a knack. In fact, this house is in pristine condition.

My mother never discusses the time, energy, or money that she spends on the house. Instead, she makes it appear effortless – the perfectly arranged flowers in the vase, the tasteful paintings on the wall, and the slightly aged Orientals on the hardwood floors. All this time I've mocked her, when in reality, she's quite gifted with interior design. It might not be my personal taste, but I have to say, she has a way about her.

Five minutes later, my alarm goes off. After a quick shower, I make my way to the kitchen, planning to grab a quick bite before heading to Flagline's headquarters. It should only take fifty minutes to drive there. However, I see my mother sitting in the dining room, reading the paper, and drinking coffee. She's set the table for two, and on the other linen placemat is a bowl of berries and a plate with an omelet, toast, and bacon that's apparently waiting for me. A coffee urn sits between the two placemats.

"Mom, you didn't have to do this. I'd be happy with just toast." I smile appreciatively as I pull out the leather backed dining chair and sit down. The omelet's delicious. She used diced onions, peppers, and mushrooms, added fresh herbs, and topped it off with a smoked mozzarella.

My mother seems at peace as she watches me devour my breakfast.

"I'm glad you called and asked to stay here. It's nice to having you home," she says as she delicately takes a sip of coffee out of a china cup.

I put my fork down and take the time to really look at my mother – who she is, here today, not how I remember her from the past. What I see is an elegant woman in her sixties, one who possesses a strong, determined face, but who is also beautiful. She's lean and fit, exuding grace in every movement. In this moment, I see how similar the house is to my mother – classic, traditional, pristine, stunning, refined and tasteful, yet longing for outside life. No doubt there are cracks and weaknesses in the foundation, but to look at either, one would never know. The blemishes are well hidden. But what might appear as flaws may actually be assets, signs of weathering a storm, of surviving, of being alone.

"I'm happy I came. Thanks for having me." I reach out and gently squeeze her hand, then let it go.

She glances down at her fingers then, smiles at me. "I know I can't go back or change what happened. But I believe that the future can be different. That is, if you want it to be." How difficult this must be for her to share her emotions. She's reaching out. I guess it's never too late. This wouldn't be happening if it weren't for Jenna.

"I'd like that." And I mean it.

We talk about the past while I finish breakfast. She offers insights that I never considered and shares missing pieces to my childhood. Slowly, things begin to make sense.

I then notice the time. I can't be late for my meeting. "Would it be alright if I stayed again, you know, the next time I have a meeting at Flagline?" I ask while folding my linen napkin and placing it on the table.

"I couldn't think of anything nicer," she says as she reaches out and delicately touches my cheek. "What a fine man you've become. I am so proud of you."

* * *

Chris meets me at the headquarters' entrance. The building's fantastic. Its modern architecture includes large floor to ceiling windows, allowing endless sunshine to enter the building. We take the elevator to the fourth floor. Chris's design team occupies half of this area. I notice the fully stocked kitchens equipped with snacks, coffees, fruit and even beer taps. There are multiple conference room areas, some with extremely comfortable looking chairs. An open space hosts air hockey, ping pong, and foosball tables.

"We find that our engineers and designers do best in a more relaxed atmosphere," Chris says, perhaps noticing my reaction to the amenities.

First, Chris and I debrief in his office. After the team reviews and approves the designs, the plant can begin to make the prototypes for the board meeting next month. I show him the blueprints for the adaptive bikes. For fifty minutes, we go over the details, discussing weight bearing, torque, and tensions. Finally, I say, "There's only one thing that's holding me back with the kids' line."

"What's that? Everything seems like it should work," he says as he tilts his swivel chair.

"I think it will work, but what if we could make it better than *just work*?" I ask, opening another drawing on my laptop.

"Go on," Chris says, looking closely at the screen.

"I was thinking about how fast kids grow. These things aren't cheap, so I doubt that parents will want to keep buying bigger versions of this bike to match their kids' growth spurts," I say.

"Good point. Where are you going with this?" he asks as he continues to scan my laptop screen.

"What if we could make the main frame adjustable, so that as the kids' bodies grew, the bike could expand with them?" I take the curser and highlight the area of change that I'm proposing.

"The trick would be not to compromise the strength of the frame," Chris adds.

"Exactly. Do you think we could bring this to the team? Maybe together we can devise a solution," I say as I bite the end of my pencil. I know I'm throwing a wrench on this design at the eleventh hour, but I want it to be flawless.

By the end of the afternoon, the team's re-engineered the bike so that it can adapt for a child's growth without impacting the integrity of its structure. After a few minor alterations, the designs are almost ready to be ready to send to production. Now I understand why there are beer taps. Suddenly there are lots of high fiving and cheers as Flagline prepares to embark on its new line of adaptive bikes.

Noting the time, I reluctantly say goodbye so that I can catch my flight back to Redmond. As I head to my rental car, I realize that a part of me doesn't want to leave. Being here, having a voice, and working with the team felt really good. Before backing out of the parking space,

I stare up at the building. This is what I'm supposed to do. I can make a difference here.

Four hours later, I'm back in our apartment in Bend, where I find Jenna curled up on the couch reading a book.

"Hey, welcome home!" She almost levitates off the sofa as she gives me a big kiss. "How was the meeting? How did it go with your mom?" she excitedly asks without pausing for either answer.

"You know, I actually had a nice time with her. She went all out for me. And the two of us talked. A lot. Hearing her stories helped me understand things from her perspective," I say as I put my overnight bag by the bedroom door.

Jenna sits down on a kitchen stool. "This was a big step for both of you. It sounds like she's starting to open up, maybe be the mother you always wanted. What did you think of Flagline? What were the headquarters like? How did that meeting go?"

"Those are a lot of questions." I smile. "Flagline's headquarters is pretty sweet. At first, I thought I'd feel intimidated, but I blended in and found my role in the group." I sit down at the kitchen table and stretch out my legs.

"Exactly as I would have predicted," Jenna says as she gets up from the stool and moves behind me to massage my shoulders.

"Did you have a good last day with Olivia and Hannah?" I ask while

I close my eyes, enjoying her firm touch.

"I hated seeing them leave. So did Sam and Bryce. They're still moping," she laughs. "Being with Liv and Hannah was so special. That baby is sweet. I never knew all that was involved with having a child, but it's totally worth the work."

As if on cue I ask, "What are you telling me? Do you want to have a baby?" I turn to face her.

She smiles, playfully smacking my butt. "Not yet, but we *could* practice." Jenna leans closer, slowly kissing my neck. Her hands move down my body, toward my belt. It's good to be home.

CHAPTER 47

Jenna

School's now in full gear, marking the second year for AGS at Northwest Crossing. This Thursday there's an artist from Seattle coming to work with the kids – to create a huge mosaic in the school's main lobby. But today my alarm didn't go off. I've overslept and am running late, so I grab a banana as I fill my travel mug with coffee before heading out.

"Hey, what are you doing next Friday?" Jackson calls from the bedroom as I'm about to leave.

Forgetting that day is October 14, the day of Flagline's board meeting, I pause. "Actually, that's an In-service Day. I'll probably work from home that day. Why?"

"Any interest in coming to Santa Rosa with me? I could show you around, introduce you to the team?"

Without giving it much thought, I say, "Sure, that would be awesome. Gotta go. See you tonight." I bolt out the door, focused on the myriad of items I must attend to before Thursday.

* * *

Ten days later, after work's calmed down, we're on a plane headed to Santa Rosa. When we arrive at Flagline, Jackson gives me a quick tour and introduces me to Chris and several other members of the design group. Then, when the board meeting's about to begin, Chris invites me to stay and watch the presentation. I sit in the back, hoping not to be noticed.

Jackson clearly impresses the entire Board. He holds each member's attention as he explains the design features of the various bikes. All present seem memorized with the prototypes displayed throughout the Board Room. In fact, when the meeting's over and people start leaving, the treasurer of the company approaches Jackson, personally thanking him for designing adaptive bikes for the company to build. I overhear the conversation. "My daughter, she's only three, but she has a degenerative disease, and soon she will lose her ability to walk. What you're doing here, well, you're giving these kids a new lease on life. Thank you." The man then turns away, seemingly in an attempt to hide his emotions.

"I am so proud of you," I whisper as Jackson stows his laptop in his backpack.

After saying goodbye to Chris and the others, Jackson leads me toward the elevator.

"Do we have time to see your mom before we go back?" I ask.

"As much as I love that idea," he says once we're in the corridor, "we have other plans."

"What are you talking about?" I'm still somewhat uneasy about surprises.

"I had a hunch that the Board would back production, so I booked us flights to go to Boulder this afternoon." That's all Jackson says as we walk into the elevator.

"Boulder? That's where Patrick is." I'd love to meet him, but why now?

When we reach the lobby, a man is waiting, standing next to a large cardboard box.

"Mr. Tait, here is your package. It won't fit in a cab, so I've arranged for the company's van to transport you and Ms. Moore to the airport."

Now I'm lost. I tug at Jackson's hand, reverting to my childlike self. "Tell me what's happening."

"This is one of the prototype bikes, and we're going to deliver it to Patrick," Jackson says, pointing to the box.

"You can *give* this bike to Patrick?" Why didn't he tell me sooner?

"Yes, Chris thought it was a great idea. This bike is similar to the samples we shared with the Board. I designed this particular bike based on Patrick's measurements and weight, as well as his disability. I could have given it to him sooner, but I thought it was important for Flagline to officially back it. Patrick will be the first person to own Flagline's newest product." The man and Jackson hoist the box in the back of the van.

Less than five hours later, we land at the Denver Airport and collect the large package from baggage claim. Driving to Boulder in a rental truck, I'm struck by how beautiful this area is. The mountains appear majestic, decorated in leaves ranging from oranges to yellows to reds.

"Last time I was here, all I saw was snow," Jackson says surveying the autumn foliage.

"They know we're coming, right?" I can't wait. Finally, I'll meet Patrick and his family.

"Mary does, but Patrick doesn't. She and I have been in communication for the past few weeks."

* * *

"Here we are," he says, once we finally turn onto Knight Street. "I texted Mary when we left the airport, so she's watching for us to arrive."

With that, the front door opens to this small, cozy ranch style home. A petite woman dressed in jeans and a flannel shirt appears on the front porch. Jackson almost vaults from the car, running to greet her. I follow.

After introductions and warm embraces, we return to the truck, all three of us lifting the large box from the back. Once we get it to the garage, Jackson opens the crate and begins to assemble the pieces. The finished product is beautiful. Black with red thin lines, the bike is a true masterpiece.

"Oh, Jackson, Patrick will love it. You have no idea what it will mean to him," Mary says as her hands move to her face in apparent awe.

"Can you understand what this means to me? It's the first time that I've been able to do something for Patrick to make his life a little bit better." Jackson pauses, inhales, then transitions to a peaceful state as he examines the bike.

"Remember, if it weren't for you, Patrick would have died that night. I wish that you could accept that you are the reason he's alive. I thought that you and Patrick settled this in January," Mary says as she frowns at Jackson. She's not letting him fall back into feeling guilty about the accident.

"You're right, we did," Jackson looks at her sheepishly.

Mary then leads us to the back of the house where we find Patrick pruning bushes.

"Honey, we have visitors," Mary calls out to her husband.

The moment Patrick sees us, he bursts out, "Holy shit, Jackson! What are you doing here, man?" Patrick's surprise is undeniable. He throws his tool and gloves to the ground.

"You're looking good," Jackson responds before giving this solid man a hug. "This is Jenna, the woman I told you about."

"Damn good to meet you." Patrick wheels toward me, pulling me in for a quick kiss on the cheek while winking at Jackson.

Mary goes back inside and grabs beers from the kitchen fridge, and the four of us sit down on the patio to catch up. Within minutes, Patrick is sharing humorous stories from their SEAL days. He has my full attention. I'm being exposed to an entirely new chapter of Jackson's life, one that he's buried.

After Patrick finishes his rendition of a southern cook who made the best grits, Jackson says, "Patrick, there's something I want to show you. Come here for a minute."

No doubt Patrick's curious as he follows Jackson into the garage. When he gets there, he sees the bike.

"What the hell is that?" Patrick's expression is priceless. He's grinning ear to ear.

"It's something that I designed for you, so you can ride. It's made with your measurements and weight in mind. I think it will work. Do you want to give it a try?" Jackson asks his buddy.

Instead of answering, Patrick wheels his chair over to the bike and begins transferring himself onto the seat. Jackson explains the various components, but Patrick doesn't need any assistance. He's got this.

Yet, it's Jackson I watch, not Patrick, as Patrick takes off down the street. Intense pride and love appear to ooze from every inch of Jackson's body. He seems immensely satisfied, in a calm, fatherly way. Not wanting to disturb the moment, I take a mental picture, capturing the way those intense green eyes sparkle, the corners of his mouth softens, and his normally clenched jaw relaxes. Finally, Jackson's let go of the guilt.

CHAPTER 48

Jackson

It's perfect – rose gold with white diamonds. Now that my income's increased, I don't have to compromise. I'm able to buy exactly what I want, what she'll love.

It's time. I'm ready, and I believe Jenna is, too. I didn't want to rush her, especially since this would be the second time – that is if she says "yes." With all of the changes she's been through – that we've been through – I needed to make sure that the moment was right. Maybe it was Jenna's reaction to Hannah during Olivia's visit that was the final sign. Whatever it was, this has to happen on our terms and our timetable. And, deep inside, I know that moment is now.

CHAPTER 49

Jenna

The cold, brisk air hits my face as I leave school. It's beautiful outside. The leaves have fallen, and we've already had our first snowfall. Jackson's at Flagline for a meeting, so I must stop by the apartment at noon to let the dogs out.

I'm not the only one enjoying this sunny November day. Sam and Bryce vigorously pull on their leashes as we walk around the neighborhood. On the way back, I check the mailbox. There are a few items, mostly junk mail. But then I notice an envelope – with Ben's handwriting. I freeze for a moment then quickly tear it open. What could this be? The last time we spoke was at Liv's wedding, over a year ago. I know that he and Maria were supposed to have been married last month. Slowly, I unfold the letter. There are two pages.

Jenna,

I hope that you are doing well. Olivia and I have been in touch, and she told me how much fun she had visiting you this past summer. It's hard to imagine Olivia being a mom.

You're probably wondering why I'm writing to you. There's something I need to share, something you deserve to know. I wish I could have told you this earlier, but I couldn't, and I hope that you can forgive me for that.

After my parent's accident, I found various documents in their safety deposit box. Knowing that these were important, I stuffed them in my nightstand drawer at Catherine and Henry's house, figuring that I could deal with it later, after I'd had some more time to process with what had happened. Then one night, before I left for my freshman year at Colgate, I started carefully reviewing these papers, wondering if there was anything I needed to deal with before I left for school.

That's when I saw it… my birth certificate. Sure, I had found it right after my parents had died, but I never read it. Why would I? But that night, as I carefully examined each piece of paper that came from my parents' safety deposit box, I discovered from my birth certificate that Catherine was not my aunt. She was my mother.

It's hard to explain how I felt — at age eighteen — having just lost my parents in a car accident. Shocked, I went downstairs and confronted Catherine, holding the birth certificate in my hand.

Instead of comforting me, showing remorse or joy at me finally knowing, she stared straight ahead as she told me what had happened. She and her boyfriend were only seventeen, too young to get married. When my grandmother found out that Catherine was expecting, she became outraged and took Catherine to Europe for the next seven months. That's where she had her baby — me.

Catherine refused to give me up for adoption to an ordinary couple, so she reached out to her sister Midge, the woman I've always known as my mother, to take me. Catherine knew that Midge and her husband, James, were unable to have children of their own. So she proposed this as the perfect solution to both of their "problems."

I had always wondered why there were never pictures of my mother when she was pregnant. I just assumed it was due to her vanity. And that explains why my parents moved to the Philadelphia suburbs right after I was born. That way no one would know that their newborn son was really their nephew. Everyone thought that I belonged to James and Midge Kelly. In the meantime, Catherine met Henry Devlin, my uncle, or my stepfather – I'm kind of confused – in college. Four years later they married.

Learning this devastated me. And instead of embracing me or even helping me deal with this news, Catherine became even colder and more distant once I knew the truth. That's when I started trying to do whatever she wanted, anything to please her. I had thought that my real mother had died when all along she was alive. But I couldn't comprehend why she wouldn't accept me as her son.

Then, when the house next to them came up for sale, Catherine approached me, offering to buy it for us. At first, I told her no. It was wrong in so many ways. But then she promised me that if you and I would move there after the wedding, she would admit that I was her son. There would be no more secrets.

Maybe now you can understand why I insisted on living in that house. I acted that way because I wanted this charade to be over, for her to be open about being my biological mother.

I am deeply sorry that I couldn't share this with you when we were together. I was afraid. I didn't want to scare you away. But that's what happened anyway, right?

I thought that explaining my story would help both of us close this chapter of our lives, so that is why I felt compelled to write to you now. I hope you can forgive me.

Love,

Ben

I stand there, my mouth hanging open. Eventually I go inside the apartment and sit down at the kitchen table, rereading the letter three more times, taking it all in. Now everything makes sense. As fucked up as it is, I finally understand why Ben acted as he did. I take a moment and imagine how I would have reacted if he had told me this when we were together. Would I have stayed with him, or would I still have left, knowing that he would always choose Catherine over me?

But then a sense of calm settles over my entire body. I was not supposed to be with Ben – he needed to find Maria. She is the one who gave him enough strength to stand up to Catherine and claim his own identity. Sure, he loved me, but I wasn't the one.

But knowing it goes both ways, he wasn't the man for me either. Jackson is. Of that I am sure.

* * *

The morning's light streaming in through the lower three inches of the window not covered by the wooden blinds wakens me. Outside, the distant railway sounds its horn, transporting livestock to western cities. I hear the Canadian Geese flying overhead, migrating south for the winter months.

In this semi-filtered light, I observe the outline of his face, his chest slowly rising and falling in rhythm. I gaze at Jackson, lovingly adoring his rugged features. As strong as his outward appearance is, Jackson's softened inside. He no longer blames himself for Patrick's injuries, nor does he resent his mother for what she could not give him. He's found peace with his past. The scar, while still slightly visible to those who know, is no longer noticeable to strangers. It's healed. He's healed.

I reach for my journal.

It's been a year and a half since I've left Boston. I came here hoping to discover my true self, my purpose, my reason for being. Instead I found a young woman filled with fears and uncertainties. I doubted myself, feared trying new things, and avoided failure at all cost. Slowly the built up, protective layers shed and allowed who I am, who I've always been, to come forth. I've realized that it's not about having the perfect life. That's no longer important. Now I am learning to nourish my own soul, leave my comfort zone, expand my horizons, and trust myself. I am taking risks with love, allowing myself to remember, and permitting myself to just be. Perhaps my spirit's becoming more aligned. Regardless, I have a clearer vision. I am beginning to live. I've found my voice.

Simone joked that there could be a correlation between the name of my new home and my personal growth. Then yesterday during yoga, my fingers actually grazed my mat. Could I finally be learning to Bend?

CHAPTER 50

Jackson

I've been waiting for the perfect moment. She deserves that. Mentally rehearsing the exact words, I make adjustments here and there. Equally important to the *how* is the *where*. Why not where it all began? That makes total sense. I smile, proud of myself.

* * *

The snow's falling at Mt. Bachelor. Already the mountain boasts a base of seventy-five inches, not bad for mid-December. The truck's packed, ready for the trip up Century Drive. In less than a half hour, we're unloading our skis and headed toward the main lift.

The powder's perfect. We both effortlessly carve through the fresh snow, leaving symmetrical tracks behind us. After multiple runs, I suggest we go inside to warm up. We order mochas then search for an empty spot by the windows, where we can look out onto the slopes. Ironically, we end up at the exact same table I sat at when I first spoke to her, when we met over a year and a half ago. When I told her to turn with her toe, not her knees.

Jenna's talking, but I'm not focused. Instead, I'm summoning the nerve for what's next. She pauses for a moment, looking down at the mug in her hand before taking a sip of the warm mocha. This is the moment.

I take a deep breath then say, "When I sat at this table over a year and half ago and watched you ski down the slope then walk into this lodge... well, I knew you were different from the rest." Jenna puts her mug down and gazes into my eyes. I take her hand in mine. "You've changed me... helped me remember who I was... taught me how to trust. I never thought I could share my life with anyone. But I was wrong. You've given me the desire to be the man I know I can be. I cannot imagine life without you. Marry me?" Slowly, I place the crushed velvet box on the table in front of Jenna.

CHAPTER 51

Jenna – Six Months Later

"Are you sure?" my dad asks, appearing very distinguished in his tuxedo. I know that he's teasing me. During his toast at last night's rehearsal dinner, he shared that he could not envision having a son finer than Jackson. Those two have bonded. Dad even went mountain biking with Jackson two days ago. Wish I could have seen that. Thinking back at what we've gone through, I could not love my father more than I presently do. Not only has he regained my trust, but he also earned my respect with the way he owned his mistake.

I'm not sure if I'm surprised or not, but my mother and Rachel are becoming quite close. In fact, my mom and I visited Rachel in Ross this past March, and the two of them went dress shopping for our wedding. That night we went to a French café in Marin, and together we polished off almost three bottles of rosé while Mom told stories of me as a little girl and Rachel shared tales of Jackson's childhood antics. I just sat there, amazed at how our families are melding.

"You look stunning, Jenna," my dad says as his fingers graze my cheek. "You've made me so proud." I can tell that he's on the verge of tears. But instead of losing his composure, he takes a deep breath, offers me his arm, and says, "Shall we?"

* * *

Garlands of wildflowers grace the rustic plank walls. Their clean lemony scent gently permeates the air inside the renovated barn. The wooden lanterns that line the aisle flicker, causing a halo effect in the dimly lit structure. I step to the rhythm of the guitarist playing Train's "Marry Me," my father's strong arm guiding me forward as we walk down the beige burlap runner. Slowly, we proceed. People turn, smile, and gaze affectionately at us.

Midway down the aisle, I pause, taking a few seconds to appreciate this moment. I lovingly take in all of our friends and family members who've joined us this evening. After making eye contact with Trisha, Mary, Marjorie, Claire, and Don, I then look toward the front row of benches. Rachel's seated to the right, beaming proudly, while my mother sits on the left. Dressed in an elegant peach dress, Mom's obviously struggling with her emotions. Her cheeks are wet from happy tears. No doubt both mothers sense the abundance of love flowing this instant for their children's future together. My gaze then moves toward the makeshift altar created out of reclaimed wooden planks from the original church in Bend.

Mollie and Simone are gorgeous in their long dusty rose bridesmaid gowns. Katy, our flower girl, tightly holds her new stepmother's hand – my best friend, who looks beyond beautiful.

To the right of the women are Patrick, Michael, and Matt, appearing incredibly handsome in their black tuxes. It took a bit of convincing, but ultimately the men agreed to my request. I appreciate the roles that these six friends and siblings have played in Jackson's and my lives. They've been our pillars, our rocks.

Then, I see him, standing by the bottom step, between the minister and Matt. Jackson waits, those sea green eyes – the ones that I first fell in love in love with over two years ago – watch as I proceed down the aisle.

I'm almost there. Only ten more steps until I join the man who I love with my entire soul and body. I take a big breath and give Jackson my best smile – he already has my heart.

Satisfied with the mental picture that I've forged in my mind and knowing that I will remember it for the rest of my life, I turn to my dad and give his arm a gentle squeeze to gesture that it's time to continue, move forward, and begin the next chapter of my life.

CPSIA information can be obtained
at www.ICGtesting.com
Printed in the USA
BVHW040212200220
572891BV00013B/200